EVACUEES AT THE WARTIME BOOKSHOP

Lesley Eames

PENGUIN BOOKS

TRANSWORLD PUBLISHERS
Penguin Random House, One Embassy Gardens,
8 Viaduct Gardens, London SW11 7BW
www.penguin.co.uk

Transworld is part of the Penguin Random House group of companies
whose addresses can be found at global.penguinrandomhouse.com

First published in Great Britain in 2024 by Bantam
an imprint of Transworld Publishers
Penguin paperback edition published 2024

A CIP catalogue record for this book
is available from the British Library.

ISBN
9781804993514

Typeset in Baskerville by Falcon Oast Graphic Art Ltd.
Printed and bound by Clays Ltd, Elcograf S.p.A.

The authorized representative in the EEA is Penguin Random House Ireland,
Morrison Chambers, 32 Nassau Street, Dublin D02 YH68.

Penguin Random House is committed to a sustainable
future for our business, our readers and our planet. This book is
made from Forest Stewardship Council® certified paper.

To my precious daughters Olivia and Isobel with thanks for all the love and encouragement, and to our new bringer of joy, my granddaughter Charlotte. Welcome to the world, beautiful girl x

Prologue

January 1942

Bermondsey, London

It was evening when the storm reached London. In a shabby area to the east of the city near the docks, six women and ten children gasped when their house was shaken by the force of it. They were gathered around the only fire in the house – a meagre fire at that – with the women sitting on a mismatched collection of wooden chairs while the children sat on benches made from wooden planks balanced across old tea chests.

The youngest woman – Victoria – attempted a smile. 'It's only the wind,' she explained, in case the children thought bombs were dropping overhead. 'Don't let your dinners go cold.'

One by one the children dipped their spoons into their bowls and continued to eat. Victoria ate, too, though she was worried about how the house would hold up in the storm and she imagined the other women were thinking much the same.

The house was at the end of a terrace and, years ago, had likely been home to a succession of single families, long gone now. Over time, as tragedy and heartache touched them, the current occupants had come to live here until they were quite the little community, terribly cramped in the small rooms but grateful for each other's support.

But a bomb had destroyed the third house along the terrace not long ago, and damaged nearby buildings, too, this house included. Newspapers had been stuffed into broken windows and buckets placed to catch the rain let in by missing roof tiles ever since, but the days of calling this place home were running out rapidly because it had been declared damaged beyond repair and marked down for demolition.

Another shudder shook the house and this time a red-haired woman spoke, doubtless in another attempt to make the children feel safe. 'It's a tasty stew, so it is.' There was a trace of Irish in Mags's voice. She'd lived in London for most of her life but had picked up the accent of her Irish parents.

'Very tasty,' the other women agreed.

The stew had been made by Ivy. She was the eldest of the women and sole carer for a little granddaughter. 'It's just veggies,' she said. 'Potatoes, carrots, turnips, onion . . .'

'Still tasty,' Mags insisted. Besides, only one gas ring on the ancient stove could be made to work so the options for cooking were limited.

They all ate quietly until a knock on the door roused them. Again, Victoria spoke. 'That'll be the rent man.'

'I'm surprised he's turned out on a night like this,' Ivy said.

'I'm not.' Mags gave a wry smile. 'The likes of Jethro Jakes won't let a storm get in the way when there's money to be had.'

Victoria got to her feet. Tall and fair, she had an air of authority and a cultured voice despite her youth. Unlike the others, who'd only ever known poverty, Victoria's early years had been lived in comfort and included a good education. Not that those times had lasted.

She lifted a dented tea caddy from the mantelpiece. There was money inside. The rent money. Taking it, she opened the door which led directly on to the street and stepped out, closing it behind her as the wind and rain whipped at her hair and clothes and made her wince. 'Good evening, Mr Jakes,' she greeted the rent collector.

'Rent's due.' Clearly, he wanted it paid quickly so he could get out of the awful weather.

'Of course.' Victoria handed over the money and watched him count it, though it must have been a difficult task in the stormy blackout.

There was no rent book for him to sign since the occupants were supposed to have left weeks ago. In letting them stay, Mr Jakes was simply making a little money on the side – money which went into his pocket rather than the landlord's.

'I've heard that the demolition men could be coming any day now,' he warned.

'We *are* looking for somewhere else,' Victoria told him, shivering in the chill.

'I should look faster or you might come back one day and find the house reduced to rubble and all your things with it.'

He touched his hat by way of farewell and, grimacing at the storm raging around them, moved on.

Back inside, Victoria encountered a sea of anxious faces. She smiled but was glad when Mags realized there was seriousness beneath the smile. 'Why don't you kids go and play upstairs?' she suggested.

Two of those children – a boy and a girl – looked at Victoria. She wasn't their mother but she'd become the closest they had to one. She nodded to signal that they should indeed go upstairs but added another smile that she hoped would allay their obvious anxiety.

With the children out of earshot, she addressed the adults quickly. 'Demolition could be imminent.'

Looks were exchanged, eloquent with fear for the future.

Hating to be the bearer of bad news, Victoria took a deep breath and continued. 'The last thing we want is to find ourselves put out on the street, but we've had no luck trying to find a place where we can all live together.'

'You're suggesting we should split up?' Mags asked.

'I don't see that we have a choice. Not for the moment. Maybe in the future we'll be able to come together again, but for now I think we'll all have a better chance of finding somewhere to stay as individual families.'

'It's a pity to break up our little household, but you're right,' Mags said. She looked around at the others but none of them argued, for they all knew it to be the truth.

'Maybe we can still live close by each other,' Ivy said.

Victoria took another deep breath. This was hard. 'Actually, I'm thinking of taking Arthur and Jenny out of London. This city – this part of it, anyway – isn't right for them any more. I live in dread of one of them being hurt scrambling over bomb sites and maybe even coming across an unexploded bomb. I also hate the way those Digwell boys from Spicer Street forage through the rubble, fighting each other for things they can sell, even though the poor families whose houses have been bombed might come back to salvage what they can. I don't want my two influenced by that. I want them well away from the constant reminders of the war for a while, surrounded by greenery with freedom to enjoy nature instead of broken buildings. Breathing fresh air, too.'

There was a moment of silence before Mags spoke again. 'Fresh air and greenery. It sounds blissful.'

The other women nodded, Ivy accompanying her nod

with a worried sigh and a glance upstairs. 'Listen to that,' she said. Her little granddaughter had a weak chest and was coughing.

'What about your job?' Mags asked Victoria.

'I'll have to leave the wireless factory and find something new.' She paused and then added anxiously, 'I hope none of you think I'm letting you down.'

'Course we don't,' Mags scoffed. 'You've only spoken the truth. We need to split up, don't we, girls?'

There were murmurs of agreement.

'It's a time of change, so it is,' Mags said. 'I've got to change my home so I'm going to follow Victoria's example and see if I can move out of this dirty city by changing my job as well. What about you, Ivy?'

'I'd love Flower to be brought up where the air is clean, but it's difficult . . .'

'I'll still send money to help out,' Victoria told her, suspecting that Ivy thought she'd be unable to manage it on her own pitiful income.

'I only wish I could do more to shift for myself,' Ivy said. She was the only one who didn't have a job. Poor nutrition when growing up had left her with rickets and it was difficult for her to walk with her legs bowing out to the sides. But she was wonderful with the children, looking after all of them while the others worked, and doing most of the shopping, cooking and washing, too.

'We'll all help you, Ivy, and anyone else who's struggling,' Mags said. 'What about the rest of yous?'

The other women looked at each other and then nodded. 'The countryside,' one said.

'A new start,' said another.

'We might have to scatter to the north, south, east and west,' Mags pointed out. 'But we're hard workers and, besides, we'll be evacuees. There must be people out there with hearts kind enough to help us. And unless I'm much mistaken, the storm is moving on. It's a good omen.'

Was it? Victoria wished she could believe it was going to be that simple.

The storm was indeed moving on. It was heading north and soon it reached Hertfordshire. When the village of Churchwood first felt its effects, it was as though the storm had sent scouts ahead to reconnoitre streets, gardens and buildings. They scooped up dry skeletal leaves from last autumn and sent them skittering across roads and pavements. They rattled gates and windows. They tested the strength of tree roots and fences.

And then, as though they'd discovered rich pickings, they beckoned the storm forward and in it swept. Winds howled and whistled so that houses trembled and trees strained to keep upright. Rain attacked windows like stones and lashed at gardens and crops, threatening to beat the life from them. Birds hunkered into their feathers and clung to their perches. Other animals scurried to find shelter. And inside houses and cottages, people huddled in front of fires and comforted frightened children.

Ever the vandal, the storm snapped twigs and branches from trees, swirled them into the air and let them fall like carelessly discarded litter. It raised a triumphant hurrah as a fence gave up the fight and collapsed, exhausted, on to a garden path. It tipped empty milk bottles off doorsteps, breaking some and causing others to roll this way and that way. In an act of particular malice, it gave one chimney the hardest shake of all and laughed when soot tumbled from it into the room below, putting out the fire that had been burning in the hearth.

Having done its worst, the storm moved on but,

mischievous to the end, it dragged all the clouds with it, leaving cold open skies to dig icy fingers into the earth and freeze pipes fit to bursting . . .

CHAPTER ONE

Naomi

Churchwood, Hertfordshire, England

'Goodness, that was quite a storm last night,' Naomi Harrington commented when her little maid, Suki, brought her morning tea upstairs. 'We've no damage, I hope?'

'It seems not, madam.'

'That's a relief.'

Naomi smiled her thanks, waited for Suki to leave and then got up to walk to her bedroom window. Foxfield had been home for most of her adult life and she loved it here. The house was the largest and loveliest in the village, and the gardens were both beautiful and extensive. Naomi's room overlooked the rear garden, and although the storm had strewn the lawn with twigs and small branches, it warmed her heart to see that all the beautiful trees, from copper beeches to oaks and hollies, remained standing.

But then a sliver of uncertainty about the future of the house – her occupation of it, rather – wriggled into Naomi's mind. She couldn't be entirely confident of keeping the house until it was held in her name alone. For the moment, though, she cast the uncertainty aside, determined to be optimistic and get on with her day.

She was downstairs eating breakfast when Suki announced, 'Mr Sykes wants a word, madam.' Sykes was the Foxfield gardener.

'Is there storm damage, after all?'

'He says not. I think he wants to talk about something else, but you know Mr Sykes . . .'

'Indeed.' Getting more than a grunted word or two out of Jeremiah Sykes took time and patience.

'He isn't waiting to speak to me now?'

'No, madam. He's getting on with his work.'

'Very well, Suki. Thank you.'

Finishing her breakfast, Naomi decided to see Sykes and then walk into the village to check that everyone else had fared well in the storm. She fetched her coat and hat from the hall cupboard, put them on in the sitting room and crossed to the mirror to be sure her hat was straight. It was.

Naomi was turning away when curiosity had her looking back at her reflection. Would a stranger who passed her in the street guess that she was a blackmailer? She certainly wouldn't be mistaken for an angel. Not even as a child had Naomi been pretty, and forty-six years on earth had done nothing to improve matters, having widened her hips, added weight to her bulldog-like jowls and scored wrinkles into her face. But in her sensible country tweeds, most people would probably dismiss her as one of those dull women of a certain age who sat on committees and did good in the world.

Naomi laughed. She was indeed one of those women, but everyone had hidden depths and Naomi was still discovering hers. With 1941 having just rolled over into 1942, the saying *Out with the old and in with the new* was in her thoughts. One of the old things she was discarding from her life was Alexander, a man she'd married in good faith more than a quarter of a century ago.

It hadn't taken long for her to realize that he was cold beneath the superficial charm, though it was only recently that she'd discovered that, in addition to betraying her in the most heartbreaking manner, he'd also fleeced her of most of the money she'd inherited from her father. That was where the blackmail came in. It wasn't a criminal misdeed against an innocent party but the righting of a wrong, the gist being that Alexander should pay back a substantial portion of her inheritance and transfer Foxfield into her name alone, or else.

He'd huffed and puffed in fury, of course, for he was an arrogant, manipulative man who hated to be thwarted. But Naomi had evidence of his secrets.

The divorce was likely to take months, but the sooner it happened, the better for Naomi. She was desperate to feel financially secure and she was equally desperate to be free to take up the offer of happiness she'd received from a different man. At her age! *In with the new*, indeed.

The old year had seen ups and downs for the village, too, not least because its beloved bookshop had literally gone up in smoke when an enemy plane had crashed into the home of its operations, the Sunday School Hall, destroying chairs, tables, equipment and most of the books, as well as the building. Much more than just a place to buy or borrow books, the bookshop had been the beating heart of Churchwood. It had brought the community together to raise spirits with fun and entertainment while war loomed over them like a malevolent cloud. And it had been the source of the mutual help and support that made such a difference to people's lives.

One life that had been changed by it was Naomi's own. Prior to the bookshop's beginning, she'd been a snobbish, bossy woman – the self-appointed Queen Bee of Churchwood – but only because she'd lacked genuine confidence. The bookshop had been someone else's idea and Naomi's involvement with it had been both reluctant and rocky at first. But through it she'd learned a lot, not least to relax, be herself and see the value in others, however humble their circumstances. That shift in attitude had brought her the sort of warm, caring friendships she'd never known before but now treasured.

Regretfully, the rebuilding of the bookshop's original home was likely to take years, but Naomi had hopes of being able to help out in the meantime. She had her eye on a house that had belonged to village resident Joe Simpson before his death. It was smaller than the Hall and would need to be kitted out, but it would offer a start and be far preferable to no bookshop at all.

Buying it depended on her divorce settlement coming through but, until then, Joe's sister, Ellen, had agreed that the house could be rented instead. It meant that the bookshop could reopen soon, but Naomi didn't want to keep Ellen and her family waiting for the purchase price for long. This was another reason why Naomi was keen for the settlement to go through and put an end to her uncertainty. It was hard to imagine how Alexander might wriggle out from under her evidence of his wrongdoing, but he was a cunning man who'd leave no stone unturned to hold on to her money.

Refusing to let thoughts of Alexander spoil her day, she turned from the mirror again and addressed Basil, her ugly but faithful bulldog. 'A walk round the garden will do you good.'

Basil looked unconvinced, clearly preferring to lie in a basket in front of the fire than face the damp chill of a winter's morning. But, being a loyal friend, he heaved himself up and came to her side. 'We won't stay out long,' she promised.

They left the house through the main door on to the front drive. More twigs and skeletal leaves lay scattered over the lawn on this side of the house but Basil seemed disinclined to investigate them. Together, they walked around to the back of the house in search of Sykes.

He was raking up storm debris from the rear lawn, a tall, thin man with an awkward, angular body. Despite the icy weather he whipped his cap off at her approach and held it – or, rather, mashed it – in his long, bony fingers, doubtless considering this to be respectful. He'd worked for Naomi for many years but still went to pieces if he had to speak to her.

'I hear you'd like a word, Mr Sykes,' she said, using the title Mr to try to boost his confidence, even while knowing it wouldn't work.

'Well, missis. It's like this.' He always called her missis, not madam or Mrs Harrington or even Naomi, the name she'd have preferred now her days of trying to rule the village were over.

Like what? she wanted to ask, but Sykes couldn't be rushed. Hiding a sigh, she waited for him to gather his words.

'Naomi!'

The shout came from behind her. Turning, Naomi saw Alice Irvine waving from over by the house. Alice was a slip of a girl less than half Naomi's age but a close friend even so. She was looking out of breath and anxious, which was concerning since she was a clever, level-headed young woman as a rule. Clearly, something was wrong.

Naomi hoped that it didn't concern Alice personally. Not after the sadness the poor girl had endured last year, a sadness that was visible in her still in unguarded moments, though she was showing a brave face to the world.

Naomi looked back at the gardener. 'Might our conversation wait a while, Mr Sykes?'

His wizened face frowned as he considered the question.

'Or do you need to speak to me urgently?' she prompted.

'I don't know that I'd call it urgent, exactly,' he finally said.

'Then let's speak later.'

'It's important, though.'

'I'll remember.' Naomi didn't like to put him off now he'd steeled himself to speak to her, but important didn't trump urgent and Alice's mission was looking urgent indeed.

'You need to come,' she said as Naomi reached her.

'Are *you* all right?' Naomi touched Alice's arm.

'I'm fine, and so is everyone else. But the bookshop . . .'

Oh, heavens. 'Let me take Basil indoors and I'll come straight out.'

Naomi walked to the kitchen door as quickly as her short legs and bad feet allowed. What had happened to the bookshop now? For something that did so much good, it was having rotten luck and, as the brains behind the venture, Alice must be feeling terrible if it was under threat again.

She'd set it up to help others, but at a time when, new to the village, she'd been lonely and nursing heartache, too. The bookshop had given her a sense of purpose and satisfaction, and she must need that more than ever after the previous year's misfortune, especially with her beloved husband, Daniel, away at the fighting.

Reaching the door, Naomi summoned Suki with a knock. 'I need to go out. I don't know how long I'll be gone,' she explained.

Basil sent her a mournful look. He was always on her side in a crisis. 'Be good,' Naomi urged, before returning to her friend.

'What's happened?' she asked then.

'I think you should see for yourself, but I doubt that we'll be opening the bookshop soon.'

It sounded bad.

The walk along Churchwood Way to Joe Simpson's old house took only minutes. Naomi was relieved to see that the house was still standing but the front door was open and she could hear shocked voices inside.

'Go carefully,' Alice advised.

The door opened straight into the centre of the large room that spanned the entire width of the house. The moment Naomi stepped inside her eyes prickled and she coughed.

'Last night's storm must have shaken a mass of soot down the chimney,' neighbour Ralph Atkinson said.

That explained the acrid blackness, but what about the water? It was dripping down walls and through the light fittings on the ceiling, while the weight of it was making the ceiling bow down ominously like a hammock that could split open at any moment.

'I lit the fire as usual last night to stop the pipes from freezing but the soot fall must have put it out,' Ralph continued.

'So the pipes froze and then burst,' Naomi finished.

A familiar bulky figure came down the stairs. Bert Makepiece, the local market gardener. He was as scruffy as ever in ancient, faded clothes but now he also had smears of soot on his face. 'I've stopped the water coming through but we'll need to do something about all the water that's already been released,' he was saying.

Seeing Naomi, he gave her a rueful look. 'Wonderful start to the new year, eh?'

It was a disaster.

'I shouldn't linger in here, if I were you,' Bert told her. 'I'm dirty already. You're not. Let's talk outside.'

He gestured towards the door and followed her through it, nodding a greeting to Alice.

'This is terrible,' Naomi said. 'Goodness knows how long it'll take to sort this mess out.'

'It'll take time and it'll take money,' Bert predicted. 'Does Ellen have the house insured?'

'I certainly hope so.'

'There's nothing you can do here, so perhaps you might call on her to find out.' Joe's sister lived five miles away in Barton. 'I'm going to punch a hole in that ceiling so the water can drain away, and then I'm going to fetch Wally Prince to make sure the chimney is empty.' Wally was the local chimney sweep. 'I suggest the clearing up begins tomorrow, when the worst of the soot has settled.'

Naomi nodded. 'I'll go to Ellen's now.'

'I should discourage her from coming for a look at the place today,' Bert advised. 'Tomorrow, too, as we'll be cleaning it up. The day after, though – Sunday – that'll be a better day for her to come.'

'I'll do my best,' Naomi said. She glanced at her watch. 'I'd better hurry if I'm to catch the next bus.'

She turned away.

'Aren't you forgetting something?' Bert asked. Naomi turned back and Bert raised an eyebrow. 'Well?' he said.

He was expecting a kiss, and why not? A greater contrast to tall, trim Alexander with his impeccable white shirts, silk ties and beautifully cut suits was hard to imagine. Bert was built like a bear and dressed like a scarecrow. And where Alexander was a crisply spoken, well-educated stockbroker who considered himself a cut above ordinary mortals, Bert worked with his hands and considered himself above no one.

Yet it was Bert who'd proposed to Naomi on Christmas Eve. Bert whom she loved and planned to marry. Despite her forty-six years, Naomi blushed, because cold-hearted

Alexander had kissed her rarely. Bert kissed her often and with passion.

Naomi reached up to kiss his cheek, only to be swept into an embrace as he kissed her soundly on the lips instead. Ah, if only she'd married Bert instead of Alexander years ago! She'd have had years of happiness with a man who loved her and she might also have had the children she'd always craved. Coldly calculating Alexander had made sure there were no children from their long marriage and now it was too late. Childlessness was a wound Naomi would carry all her life, but she wasn't going to let it stop her from treasuring the happiness Bert had to offer. Not that she was entirely comfortable with these public shows of affection. They delighted and flustered her in equal measure.

Releasing her at last, he grinned at her blushing cheeks before turning serious again. 'Here's hoping Ellen can reassure you about the insurance. This place is going to cost a pretty penny to put right, and if it isn't insured . . .'

That would pile catastrophe on top of catastrophe.

Naomi was sitting on the bus when she remembered Sykes. Oh dear. He worked short hours during the winter months and would probably have left by the time she returned home. She felt bad, keeping him waiting when he found it hard to speak to her, but it couldn't be helped. She'd catch up with him another day.

CHAPTER TWO

Alice

The best that Alice could say about Joe Simpson's house when she went along to help clear up after the previous day's disaster was that water was no longer actively running down walls or through the ceiling lights. It was under their feet, though, and the air felt saturated with its smoky chill.

There was rubble under their feet as well, the remains of the ceiling Bert had knocked down before it fell on someone's head. Looking around, Alice felt a pang of distress. She'd begun the new year determined to be cheerful after the setback of the previous year, but to see this calamity . . .

This wasn't the time for wallowing in regret, though. This was the time for action.

She walked up to Bert. 'Did Naomi manage to see Ellen yesterday?'

'She did, and the poor woman is devastated by what's happened to her brother's house.'

'They were very close,' Alice said.

'As for insurance, Ellen isn't sure what Joe had. She's going to look through his papers.'

'Fingers crossed she finds an insurance certificate.'

'Fingers and toes crossed,' Bert agreed.

With that, Alice went to join her father, who'd also come to help. A doctor for many years, and long widowed, he'd retired to Churchwood hoping for peace and quiet but had gradually been drawn into the life of the village despite himself. Alice was glad of it. Much as he needed to relax and enjoy having time to indulge his interest in studying ancient civilizations, it wasn't good for him to be alone too much.

May Janicki – another member of the bookshop organizing team – and several other village residents had also come to help. They were young women like May and old men like Alice's father, since younger men were away at the war.

'It'll be dirty work so I hope we're all in our oldest clothes,' Bert said.

Alice was certainly in her oldest clothes, though trousers would have been more practical than her faded flannel skirt and lisle stockings. Tall, slender May was wearing trousers and also had a duster tied around her hair. It was an odd look for her since she was normally the epitome of style, having overcome the challenge of an orphanage upbringing to carve out a career as a designer and manufacturer of clothes in London. She'd stepped away from that career now but still dressed with elegance. Usually.

This wasn't a usual situation, though, and May acknowledged it with a wry look as she passed another duster to Alice. 'Let's at least try to keep our hair clean,' she said.

'Where are the children?' Alice asked. May had never wanted children of her own – she'd loved her career too much – but the war had brought her three Polish refugee children in the form of the nieces and nephew of her husband, Marek, who was away fighting in North Africa, as was Alice's Daniel. It had been the need to provide the children with safer lives that had led to May leaving her job and moving to Churchwood.

'Janet's looking after them,' she explained.

Janet Collins helped to organize the bookshop, too. She was also a wonderfully caring mother and grandmother, so May's Rosa, Samuel and Zofia couldn't have been in better hands.

'The first job is to get rid of all this fallen plaster,' Bert said. 'I've brought sacks to put it in. Wear gloves, everyone. We don't want to be troubling Dr Lovell with any cuts or other injuries.' He nodded towards Alice's father, who was often called upon to help Churchwood's residents with their ailments despite his retirement, since the nearest practising doctor lived in Barton.

They began filling the sacks with debris. Alice couldn't work quickly given that an accident a couple of years ago had left her with a scarred and weakened hand, but she did her best.

Inevitably, the water had mixed with soot to form a soupy ooze and it wasn't long before everyone was smeared with black filth. But eventually, all the debris had been collected. The floor was swept and then buckets were filled with water at Ralph Atkinson's house next door for washing down walls, windows and paintwork.

'I think I'm just redistributing soot,' May complained, but more villagers arrived with cloths and old newspapers, and Bert organized a chain of people to pass buckets of clean water along so progress was eventually made.

'It may be that a plasterer will advise that some of these walls will have to come down like the ceiling, but let's hope not,' Bert said.

Time was marching on and Alice excused herself since she was due at Stratton House, the local military hospital where she was a volunteer visitor. Feeling her father had earned a break, she encouraged him to leave too, and they headed home to The Linnets, their picturesque cottage.

There she washed, changed and served a quick lunch before setting out on the long walk up Brimbles Lane.

She'd made the walk many times since moving to Churchwood and it had mixed memories for her. On the positive side of the equation, it was in this lane that the idea for the bookshop had taken shape. At the time, Alice had been feeling heartbroken over a misunderstanding with Daniel and full of fear that the injury to her hand might leave her unemployable and for ever dependent on her father.

In visiting the hospital, she'd aimed to do some good while lifting herself out of a pit of misery, but she'd come to realize that the patients were desperately in need of books to read. Setting out to change that, Alice had crossed paths with her dear friend Kate, who lived at a farm along Brimbles Lane. Like Alice, Kate was motherless and lonely, but was also disadvantaged by being a member of the notoriously rough and universally despised Fletcher family.

Together, they'd sought donations of books for the hospital and, on discovering that the village community wasn't actually as close as it might have been, had set up the bookshop in the Sunday School Hall as well. More than just an ordinary bookshop, it was a place where people could come to chat over cups of tea, hear stories read out, listen to talks and join clubs for knitting, woodworking, gardening, board games . . . Social events were held, too, beloved by hospital staff and patients as well as village residents. And if anyone needed help because of illness or any other problems, it was the place where support could be arranged.

Naomi, Bert, May and Janet had joined them as organizers along the way. So had the new vicar, Adam Potts. A small young man with an abundance of untidy brown hair, Adam made up for his scruffiness with sweetness and enthusiasm. The bookshop had made friends of them all.

Yet it was also on Brimbles Lane where, the previous November, less than three months after marrying her darling Daniel, Alice had collapsed as she miscarried their child. The miscarriage had affected her badly, especially since Daniel was serving far from home so they were unable to comfort each other. Alice was trying hard to appear more positive now, but it was a struggle she mostly kept secret from everyone else.

As a doctor's daughter, she knew better than most people that miscarriages were common and rarely caused by anything the mother had or hadn't done. She also knew that many – perhaps even most – women who miscarried went on to have healthy babies so she shouldn't despair.

Alice also knew she was lucky to have a roof over her head and, with part of Daniel's service pay being made over to her, she wasn't precisely short of money even though she didn't have a job.

And yet . . .

She couldn't help grieving the baby she'd lost – her beloved Daniel's baby, too – and it was hard to feel optimistic about conceiving another baby in the future when he was so far from home and in danger. And, while she had enough money to get by, she wanted badly to build a nest egg towards setting up a home of their own once Daniel returned from the war. He'd designed racing cars in the past but there was no guarantee that he could walk straight back into that or any other job, and they might struggle for a while.

Alice yearned for the satisfaction and fulfilment of working, too. Prior to the accident she'd been a skilful typist who had managed all aspects of her father's medical practice, from welcoming patients to keeping accounts. Now she could only type one-handedly and her speed was pitiful. For a few months she'd found work helping an elderly gentleman with his memoirs, but since then no prospective employer seemed able to see past her injury to the fact that she was highly efficient at office organization.

She'd thought about trying to earn an income from her kitchen table by writing stories for magazines, but when she'd sat down to begin one, she'd frozen in panic. It wasn't hard to guess the reason. The miscarriage, the lack of a job, the problems with the bookshop . . . they were all combining to make her feel a failure and, try as she might, she couldn't seem to shake it off.

But the post had brought her a glimmer of light. Home leave from North Africa was difficult due to the distance but Daniel had written to say he was being considered for some training which could bring him back to England. *I don't have a date or any certainty at all but I'm keeping my fingers crossed*, he'd said. *I can't wait to hold you in my arms again, darling.*

Alice couldn't wait either. Perhaps then she'd start to feel steadier. Not that she wanted Daniel to find her weak and troubled. He had enough to cope with as a soldier without worrying about his wife's feebleness. She needed to pull herself together and find some strength of her own.

Perhaps her first step should be to write a story. It would give her a real boost to be able to tell Daniel that she'd sold it.

Reaching Brimbles Farm, Alice saw Kate's distinctive figure in a field and called out to her. Kate bounded over. She was a beautiful girl, being tall and slim with fresh skin, warm brown eyes and a mass of rich chestnut hair which she wore in a single braid down her back.

23

'Have you heard the news?' Alice asked, for the farm was some distance from the village.

'What news?'

'A pipe in the new bookshop burst and caused a lot of damage.'

'Oh no! It's repairable, though?'

'Hopefully, though it'll cost money and I'm not sure if the house was insured. Besides . . .'

'Builders and building materials are in short supply with the war on,' Kate finished. 'So it might be ages before the bookshop can reopen.' She looked gloomy.

Not wanting to be the bearer of only bad news, Alice added, 'Daniel may be coming home.'

'That's wonderful!'

'It isn't definite yet, but we're hopeful. Have you heard from Leo?'

To Alice's delight, Kate had met and fallen in love with a flight lieutenant in the RAF. Unfortunately, Leo had been shot down and injured, and currently he was in hospital in Manchester, recovering from burns and a broken arm.

Kate's pretty features softened. 'I'm expecting a letter any day.'

'Hopefully, he'll be out of hospital soon.'

'Yes,' Kate agreed, but Alice was surprised to see what looked like anxiety in her friend's expression.

'You *are* keen for Leo to leave hospital?'

'Of course!' Kate assured her.

Perhaps Alice had imagined that look. Or maybe Kate was simply thinking that the sooner Leo left hospital, the sooner he might be sent back to active duty to face danger all over again.

The girls parted with a hug and Alice walked on to the hospital.

Matron, Alice's nursing friends Babs Carter and Pauline Evans and the patients were all crestfallen to hear about the damage to the bookshop's new home. 'You know how the patients love the socials,' Matron said. 'As do we all.'

'Hopefully, the repairs can be done soon,' Alice said.

She went about her usual business of collecting in the books that had been read and distributing those that had become available, though they were few in number since the books were shared between the hospital and the village and many had been destroyed in the plane crash.

Time and again she had to tell patients that she had nothing for them, and the disappointment on their faces tugged at her heartstrings.

'I'll try to buy some books soon,' Naomi had promised, but she was waiting for her divorce settlement to go through before she could be sure of her finances.

For the moment, Alice could only make the most of her compendium of short stories. 'Who'd like to hear one of these?' she asked, holding it in front of her, and a forest of arms went up.

'Today's story is called "Tom Smith and the Mysterious Package",' she announced and, making a mental note to consider how the writer had put the story together, she began to read. '"Tom Smith was in a bad mood. Work had kept him late and not only had an old man sat next to him on the bus home, but that old man had chattered Tom into exhaustion. Then the bus had broken down and Tom had needed to walk the final three miles to his house. Letting himself in through the front door at last, he hung up his coat only to pause. There was something in the pocket. Removing it, Tom saw that it was a package. There was no writing on the outside but inside Tom found money. A lot of money . . ."'

She was pleased to see that her audience was rapt but

later, when she was back at home and thinking about writing a story of her own, the fear of failure crept over her again.

CHAPTER THREE

Kate

Kate thrust the fork into the ground with as much power as she could muster. Last night's clear skies had hardened the earth with frost, making it difficult to move, but she also wanted to vent her frustration. For a moment she thought of her private troubles – and gave the fork another savage thrust – but, seeing nothing to be gained by dwelling on them, she turned her thoughts to the bookshop instead.

Getting away from the never-ending farm work had always been a struggle but the bookshop – and Kate's friendship with Alice – had become lifelines. They'd kept her going in those dark days when she'd been shunned by the village. They'd also introduced her to a new world of information, adventure and joy. A world in which she was valued and liked as a person. Kate *needed* the bookshop and she wasn't the only one. For them all to be cheated of its benefits by the weather . . . *Grgh!*

She thrust the fork in once again but the day was advancing and it was time for the mid-afternoon cup of tea. Dusting earth from her hands, Kate headed for the farmhouse.

Inside, she found the two land girls who'd come to work on the farm. Six feet tall and wiry, Pearl – or Gertie Grimes, as she'd been christened – worked as hard as any man and needed feeding like one. Just now she was watching Ruby slice bread with eager anticipation, but she managed to drag her gaze away and turned to Kate, saying, 'I shifted those cabbages.'

'Well done.'

Ruby arranged the bread on a platter. She was Pearl's opposite in appearance, being short, curvy and pretty. And while Pearl couldn't have cared less about such things, Ruby dyed her hair white-blonde and wore cosmetics, even on the farm.

Their backgrounds were different, too. Pearl was from a well-to-do family that found her clumsy ways and tastes exasperating. Ruby was from London's East End, where she'd hoped to train as a hairdresser only to fall prey to the owner of the hairdressing shop, who'd left her pregnant at just sixteen, much to the disgust of her family. Her son, Timmy – a lovely boy – had been coached to describe Ruby as his sister and most people still believed that to be the truth. Kate was one of those who knew differently. Timmy was, in fact, the reason Ruby had become a land girl despite loathing dirt and physical labour. He'd been unhappy when evacuated to another farm so Ruby had carved a niche for herself here and, in time, had been given permission to bring the boy to live with her.

Ruby had recently found love with Kenny, the eldest of Kate's four brothers. The most handsome brother, too, as he was tall with a full head of chestnut hair, though in the past his looks had been spoiled by his morose personality. Amazingly, Ruby was turning him into a civilized man. Almost.

Whether Pearl had a romantic interest was hard to say. She was close to Fred, one of the twins who were Kate's youngest brothers, but the relationship consisted mostly of them bickering and criticizing each other.

'Was that Alice I saw in the lane?' Ruby asked.

'It was,' Kate confirmed, 'though I'm afraid she brought bad news.'

'Oh?'

Kate explained about the bookshop's woes and saw both land girls' faces fall in disappointment. The three girls were company for each other but life on the farm sometimes felt remote to all of them. Bookshop activities had got them out meeting other people.

'Timmy's going to be disappointed, too,' Ruby said. 'Adam's been promising a children's club that would run once or twice a week after school and perhaps on a Saturday or Sunday as well. He had games and crafts in mind.'

'With luck, it won't be delayed for long,' Kate said, hoping that really proved to be the case – for all their sakes, but perhaps especially for Alice, who'd been through a tough time recently and needed the bookshop to take her mind off it.

She washed her hands and helped Ruby to carry cups and saucers to the table. Most of the crockery was chipped but Kate's skinflint father, Ernie, had neither a taste for finery nor a willingness to spend money. The chipped crockery suited the ramshackle farmhouse anyway, as it was maintained only enough to stop it from falling down.

The others began to arrive. Fred came first, banging on the door to be let in because he couldn't yet manage to open it from the wheelchair he needed to use these days. Pearl took a giant bite of bread and strolled leisurely to the door.

'You took your time,' he grumbled.

'Saw no reason to rush.'

'It's freezing out there!'

'Then you should have put a blanket over your lap.'

Fred rolled his eyes and wheeled himself to the sink to wash his hands.

Despite being exempt, as farmworkers, Fred 'n' Frank

had signed on with the army expecting larks and adventures, only for Fred to lose his legs – one below the knee and one above. The injuries had turned him from a laughing, joking, powerful young man into a bitter echo of his former self but, after everyone else had tried to tiptoe around his sensitivities, Pearl's blunt lack of sympathy had been exactly what he'd needed to perk up.

Kenny entered next and was followed by middle brother Vinnie. Handsomeness had passed Vinnie by, since he took after their father in being ferret-faced with sparse ginger hair, but he too was showing signs of improvement. He was still tactless, but his spiteful streak was fading now Ruby and Pearl took him to task for it.

Ernie arrived last. All his children called him Ernie at his insistence, probably because he was emotionally stunted as both a father and a man.

'Where's the tea?' he demanded, glowering at Ruby. 'We haven't time to stand here waiting. The daylight is going already.'

Ruby simply glowered back but Kenny stepped towards her protectively. 'Don't be mean,' he told Ernie. 'Ruby works hard.'

Ernie made a mocking sound. 'Soft in the head, that's your trouble.'

'And your trouble is—'

'Here comes the tea,' Kate interrupted. Living with Pearl and Fred's petty squabbling was bad enough without Kenny and Ernie going into battle.

Just then Timmy arrived home from seeing friends in the village. Urchin-faced at seven years old, his nose was red from the chill of the long walk. 'Did you hear that they forgot to get the chimney swept in the new bookshop? The storm last night made soot fall down and it went everywhere. Whoosh!'

He told that part of the story with relish but then the consequences of the drama had him frowning. 'Is it true that the children's club won't be able to start for ages now?'

'We'll have to wait and see,' Ruby told him.

'It sounded the best thing ever.'

Kate imagined there were many disappointed people in Churchwood just now, children and adults alike.

There was more work to be done after tea. Even darkness creeping stealthily over the fields didn't signal the end of the farming day, as they merely transferred to the barn and outhouses to clean, oil and repair tools. Ernie cared nothing for personal grooming and creature comforts, but tools were treated well because they were expensive.

Kate locked up the chickens for the night and, after washing her hands again, went back out to unpeg the washing from the clothes line. She walked into the kitchen with the basket under her arm and Ruby turned from the stove as though she'd been startled from a daydream – and not a happy daydream, either. She summoned a quick smile but it didn't fool Kate.

'Is something wrong?' Kate asked.

'Why should anything be wrong?'

'I don't know, but if something is bothering you . . .'

'It isn't. Now, pass that basket over and I'll get stuck into the ironing. I've already got the irons warming in the fire.'

Ruby took the washing basket and set to work. As a land girl, she wasn't supposed to carry out domestic tasks, but since she much preferred them to outdoor work, they'd agreed that it was better for everyone if she helped to run the house and freed Kate to concentrate on the farm.

Ruby was cheerful for the rest of the evening. It sounded like forced cheer to Kate, but perhaps she was overreacting. Everyone had their moods and a night's sleep might restore Ruby to her usual self.

Kate went up to bed in the tiny room tucked under the eaves that had been hers for all of her life. It was icy in winter but the only place where she could be alone and for that reason it was precious. Getting into bed, she pulled the covers to her chin but kept her lamp lit as she turned her thoughts to Leo.

He wasn't traditionally handsome in the clean-cut way of Alice's Daniel, but he was tall, trim and extraordinarily attractive with his ready smile and laughing blue eyes. Kate wasn't the only person to think so, judging from the admiring looks she'd noticed on the faces of other girls.

His injuries had changed him a little. Burns now scarred the left side of his face and neck as well as his left hand, but Kate didn't care a jot about them except in relation to the pain and discomfort they'd caused him.

She loved him deeply and still felt stunned by the fact that he loved her in return. After all, Leo was a highly educated flight lieutenant who was dashing, debonair and full of fun, while she was a farmworker who'd barely been to school and dressed mostly in the patched breeches, ancient shirts and misshapen jumpers that were handed down from her brothers. Despite her lack of sophistication, Leo insisted that he adored her, and when he looked at her with warmth in his eyes and kissed her . . .

Kate hugged the memories close like precious things. But then the doubts crept into her mind.

She'd been thrilled when Leo had written to say he was expecting to leave hospital soon, but then he'd added: *I'll be required to convalesce for a while, but I don't yet know whether I'll be sent to a convalescent home or allowed back to my parents' house. Wherever I go, I hope you'll come and see me, perhaps staying for a day or two. I can't wait to be with you again, my darling . . .*

Kate couldn't wait to be with him either and would gladly visit him in a convalescent home. She'd stayed in a bed-and-breakfast lodging when she'd visited him in hospital in Manchester and would be happy to make the same sort of arrangement again.

But what if he returned to his parents' house? Would she be expected to visit him there? Perhaps even stay the night? The thought of it filled her with alarm.

Kate hadn't yet met Leo's family, but she'd learned enough about them to know that they were far higher up the social scale than the rough-and-ready Fletchers. The Kinsellas lived in a large house in Cheltenham with servants and a tennis court in the garden. They'd given their son a private education, too. Leo was no snob, but what about them?

An only child born to his parents when they'd given up hope of a baby, Leo had given her the impression that they doted on him and he adored them in return. Doubtless, they wanted his happiness, but would they agree that a country bumpkin – whose only wealth was a few pounds in a Post Office savings account – was the girl to make him happy? Might she visit only to see them turn their refined noses up at her?

Of course, if she and Leo were to make a real go of their relationship, Kate would have to meet his parents eventually. But that was in the future and, amid the perils of wartime, it felt like tempting fate to look too far ahead. It was the here and now that concerned her, and the thought of a trip to Cheltenham . . .

But perhaps it wouldn't come to that. With luck, Leo would be sent to a convalescent home miles from his parents' house.

With luck.

CHAPTER FOUR

Naomi

'I'd like to say it isn't as bad as it looks, but I'm afraid that would make me a liar,' Bert told Joe's sister, Ellen, when she came to inspect the damage the day following the clean-up. 'As you can see, we had to knock the ceiling down, but it's likely that a wall or two will need to come down, too, both here and upstairs. Then there's the electrics. I haven't switched the light on because there was an ominous crackling sound when I tried it earlier.'

Ellen looked distraught and Naomi thought she knew the reason. So did Bert, judging from his expression. 'Perhaps insurance will cover the work?' Naomi suggested tentatively.

Distress worked pleats into Ellen's forehead. 'Joe's insurance lapsed when he was ill. It didn't occur to me to ask him about it any more than it occurred to me to have his chimney swept. I've been such a fool, and I've let everyone down – Joe, you, your bookshop . . .'

Naomi patted Ellen's arm. 'You simply had too much on your mind, caring for Joe in his last months as well as looking after your own family.'

Ellen's son and daughter were grown up with children of their own, but her son was unable to work for a while following a fall from a tree he'd been pruning, and her daughter was struggling with three small children and a fourth pregnancy while her husband was away training to be a wireless operator. The demands on Ellen's time and funds had been considerable even before she'd nursed her brother through his final months, and it wasn't as though she had a husband to help – she'd been widowed for many years.

'I made sure Joe's usual bills were paid. Rates, electric and so on. But insurance . . .' She shook her head.

Which left the delicate issue of how the repairs could be financed. If Naomi's settlement had come through, she'd have paid for them without hesitation, but until then she needed to keep a careful eye on her spending.

Bert cleared his throat and said, 'Perhaps I might lend you the money, Ellen. You could repay me when Naomi finally buys the house. No one else needs to know about it.'

'Oh, no.' Ellen was a proud woman. 'It's kind of you to offer, but Joe left a little money as well as the house. I was hoping . . . But that doesn't matter. The important thing is to get this place repaired.'

'I imagine you were hoping to use Joe's money to help your children,' Naomi said.

'The children will have to wait,' Ellen insisted. 'I'll look into getting the work done as soon as possible.'

'You'll need a plasterer, a plumber and an electrician, though you might find a building firm that offers all three services,' Bert advised. 'If you need any help finding one . . .'

'You've already done more than enough,' Ellen told him. 'Now I need to catch my bus. I'll let you know when I've found someone to do the work.'

'We'll make sure there are no more burst pipes in the meantime,' Bert promised. 'The chimney should be fine now it's had a thorough sweep.'

'Something else I have to thank you for,' Ellen said. With a smile that trembled a little, she went on her way.

'Poor woman,' Bert said.

'She didn't deserve for this to happen when she had so much on her plate already.'

'Sadly, disaster doesn't discriminate between good and bad people.'

'More's the pity. It was nice of you to offer to fund the repairs, Bert.'

'I'm a nice man,' he said. 'That's why you're marrying me as soon as you can get rid of the icicle.' The icicle was Alexander, of course. 'Pleasant though it is to spend time with my beloved, I have a delivery to make in Eshton,' he said, moving the day along. 'Do you want a lift home first?'

'Save your petrol,' Naomi told him. 'I can walk.'

'I'll say goodbye, then, and you know what that means.'

Another kiss. It was delicious but, walking home afterwards, Naomi's thoughts turned sombre again. Would Ellen have enough money to cover the repairs? If not, could she be persuaded to accept Bert's help? And how long would the work take, given the shortage of labour and materials?

Reaching Foxfield, she let herself into the house and realized her cook-housekeeper must have been listening out for her, because Mrs Kitts emerged from the kitchen. 'Might I have a word, madam?'

'Of course.' Naomi led the way into the sitting room.

'I'm wondering if you've made any progress with finding my replacement?' Mrs Kitts asked. She wanted to retire.

'I'm afraid I haven't.'

'You've been busy.'

True, but Naomi had also been dithering about what was best to be done and asking herself if she might manage without a cook-housekeeper for a while. Given the uncertainty over her finances, it would be useful to save on the cost of the wage, and it wouldn't hurt Naomi to learn to shift for herself. In fact, it might be good practice for when she married Bert. They hadn't settled on where they would live – at Foxfield or at Bert's house – but flitting between the two properties seemed likely, at least in the early days, and Bert kept no servants. On the other hand, she suspected that, even if she attempted some of the Foxfield work herself, the lack of a cook-housekeeper would still increase the pressure on Suki and Beryl, the cleaning lady.

'Madam?' Mrs Kitts prompted.

Naomi roused herself. 'Please don't let my delay influence when you leave. You've earned your retirement.'

'I'm happy to hang on a bit longer.'

'That's kind of you, but the moment it becomes inconvenient . . .'

'I'll let you know, madam.'

Mrs Kitts went on her way but the conversation reminded Naomi that she still hadn't spoken to Sykes, since he didn't work on Saturdays or Sundays. Still, something that was important but not urgent didn't sound like too big a problem. At least, Naomi hoped it wasn't.

CHAPTER FIVE

Kate

Darling Leo,
I'm so glad to hear that you're recovering well and expect
to be allowed home soon. Of course, I'll visit you – wherever
you like.

Kate paused, exhaling slowly because writing those last three words had filled her with trepidation. She hadn't been brought up to follow religion but she'd found herself chanting over and over inside her head: *Please let Leo be sent to a convalescent home.*

Brooding about it wouldn't help, though. Pulling herself together, she wrote about life on the farm and the setback to the bookshop and then, assuring him of her love, she signed off with kisses and sealed the letter inside an envelope.

She'd left her boots by the kitchen door so walked down the wooden stairs in her socks. She must have been quiet because she reached the kitchen to see Ruby shrugging off a hug from Kenny. 'What's wrong?' he asked.

'I'm just busy.' Ruby picked up a potato and peeled it almost viciously.

Were Ruby's feelings for Kenny cooling? It would be sad for Kenny and awkward for everyone else at Brimbles Farm if so.

Kate waited for Kenny to go outside then said, 'Ruby, I don't wish to pry, but if something is wrong . . .'

'What could be wrong?' Ruby asked. Defensively, Kate thought.

'I couldn't help seeing what just happened.'

'Me giving Kenny the brush-off?' Ruby forced a laugh. 'He needs to learn that there's a time for romance and it isn't when I've a meal to prepare. That's all.'

Was that really all? Kate was unconvinced but clearly Ruby didn't want to talk about her troubles. 'I hope you'll always remember that I'm your friend.'

'I know that!' Ruby laughed again as though Kate was making too much of what amounted to a mere nothing. 'Now then, would you prefer tonight's potatoes mashed or baked?'

'Either. You're an excellent cook.'

'I'm a better cook than farmhand, that's for sure.'

Timmy burst into the kitchen, fresh from school, and Ruby looked relieved by the diversion. 'Good day?' she asked him.

'Jack Fenton brought in a whale!'

'Not a real one?' Ruby guessed.

'Course not, silly. His uncle made it from wood. I want to try making a wooden animal, too.'

'It's called whittling,' Kate said. 'Carving wood in that way.'

Timmy's eyes brightened. 'Do you know how to do it?'

'I'm afraid not.'

'I still want to try.'

'Then I suggest you fetch a small log from the barn,' Kate told him. 'I'll look out a knife for you.'

'A knife?' Ruby looked alarmed. 'I don't want you cutting your fingers off, Tim.'

'It won't be a sharp one,' Kate promised.

Timmy ran out again and returned with a log. He sat at the table but seemed unsure how to proceed.

'I should start with a simple shape like a fish,' Kate suggested. 'You could draw one on a piece of paper and then cut it out to use as a guide.'

Timmy followed her suggestion and held the paper fish against the wood. 'I think the idea is to scrape the wood away to leave the shape,' Kate said.

Timmy got to work.

'Careful with that knife,' Ruby pleaded.

Pearl arrived for the mid-afternoon cup of tea. 'What are you making?' she asked Timmy. 'A caterpillar?'

'It's not a caterpillar. It's a fish!'

'I see,' Pearl said, though she sounded doubtful.

Kenny, Vinnie and Ernie arrived, too, and Fred wheeled himself in from the downstairs room in which he slept.

'Do *you* know how to wriggle?' Timmy asked Kenny.

'Eh?'

'Whittle,' Kate corrected.

'Me? No,' Kenny said.

'Me neither,' Vinnie said, not having an artistic bone in his body.

No one bothered to ask Ernie, of course.

Gradually, the fish appeared. It resembled no fish that had ever swum the waters of planet earth, since it was a mess of sharp angles, but everyone except Ernie admired it.

'It needs eyes, though,' Fred said.

Timmy gouged two holes, lopsided and differently sized but recognizable as eyes.

'And scales,' Fred added.

'I don't know how to do scales,' Timmy admitted.

'Give it here.' Fred gestured at the fish.

He studied it for a moment then picked up the knife and made a pattern that looked extraordinarily like a row of fish scales.

'Cor!' Timmy's eyes were wide and admiring. 'Can you make more?'

Soon the fish was covered in scales and feathery fins.

'Thanks!' Timmy said.

'About time you did something useful around here,' Pearl told Fred, who rolled his eyes.

'Can you make more animals?' Timmy asked him.

'I can't make anything,' Fred answered.

'You just can't be bothered,' Pearl said. 'I vote that you don't get any supper until you promise to make a whole Noah's Ark of animals.'

'Are you deaf? I just said I don't know how to make anything!'

'You can try. There, it's settled. Fred's going to make more animals or he doesn't get fed.'

'You're nuts,' Fred told her, but Pearl only grinned and Kate thought the land girl was on to something.

Clearly, Fred had at least some talent. It would do him good to have a challenge and, with luck, he might be pleased by the outcome. He needed to stop feeling useless.

After supper Kate cycled into the village to post her letter to Leo. Returning, she patched a pair of Ernie's breeches but cast sidelong looks at Ruby now and then, still suspecting that something was wrong.

Kate supposed she'd have to wait and see what happened with Ruby, just as she'd have to wait and see what happened with Leo's parents. On that thought, her stomach crumpled with nerves and she pricked her finger on her needle.

CHAPTER SIX

Naomi

'Naomi!'

Leaving the post office, Naomi saw Ellen approaching from the bus stop and waited for her to catch up.

'Good news,' Ellen announced as she reached Naomi. 'I've found a builder with all the materials he needs, so he can start on Joe's house straight away.'

'That's marvellous!' It was exciting to know the bookshop could be opening much sooner than anticipated.

'I'm told the work should take no more than a couple of weeks,' Ellen said. 'Plumbing, plastering and electrics – my builder can see to them all. Such a relief!'

'And the – er – cost?' Naomi hoped she didn't sound insensitive.

'Manageable from the money Joe left and a little of my own that I'd put by.'

'You really are the bearer of good news today, Ellen. Can I offer you a cup of tea or even a sherry to celebrate?'

'Bless you, but I've promised to call in on Edna Hall. I just wanted to let you know about the builder and ask if you'll mind keeping an eye on him? His name is George Gregg.'

'I'll be glad to. So will Bert.'

'He's a good man, is Bert.' Ellen's eyes twinkled. 'Quite a catch in his way.'

'I'm a lucky woman,' Naomi admitted.

They parted just as Naomi saw Churchwood's biggest gossip, Marjorie Plym, hastening towards them, doubtless hoping for a titbit of tittle-tattle to spread around the village. She looked crestfallen at having missed Ellen, so Naomi took pity on her and told her Ellen's news.

Seeing Marjorie's plain features light up in pleasure, Naomi felt her conscience stir. Marjorie could be tiresome, especially when she let her love of gossip run away with her, but she'd been a loyal friend to Naomi for many years.

'I've time for a cup of tea if you'd like to join me?' Naomi said, sacrificing peace and quiet for friendship.

Marjorie flushed with delight. 'Lovely!'

Sykes was out in the front garden when they reached Foxfield. 'I haven't forgotten that you'd like a word,' Naomi told him. 'I'll come and find you when Miss Plym has left.'

Sykes gave Marjorie a long look. For all that he didn't mix in the village, he couldn't live in Churchwood without knowing that once Marjorie got her feet under Naomi's table she was hard to shift.

Naomi led Marjorie inside, encountering a sympathetic look from Suki, who also knew Marjorie well. 'Tea, madam?' she asked.

'Yes, please, Suki.'

The maid took their coats and Marjorie looked around the sitting room in the ill-concealed hope of finding something new to report to others. She wasn't malicious, but the passing years hadn't delivered her the sort of life she'd once expected. Marjorie's family had been wealthy in her youth but that wealth had dwindled over time, and now she lived alone in a drab little house, eking out every penny. Gossip brought both spice and a sense of importance into her life.

'How are you, Naomi?' she asked. 'I know you have Bert now, but how is dear Alexander, too?'

Naomi's husband had loathed Marjorie but she'd stood in awe of him. She was desperate to know the details of Naomi's separation but, not wanting the sorry story to become public property in the village, Naomi had told her only that they'd decided to part.

'He's well, thank you,' Naomi said, and brought the conversation back round to the bookshop.

An hour passed. 'What a pleasant time we've had,' Naomi declared, getting to her feet, since only the strongest hints penetrated Marjorie's brain.

It still took more than five minutes to get her through the door, but at last it was done.

'More tea, madam?' Suki asked, probably thinking that Naomi needed a pick-me-up after one of Marjorie's visits.

'Thank you, Suki, but it's time for Basil's walk.'

Basil gave the chilly day a grimace but left the house uncomplainingly. Sykes was still at work at the front of the house and Naomi headed straight for him. 'At last we can talk, Mr Sykes. What is it you'd like to tell me?'

He snatched his cap off his head and gave it another mashing. 'Well, missis, the thing is—'

He broke off as they heard frantic barking out in Churchwood Way. 'No, stop, I say!' a female voice implored, but it was followed by a cry of alarm and then the sound of something – or someone – falling hard.

CHAPTER SEVEN

Naomi

Rushing out to investigate, Naomi saw a dog yapping and dancing around a young woman who, along with her bicycle, had fallen into the ditch that bordered the opposite side of the road. 'Could you secure the dog?' Naomi called to Sykes as she hastened towards the young woman. 'But take care you're not bitten.'

'No one's getting hurt.' Alec Mead, who farmed the land beyond the ditch, appeared. He looked as he usually did: highly irritated.

'I think someone has already been hurt,' Naomi pointed out.

'Indeed, yes,' the young woman said, dashing dishevelled honey-coloured hair from her face. It was a pretty face but smeared with dirt and blood. As was her hand.

'You're not badly hurt?' Mr Mead asked, though Naomi suspected it wasn't the girl's welfare that concerned him as much as the possibility of being reported to the police for keeping a dangerous dog. 'The dog's a young 'un, that's all.'

'If he's untrained, he should be kept where he can do no harm,' Naomi said.

'He was in the barn but my boy let him out by accident.' Mr Mead took the dog from Sykes and Naomi helped the young woman to climb out of the ditch, bringing her bicycle with her.

45

'There's no damage, as far as I can see,' the girl said, after giving the bike a quick inspection.

'It's a pity the same can't be said of you,' Naomi told her.

'Come up to the farm and my wife will help clean you up,' Mr Mead offered.

'My house is nearer,' Naomi said.

The girl smiled at her. 'I'd welcome a chance to clean off some of this dirt. Being thrown into a muddy ditch hasn't given me the sort of smart appearance I was hoping to achieve today. Not when I'm trying to find a job.'

'A job in Churchwood?' Naomi asked.

'I applied for a job in Barton. It wasn't suitable but someone mentioned that there might be an opening here since a housekeeper is retiring. The employer is a Mrs Naomi Harrington who lives at a house called Foxfield. Do you know it?'

'I'm Naomi Harrington and Foxfield is just through those gateposts.'

The girl looked dismayed. 'It's a pleasure to meet you, Mrs Harrington, but I'm afraid I've made a terrible impression on you.'

'It wasn't your fault a dog jumped up at you. Now, it's a chilly day so I suggest you come inside and Mr Mead takes his dog home without delay. Mr Sykes, we'll have to speak tomorrow.'

The gardener was crestfallen, but it couldn't be helped. Naomi nudged the young woman forward.

'I'm Victoria Page,' the girl said. She offered a hand but, realizing it was filthy, she smiled ruefully and drew it back.

Suki's eyes widened when she opened the door and saw Victoria in all her mud and twigs. 'Miss Page has had an accident, Suki,' Naomi told her. 'Could you make tea and bring fresh towels upstairs, please?'

46

'Of course, madam.'

They removed their shoes before mounting the carpeted stairs to Naomi's large bathroom. 'Would you like a bath?' Naomi offered.

'I'm sure that won't be necessary, but thank you. I'll just wash my face and hands.'

'Perhaps your hair, too?'

Victoria studied it in the mirror and grimaced. 'Good idea.'

Suki came in with towels. 'Could you also fetch my dressing gown?' Naomi asked. 'Miss Page can wear it while we clean up her clothes as best we can.'

The maid brought the dressing gown and slippers, too. 'I'll take the clothes down to the scullery,' she offered. 'Cook and I can clean them up.'

Naomi thanked Suki and advised her unexpected visitor to come down when she was ready. 'I'll leave the sitting-room door open so you can find me,' she said.

Naomi wasn't kept waiting for long before Miss Page appeared. She was a tall, slender girl so the dressing gown was too short, but this wasn't a fashion parade.

Naomi invited her to sit and poured the tea that Suki had brought. 'What happened in Barton, if you don't mind my asking? I don't mean to pry into your private business.'

'The reason I didn't get the job had nothing to do with my abilities but with the fact that I need a live-in position,' Miss Page said. 'Not just for me but for two children, too.'

'You're a mother? Forgive my surprise, but you look so young.' The girl wasn't wearing a wedding ring, either.

'I'm twenty-two but I'm not actually related to the children. Their father was a dock worker who was killed in an accident before the war. Their mother died some months ago. She had a heart disorder but didn't know it until she collapsed suddenly.'

'I'm sorry. Was she a friend?'

'We worked together in a factory making wireless parts. War work. We came from different backgrounds but I admired Joan for her courage and laughter in the face of adversity. She was a loving mother, too. And yes, we became friends. When she knew she was dying she asked me to take care of her children since there was no one else. She didn't want them to be sent to an orphanage.'

Naomi felt sadness for the woman she'd never met. 'I'm glad she had you to help. But if you were working in a factory, I can't quite see . . .'

'How I'm qualified to be a housekeeper?'

'Yes.'

'I haven't always worked in a factory. My mother was a . . . nervous sort of woman who'd been brought up with a full complement of servants. We still had servants when I was young, since my mother inherited money, but neither she nor my father were the sort of people who could manage their finances efficiently and while my father wrote books for a living, they were scholarly books and didn't sell well. I only realized my parents had run out of money when I arrived home to find the servants had quit because they hadn't been paid, poor dears. My school fees hadn't been paid either, so I had to leave.'

'That must have been hard. Unless you were glad to leave?'

'I enjoyed school, actually. I even thought I might become a teacher. But it wasn't to be. I took on the care of the house and garden, teaching myself to cook from books borrowed from the library. I also became an assistant in a grocery shop, since we needed an income. Not that I earned much as a fifteen-year-old, but the grocer boosted my wages by giving me stock which had damaged packaging. He gave me the broken biscuits from the bottom of the tins as well. There were two biscuit tins – one for plain biscuits and one for creams. It was a treat to be given the broken creams.' She laughed at the memory and Naomi realized Victoria Page was a plucky young thing.

'It mortified my mother to have a daughter working in a shop,' she said then, 'but I don't see that there's anything wrong with an honest day's toil, do you?'

'I certainly don't.'

'Anyway, it meant we didn't starve, but when I was eighteen both of my parents died within a few months of each other. The house was rented and the furniture, china and other contents had to be sold to pay off debts. I think it only honourable to pay off debts. Needing a home as well as an income, I became a live-in housekeeper in London.'

'Wasn't it difficult to persuade someone to take you on in that role at such a tender age?'

'I made the employer an offer. I'd work for a month for no wages and if I didn't prove myself within that time, I'd walk away without complaint.'

'Enterprising of you.'

'Necessary. Even if I say so myself, I did well in the position and have a glowing reference to prove it. But when my employer moved into her daughter's house she no longer needed me, and I decided it was time I contributed to the war effort. Hence the wireless factory. But now I need to build a new life for the children away from London.'

'Weren't the children evacuated at the start of the war?'

'Yes, but they hadn't long lost their father and they were desperately unhappy, so Joan took them home when the Blitz ended.'

'Wouldn't they prefer to stay in London now? In a familiar place, I mean?'

Victoria shook her head. 'The Blitz may be over but bombs are still dropped sometimes, and then there are all the unexploded ones still around that could go off at any time . . .'

Naomi had once been caught up in the devastation caused by an unexploded bomb going off. It had fallen into the space between two buildings and no one had known it was there.

'And who's to say there won't be another Blitz?' Victoria asked. 'Besides, where we're living now . . . It's far from satisfactory.'

'Oh?'

'We're sharing a house with a group of other women and children who've all been touched by tragedy of one sort or another, but the building is due for demolition. We're all looking for new places to stay as a matter of urgency.'

'Do they all want to leave London?'

'If possible. It means we'll have to split up, which is a pity, but the countryside will be better for the children. Safer, with healthier air and space to run and play.'

'Not entirely safe.' Naomi told Victoria about the German plane that had crashed into the Sunday School Hall. 'But a place like Churchwood will never be a primary target for bombing raids.'

'That's what I thought.'

'Your young orphans are lucky to have you to take care of them,' Naomi said.

'I like to think the luck is on my side,' Victoria countered. It was hard to keep thinking of her as Miss Page when she was sitting in Naomi's dressing gown and talking about her life so openly.

'Arthur is eight and a lovely boy,' Victoria continued. 'He's so kind to his little sister, Jenny, who's four and just as lovely. He's taken another child under his wing as well. She's the granddaughter of a woman called Ivy whose daughter went off, leaving Flower with her. Actually, her name is Daisy, but everyone calls her Flower. She's four, too, but tiny. She has a weak chest and falls ill a lot. I think she brings out Arthur's protective instincts and in turn she dotes on him. She treats him like her hero.'

Naomi smiled but talking about children was always difficult since it reminded her of her own childless state. Oh, she did the best she could to hide it – the bookshop often teemed with children and Naomi forced herself never to refuse to help with them – but it was hard all the same.

Lost in her own thoughts, Naomi only just caught the shadow that passed over Victoria's face. 'Is there a problem with the children?' Naomi asked.

Victoria looked as though she wanted to deny it but then she sighed. 'It's just that losing their parents has been difficult for them. Jenny's reaction has been to cling to me, but Arthur seems to feel that he needs to be a man now. He wants to help all of us with money, but I worry that he'll take that wish too far.'

'By stealing?'

'Arthur would never do anything dishonest. Not knowingly. But I'm worried he might be led astray by older boys who could take advantage of his naivety. I'd like to give him a comfortable home so he doesn't have to worry about rent or the price of coal and can regain his childhood, if that makes sense?'

'It does.'

'I know I must have made the worst possible impression on *you*, Mrs Harrington, but if you hear of any vacancies that might suit me, would you let me know? I'll take on any job if it'll help me to provide a home for the children and spend a little time with them. I'm not asking for sympathy for myself and I'm not looking for charity. I want to work hard. To give good value for my wage and accommodation.'

'I understand. I don't know of any vacancies at present, but I'll gladly keep my eyes and ears open.'

'Thank you.'

'Just to be clear, you haven't made a bad impression on me,' Naomi added, 'but while it's true that my current housekeeper is retiring, I don't feel I can offer what you need. You've been frank with me, so I'll be frank with you. My husband and I are divorcing.'

'I'm sorry,' Victoria said, her green eyes warm with sympathy.

'It's for the best, I assure you, because I'm also getting married again once the divorce comes through. That makes me sound as fast as a giddy girl, though I've never been fast in my life. The thing is that, while I hope to keep this house, I'm unsure of what I'll do with it once I've remarried. Live in it, sell it, get a tenant for it . . .' She shrugged. 'I can't offer the sort of stability you and your children need.'

'Even a temporary position will give us breathing space and a chance to look around for something more permanent without the pressure of having to vacate a building that's facing demolition,' Victoria said. 'But forgive me, Mrs Harrington. I'm putting you in an awkward position, which is especially wrong of me after you've been so kind.'

'You're concerned for the children and that does you credit. Let me pour you another cup of tea and then I'll ask Cook to include you in the lunch.'

'Oh, no! I've intruded on your day enough.'

'I insist.'

Naomi went out but didn't head straight for the kitchen. Instead, she lingered in the hall, trying to sort through the jumble of thoughts and emotions that circled her head like an out-of-control carousel.

Victoria's story had touched Naomi's heart and she felt a strong urge to help the girl. But the only way which sprang to mind was to offer her the position of cook-housekeeper here, and that was surely a bad idea. Naomi had spoken truthfully when she'd said the future of the house was uncertain, but that wasn't the only consideration. Money was an issue, of course. A wage to pay and three more mouths to feed. More concerning was the fact that Naomi barely knew Victoria and hadn't met the children at all. The children might struggle to settle down to a life so different from anything they'd ever known before, and their rampaging might have the house in uproar.

Even if they did settle down well, they might threaten Naomi's peace of mind, for it was one thing to spend a limited amount of time with other people's children and quite another to have them around her constantly. There'd be no escaping the reminders of her own lost chance of motherhood.

Unable to decide what to do, but not wanting to be found wringing her hands in the hall, she moved on to the kitchen where Suki and Mrs Kitts were working on Victoria's clothes. 'They're coming along nicely,' Suki reported.

'That's wonderful. About lunch . . .'

'I've already assumed the young lady will be staying,' Mrs Kitts said.

'You're a mind reader,' Naomi told her.

'I just know you're a kind woman.'

A kind woman? Naomi didn't feel kind. She felt selfish.

They ate at the small table in the sitting room instead of in the formal dining room, and every line of conversation only reinforced Naomi's impression of Victoria as a courageous young woman who'd set aside her own interests to help others. The friends who shared the condemned house sounded heroic as well. They were all trying to do right by their children. All trying to evacuate from London and start afresh in safer, greener places.

Naomi wished them well, but that wasn't enough for her conscience, which seemed to be sitting at the table with them, nudging her constantly and saying, *Perhaps you can't help all the women, but you can help this one – if you choose.*

Naomi fought back with reminders of the uncertain future, the wage bill, the likelihood of chaos and the risk to her own emotions.

Selfish, selfish, her conscience chided. *The girl has said even a temporary position would be welcome, but you're too wrapped up in your own needs and wishes to give her a chance. Not good enough.*

The meal finally came to an end. 'That was delicious,' Victoria said. 'I'll leave you in peace now, but thank you so much for your kindness.'

Kindness? Bah! Naomi's conscience huffed.

'We need to be sure your clothes are dry before you leave,' Naomi said. 'You'll catch a chill if you go out in damp clothes on a cold day like this.'

'I'll soon warm up on the bicycle.'

'At least let me check that they're not soaking wet.' Naomi went back into the hall but her conscience followed.

You're running out of time, it told her.

All right! Naomi snapped back. *I give in, but mark my words: I could be making a terrible mistake.*

She continued into the kitchen.

'Almost dry,' Suki said, holding the iron close to Victoria's trousers.

'Thank you, Suki.' Naomi turned to Mrs Kitts. 'It seems Miss Page is looking for housekeeping work. I wonder if you might show her around the house, explain your role to her and give me your impression of her afterwards?'

'I'll be glad to, madam.'

Naomi returned to the sitting room. 'Victoria, I meant it when I said the future of this house is uncertain but, if you're interested in working here on a temporary basis, would you like to discuss it with Mrs Kitts, my current cook-housekeeper?'

'I'd love that, Mrs Harrington!'

'It's only a chat to help you understand what's involved, and there's no obligation on either side to take it further. We may find we wouldn't suit.'

'Of course. Do I need to dress first?'

'I think we left formality behind when you fell into that ditch.'

Victoria laughed. 'It wasn't my most dignified moment.'

Naomi took her into the kitchen and left her there.

I should think so, too, her conscience said.

Half hoping that Victoria would decide that the job wouldn't suit her, Naomi paced the sitting room, as was her habit when under stress. Basil watched her from his basket – always her companion in challenging times – and when she threw herself into a chair, he came out to nuzzle her fingers. 'What did you think of Victoria?' Naomi asked him.

His only answer was a mournful look, but mournfulness was his natural expression and Naomi was sure he'd have warmed to their young visitor.

In time, she heard Mrs Kitts showing Victoria around the house. Naomi couldn't catch their words but it seemed to be an equal sort of conversation. Victoria must be making a good impression, since Mrs Kitts tended to go quiet when she disapproved of anyone.

When Victoria returned to the sitting room, she'd changed back into her trousers. 'You have a beautiful house, Mrs Harrington. I'd like to work here very much, but I'll quite understand if you feel I'm not right for the job or if you're worried about the noise and bother of the children.'

A little noise and bother? Naomi's conscience scoffed. *They're a small price to pay for helping a woman and two children in need.*

Oh, shut up! Naomi told it. Out loud, she said to Victoria, 'Will you excuse me for a moment?'

Victoria gave a consenting smile.

'Well?' Naomi asked, in the kitchen.

'She may be young but she has a sensible head on her shoulders and a good attitude to work,' Mrs Kitts pronounced. 'Not a slacker, if you take my meaning. She's cheerful, too, which never hurts. You could do a lot worse, in my opinion.'

'Did she mention the children?'

'Children, madam?'

'She's taken on two young orphans and wants to evacuate them from London.'

'Then I have to admire her pluck. But two children running around this place . . . It would take some getting used to.'

It certainly would. Naomi's peace and quiet might be destroyed.

Back in the sitting room, she said, 'I have a suggestion for you to consider, Victoria, which is that you work beside Mrs Kitts for a trial period of a week. On your own, though. It wouldn't be fair to the children to uproot them only for a trial. Will your friends look after them for you?'

'I'm sure they will. We're a little community in our condemned house. We often look after each other's children.'

'Then, when would you like to start?'

'Now, if possible. I'm not expected home tonight, as I figured it might take a while to secure a position. I was planning on finding a B&B or something similar. I could send a telegram explaining that I won't be back for several days.'

'There's a post office in the village.'

'Thank you, Mrs Harrington. I'm grateful!'

'It's only a trial,' Naomi reminded her.

'Yes, but you won't regret it.'

Naomi certainly hoped not. 'I'll leave you to send your telegram and then I suggest you report to Mrs Kitts,' she said. 'I need to go out now.'

'Of course,' Victoria said.

Wanting desperately to talk to someone about her rash decision, Naomi headed into the hall for her coat.

CHAPTER EIGHT

Naomi

'Out with it, woman,' Bert said, when Naomi arrived at his market garden after taking her usual route through the woods behind Foxfield. 'I see you have troubles on your mind.'

'I've done something momentous, and I hope I'm not going to regret it.'

'That word, momentous, covers a lot of territory,' he told her. 'Good, bad and all stations in between.'

'I've taken on a new cook-housekeeper.'

'Should I be worrying that you're about to break off our engagement?'

'Of course not! I've made it clear that it's a temporary position and it's only a trial at present.'

'So why are you anxious? Is she a former lady of the night with dubious morals or something equally shocking?'

'She's a polite and well-spoken young woman. She reminds me of Alice in some ways.'

'If she has any of Alice's qualities, I'd say you're on to a winner.'

'The thing is, if I allow her to stay after the trial, she'll bring two children to live with her.'

'She's a widow? Or is her husband away at the war?'

'Neither. She's only twenty-two and unmarried. The children are orphans and Victoria took them on because their mother was a friend.'

'She adopted them?'

'I don't know the legalities of the situation, but in practice . . .'

'It's the sort of thing Alice would do. What do you know about these children?'

Naomi told him what she'd learned. 'I believe they're East End children. Cockneys, I suppose. I hope they fit in.'

'They'll run you ragged, woman, but you're not in your dotage yet. You'll manage, and you can always come to my house whenever you need to escape.'

'You don't think I've been foolish?'

'I think you've been kind. It's one of the things I love about you.'

There was that word again: kind. Naomi still didn't feel kind. She felt pummelled by conscience. Nervous, too. Even a little scared. 'I hope you'll help to keep the children in order, if the need arises.'

'Play Bert the Ogre, you mean?'

'Something like that.'

'I'll do everything I can to support the woman I love. We've faced challenges before and come through them. We'll come through again.'

Naomi hoped he was right.

Sykes was on the lookout for her when she reached Foxfield. Poor man! She'd forgotten all about him.

She walked towards him and said, 'At last we can talk, Mr Sykes.'

He took his cap off and crushed it between his fingers. 'It's about my shed.'

Her shed, actually, but Naomi's garden was Sykes's kingdom.

'Someone's been inside it.'

'A thief?'

'Nothing's been taken, as far as I can see. But things have been moved.'

'Could an animal be responsible? A squirrel, perhaps?'

'There's no squirrel or other wild creature hereabouts that's strong enough to move my lawnmower. Heavy, it is.'

'A person, then. Was this intruder looking for something, do you think? Food? Drink? Items to sell?'

'I only know he's been in my shed and moved my mower.'

'More than once?'

'Two or three times, I'd say.'

Naomi thought about it. 'Might he have moved the mower so he could lie down and sleep?'

'I suppose.'

Sleeping sounded harmless enough but Naomi was only guessing that the intruder was seeking shelter. He might still be working his way up to taking something. 'The shed isn't kept locked?'

Sykes drew himself up a little. She'd insulted him. 'For sure, it's kept locked. But the hasp is old and the screws are weak. I reckon this man is unscrewing it and then screwing it back on when he leaves.'

'Could you get a stronger lock?'

'I could.'

'Then please do so, and let me know if you see anyone loitering near by.'

He nodded, put his hat back on and shuffled away.

Naomi headed for the house. There'd been a stranger in Churchwood once before – John Gregson, who'd camped in the woods and existed on milk stolen from doorsteps and vegetables taken from gardens. Only after he'd died – caught in the blast when the plane crashed into the bookshop – had they learned his story. A sensitive man, he'd deserted from the army after being horribly

60

bullied and come to Churchwood to be near his wife and children, who'd recently moved to the village. Evelyn Gregson and the boys, Alan and Roger, lived here still.

Was Naomi's intruder another piece of flotsam from the war that had disordered so many minds and left so many people homeless? He might just be passing through but he'd lingered for several days already, so, just in case he became a problem, she decided to mention him to Bert next time she saw him. It wouldn't hurt to let a few others know about the intruder, too, starting with Alice. Hoping to find her at home, Naomi crossed the road to The Linnets.

CHAPTER NINE

Alice

Alice put down the newspaper with a sigh. There wasn't a single job in the 'Situations Vacant' column that might suit her. As for the notebook in which she planned to write a story, the pages remained blank.

Sweeping the newspaper under a tea towel, she got up to attend to her caller.

'Naomi! Come in.' Alice led the way into the kitchen. 'Tea?' she offered.

'I won't stay long, as I've a lot to do, but I want to make you aware of a couple of things.'

'Not bad things, I hope.' Alice gestured to a chair.

'One of them is a little worrying.' Naomi explained about the Foxfield intruder.

'I haven't seen a stranger around the village but I'll keep an eye out for one,' Alice promised. 'Many people have been made homeless by this war, so I suppose it isn't all that surprising that we should have a second stranger here so soon after the first, even if Churchwood is merely a small dot on the map of England.'

'True. I've asked Sykes to buy a stronger lock for the shed, since I don't want anything stolen. Maybe that will persuade the intruder to move on.' Naomi looked conflicted by what she'd done. 'I don't mean to be unkind if the intruder is in genuine need, but there may be children at Foxfield soon.'

Alice was intrigued. 'This is your other news?'

Naomi told her the story of Victoria Page and her cockney children.

Alice smiled. 'It's good of you to take them on, Naomi, but you must ask for help, if needed. Ruby Turner is from the East End so she might have some insight into what Victoria's children are used to, and Timmy Turner might befriend them, too. I know Brimbles Farm takes up a lot of their time, but even so . . .'

'Good idea,' Naomi approved.

'Evelyn Gregson and her boys might be willing to help make the newcomers feel welcome, too. They know what it's like to be outsiders.'

'Another good idea.'

'When are the children coming? Assuming Miss Page's trial goes well and you offer her the position.'

'I'm not sure, but I imagine Victoria will want them here as soon as it can be arranged.'

'Life is never dull in Churchwood!' Alice said, smiling and wishing she could drag herself out of her rut to appreciate what she had instead of moping about her failures.

Naomi left and Alice decided to walk into the village to buy bread and do what she could to shake off this low mood. Lost in thought, she failed to notice who was on the opposite pavement until Evelyn Gregson ran across the road and touched Alice's arm.

'Sorry, my head was away in fairyland,' Alice apologized.

'I just want to share my news,' Evelyn told her. 'I'm replacing Miss Forrest at the village school after she retires at Easter.'

'Evelyn, I couldn't be more pleased!'

'We had a rocky start in Churchwood but we're settled now and want to stay.'

'You and the boys have friends here.'

'We do. Thanks to you, Alice.'

Alice waved the compliment away. 'We may have some more new people coming.' She explained about Victoria and her children. 'Nothing is certain yet, though.'

'Anything I can do to help . . .' Evelyn said, and they parted with a hug.

Alice walked on, reflecting that Evelyn was looking well and happy, which was remarkable after she'd lost her husband only last year and for a while had been shunned by the village. It was to her credit that she was forging a good life for herself and her boys after so much adversity. Alice knew she had to pull herself together, too. If only it were as easy to do it as to think it.

CHAPTER TEN

Kate

I'm being discharged from hospital next week and I'm definitely going to my parents' house to recuperate! Leo had written. *It'll please the old dears and mean the next time you visit me will be in Cheltenham – if you're still willing to come? Perhaps for a night or two? I'll suggest a date as soon as I've settled in . . .*

Oh no. Nerves cramped Kate's stomach. Alice would tell her to hold her head high because only fools wouldn't cherish her as their son's sweetheart. Alice believed fervently that a person's values and kindness mattered more than their social class. In fact, she considered the very idea of judging people by their social class to be ridiculous, as rich people could be bad while poor people could be good. Kate agreed, but would Leo's parents think differently?

Driving the cart into the village for some shopping later, she was trying to talk herself into a more positive frame of mind when she noticed Alice staring up at Joe Simpson's old house.

'What's so interesting?' Kate asked, drawing the cart into the kerb.

'I'm wondering when Ellen's builder will start. It's been a few days since she said he'd start straight away.'

'Maybe he exaggerated his availability to be sure of getting the job,' Kate suggested.

'Maybe he did.' Alice put her head on one side as though assessing Kate. 'Is everything all right?'

'Leo goes home next week.'

'That's good, isn't it?'

'Of course. But he wants me to visit him at his parents' house.'

'You're worried you won't fit in,' Alice guessed.

'It's easier to tell myself I should hold my head high than actually do it.'

'They may be as nervous of meeting you as you are of meeting them,' Alice suggested. 'They may be afraid you'll think them old and boring.'

Was that likely?

'It's normal to be nervous of meeting a sweetheart's family,' Alice continued. 'Just don't let your nerves run away with you and spoil the joy of seeing Leo again. When are you going?'

'I don't know yet.' An awful thought slid into Kate's mind. What if the Kinsellas refused Leo permission to invite her because they didn't like what they'd heard about her?

'I'm sure May will lend you some clothes,' Alice said. 'That'll help your confidence.'

Tall, stylish May was generous like that. She was the perfect person to advise on grooming, too, from hair arrangements to cosmetics. 'I'll wait to see if an invitation actually arrives before I ask her,' Kate said.

'I suspect Leo can't wait to invite you.' Alice's eyes twinkled.

He might feel like that now. But once he was at home and under the influence of his well-to-do family . . .

'Is Daniel still hoping for some leave?' Kate asked, not wanting her worries to dominate the conversation.

'As far as I know.' Uncertainty was a fact of life in wartime.

As ever, work awaited Kate back on the farm, so she said

goodbye to Alice and moved on to the shops. Returning home, she found that Fred had monopolized the kitchen table for his whittling. There were drawings, knives, wood shavings and several animals in progress.

'Don't blame me for the mess. Blame Timmy,' Fred complained. 'He doesn't stop asking for things. A dog, a cat, a cow, a sheep . . . It's driving me nuts.'

No, it wasn't. Fred had found a purpose and he was enjoying it.

'You're improving,' Kate said, picking up a sheep. 'How did you make the wool look curly?'

'Dunno, really. I tried making swirls with one of the smaller knives, that's all.'

'It's good.'

'You're just saying that.'

'I can assure you I'm not. If someone had asked me a few weeks ago whether you had an artistic bone in your body, I'd have laughed and said not even a tiny one. It seems I'd have been wrong. If you keep this up, Timmy will be the envy of all the boys at school.'

'Don't talk soft.' Fred pulled a disbelieving face but couldn't quite hide his pleasure.

Unpacking the shopping, Kate thought that it had been a good day for Fred. She wished she could say the same for Ruby. Despite her efforts to appear cheerful, there were signs of unhappiness within. Occasional slumps in her shoulders . . . the speed with which smiles fell from her face . . . the way she stared into space . . . Even insensitive Kenny had noticed, judging from the puzzled looks he sent Ruby now and then.

They didn't appear to have argued, but not all romantic affection stood the test of time. Was Ruby thinking that she should stick things out for Timmy's sake? He loved it here and it wasn't as though Ruby had anywhere else to take him, except perhaps to the parents who'd never forgiven her for falling pregnant without being married, even though it hadn't been her fault.

Yet sticking it out wouldn't only mean sacrificing her own happiness. It would also be unfair to Kenny.

Catching Kate watching her, Ruby tilted her chin as though to hide behind a show of good cheer. 'Sausage and onion hotpot tonight,' she announced, and no one who hadn't seen her brooding would have thought that anything was wrong.

Problems . . . problems . . .

CHAPTER ELEVEN

Naomi

'I've changed my mind,' Naomi told Sykes.

'Eh?'

'I want the shed left unlocked.'

It had rained heavily last night. Icy-cold rain that must have been miserable for anyone spending the night shivering under a tree or in a makeshift shelter somewhere. She'd walked down to the shed early this morning and seen fresh footprints in the ground in front of the door. Long footprints that suggested they'd been made by a slender-footed man wearing shoes rather than boots. Had he come hoping to spend another night here, only to be bitterly disappointed at being unable to get inside now Sykes had installed a stronger lock?

Naomi had been imagining his distress when a sense of being watched had suddenly stolen over her like a cloud passing over the sun. She'd looked around and studied the furthest reaches of the garden. Had the intruder been observing her from the woods beyond it?

Trying to jettison the spooky feeling, she'd given herself a shake and come in search of Sykes, who started early at this time of year to make the most of the limited daylight hours.

'The intruder might simply need a place to shelter overnight,' she explained. 'I'm sure the lawnmower can survive being moved to make room for him. I'm going to put a pillow and some blankets in the shed later. Some food, too.'

'If that's what you want, missis,' Sykes said, clearly thinking she'd taken leave of her senses.

'It is, Mr Sykes.' Of course, the intruder might actually have moved on elsewhere after finding the shed locked against him, but time would tell.

Heading back to the house, she saw Victoria coming around the side as though aiming for the kitchen door. Victoria noticed Naomi, too, and waited for her to draw level. 'Have you been for a walk?' Naomi asked, thinking that perhaps the young woman liked some air and exercise before she settled into her day's work.

'I went out to post a letter. The telegram I sent yesterday was short, so I thought it might help the children if I wrote in more detail about where I am. I also wanted to thank my friends properly for taking care of the children while I'm here. I thanked them in my telegram but only briefly.'

'Telegrams are too expensive for much more than *Arrived safely – stop – will write – stop . . .*'

'So true!' Victoria's smile was warm and rueful. Naomi liked her more and more.

'I'll go in and see to your breakfast,' Victoria said.

'There's something I should tell you first.'

'You're not happy with my work?' Victoria's face registered dismay. Anxiety, too.

'Nothing like that,' Naomi assured her. She went on to explain about the intruder. 'I don't know if he's still in the area, but I thought I should warn you about him.'

'Poor man. He must be desperate. Well, as someone who's benefitting from your kindness in being given a place to stay and food to eat, I can't object if you extend that kindness to another. It isn't as though he's shown signs of being a threat, is it?'

'Not so far.'

'Let's hope it stays that way.'

Victoria went inside and Naomi looked down the garden again. There really was no reason to suspect any watcher of intending harm to her or anyone else. Even so, the idea of being spied upon was disconcerting.

Aware that her imagination might simply be playing tricks on her, Naomi set about her day. It took her into the village and she frowned when she saw that Joe's house still looked empty. Ellen had given her a key, so, just to be sure, she unlocked the door, popped her head inside and called out, 'Hello!'

She was met only by silence and emptiness. No ladders, buckets, toolboxes or anything else that would suggest the builder had even called in.

After lunch she set out for Bert's to ask for his views on the builder's non-appearance. With her thoughts full of this latest worry, she took her usual route through the woods, forgetting all about the intruder – until a figure suddenly burst from a bush up ahead of her and ran into the distance.

Naomi's heartbeat skittered in panic. She put a hand to her chest to try to steady it, the rational part of her brain pointing out that the figure had run away from her rather than towards her to do her harm. Even so, she walked on hurriedly, keeping a wary eye out in case the man turned around and followed her.

'You look like you've seen a ghost,' Bert remarked when she passed through the side gate into his market garden and made her way to where he was working.

'Not a ghost. A person.'

'The intruder?'

'I expect so. A man, I think. Tall, with stick-thin arms and legs. I didn't see his face and he had some sort of

71

blanket or sack over his head and shoulders. He startled me but then he ran away. Fast. I don't think he can be very old.'

'It sounds as though he was more scared of you than you of him.'

'I expect you're right. Anyway, I've decided to help him by leaving the shed unlocked.'

'Some food wouldn't go amiss,' Bert suggested.

'I'm going to put some in the shed along with a pillow and blankets. And I'll leave a note suggesting he knock on the door if he wants help.'

'He's probably just an ordinary person who's down on his luck, but if you'll forgive an old man for being protective, I'd rather you walked along Churchwood Way instead of through the woods on your way home. Is the intruder the reason you're here? Or have you come to drink in the sight of my handsome good looks and enjoy my riveting company?'

He was teasing. Bert was neither handsome nor conceited.

'I came to talk about Joe's house. There's still no sign of the builder. He could be unwell or out on a more urgent job, of course.'

'Or he might just be slacking now he knows he's got the job,' Bert said.

'Ellen may have given him permission to start later, but do you think I should mention his absence to her, just in case she's unaware of it? She might be able to give him a nudge.'

'Hmm.' Bert mulled the question over. 'I know we want the bookshop up and running as soon as possible, but Ellen already feels bad about what happened to the house. You don't want to make her feel bad about delays to the repairs as well.'

'That's why I'm hesitating,' Naomi said.

'Let's see what tomorrow brings and decide what to do then.'

It was good advice, since Naomi might be worrying over nothing.

'How's your new cook-housekeeper?' Bert asked, changing the subject.

'Doing well.'

They went indoors to chat over a cup of tea before Naomi made her way home – along Churchwood Way this time, with Bert walking at her side.

As dusk approached, she gathered together a pillow, blankets, sandwiches and a flask of hot tea then sat down to write a note.

Dear . . .

She paused. Dear what? *Dear Intruder? Dear Stranger?* Neither felt particularly friendly.

Dear Visitor, she decided.

Please feel free to use my shed as an overnight shelter, together with the bedding I've provided. There's also food and a hot drink for you. If you need anything else, please ask for it. Churchwood is a kind village and will help you.

With every good wish,
Naomi Harrington

She took the supplies down to the shed and left them on the workbench, securing the note with the flask so it wouldn't float away. Back outside, she paused to stare into the trees and bushes. Again, she felt a tingle that suggested she was being watched, but it was hard to separate reality from imagination. She still walked back to the house at speed.

CHAPTER TWELVE

Alice

Alice had just returned from the grocer's when Naomi emerged from between the Foxfield gateposts. 'I'm glad I've seen you,' Alice said. 'I want to let you know that I met Victoria at the shops and I like her very much. She has a smile for everyone, and kindly let Humphrey Guscott go in front of her in the queue at the baker's. He was looking a bit unsteady but she handled it tactfully by saying she needed a moment to make up her mind about what she wanted to buy.'

'She's a lovely girl,' Naomi agreed. 'I'm off to see if the builder has started work on Joe's house.'

'I can save you the walk because I looked through the window on my way past and there's still no sign of him.'

Naomi looked thoughtful. 'I think I'll have a word with Ellen, just to find out what's going on. I don't want to nag her, but— Actually, this looks like Ellen coming now.'

Alice turned and saw that Ellen was indeed approaching. Quickly, too, though whether her frown owed its existence to breathlessness or anxiety was hard to gauge.

'I was just coming to see you, Naomi,' she said, breathing heavily. 'I came to check how the builder was getting on but he doesn't seem to have started yet.'

Oh dear.

'We haven't seen him at all,' Naomi said. 'We wondered if he'd changed his starting date.'

'I haven't seen or heard from him since I agreed he should do the work,' Ellen told them.

'Is he on the telephone?' Alice asked.

'I don't remember him mentioning a telephone.'

'Might you visit him, then? Or dash off a letter asking him to get in touch?'

'That's a good idea,' Ellen agreed, but then she appeared to lose herself in thought. 'I was just trying to remember where I put his address.'

Alice exchanged an uneasy look with Naomi then said, 'He definitely gave you his address?'

'He must have done, mustn't he? I recall him saying he lived in Rawley, so I must have got the rest of his address from him, too.'

Alice couldn't see that one thing necessarily followed the other but didn't like to point this out.

'I'd better go home and find it,' Ellen said.

'Would you like to come in for a cup of tea first?' Alice invited, as the poor woman was looking flustered.

'Kind of you, but the sooner I get a letter in the post, the better. I'm so sorry about the delay.'

'Please don't worry about us,' Naomi said, doubtless equally reluctant to add to Ellen's woes. 'But would you telephone me later? Just to keep me informed?'

'Of course.'

Ellen bustled off again. 'I have a bad feeling about this,' Alice said.

'Me too,' Naomi admitted. 'But let's not go jumping to conclusions prematurely.'

'Wisely said. Is your intruder still loitering in Churchwood?'

'He is. I left food in the shed for him last night and it all got eaten. The blankets I'd left were used, too, judging from the way they were folded – untidily, though effort had been made. I also left a note inviting him to knock if he needed help. He wrote *Thank you* on the bottom but didn't show himself.'

'Too ashamed. Too proud. Too frightened,' Alice suggested.

'Like poor John Gregson when he was taking milk off doorsteps,' Naomi said.

'Let's hope this poor man doesn't meet a tragic end as well.'

'I'll leave another note and more food tonight. Hopefully, I'll build his trust so he'll come into the open. I saw him in the woods, by the way.'

'You *saw* him?'

'I think it must have been him. He ran away before I could get a good look at him, but he didn't strike me as old or infirm. Quite the opposite.'

'Do you think we should warn other people that there's a stranger around?' Alice asked.

They'd wrestled with the same question when John Gregson had first made his presence known by taking milk off doorsteps.

'This may be bad advice, but I suggest we give him another night in the shed first and hope it persuades him to seek help,' Naomi answered.

'So we wait to see what our stranger does, just as we wait to hear from Ellen,' Alice summarized. 'I hate waiting.'

'So do I.'

At least the wait to see Daniel was almost over. According to a telegram Alice had received, he was on his way back to England. Would she be able to shake off this feeling of failure and greet him with the clear-eyed purposefulness of old? Alice could only hope so. It was absurd to feel so powerless, but she couldn't seem to help it.

CHAPTER THIRTEEN

Kate

I'm home! Leo had written. *It's liberating to be out of the hospital and living a more normal life. Not quite normal, of course, as I'm convalescing instead of working and I'm being fussed over by my parents, bless them.*

I'm desperate to see you but my parents think I should settle in before receiving visitors and I don't wish to upset the old dears by resisting. I'll write again soon to suggest a date for your visit and I'll cross my fingers that it'll be convenient to you. In the meantime, please write back at the address above.

All my love, Leo x

Hmm. There was no doubt that Leo needed to rest and entertaining a visitor for a couple of days would be far more tiring than short visits in hospital. But were his parents really against *any* visitors yet, or was it Kate in particular they were reluctant to welcome? Were they hoping that time would diminish his ardour for her, helped along by reintroducing him to girls who were more their sort so he could see the difference?

She looked at the address at the top of the letter: *Claremont, Cavendish Place, Cheltenham.*

Kate's own address was similar in terms of format: *Brimbles Farm, Brimbles Lane, Churchwood.* But she suspected that the similarity between Claremont and Brimbles Farm ended there.

Sighing, she pushed the letter into her pocket and became aware that Kenny was hovering near by, looking awkward. They were alone in the kitchen, Ruby having gone out to collect eggs and Fred having gone out to choose more wood for his whittling.

'Um,' Kenny began, glancing towards the kitchen door as though fearing an interruption.

'What is it?' Kate asked.

'It's Ruby. Do you think she's all right?'

'Don't *you* think she's all right?'

'She says she's fine but . . . I don't know. I'm not good at all this talking lark.'

'Have you done anything to upset her?'

'I don't think so. But she keeps going kind of . . . quiet. And one time she snapped at me for hugging her when I had dirt on my shirt.'

'I expect she didn't want you to get dirt on *her*. You know she's always trying to make you cleaner.'

'Yes, but she's never snapped at that sort of thing before. She's just rolled her eyes.'

'Maybe she thinks the eye-rolling isn't getting the message across about cleaning up before you touch her.'

Kenny merely looked glum.

Kate sighed again. 'Ruby hasn't said anything to me about being unhappy.' Whatever was troubling the land girl, she was keeping it to herself.

'Could you . . . *you* know? Speak to her? Find out which way the wind is blowing?'

'I can try, but I can't promise she'll want to talk.'

'Just try, yes?'

Fred entered then, accompanied by an icy breeze that blew curls of whittled wood from the table to the floor. Kate fetched the brush to sweep them up and, after a moment of dithering uncertainty, Kenny went back out to work.

Ruby returned with the eggs. 'It occurred to me that you haven't made a wooden chicken yet,' she told Fred.

'It's on my list of animals I want to make.'

'My favourite so far is the cat,' Ruby said. 'Timmy's favourite is the lion with the big mane. His friends at school loved it, apparently.'

Watching Ruby now, there appeared to be nothing wrong with her. It was only in unguarded moments that her mood showed.

This was neither the time nor the place to attempt a heart-to-heart with her, but when Kate went out to work she took a detour to the barn where Pearl was cleaning tools. 'If you're bored, I could take over cleaning and you could sow broad bean seeds in pots ready for planting out later,' Kate said, to open the conversation.

'I don't mind sticking with this job,' Pearl told her. 'I've nearly finished, anyway.'

'You're still enjoying working here?'

'There's nowhere I'd rather work. You know me, Kate. I *need* to get stuck into digging or ploughing or even cleaning tools. I wouldn't know what to do with myself if I didn't have work. Besides, farm work is the only thing I've ever been good at.'

'I'm glad you're happy,' Kate said. 'You're such an asset to the farm.'

Pearl gave a dismissive snort but her plain face flushed endearingly.

'How about Ruby?' Kate asked. 'Do you think she's still happy?'

'Timmy loves it here so Ruby loves it here too.'

'She's a wonderful mother. But I wonder . . . do you think she looks a little low sometimes?'

Pearl glanced up from the shears she was cleaning. 'I haven't noticed, but I suppose the weather could be

79

getting her down. It's cold the way the wind whips across the fields and it's a long walk into the village for someone who's used to living in a big city like London. Get the bookshop up and running with a party and she'll soon cheer up. Why? Do you think she's low?'

'I just want to be sure you're both all right.' Kate didn't want Ruby to hear that she'd been asking questions about her.

'Does the Women's Land Army expect you to check on us or something?'

'I'm responsible for your welfare, yes. But I care about you anyway. You're my friends.'

Pearl flushed again and said, 'Crikey!'

Back in the kitchen later, Kate was washing her hands in the sink when Pearl entered. 'Alice walked past a few minutes ago,' she reported. 'She asked me to tell you there's a meeting of the bookshop team tomorrow.'

'Oh?'

'It's at Alice's cottage at seven o'clock if you can make it. Maybe there's good news about the bookshop.'

Or maybe there was bad news about the bookshop instead.

CHAPTER FOURTEEN

Naomi

'I'm glad you could make it,' Naomi whispered to Kate as the tall girl strode into the dining room of The Linnets, where the bookshop team was meeting. The cottage had a pretty sitting room but Alice insisted that her father use it as his study, leaving her with the dining room for entertaining guests. The furniture had come from their much larger house in London so was too big for the space available, but there was just enough room around the table for all of them: Alice, Naomi, Bert, Adam, May, Janet – and now Kate.

'I thought it might be helpful to talk about the problems with the bookshop,' Alice began.

'More problems?' Kate asked.

'I'm afraid so. You spoke to Ellen, Naomi,' Alice said. 'Would you like to explain?'

Naomi nodded. 'Ellen's builder seems to be some sort of con man. Not only has he failed to do the work, he's also made off with Ellen's money. He talked her into paying the full amount in advance and omitted to give her his address except for saying he lived in Rawley.'

'That's just a village,' Janet pointed out. 'Someone there will know him.'

'That's what Ellen thought, so she took the bus there.'

'Let me guess,' Kate said. 'No one in Rawley had ever heard of him.'

'Presumably, he lied about where he lived to cover his tracks,' Naomi confirmed.

'Can the police trace this man and get her money back?'

'I've suggested she contacts the police as soon as possible,' Naomi said, 'but I think we have to assume they won't be successful. Unfortunately, the money she paid included every penny Joe left her and her own savings, too. She's very distressed and blames herself for everything – forgetting the insurance, forgetting to get the chimney swept and handing over money without checking she was giving it to a genuine builder. She feels she's let everyone down.'

'Poor Ellen,' Kate said. 'And poor bookshop. Is there no chance of getting it repaired now?'

'It might be possible to set up some sort of loan arrangement,' Bert said, 'but Ellen is a proud woman and may need time to come to terms with what's happened first.'

'The purpose of tonight's meeting is to ensure you all understand the position,' Alice said. 'People were excited when they thought the bookshop might open again soon. If anyone asks why no progress is being made, I suggest we simply say there's been a delay, without going into detail.'

'I agree,' Adam said. 'Ellen is already feeling humiliated. We should do everything we can to avoid adding to that embarrassment.'

'There's another thing to mention,' Naomi said. 'Someone – a stranger, I think – has been sleeping in my shed.'

'There's another thief about?' May was shocked. 'Not that I mean to call John Gregson a thief, because he only took milk from doorsteps when he was desperate.'

'I'm not aware that this man has stolen anything,' Naomi reported. 'He actually wrote *thank you* for the food and blankets I left for him, so he seems to be harmless.'

'Have you seen him?' Janet asked.

'I might have seen him in the woods – I had the impression of someone tall and thin – but he ran away.'

'Scared,' Bert suggested.

'What do you want us to do?' Janet continued.

'Nothing for the moment,' Naomi said. 'Let's wait and see if he moves on or asks for help.'

The meeting broke up and Naomi walked back towards Foxfield with Bert. 'Here's hoping Ellen will let me lend her some money,' he said. 'It's hard to see any other way forward.'

'If only my divorce would go through quickly, I could buy the house in its current state. Ellen wouldn't have to be involved in the repairs at all and she'd have enough money to give her children all the help they need.'

'Life isn't as convenient as that.'

'You could be out of pocket for a long time if you lend Ellen the money, Bert.'

'I'll manage. I'll help you pay Ellen rent on the house until you can buy it, too. I know it'll stretch you financially to pay it all yourself, especially as you've now got young Victoria and possibly a couple of kids to support.'

'You shouldn't feel obliged to help.'

'Obliged? What nonsense! The bookshop is for all of us. Besides, I'll be marrying you as soon as it's legal and we'll be exchanging vows, too. *All our worldly goods we thee endow*, or however the words of the ceremony go. I love you, woman.'

The declaration never failed to move her. 'I love you too, Bert.'

'That's good to hear.' He took hold of her arm and linked it through his.

'Lending Ellen money for repairs may help get the bookshop off to a start but it won't help her children,' Naomi said. 'She won't accept loans for them.'

'It's a mess,' Bert agreed. 'But the rent we pay should go some way towards helping them. If I could get my hands on the man who conned her . . .'

'I feel the same way,' Naomi said. She paused and then added, 'I'm thinking of confirming Victoria as my cook-housekeeper. She's so hard-working that I've no grounds for refusing her.' Naomi's heart wasn't hard enough, either. 'What do you think? Is a new cook-housekeeper an extravagance on my part?'

'Foxfield is a big house. It needs people to look after it.'

'You don't think I should roll up my sleeves and learn to cook and clean?'

'You'll learn soon enough when you're married to me. Besides, the village is better off with you being available to give help when it's needed – visiting the sick and lonely, doing their shopping . . . With luck, there'll be the book-shop to get up and running, too.'

'Even so.'

'You do good in the world, woman. Unless I'm much mistaken, you're not just thinking of your own comfort in taking Victoria on, but also that of her and those little kiddies.'

She *was* thinking of those kiddies but, while she wanted to help them, she was still worried sick about the heartbreak they'd stir in her own breast. She roused herself. 'Would you like to come in for a sherry?'

'Tempting, but I've got strawberry nets to mend. It may not be strawberry season but these dark winter months are all about getting ready.'

He kissed her goodbye – so lovely! – and went on his way.

Victoria's eyes shone with joy when Naomi told her the job was hers. 'Mrs Harrington, you won't regret it.

I'll work hard and I'll make sure the children are well behaved, too.'

'When will you fetch them?'

'I'll speak to Mrs Kitts about a convenient date, though I'll write to the children and my London friends straight away to let them know I have the job. Thank you so much for this opportunity.' Victoria seized Naomi's hand and squeezed it. 'I'm truly grateful.'

'As I said before, it's only—'

'Temporary. I understand. But it's a new start in a lovely place and I couldn't be more grateful.'

Naomi smiled through her unease.

Later that evening, she looked out of her bedroom window, unable to see the shed in the darkness but picturing the intruder wrapped in her blankets and eating the picnic she'd left. She hoped he was warm and well.

Washed and dressed the following morning, and assuming the intruder had slipped away with the dawn, she walked down to the shed before breakfast to retrieve the flask for washing up.

She opened the door only to come to a sudden, shocked halt. Far from having slipped away, the intruder was still there. Still sleeping. Naomi breathed out slowly to still her fast-beating heart and wondered if she should creep away again to avoid startling him. But as she stared at him – at the half-covered face and the adolescent fluff of a boy who hadn't shaved in a while – a bigger, deeper sense of shock rose up in her like a tsunami. And Naomi felt herself transported in her mind back to that awful afternoon at Marcroft's Hotel . . .

CHAPTER FIFTEEN

Naomi

Suspicion had taken Naomi into London that day: the suspicion that Alexander might be having an affair. Following him into the hotel and taking a seat in a quiet corner of the restaurant from where she could observe him without being seen, she'd expected him to be meeting a lover. But when she saw that he wasn't only sharing his table with a pretty fair-haired woman but also with two children, she thought she must be mistaken – until she realized how much the boy resembled Alexander with those long limbs and imposing nose.

She didn't confront Alexander immediately. She staggered from the hotel instead, utterly distraught. It was bad enough that Alexander had betrayed her. Bad enough that he'd obviously married her only to get his hands on her father's fortune. But much, much worse was the fact that he had a secret family. All her adult life Naomi had yearned for children but, in barely touching her, Alexander had denied her the chance of motherhood while fathering children of his own with someone else. Someone who wasn't merely a source of funds but a woman he loved.

Only later did Naomi confront him. By then she had evidence that he'd gone through a marriage ceremony with his Amelia Ashmore despite being legally married to Naomi. Threatening to expose his bigamy didn't relieve the pain she felt but it forced him to agree a divorce settlement in which he was to transfer Foxfield into her sole name and return some of the trust fund he'd pilfered from her over the years.

That had been months ago now but ever since, she'd suspected he might try to overturn that agreement somehow. It made no sense that he'd have sent this boy as either his spy or his emissary, though. So what *was* the boy doing here?

Several minutes passed and Naomi used them to try to decide what to do. But the situation was so strange that her mind simply recled. When the boy opened his eyes at last, they looked blank for a moment, until misery settled into them, probably at remembering his sorry whereabouts. But then he must have noticed her shoes. His gaze moved upwards in growing horror until it reached her face and with a strangled cry he tried to leap to his feet, only to be caught up in the blankets and stumble into the lawnmower.

'Careful!' Naomi cautioned.

'I need to leave,' he said, unable to do so because she was blocking his way. 'I haven't done any harm.'

'I'm not suggesting you have. It's William, isn't it? William Harrington?'

His face had already looked white and gaunt, his clothes and hair dishevelled. But he looked even whiter at this. 'You know me?'

'I saw you once.' This was Alexander's secret son, the boy she'd seen in Marcroft's Hotel that terrible day. 'Come into the house,' she said.

'I can't do that!' He looked appalled.

'You need to explain what you're doing here. And no offence, but I'd rather talk to someone who's clean and odour-free.'

William blushed. 'I didn't come here to be your *friend*.' He injected contempt into the word.

'I don't suppose you did. But neither do I suppose you

came here because you fancied camping in my shed in the depths of winter.'

The boy looked embarrassed, but made an effort to fight back. 'I came to confront you!'

'There's no reason why you can't confront me indoors.'

She turned and headed for the house, hoping he'd follow. He did, but only, she guessed, because he was at a loss for something else to do. She led him through the kitchen door, much to Suki's consternation. 'We'd like tea, please, Suki,' Naomi said. 'A sandwich, if possible, too. But wait twenty minutes.'

'Yes, madam.' Suki's eyes were wide as they studied William.

Naomi reached the door that led into the main hall. 'Would it be too much to ask you to remove your shoes?' she asked the boy. 'They're muddy.'

His face was mutinous. Clearly, he didn't want to agree with anything she suggested, but he looked down and must have seen how very dirty they were because he eased them off.

'I'd prefer you didn't dirty my furniture, either, so perhaps a bath?'

He hesitated, looking mulish, then shrugged as though trying to protect his pride by pretending it was a matter of indifference to him.

She took him upstairs and fetched a clean towel and an old shaving set that Alexander had left behind. 'Take as long as you wish,' she said.

'Humph.'

Naomi imagined he didn't know what else to say.

Leaving him, she walked along the landing to her own bedroom, where she sat on the bed, wondering what on earth had brought William Harrington to her door. A confrontation, he'd said, but what did that mean? Naomi was surprised he even knew of her existence. It still seemed doubtful that Alexander had sent him, though if William was here of his own free will, why had he spent more than a week camping in her shed? Had he come fired up with purpose, only to lose his nerve? It would explain the way his anger vied with his vulnerability.

She listened to him filling the bath. But then it occurred to her that he might have no clean clothes to change into. He had a bag but all his clothes might be filthy.

Hastening downstairs, she grabbed her coat and crossed the lane to The Linnets, relieved to find Alice at home. 'I'll explain why another time, but just now I'm in a hurry,' Naomi said. 'Did Daniel leave any clothes behind? If so, might I borrow them?'

'Yes, he did, and yes, you can, though I'm intrigued about why you want them. Come in and wait in the warmth while I fetch them.'

Naomi stepped into the hall and Alice ran upstairs, returning a few minutes later with a bag. 'Trousers, shirt, sweater, underwear and socks. Also some shoes.'

'You're an angel.'

'I hope they fit whoever needs them. I'm looking forward to learning who he is.'

'I don't know the full story myself yet.' Naomi turned to leave.

'Good luck!' Alice called.

At home, Naomi was glad to find that William was still in the bathroom. She could hear water splashing. 'I'm leaving some clothes for you outside,' she called through the door. 'They may not fit perfectly but at least they're clean.'

The splashing had stopped so she was sure he'd heard her, but he stayed silent and she guessed he was fighting a battle between good manners and the hostility that arose from whatever grievance had brought him here.

Naomi returned to her bedroom to wait and soon heard the bathroom door creak open. Just a crack, she estimated. She pictured William peering out to be sure she wasn't lurking on the landing then snatching up the clothes. Seconds later the door snapped shut again.

Naomi walked back along the landing. 'Tea downstairs and a sandwich, too, if you're hungry,' she called.

Suki was carrying the tray into the sitting room when Naomi reached the hall. 'Thank you, Suki.'

'Will that be everything, madam?'

'For the moment.'

Suki left but was clearly desperate to know more about this unusual visitor. Soon Naomi heard William's hesitant footsteps on the stairs. 'In here!' she called.

He shuffled along the hall and stood in the doorway. 'Tea,' she said, placing a cup on the small table beside the sofa that stood opposite her armchair. She put the sandwich beside it.

The boy tilted his chin as though it would degrade him to acknowledge her existence but sat down with as much dignity as he could muster. Daniel was trim but William was skinny, all spidery legs and arms in the unfamiliar clothes. He stole several looks at the tea before he could resist it no longer. He picked it up and took a sip. A sip soon became a gulp of pure relief. He ignored the sandwich but Naomi guessed it was calling to him because his gaze kept straying towards it and she could practically see him salivating. She half turned away to look out of the window and William seized the moment to grab the sandwich and take a giant bite.

She gave no sign of having noticed but simply turned back and picked up her own cup, sipping her tea until the sandwich was no more. It didn't take long.

'So . . .?' she said then.

Emotion worked over the youthful face and his Adam's apple bobbed up and down as he swallowed. 'You've ruined everything!' he accused.

Naomi nodded to show she was giving his accusation some consideration before asking gently, 'I wonder if you might explain?'

'We were happy. Or at least not as *un*happy. An ordinary family, anyway. But now my father says we're going to be poor because of you. He's furious, and my mother . . . Well, she's upset and so is my sister.'

'Your father told you this?'

'Not exactly. I heard him tell my mother. Shout it, rather. It was awful.'

'William, do you know who I am?'

'Naomi Harrington.'

'Yes, but do you know my relationship to your father?'

'You're . . . you're . . .' He swallowed again. 'You used to be married to my father but you made him unhappy and when he fell in love with my mother you wouldn't let him go, so they had to pretend to be married. Now you want to divorce him but you're taking all his money out of spite. A lot of his money, anyway.'

'You heard your father telling your mother this, too?'

'I asked him and he explained.'

'William, I didn't know you, your sister or even your mother existed until a few months ago. Your father has never asked me for a divorce. We're only getting a divorce now because I want it.'

'That isn't true. My father wouldn't lie.'

'I'm not going to argue, William. It's understandable that you love your father and don't want to think badly of him.'

He looked startled at that, and Naomi wondered if his feelings for his father were rather more complicated.

He thought for a moment before fighting back with, 'Whatever happened in the past, you're taking our money now.'

'I had a trust fund of fifty thousand pounds when I married your father.'

The sudden widening of his eyes signalled that this was the first he'd heard of Naomi having money of her own.

'It was set up by my father using money he'd received from the sale of his business. All I want now is this house – a large house, but hardly a mansion in Mayfair – and the return of just some of my trust fund. Your father can keep the flat in London and any other property he may own. He can also keep any other investments and all the money he earns in the future. Does that seem unreasonable?'

His face showed his urge to retort that of course it was unreasonable – but something held him back. A sense of fairness, she hoped, or at least a dawning recognition that his father's words might not have painted a complete picture of the situation.

'I don't know how much money your father has. Or your mother,' Naomi said.

'She has nothing!'

So the house in Virginia Water in which Alexander's lover lived with their children hadn't – as he'd claimed – been bought from inheritances she'd received. He must have supplied most of the purchase price from Naomi's money.

'Your father has a good job, and investments, too,' Naomi pointed out. 'Are you really afraid that you'll be poor?'

The boy shrugged.

'Is it the thought of being taken out of school that troubles you? Are you worried about the fees?'

'I wouldn't care if I never set foot in that school again!'

'You don't like it?'

'I hate it. I'm not . . . clever enough. Not for my father . . .' He let his words trail off then gave Naomi another harsh glare. 'It'll be even worse if the other boys hear that my mother isn't married to my father.'

'Who would tell them?'

'I don't know. But if one person finds out, it'll be all over the school in five minutes, and the boys will be . . . They'll be vile, and there'll be no escaping them.'

'It's a boarding school?'

'Of course it's a boarding school! That sort of thing matters to my father!'

'Status, you mean? Social standing?'

He shrugged his thin shoulders again.

'Does your sister feel the same?'

'Not as much. But she's at a girls' day school and anyway, she's . . . Things are easier for her.'

'Your father expects higher standards from you than from your sister?' Naomi guessed, and it seemed she'd hit the nail on the head because William didn't answer.

'She's cleverer, though,' he finally admitted, and Naomi liked him for his fairness.

'You don't strike me as being stupid, William,' she said.

'I'm not. I'm in the middle in most classes. Average.'

'But that isn't good enough for your father. What about sports? Music? Things like that?'

'I once came tenth in a cross-country run but I'm no good at cricket or rugby. And I've been told I'm tone-deaf so I'm no good at music, either.'

Poor boy. 'Can't your mother ask your father to be a little more . . . gentle with you?'

He looked at Naomi as though she'd just floated down from the moon. 'My mother wouldn't dare argue with my father. She isn't like you.'

93

No. She was pretty now and must have been a stunning golden-haired angel in her youth. But William hadn't been thinking of appearances. 'She isn't strong, I mean,' he explained.

'If I'm forceful, it's only a recent change,' Naomi said. 'When I was married to your father I rarely stood up to him.'

'He's a bully,' William declared.

Naomi agreed but didn't like to tell this troubled boy so. She poured him another cup of tea and tried to steer the conversation round to the reason he was here.

'You mentioned confronting me. What is it you want me to do?'

He drew himself up, doubtless remembering that she was supposed to be his enemy. 'I want you to stop fleecing my father for money.'

Something in her face must have reminded him that the boot had been on the other foot when it came to fleecing. He slumped a little, clearly at a loss. 'I want him to stop shouting. All through the Christmas holiday he was shouting and being mean. To my mother. To me. Even to my sister a little bit.'

'Is that how you found out about me? From the shouting?'

'He just called you "that woman" so I didn't know you were his wife at first. It's against the law, isn't it? To be married to two people at once?'

'It's called bigamy.'

'My father would never admit to doing something bad. But I sneaked downstairs one night and looked through his study. That's where I found your name and address. On papers from a lawyer. I didn't know what to do at first. I went back to school but I couldn't think straight. And then I flunked a maths test and I knew Father would be furious.'

'So you ran away, hoping that if you managed to per-suade me to withdraw my claim for money, your father would calm down and not be quite as angry?'

'I wanted him to stop shouting at my mother, too,' he said, and Naomi understood that running away hadn't only been a selfish act.

'But you didn't speak to me when you got here,' Naomi pointed out.

'I . . . didn't know how to go about it. And then I watched you – in the garden with your dog, talking to the people who work here and visitors, too.'

'You realized I wasn't quite the monster you expected.'

'I don't know,' he said, and he sounded helpless, as though his reality had been shaken to its core.

'Does your father know you're here?'

William's face registered horror. 'No.'

'Does he even know that you're safe?'

He gave her another tortured look which clearly meant no.

'I'm sure the school must have told him you're missing,' Naomi said. 'Everyone must be frantic about you – the school, your father, your mother and your sister.'

He'd come here fired up with a mission, only to question it and lose his nerve. Now he was stuck.

'You can't send me back,' he said suddenly. 'I won't go!'

'That isn't for me to decide, but we must let your par-ents know you're safe.'

He sat forward, his hands covering his face in defeat. He knew she was right.

'Shall I telephone on your behalf?' Naomi offered. She wasn't afraid of Alexander any more. He could shout all he liked and his anger would bounce off her.

'Would you? I could telephone my mother but . . .' His mother would then be tasked with telling his father and the anger would rain down on her like savage darts.

'Is he likely to be in his office?'

'Probably.'

Which meant that Alexander wouldn't vary his routine for the trifling matter of a missing son. 'I'll telephone from the study,' she said, not wanting the boy to hear the fury that would doubtless come down the line. If Alexander was angry at his son for running away, he'd be incensed to learn that William was with Naomi.

Thinking about everything the boy had told her, she was struck by how wrong a person could be. Ever since she'd learned of Alexander's secret family, she'd imagined it as blissfully happy.

Not that she was glad it had its problems. Not when William was sitting on her sofa, filled with misery.

She looked at the phone, bracing herself, then picked it up and asked to be connected to Alexander's office. She reached his secretary first, the crisp Miss Seymour. 'I'll need to check if Mr Harrington is available,' she told Naomi, an obvious ploy to give him a chance to decline the call.

But moments later his voice sounded in her ear, brusque and irritated. 'What do you want, Naomi? If you want more money, you can—'

'I'm not calling about money. I'm calling about your son.'

A moment of surprised silence followed. 'What about him?' Alexander asked then.

'I'm ringing to let you know that he's safe.'

'What do you mean? What do you know of William?'

'I know he's in my sitting room.'

'*What?*'

'He's here. At Foxfield.'

'But why? Have you lured him there with—'

'Don't be ridiculous, Alexander. And save your breath

96

if you're thinking of shouting. I won't listen. I'm merely letting you know that William is safe. Upset, but safe.'

'Have you been harbouring him in some twisted game of revenge?'

'What did I just say about being ridiculous? I've never spoken to him before today.'

'But why is he there?'

'It seems he came to persuade me to cancel our agreed settlement because it would leave your family poor. Obviously, he didn't understand the circumstances, but I've put him right now.'

'You're poisoning him against me.'

'I think you're achieving that all by yourself. Anyway, isn't the most important thing his welfare? You haven't asked how he is.'

'You'd have said if he wasn't all right.'

Maybe she would. But in failing to ask, Alexander had shown his coldness.

'I suppose I'll have to come and get him,' he said. 'Unless you can put him on the train and send him home?'

'To save you the bother of the journey?'

'I'm a busy man.'

'You're certainly a horrible one. I'm not going to do anything today and I'm not going to let you into the house if you come here. In fact, I'm not going to let you into the house at all until I telephone again to give you permission to visit. You need to calm down and William needs to recover from his ordeal. The poor boy has been sleeping rough.'

'More fool him.'

'Every word you say makes me so glad that I'm divorcing you. I'm ringing off now. I'll leave it to you to tell William's mother that he's safe. I'll telephone again in a day or two. In the meantime, I suggest you ask yourself why William's life is so miserable that he's had to run away from school.'

'How dare you—'

Naomi put the phone down and returned to William in the sitting room. The boy looked scared. 'Did you speak to him?'

'I did.'

'Is he coming to drag me back to school?'

'Not today.' She smiled. 'I told him I wouldn't let him in the house.'

William looked surprised but then he grinned. 'He's met his match in you, Mrs Harrington!'

'I only wish I'd stood up to him long ago. But we can't change the past. We can only look to the future.'

The boy's face fell. His future promised ill.

'Thinking about the immediate future, you can't spend another night in that shed. You can sleep here. Have some dinner here, too. We'll decide tomorrow what's best to be done.'

He blinked and Naomi saw tears in his eyes. 'Thank you.'

'I've a few things to be getting on with now. Why don't you take a book from that bookcase and relax for a while? You'll find it pleasant to sit in front of the fire.'

Not wanting to embarrass him in case his tears began falling, Naomi left the room to tell Victoria that there'd be one more person at lunch and dinner. 'He's no ration book with him, of course, but we'll manage.'

Creeping back to the sitting room, she saw that William had taken a book only to fall asleep before he'd even opened it. She was glad since he couldn't have slept well shivering in the shed. Needing to think for a while, Naomi returned to the study and sat in the chair behind the desk where Alexander had formerly sat.

She might no longer be afraid of him but it was

unpleasant to have to deal with him again, and doubtless she'd have to face more of his anger before William was restored to his school or home. How unhappy the boy must have been, and how unhappy he'd be again if his life continued in the same way as before.

Of course, at around sixteen or seventeen, he wasn't many years from adulthood and then he'd be free to make his own choices. It would be hard for William to break away from his family to live a life that differed from his father's expectations, though. Alexander wasn't a forgiving man and it stretched Naomi's imagination hardly at all to picture him cutting off his son without a penny if William's choices displeased him. With his mother unable or unwilling to fight for him, William was at his father's mercy.

Wanting to talk to someone, Naomi telephoned Bert, keeping her voice soft so she wouldn't be overheard by William if he woke and walked into the hall. 'You'll never guess what happened just now.'

'Knowing you, woman, I expect it involved helping someone in need.'

'I came face to face with the intruder and he turned out to be Alexander's son,' she said.

'The icicle's boy? Well, well, well. That promises to be an interesting story. Shall I come over to hear the full version?'

'If it's no trouble.'

'Not for you, my love. Expect me in a few minutes, so get the kettle on.'

Soon his ancient truck could be heard on the drive, sounding like the death throes of a metal leviathan from the ocean deep.

A peep into the sitting room established that William was still sleeping, so Naomi and Bert drank their tea in the study. Bert glanced around the room and Naomi wondered if he was picturing Alexander sitting here in the past.

'A house is just bricks and mortar, and furniture is just chopped-down wood,' he said, to disabuse her of any notion that reminders of Alexander might upset him. Bert had an uncanny ability to read her thoughts. 'I'm more interested in that boy.'

Naomi told him what had happened and was surprised that Bert was *un*surprised. But then, he hadn't been tortured by fantasies about Alexander's new family living in loving bliss. Down-to-earth Bert had a much shrewder understanding of Alexander. 'A horrible man and a horrible father,' he said. 'No wonder the boy ran away. The question is, what happens to him now?'

'I've no right to interfere on William's behalf,' Naomi said. 'I expect it's against the law to come between a man and his son when that son is still a child.'

'I expect it is. But I imagine you won't let a minor inconvenience like the law of the land stop you from doing what you can for the lad.'

'I don't know what to do, but at least I've stopped Alexander from dragging William away today.'

'It's a start,' Bert agreed. 'If you want my advice, I'd stop him from getting the boy back tomorrow, too. An extra day will help William recover some strength and maybe it'll take some of the fire out of the icicle's temper.'

'I'll telephone Alexander again tomorrow before he has a chance to set out,' Naomi agreed, 'though whether he'll take any notice remains to be seen.'

'The lad disappeared once and he can disappear again,' Bert pointed out.

'You wouldn't actually encourage him to disappear?'

'Let's just say I might not stop him. But we shouldn't

get ahead of ourselves. We need a chat with the lad once he's woken and got some hot food inside him.'

Bert returned to his market garden and Naomi went upstairs with Victoria to prepare a bedroom for William. 'I'm sorry I couldn't give you warning of his arrival,' Naomi said, but Victoria only smiled.

'I'm glad to help. I saw your guest when he walked up from the shed and he looked to be in a sorry state. I'm glad he's found kindness with you, Mrs Harrington.'

What a nice girl Victoria was. Bert thought so, too. 'Welcome to Churchwood,' he'd said on first meeting her. 'You've been living in London, I believe. Interesting city, but I'm more of a country man.'

'It is an interesting city,' Victoria had agreed. 'A great city, in fact. But not right for children in wartime.'

He'd spent a few minutes drawing her out about the children and her life in general, reporting to Naomi afterwards, 'You've got a fine young woman there. It's the courage that reminds us of Alice. The kindness, too.'

Another couple of hours passed before William awoke. Naomi went to join him as he staggered noisily into the hall, his hair dishevelled and his eyes blinking like those of a baby owl.

He jerked a thumb back towards the sitting room. 'I didn't mean . . .'

'To fall asleep? You needed the rest, William, and I hope you feel better for it.'

He rubbed a hand across his face as though rubbing away traces of sleepiness. 'I think I do. Thanks.'

'There'll be three of us at lunch today. I've invited a friend and neighbour, Mr Makepiece.'

William looked fearful and Naomi guessed that he didn't rate his social skills highly, especially when the circumstances were awkward.

'We'll be eating in about an hour when Mr Makepiece returns from his market garden. In the meantime, let me show you where you'll be sleeping.'

She led him upstairs to a guest room. 'I didn't like to look in your bag without your permission, but if you've other clothes that need washing or pressing, I suggest you let me have them now.' She almost added that a clean, neat appearance would create a more favourable impression on his father, but didn't like to remind him of the confrontation that was inevitable, sooner or later.

His clothes were filthy and smelly, but Naomi suppressed a grimace and took them down to the scullery.

'Oh my goodness,' Suki said, recoiling from them. 'I'm not sure there's enough soap in the house to get these clothes smelling fresh, but we'll do our best, madam.'

'Thank you, Suki. Don't worry about laying the dining table. I'll see to it.'

She set places for the three of them and called William down when Bert arrived.

Alexander knew nothing of Naomi's engagement to Bert. He'd looked down on the market gardener even as her friend and he'd be cruel in his comments if he learned that she planned to marry the man. Not that the criticism would trouble Bert, coming from a person he despised. Besides, Naomi's instinct warned her that Alexander would try to use the engagement against her somehow. All things considered, she decided it was wiser to introduce Bert to William in the same way she'd described him earlier – as a neighbour and friend.

Having no taste for finery and never judging a person's worth from their clothing, Bert had turned up in his usual out-for-a-meal outfit of shirt, trousers and jacket that had all faded and grown limp with the passing of many years. 'Pleased to meet you,' he said, shaking William's hand.

Naomi suspected that William's handshake was weak and lacking in confidence but Bert gave no sign of having noticed.

William's face showed puzzlement over this man who was to share the table. At home and at school, people like Bert – unpolished and scruffy with voices that made no attempt at refinement – probably ate in the servants' quarters. But, to his credit, there was no distaste in William's expression.

Neither Naomi nor Bert put pressure on him to converse. Instead, they began an everyday sort of conversation about Bert's market garden, pretending to be unaware that skinny William was spooning soup into his mouth and chewing on bread like someone who feared starvation. But as the worst of his hunger eased, Naomi realized that William had begun to listen intently. She smiled an invitation for him to join in.

'You grow food?' he asked Bert.

'Pretty well all the vegetables in this soup came from my market garden.'

'And very tasty they are,' Naomi said.

'Tasty,' William agreed.

'Have you ever tried growing food?' Bert asked him.

'Not really. There's a Dig for Victory garden for the boys at school, but some of the other boys have taken it over and a chap has to be in with that group to take part.'

Clearly, William wasn't in with that group.

'They're not really bothered about growing anything except as a competition,' he added. 'Who can dig the fastest . . . That sort of thing. The school has a kitchen garden, too, but the boys aren't allowed anywhere near that.'

'If you're interested, you could come along to my place tomorrow and have a look around. You could get your hands dirty, too, if you've a taste for it.'

'I'd like that,' William said, but then he looked at Naomi. 'Will *he* be coming tomorrow?'

There was no need to explain who *he* was.

'I could suggest that your father lets you stay here another day if you think it might help to cool his temper.'

'I'm not sure it will help exactly, but I'd like it. If I'm not in your way? I have a bit of money to pay for my food but not much.'

'I don't think we need to worry about the cost of your food,' Naomi said, and saw relief lighten his thin features. His funds must be low.

Still, the offer of payment gave her the chance to relieve her curiosity about something. 'How did you manage for food while you were sleeping rough?'

'I brought some food from school on the journey here,' William explained. 'When that was gone, I walked to another village – Barton, I think it's called – and bought more there. I didn't like to go to the Churchwood shops in case . . .' He shrugged.

In case the village was suspicious of the dishevelled stranger in their midst and told Naomi about him. Barton was a safer distance away.

'I can't promise your father will agree to your staying here longer,' Naomi said.

'But neither will we throw you into your father's arms if he insists on turning up,' Bert told William, and for the first time the boy grinned.

It looked to be an unfamiliar movement for him, but one Naomi hoped to see again.

CHAPTER SIXTEEN

Alice

Alice threw the notebook on to the floor in disgust. She knew she was capable of writing a story, even if it wasn't good enough for publication, but every time she attempted it a mist of dark doubt stole around her and whispered that anything she wrote would be terrible. The frustration was—

The kitchen door opened and her father looked in. 'Everything all right, my dear?' he asked.

Alice swallowed hard to quell her temper. 'Fine. I just dropped my notebook.'

The last thing she wanted was her father worrying about her. She swooped down to pick up the notebook, dusting it off and saying, 'No harm done.'

'Have you been looking for a job?'

Alice realized that she'd left the newspaper open at the 'Situations Vacant' pages and her father was staring down at it. 'I just looked to see if there was anything interesting available. There wasn't, but it doesn't matter. I'm hardly in desperate need of an income. Not with—'

A knock sounded on the cottage's front door. Alice wasn't in the mood for company but she suppressed a frown for her father's sake and went to greet the visitor.

She gasped when she saw who was in the porch. For a moment all she could do was blink in disbelief. But then she launched herself into the visitor's arms, emotion bringing tears to her eyes.

'Sorry I didn't tell you exactly when I'd arrive,' Daniel said, cradling her tightly as though he never wanted to let her go. 'It became a choice between sending another telegram and missing the next train or catching the train and seeing you sooner.'

'You chose well,' Alice assured him.

His grip relaxed enough for her to raise her face so they could look at each other. 'It's so good to see you, darling girl,' he said, his voice husky and raw, and then he kissed her.

It was a long kiss, full of love, desire, and comfort too, for this was the first time they'd met since her devastating miscarriage.

In time the kiss ended but Daniel continued to hold her close until the sound of a discreet cough had them turning to see Alice's father step out of the kitchen.

'I guessed it must be you, Daniel,' he said, smiling. 'No one else could make my daughter forget to close the door against the cold. It's good to see you, boy.'

The men shook hands. 'I'll leave you two to talk,' Alice's father said then. 'I just wanted to welcome you home, Daniel.'

'It's appreciated, sir.'

Alice led Daniel into the kitchen as her father returned to his study. 'Tea?' she offered.

'Yes, please.'

'I expect you're hungry, too.'

'You know me well. A sandwich, perhaps? Or anything else that's quick to prepare. I want you beside me, not flitting around the kitchen.'

He sat at the little table and Alice was aware of him watching her as she worked. Glancing back at him from time to time, she saw softness in his dark-brown eyes. 'I like looking at you,' he said.

Alice smiled, hoping he didn't think she looked peaky. 'You're not too terrible to look at either,' she joked, and was relieved when his even white teeth showed brightly in his Africa-tanned face as he grinned. The strains of war had given him the first hint of creases around his eyes but he was as handsome as ever with his smooth, wide forehead and clean-cut features.

Alice sat with Daniel as he ate soup and a sandwich. 'That was delicious,' he finally said, patting his stomach.

Alice smiled but then tears came to her eyes and he drew her on to his lap, holding her as they talked about their lost baby at last. 'I'm sorry I couldn't hold on to it,' Alice said. 'I don't *think* I did anything wrong but—'

'You're not blaming yourself?' Daniel looked horrified. 'Miscarriages are common and happen for no obvious reason, as I understand it.'

'True.' But what Alice knew in her head couldn't quite drive out the sense that she'd somehow let down their baby and Daniel, too.

'Promise me you'll rid yourself of any notion that you were at fault.'

'I promise,' Alice said, meaning she promised to try.

Daniel kissed her on the temple. A tender kiss of healing. 'Better?' he asked, and Alice nodded.

'I hated being apart from you when you needed me,' Daniel said then. 'When I needed you, too.'

'I know this war is necessary if the evil of Adolf Hitler and his supporters is to be stopped, but I hate it,' Alice said.

'Likewise. But let's enjoy being together, hmm?'

'Of course. How long can you stay?'

'Probably no more than a few days. I'm awaiting further orders. I'm only home at all for some training.'

'Training where?'

'London first. But enough of the war. Tell me about Churchwood.'

Alice had already mentioned Naomi's engagement in a letter. Now she spoke of Kate's fears over meeting Leo's parents. 'That girl needs more confidence,' Daniel said. 'She's beautiful, intelligent, kind . . .'

'I agree. But it's hard for her to believe it after being undervalued by her family all her life.'

Alice also spoke of the woes that had befallen the new bookshop.

'So this disgusting con man is happily spending Ellen's money somewhere,' Daniel said. 'Has anyone tried to find him?'

'I think Ellen has, but she's had no luck so far.' Alice felt the stirring of an idea at the back of her mind. Why didn't *she* try to find him? It had to be better than moping and, if she could recover the stolen money, she'd have the satisfaction of helping Ellen and the bookshop, too. She might even reawaken her own sense of purpose.

She realized Daniel was watching her. And smiling. 'I'm not here for long, so we'd better get started,' he said.

'On what?'

'On finding this rogue builder, of course. That's what you were thinking about just then, wasn't it?'

'Yes, but I didn't intend for you to look for him, only for me to try it after you'd left for your training. You need to rest.'

'Nonsense. All I need is a bath and a change of clothes. I can sleep later.'

But Alice wasn't having that. Despite his denial she could see tiredness in his eyes. 'We'll start tomorrow,' she insisted, getting up to answer another knock on the door. 'Maybe.'

This time the caller was Naomi – whose eyes widened as Daniel followed Alice into the hall.

'How lovely to see you!' Naomi said, accepting a hug from him. 'When did you arrive?'

'Less than an hour ago. I've been hearing all about poor Ellen Bates and her rogue builder and we're thinking of trying to find him.'

'Not today. You need to rest.'

'Are you and my wife in a conspiracy?' Daniel joked. 'That's exactly what Alice said.'

'Quite right, too. Well, I won't keep you standing on the doorstep. I came to ask if you'd left your gardening clothes here and if I might borrow them?'

'You want to wear my gardening clothes?' Daniel asked, mystified.

'Not me! An unexpected visitor. I'm planning to send him to Bert's today. I think he'll enjoy it.'

'Then I'll be delighted to lend him my clothes.' Daniel ran upstairs to fetch them.

Alice raised an eyebrow. 'The identity of this visitor is . . .?'

'William Harrington.'

'William . . . Good grief, you don't mean—'

'Alexander's son,' Naomi confirmed.

Alice was stunned. 'But how? Why?'

'He ran away from school. Apparently, life in Alexander's secret family isn't as blissful as I'd assumed. Thank you, Daniel.' Naomi took the clothes from him. 'I'll let you know how things develop.'

'Please do.' Alice was agog to hear more.

'What's happened?' Daniel asked as they waved Naomi off.

Alice filled him in. 'And to think that Churchwood looks such a quiet place,' he said.

At Alice's urging, Daniel returned upstairs for a long, relaxing bath while she sat in the kitchen, thinking – about Daniel with joy, William Harrington with curiosity and the hunt for the rogue builder with hope. After all, the hunt was partly a quest to rediscover herself.

CHAPTER SEVENTEEN

Naomi

Naomi telephoned Alexander the moment she returned to Foxfield with the gardening clothes. She rang him at home, having asked William for the number. Might Amelia Ashmore answer? The possibility was disturbing, though the more Naomi learned about Alexander's lover, the more she suspected that the woman was weak and unintelligent, even if she was also beautiful. Naomi was connected to a maid, however, and a moment later Alexander came on the line.

'You need to put the boy on a train *today*,' he insisted. 'I'll refund the ticket price, if that's what's stopping you.'

'I'm not bothered about the money, Alexander.'

'Then you've changed your tune after all your demands.'

'You call my wish to have some of my trust fund money restored a demand?' But she didn't want to talk about the divorce. 'William would like to spend another night here.'

'I won't hear of it. Tell him that if I have to come all the way there to drag him home, I'll be even more displeased than I already am.'

How cold Alexander was. He hadn't shown an ounce of concern for his son's well-being. He was more concerned with the inconvenience to his routine and he especially disliked the fact that his son was establishing some sort of relationship with Naomi. 'Not today,' she told him, in tones that brooked no argument. 'Short of locking William in a room, I can't stop him from running away again if you appear.'

'Lock him in a room, then!' She guessed he wanted to add 'you stupid woman' but was held back only because she was the key to getting William to toe the line.

'I'm not locking him anywhere. We can speak again tomorrow, by which time I hope it will have occurred to you to think about William's welfare.'

He began to splutter a response but Naomi didn't listen. 'Goodbye,' she said, putting the phone down.

If only she'd been half as assertive during their marriage! Still, better late than never.

William was grinning when he appeared in Daniel's old gardening clothes. 'My father would be apoplectic if he saw me like this!'

'I'm sure he would!' Naomi agreed. 'Now, the main entrance to Mr Makepiece's market garden is along Churchwood Way, the road that runs from the village. We'll take a different route, though.'

She wrapped herself up warmly and took him into the woods behind Foxfield and around the lake that lay there. 'I expect you've seen this lake before,' she said.

William nodded. He was looking around thoughtfully, doubtless remembering how hard his week in these woods had been and how unhappy he'd felt. Perhaps also remembering the situation that had driven him there.

'You know, few situations last for ever,' Naomi said. 'Time changes things, especially when we're young. You may be under your father's authority now, but that won't be for more than a couple of years or so.'

She was giving him a holiday from his troubles, but it couldn't go on indefinitely, and the best thing she could do to help him was to encourage the resilience he needed to endure them until he came out on the other side. 'Does your father want you to follow him into stockbroking?' she asked.

'Stockbroking or something else in finance. Or law. He wouldn't mind if I became a lawyer.'

'The law doesn't interest you?'

'Not really, and I don't think I've the brains to be a top lawyer.'

'Not everyone has to be at the top of his profession. Happiness and contentment . . . they're the most important goals.'

'My father doesn't see it that way.'

To be fair, neither had Naomi in her first years in Churchwood when, desperately lacking in confidence, she'd compensated by using her wealth and position to boss the village about.

'It might help if you have an idea of what you'd like to do instead,' she suggested. 'Your father might not agree with your choice, but if you can show how it might work in practice – how you might earn a living from it – then he'll see that you're serious about your future. In time, he'll *have* to allow you your independence.'

'I don't know what I want to do,' William said regretfully. 'It would need to pay enough for me to live on from the beginning, because my father would never help out if I trained for a job he disliked.'

It was a reasonable point. Apprentices and young people in other junior roles were paid next to nothing since it was assumed they'd live at home.

There was another point Naomi wanted to make. 'I'm not suggesting you fix on something definite. Just as situations have a habit of changing, so do we as people. It would be unwise to burn your bridges now for an uncertain future. The more you achieve at school, the more options you'll have for earning a living, not just when you're young but when you're older, too.'

'You mean I might change my mind about what I'd like to do with my life?'

'Exactly. I'm much older than you' – probably he thought her ancient – 'but I've changed my mind about a lot of things in recent years. It really doesn't hurt to keep our options open.'

He shrugged, a gesture she took to mean that he thought she was probably right but was still daunted by the prospect of his immediate future.

Deciding she must have given him enough food for thought for the time being, Naomi turned the conversation to the market garden. 'Bert will be glad of your help today. It may be winter but work never stops in a market garden. He has a boy helping him for a few hours a week – Luke Carpenter – but mostly Bert manages himself.'

'It must be wonderful to see something grow from a seed into food.'

'Bert certainly thinks so. He loves the whole process of nature at work. He may point out some of the local wildlife, if there's time.'

'I've seen some birds,' William said. 'Chaffinches, woodpeckers, fieldfares, thrushes . . . I have a book about them. A little book that fits in a pocket. I take it on walks around the school grounds sometimes.'

It helped him to escape the day-to-day misery of being a round peg in a square hole, Naomi guessed.

'Here we are.' They'd reached the narrow lane that bordered Bert's land.

A small gate stood in a gap in the hedge. Naomi gestured to William to pass through it and they saw Bert over by a greenhouse. 'Good morning!' he called, waving.

They joined him. 'I see you've got Daniel's gardening

togs on.' Bert looked William up and down approvingly. 'I've an old jacket here for you, and some gloves. A cap, too, if you want it. It's no fashion parade here.' He looked at Naomi. 'Are you staying?'

'Not today.' She wanted to be close to home just in case Alexander took it into his head to come and try to drag his son away.

Bert nodded his understanding. 'Don't worry about William. He'll be fed and watered as well as any of my plants.'

Of course he would. Bert might not be a father but Naomi was sure he knew far better than Alexander what a boy of William's age needed.

CHAPTER EIGHTEEN

Naomi

William was bright-eyed when he returned from Bert's. Naomi didn't need to ask if he'd enjoyed his day because she could see that it had brought him to life. But she asked him anyway, curious about how he'd answer.

'I had the best day ever!' he told her. 'We did some planting and harvesting. We packed some produce, ready for delivery, and then we did some maintenance because Bert says he's too busy to do it in the summer months.'

Bert had said a lot, it seemed – about seedlings, pricking out, fertilizing, discouraging pests, encouraging sunlight . . . Much as she loved Bert, his horticultural wisdom became a little too much for her after a while. Not, apparently, for William.

'You got along with Bert all right?'

'I did. He's very . . . Oh, what's the word?'

'Relaxed? Shrewd? Philosophical?'

'All three. I can see that he'd stand up for what he thought was right, but he's patient and never shouts. Unlike . . .' William's words trailed off. 'Have you heard from him?'

'Not since I spoke to him this morning, but I need to telephone him again soon. Even leaving aside your personal relationship with him, it isn't a good thing to be missing school.'

'I've learned more from Bert today than I'd have learned

from any of the masters at school,' William argued. 'It's far more useful to know how to grow food than how to work with Pythagoras' theorem.'

'I'm sure,' Naomi said, knowing nothing of Pythagoras or his theorem beyond the fact that they were something to do with mathematics. 'But, as I said earlier, it would be wise to keep all of your options open regarding your future. You're young. You don't know what you want to do with your life.'

'Actually, I do know now. I want to do something useful like Bert. I'd like to grow things like he does or make things from wood or . . . Oh, anything like that. I don't want to work in a stuffy office. I like being outside. Bert pointed out lots of birds to me today – a sparrowhawk, a kestrel, a goldcrest . . . He taught me how to recognize the shapes of their wings and bodies when they're in flight. To identify the different birdsongs, too. It made me feel . . . peaceful. At ease with myself. Unlike sitting in a soulless classroom staring at equations I don't understand. I don't care about having lots of money and I don't care about impressing the sort of people my father seems to think matter most. Cocktail parties, fine dinners, golfing tournaments . . . I can't think of a more miserable existence.'

Bless him. He was a boy after Bert's own heart, though many years younger and pitifully vulnerable.

'I'm glad you're beginning to think about the sort of life you'd like to lead,' Naomi said. 'But there's a hill to climb before you can get there.'

'The hill being my father and school?'

'You'll reach the top of that hill in just another year or so and then you'll be on the downward slope.'

'I'll be running away from that hill as fast as my legs will carry me.'

'Maybe so. But for the moment the hill still lies ahead.'

William looked crestfallen. 'When do you want me to leave? In the morning?'

'If it were up to me, I'd consider a different school for you – perhaps a day school – and encourage you to develop your interests alongside your schoolwork so you'll have a clearer idea of the path you want to take when school is behind you.'

'I wish you were my mother!' he declared fervently. But then he frowned. 'I don't mean that exactly. I know you have no reason to care for my mother, but I love her.'

'There's no need to apologize, William. It's natural to love your mother. I think what you mean is that you wish you could exchange my views for your father's.'

'Yes,' he said. 'That's exactly what I mean.'

'It can't be done, I'm afraid. I don't want to force you out, but we can't keep your father away indefinitely. What I suggest is that we ask him to come here and talk.'

'He'll never listen. Not to me.'

'He might not listen to me either, but I still think we should try it.'

William hung his head but finally nodded agreement.

'I'll telephone him later. In the meantime, you might want to wash and change ready for dinner.'

'I brought some potatoes and carrots back. Bert said it would do me good to eat vegetables I'd pulled from the ground with my own hands. It would be even better if I'd planted them, too, but Bert says it's a start.'

Bert says . . . It was going to be a long evening.

'He says I can call him Bert, by the way. Instead of Mr Makepiece. I wasn't being impertinent.'

'I never thought you were. You can call me Naomi.'

William grinned. But then his face fell again – thoughts of the forthcoming confrontation with his father intruding, Naomi guessed. He loped from the room to change.

Naomi sat back and sighed, wondering how things were going to turn out. Only a handful of people knew about Alexander's secret family but, while William was at Bert's, she'd decided to call Victoria and Suki into the sitting room to tell them that William was Alexander's son. Telling them straight seemed a better option than leaving them to speculate and ask questions in the village.

'I did wonder,' Suki admitted, clearly having been struck by the physical similarities between father and son, 'but I haven't said a word to anyone.'

'You can rely on me to be discreet as well,' Victoria said.

'I know I can rely on both of you,' Naomi told them.

'If anyone asks, shall we simply explain that William is a distant relative on Mr Harrington's side?' Victoria asked.

'That will be perfect.' It would be uncomfortable for William if word got out about his true origins. It would be uncomfortable for Naomi, too. She was lucky to have Victoria and Suki on her side.

'If you're going to splutter insults at me, I'm going to hang up on you,' Naomi warned Alexander when he began abusing her the moment he came on the telephone line the following morning.

'You've no right to interfere in matters that don't concern you. Matters like my son!'

'William became my concern the moment he began sleeping in my shed.'

'It's still *our* shed, Naomi. The divorce hasn't gone through yet.'

'Is that some sort of threat? Save yourself the bother because threats won't work.'

'You're interfering out of spite, aren't you? Because I have children and you don't? You're jealous.'

The knife of regret she'd long carried over her

childlessness plunged into her heart and grief flooded out like blood. But she swallowed and fought her way back to self-control. 'You can think whatever you like because I really don't care a jot for your opinions. But William is here and we need to talk about what's to become of him.'

'There's no *we* about it. William already has a mother and she isn't you!'

Another plunge of the knife. 'That fact takes nothing away from the reality that he's here with me and we need to settle his future.'

'Just keep your nose out of my business and put him on a train.'

'I'm not doing that. I'm inviting you to come here for a chat. Bring his mother, if you like.'

Goodness, what a challenge that would be for Naomi to face. 'Tomorrow will be convenient,' she added.

'Convenient for you, but not for me. I'm playing—' He broke off suddenly.

'Playing golf?' she suggested, picturing his chagrin at having his shallow sense of priorities exposed.

'Playing golf with clients,' he corrected. 'I need to earn a living. Especially now—'

'Now I want some of my trust fund restored,' she finished. 'I'm bored with all your money talk, Alexander. If you don't want to come tomorrow, come on Friday. I'll expect you after lunch.' She wasn't going to feed the man.

'That boy is missing school. A school that costs me a fortune in fees.'

'You're talking about money again. How tedious. Goodbye, Alexander. I'll see you on Friday.'

CHAPTER NINETEEN

Alice

Alice was glad she'd insisted on Daniel staying at home yesterday. The rest had done him good and the sparkle was back in his dark eyes.

She glanced at her watch. 'There won't be a bus to Barton for another hour.' They'd agreed to start their enquiries with Ellen. 'It'll be quicker to walk – if you can manage five miles?'

'Five miles and more.'

They left the cottage and stepped on to Churchwood Way just as Bert drove between the Foxfield gateposts. Stopping the truck, he wound down the window. 'Welcome home, Daniel.'

'It's good to be home and back with my darling wife.'

Bert nodded, and Alice guessed he was thinking of all that she'd suffered with her miscarriage. 'Have you been calling on Naomi?' she asked.

'Naomi and that long streak of a boy called William. He helped in my market garden yesterday and he's going to help again later. He seems a nice boy at heart.'

'Naomi's kindness must be doing him good,' Alice suggested.

'That's my woman, all right. Where are you two heading? Out for a stroll?'

'Out to try to right wrongs,' Daniel told him, explaining where they were going and why.

'You've plenty of brains between you, so if anyone can find the con man, it'll be you. Tell you what.' Bert heaved his substantial body down to the pavement. 'I was on my way to Barton to deliver this produce.' He nodded at the crates and baskets in the truck bed. 'Why don't you save yourselves the walk by dropping this lot off at the greengrocer's for me and seeing Ellen straight after?'

'We can borrow the truck?' Daniel asked.

'As long as you don't drive it into a ditch. The gearstick needs a shove sometimes and you'll need to allow a lot of space for turning,' Bert advised. 'Imagine you're piloting a ship and you'll get the idea.'

They drove into Barton and delivered Bert's produce without mishap. 'Looks like she's at home,' Alice said, observing the smoke emerging from Ellen's chimney.

They parked outside the house and knocked on the door. 'Come in and warm up with a cup of tea,' Ellen invited, leading them inside her comfortable but modest little home. 'You're here about that horrible builder, I suppose, though I've nothing helpful to add to what I've already shared. I was a silly old woman for letting him take advantage of me.' Her distress ran deep.

'Any of us could fall for the lies of a con man,' Alice soothed.

'That's right,' Daniel agreed. 'The reason people succeed as con men – or women – is because they sound so credible and trustworthy.'

'Bless you both,' Ellen said. 'I still feel foolish for parting with all that money in advance.'

'Easy to be wise after the event,' Alice said.

Ellen brought the tea and with Daniel chatting to her about how good it was to be home on leave, some of the tension left her. 'Just talk us through what happened,' he invited then. 'Assume we know nothing. Start at the beginning and we'll see how we get on.'

'The builder turned up at my door a couple of days after the storm hit. I had some pies in the oven and half of my mind was on them, since I didn't want them to burn.'

'Could you describe him?' Alice asked. 'Close your eyes if it might help.'

Ellen looked as though closing her eyes would embarrass her. 'He was my age or thereabouts. In his fifties.'

'What made you think that?' Daniel asked.

'Why, he just *looked* my age,' Ellen said, surprised. She paused and finally closed her eyes. 'He had thinning hair. Pale brown, I think, but with grey mixed in. He had the sort of face that reminds me of uncooked pastry. Doughy, rather than clean-cut. Large nose. Lots of creases. I didn't notice the colour of his eyes. They weren't a piercing blue or a warm brown so I suppose they might have been muddy brown. He smiled a lot but his teeth weren't good. Some were missing.'

'Height?' Alice prompted.

'Average. But he looked strong, being a builder. His stomach overhung his trousers, though.'

'What were his clothes like?' Alice asked next.

'Oh dear. I think they were doughy-coloured, too. Not smart. Not bright. Beige, perhaps. Old and faded.'

'Trousers and a shirt?'

'With a jacket over the top but hanging open. That was how I could see his belly.'

'Shoes?'

'Work boots? I don't remember.'

'What else did you see when you opened the door? Did you notice a vehicle?'

'I think there may have been a van parked outside. Beige.'

123

'Any lettering along the side?'

'Not that I recall.'

'What did he say, exactly?'

'He apologized for interrupting my baking – he must have been able to smell the pies – but said he didn't want to miss the chance to call because he'd heard I had a problem and he could fix it for me.'

'The problem being the damage from the burst?'

Ellen nodded. 'He said a lot of pipes burst at this time of year and he'd been replastering ceilings over near Churchwood for precisely that reason. He introduced himself as George Gregg and said perhaps I'd heard of him. I hadn't, of course, but the way he spoke suggested he was proud of the name because he had a good reputation.'

'He was trying to reassure and impress you,' Daniel guessed.

'When I told him I was unfamiliar with the name he said it didn't matter because he was here now and, as he knew where he could get a good supply of plaster, I just needed to say the word and he'd get started. That's when he came into the house. So he didn't keep me standing with the door open and letting the cold air inside, he said. It made him sound . . . considerate.'

'Did he mention who told him about the problems at Joe's house?'

'No, but I didn't think anything of it, since lots of people were saying what a shame it was.'

'He told you he lived in Rawley?'

'Mmm. He boasted that there were many people in Rawley and the surrounding villages who'd speak highly of both his work and his integrity. That was the word he used. Integrity.' Ellen looked bewildered by the dishonesty of it all. 'I wouldn't say he was charming, exactly, but he gave the impression of being on my side and wanting to help.'

'When did he ask for the money?'

'When I questioned how much he'd charge. He said I was safe in his hands as he prized his reputation in these parts.' Ellen winced. 'Anyway, I was worried about my pies and asked if I could have time to think about his offer. He said of course I could, as he wasn't the man to put pressure on people. But then he said he couldn't guarantee the plaster would be available for long . . .'

'He put pressure on you anyway,' Alice said.

'I suppose so, but he made it sound as though he'd regret having to let me down. He was . . . sorrowful about it. Not *really* sorrowful, considering the way things turned out, but pretending to be.'

'He was manipulating you.'

'And I let him. I found myself agreeing to pay the whole amount in one go – I could smell the pies burning by this point – as it meant he could get started straight away without having to keep bothering me. Or so he claimed.'

'You had the money in the house?'

'Joe had cashed in his savings, so yes. And I had a little of my own put by to make up the shortfall. More's the pity.'

'What happened next?'

'He put the money in his pocket and left. I saw him to the door but went straight back in to save the pies.'

'There's nothing more you remember?'

Ellen shook her head regretfully, but then, as though surprised by the recollection, said, 'Now you ask, I remember he limped when he walked. And I heard him calling, "Quiet now, Samson," or something like that, anyway. I suppose he was calling to a dog, though I didn't hear it barking. Does that help?'

'Let's hope so,' Alice said. 'Were any of your neighbours outside when he arrived or left?'

Ellen consulted the inner recesses of her mind. 'Beryl Dowd from across the road was out. I waved to her. She's at number eleven. The house with the aspidistra in the window, if you're planning on speaking to her. Anything you can do to get the money back will be much appreciated, since I've no other way of paying a builder unless I take on a debt, and the thought of that . . .' She shuddered. 'But you shouldn't spend all your time trying to put right my foolishness. You need to enjoy your leave, Mr Irvine.'

'It's Daniel, and I enjoy a challenge.'

Bidding goodbye to Ellen, they crossed the road to number eleven, Ellen lingering on her doorstep to nod to Mrs Dowd when she opened her door. 'It's all right, Beryl,' she called. 'They're trying to help me, so if you can answer their questions . . .?'

Beryl waved back and invited Alice and Daniel inside.

No, she told them, she couldn't remember anything about the van except that there was a dog in the front.

'No lettering along the side? Nothing on the top?'

'Now you mention it, I think there was a ladder strapped to the roof. Mostly I was irritated because the dog kept barking. A big dog, it was. Long snout. Large teeth. *Very* large teeth.' Mrs Dowd shuddered.

'What colour?'

'Black and . . . tan, I suppose you'd call it.'

'You don't know the breed?'

'A big dog, that's all I know. I'm not interested in dogs except when it comes to steering clear of their teeth. I don't like the way they jump up. And as for all that sniffing! Indecent, I call it.'

'Thank you, Mrs Dowd. You've been helpful,' Alice said.

'Was anyone else out in the street?' Daniel asked.

'Ooh, you ask some questions!'

'Sorry. If you can't recall . . .'

'No, I'm glad to help. Poor Ellen's taking it badly, being fleeced. The money was Joe's savings, you see. Just give me a moment to think . . .'

She screwed up her face. 'Cyril Bentley,' she announced then. 'Cyril was out for his daily constitutional. He might have noticed something.'

'Mr Bentley lives . . .?'

'Number twenty-three. You should find him at home, as he's already been out on his constitutional today. Don't be offended if he's a bit sharp. He's sharp with everyone.'

'We'll consider ourselves warned,' Daniel told her.

The sharpness was in evidence the moment Mr Bentley opened his door. His face was tight with grievance. 'Yes?' he demanded. 'Well, spit it out. I haven't got time to stand chatting and letting cold air into the house. What do you want?'

Daniel explained about the builder.

'There was a van,' Mr Bentley confirmed. 'But if you think I'm the sort of gossip who's got nothing better to do than waste time on other people's business, you're sadly mistaken.'

'We don't think that,' Daniel assured him. 'But we do think you're the sort of man who objects to criminals getting away with their crimes. The man with the van obtained money under false pretences from Ellen Bates and we're trying to recover it. So, if there's anything you can remember about the man – or his van or dog – you'll be on the side of justice by telling us.'

'The van was beige, with a paint-spattered ladder on the roof. The man looked uncouth.'

Mr Bentley described him but had nothing to add to

the information Ellen had already shared. 'I heard him call something ridiculous to the dog. "Daddy Mick is here now," I think it was. As I said, ridiculous coming from such a man and to such a dog. It was an Alsatian, and it didn't look friendly.'

'We won't keep you standing in the cold any longer,' Alice said. 'If anything else occurs to you, perhaps you could mention it to Ellen.'

'Humph.' Chatting to a neighbour appeared to fall into the category of gossip.

He stepped back into his hall and closed the door.

'We need to get the truck back to Bert,' Alice said. 'But we've a clearer description of the con man now. We also know his name might be Mick rather than George. And that he goes around with an unfriendly Alsatian called Samson.'

'We can come again tomorrow and ask people in shops and on the street if they've anything to add to the picture,' Daniel suggested. 'We can ask in other villages, too, though it'll take a long time if we have to walk or catch buses everywhere.'

'I don't want you getting overtired.'

'I'm not an invalid, but it's sweet of you to worry about me.' He wrapped an arm around Alice and kissed her. Only lightly, though. 'I don't want to scandalize Barton,' he explained.

'Any luck?' Bert asked, when they reached his market garden.

They told him what they'd learned.

'Sounds as though the net may be closing in on this con man,' Bert told them. 'You can borrow my truck again tomorrow if you can make more deliveries for me.'

'We'll be glad to,' Alice said.

'Meanwhile, let me introduce you to Spider-legs over there.'

William was watching them from a distance, looking unsure about whether he should come forward to meet them or stay in the background. Bert beckoned him over and the introductions were made.

The boy was polite, even enthusiastic. Alexander was there to see in the tall, thin body and imposing nose, but William's sweet smile was all his own.

'Welcome to Churchwood,' Alice said. 'Naomi is a dear friend of ours.'

'Yes,' he said, as though he'd begun to realize that Naomi was nothing like the money-grabbing ogre Alexander had probably described.

'Glad to see the clothes are proving helpful,' Daniel told him, smiling because they hung off William's skinny limbs.

'They're yours? Thank you,' William said, blushing rather endearingly.

Still mindful of wanting Daniel to rest, Alice suggested heading home.

'It's been a good day,' Daniel remarked as they walked.

For all sorts of reasons, Alice agreed. She'd spent time with her beloved Daniel. They'd uncovered useful information about the con man. And, like a sip of brandy warming her veins, she was beginning to feel something of her old energy returning.

CHAPTER TWENTY

Kate

'Daniel!' Kate brought her bicycle to a skidding halt as she saw Alice and her husband walking towards The Linnets. 'When did you get back?'

Daniel gave her a friendly grin. 'Hello, Kate. It's good to see you. I arrived yesterday.'

She hopped off the bike to hug him then turned to Alice, glad to see that her friend looked happier now she had Daniel by her side. 'Been calling on Naomi?' she asked, since they'd come from that direction.

'On Bert. We thought we'd leave Naomi alone today now William Harrington has come to stay,' Alice told her.

'William Harrington?'

'Alexander's secret son.'

'Obviously not so secret any more!' Kate was shocked. 'What's he doing here? Not making trouble for Naomi, I hope?'

'I believe he came with that intention, but now he's getting to know her, he's having a change of heart.'

'Ha! That's one in the eye for Awful Alexander!'

'Isn't it? But I suggest we don't tell anyone else that William is here. It's for Naomi to decide what she wants people to know.'

'No one will hear of it from me,' Kate promised. 'I particularly won't breathe a word to Marjorie. If she catches even a sniff of the news, she'll be running down

Churchwood Way and hammering on Naomi's door demanding to meet the boy.'

'Perish the thought,' Alice said.

'We've been playing amateur detectives,' Daniel announced. He described their mission to Barton.

'Well done!' Kate approved.

'Are you heading for the shops?' Alice asked, and Kate felt anxiety squeeze inside her.

'To May's house, actually. I've had another letter from Leo – two in four days – inviting me to visit for a couple of days next week.'

'That's excellent news!' Alice cried, but then she took stock of Kate's expression. 'You're nervous.'

Kate shrugged.

'Leo is a lucky man, and if his parents don't share that opinion, the problem lies with them, not you,' Daniel said.

He was always gallant. 'We'll see,' Kate said.

'May will lend you everything you need and you'll look sensational,' Alice promised.

Hmm. If Kate could look . . . appropriate, that would be good enough.

'I'd better get on,' Kate said, 'but I hope to see more of you before you leave, Daniel.'

'Likewise.' He kissed her cheek and stood with Alice, waving as she pedalled away.

'You've come to the right place,' May assured her, when Kate explained her reason for calling. 'Let's draw up a list of what you might need.'

May's house was immaculate despite having three children in her care. Not that May was a tyrant when it came to tidiness. She was simply efficient and bringing up Rosa, Samuel and Zofia to show respect for their home while still allowing it to be a place of creativity and fun.

Kate talked to the children while May made tea and then joined her at the table. May had a notepad and pen at the ready. 'Do you know what you'll be doing during your visit?'

'I don't. Sorry. That isn't helpful, is it?'

'No matter. We'll just have to allow for different possibilities. Firstly, travelling clothes. It'll be cold, so I suggest smart trousers worn with a practical blouse and a jacket. Flat shoes, too, and a decent handbag. Oh, and you'll need a case to put everything in. Do you have a case?'

'I don't have a case *or* a handbag.'

'Luckily, I have both.' May wrote them on her list. 'Nightwear,' she said then. 'What do you sleep in?'

'An ancient shirt that belonged to my brothers.'

'I'll lend you a nightdress, dressing gown and slippers. I suggest smart but practical outfits for the daytime. As for the evenings, you may be expected to change. I'll add an elegant evening dress in case they smarten up for dinner, and an ordinary dress in case they're more informal. You'll need accessories, of course. A nice scarf and gloves, and some jewellery. I can't offer diamonds and pearls, but I have some pretty strings of beads.'

'So much stuff!' Kate said, awed, when the list was complete.

'Leave it with me and I'll look out what I think may suit you. I'm forgetting a washbag.' May added it to the list.

'A what?'

'For your toothbrush, creams and so on.'

'I don't have any creams except for a jar of Vaseline that I put on my hands to stop them becoming chapped from all the farm work. Are you sure you don't mind lending me so many things?'

'Quite sure. I'm going to enjoy imagining you taking Cheltenham by storm.'

There was no chance of that. Kate was hugely relieved and grateful to have May's help but it didn't ease her nervousness by much. May meant well, though, so Kate gave her a smile.

Cycling home, her thoughts turned back to Leo's latest letter. The words were scored across her brain.

I have a date for your visit and I'm crossing my fingers — my toes, too — that it'll be convenient for you. Might you come next Tuesday and stay until Thursday? I miss you dreadfully — so dreadfully that I insisted to my parents that the only thing that would make me rest and get well was a visit from you. Luckily, they relented . . .

Relented? It sounded as though their arms had been twisted up their backs. Far from welcoming her, they were having her company foisted on them. It didn't bode well.

CHAPTER TWENTY-ONE

Naomi

'I've had a telegram from one of my friends,' Victoria told Naomi. 'She says she's happy to bring the children here on Saturday, if that suits you? It'll save me making a trip to London.'

'If it suits you, it suits me,' Naomi said. 'But if you'd prefer to go to London to say goodbye to your other friends, that will suit me just as well. Don't worry that you can't take the time because Mrs Kitts leaves today.'

'Thank you, but I'll let Mags bring the children. Once they've been here for a week or two, I can offer them a trip to see their old friends as an adventure.'

What a thoughtful girl she was. 'If you're sure . . . You'll let me know when Mrs Kitts is ready to go? I don't want her to sneak out without saying goodbye, despite her insisting that she doesn't want a fuss.'

'It was kind of you to offer to host a farewell gathering for her.'

'She'd have deserved it.'

But Mrs Kitts had turned the suggestion down. 'A fuss over me? I've said my goodbyes already and I don't need a bunch of people staring at me, thanks all the same.'

It wasn't long before Mrs Kitts knocked on the sitting-room door. 'I'm all set to go, Mrs Harrington. You've been a more than fair employer to me, especially over the last couple of years, and I'm glad I'm leaving you in capable hands.'

'You've been wonderful.' Naomi handed over an envelope.

'What's this? You've already made me a present of a new watch.'

'Just a little money as an extra thank you.'

'You shouldn't, madam.'

'I insist.' Naomi's funds were draining fast but she wouldn't have felt right if she'd been miserly with her parting gift to a loyal employee.

They said goodbye and wished each other well, and Bert came in to say he had the truck waiting to take Mrs Kitts and her luggage to the bus stop.

'I'd take you all the way to your sister's house if I had petrol,' he said.

'But you don't, and the bus stop will do just fine,' Mrs Kitts said.

Naomi saw them to the door and then went back inside. Another era was beginning with Victoria's children arriving soon. She was determined to do her best by them but, oh! Her heart was going to ache over never having had a child of her own.

CHAPTER TWENTY-TWO

Alice

Poring over a map of the area, Alice and Daniel plotted a route that would suit Bert's deliveries as well as their own quest.

They headed first for Barton, but no one they questioned on the street and in shops knew anything of Mick, his van or his dog. 'Do you think we should ask Ellen if she mentioned the problems with Joe's house to anyone living *outside* Barton and Churchwood?' Alice wondered.

'Definitely. Tracing how Mick heard about the burst pipe might lead us to Mick himself.'

They found Ellen at home again. 'I remember telling Ivy Painswick and Miriam Roberts,' she said.

She consulted a small address book and read out the addresses as Alice wrote them down. 'It's obvious that man was conning me, now I look back on it,' Ellen said.

'You're not to blame for anything. He is,' Daniel insisted, but clearly Ellen wasn't letting herself off the hook of responsibility and Alice wanted to get her money back more than ever.

They went next to the village of Burfield, where they unloaded some of Bert's produce but came away with no information. Esholt was the next village along and there they called on Ellen's friend Ivy. 'How anyone could cheat a nice woman like Ellen . . .' Ivy was full of outrage but the description of Mick, his dog and his van meant nothing to her. 'I can only tell you he doesn't live around here.'

'On to Ornsford,' Alice said, but it was no more than a hamlet, so they continued to Upper Beech where Miriam lived.

'This Mick can't be local,' she told them, echoing Ivy, but then she added, 'I think I might have mentioned Ellen's situation in the grocer's but I couldn't swear to it.'

Alice and Daniel headed for the shop only to draw a blank there, too, but a man was entering as they were leaving and they paused to question him. 'I don't know anyone called Mick or George Gregg,' he said. 'I can't remember seeing a van. But I do recall seeing an Alsatian dog. Snarled at me, it did, and I had to jump out of its way. Me an old man, too! The owner just sniggered.'

'Can you describe him?' Alice asked.

'Big chap. Too much weight around his middle. He wore overalls, spattered with paint or something like that.'

This sounded promising. 'Age?' Daniel queried.

'Younger than me. Older than you.'

'Did you notice where he came from or where he was heading?'

'I didn't notice where he came from but I looked back after I'd passed because I was thinking of raising my fist to him. I feared he'd set the dog on me, though, and that wouldn't have been a fair fight. He turned into Acer Street.'

'Perhaps he'd left the van there,' Alice suggested as she and Daniel walked on.

Reaching Acer Street, they saw a woman cleaning her windows. 'I remember the dog because it cocked its leg over my gate,' she said. 'Its owner only glared when I went to shoo it away. I remember the van, too, because it coughed smoke and I feared for my clean curtains.'

'Did you see which way it headed?'

'On to the High Street, I think.'

From there it could have gone anywhere. It was time to return to Churchwood, since Alice was due at the hospital. She'd offered to pause her hospital visiting while Daniel was home but he didn't want her to disappoint the patients. 'Time must hang heavily for them and you'd cheer up the gloomiest day,' he'd said. 'I'd like to spend time with your father, anyway.'

Alice was keen for that, too. Her father adored Daniel.

'We may not have found Mick yet but we've made progress,' Daniel said when they restored Bert's truck to him. 'We'll resume the hunt tomorrow.'

'Are you sure about tomorrow?' Alice asked as they walked back to The Linnets. 'You should be resting.'

'I'm spending time with the woman I love and we're working together to try to right a wrong. That's a better use of my leave than lounging on a sofa. Besides, being with you makes me feel truly alive, my darling.'

He drew her to him and kissed her – until some awkward foot shuffling in the cottage's porch alerted them to the fact that they weren't alone.

'Sorry to – er – interrupt,' old Jonah Kerrigan said. 'I was just coming to call on you, Alice.'

Alice blushed but Daniel only grinned.

'Come in, Jonah,' she invited.

'Better not. I don't want to spread germs. I haven't been well.'

'I'm sorry. I didn't know.'

'No one gets to know much of what goes on around here now we've lost the bookshop. Back when it was thriving, you'd have noticed if I'd missed a couple of sessions and come round to check on me, bringing soup or something like that.'

The bookshop had indeed acted as the village safety net for people who were struggling with illness or other problems.

'Can I do anything for you now?' she asked.

'Thanks, but I'm on the mend. It's just that I've been hearing about the man who ran off with Ellen's money. Well, a few nights ago – I can't be sure which one – I heard noises across the road at Joe's house. It seemed odd since the house was empty, so I stepped outside to investigate and saw a man on the pavement. I can't be sure he'd come out of Joe's garden but it looked that way. "Can I help?" I called, but he just shook his head.'

'Can you describe him?'

'It was dark but I could see he had a belly on him. A big belly. And he had a dog. Not the sort you'd let loose near young 'uns.'

'An Alsatian?'

'I think that's the breed. Anyway, I got taken over by one of my coughing fits, and when I looked up again he'd gone. I thought I'd mention him in case he had something to do with what happened.'

'We'd been wondering how this man got to know about the sort of work Joe's house needed.'

'Then I'm glad I told you. Get yourself indoors now, Alice. You too, Daniel. It's good to see you home and looking in fine fettle, young man.'

'Let me know if you need any help,' Alice called as Jonah walked away.

They didn't have a complete picture of the rogue builder, but it was taking shape.

CHAPTER TWENTY-THREE

Kate

'I'm going away for a couple of days,' Kate told Ernie.

Unsurprisingly, he scowled. 'Again? There's work to be done.'

'Yes, and I always do my fair share of it.'

'More than your fair share!' Ruby called. 'Don't worry, Kate. We'll manage.'

'We will!' Pearl yelled.

Ernie muttered a curse but didn't argue further. More and more, his bullying was being beaten down, which was better for everyone.

Kenny suddenly sent an impatient curse into the air. He was rifling through the dresser drawer where invoices, bills and correspondence were kept. Some of them spilled on to the floor.

'What's wrong with you?' Pearl demanded.

'I can't find Pearson's last invoice. I want to check their prices.'

'I've got a solution to that,' Pearl said.

She scooped up the fallen papers and shoved them back into the drawer, which she tugged from the dresser and plonked on the table beside Fred.

'Oi! You're spoiling my animals!' Fred protested.

'Move them aside. You've got a different job.'

'Eh?'

'Putting these papers in order. Bills in one pile . . .

Invoices in another . . . Then make a pile for each supplier or customer and put them into date order. Does that sound right, Kenny?'

'Well, yes.'

'Off you go, then, Fred. Your animals will have to wait.'

'But I'm no good with papers and stuff.'

'Have a go and you might discover you have a brain. Not a big one – I don't expect miracles – but maybe one the size of an acorn.'

'You're horrible, you are!'

Pearl only shrugged. 'You should look after all the paperwork in future. That way we'll know who to blame if it isn't done right.'

Fred began to whine again but Ruby cut him off. 'Be thankful you've only got one drawer of papers to sort out. We all need to count our blessings.'

Was that what Ruby was doing? Counting her blessings and settling for Kenny to avoid having to uproot Timmy and herself? Kenny appeared to think the hiccup in their relationship was over, but if Ruby was only pretending to be happy, Kate couldn't imagine her keeping it up indefinitely. Hopefully, Ruby's resolve wouldn't fall to pieces while Kate was away.

CHAPTER TWENTY-FOUR

Alice

'We don't have the use of Bert's truck today so I suggest we catch the bus to Hatfield and look for our man there,' Alice said. 'It's quite a large town so there should be plenty of people out and about, and we only need one of them to lead us to him.'

They stepped off the bus in the town centre. 'We could start asking questions here and move outwards in ever-increasing circles,' Daniel said.

They got to work but for the first hour had no luck at all. Then one man gave them a glimmer of hope. 'An Alsatian, you say? I've seen a man with a dog like that. Wearing decorator's overalls, too. The man, I mean. Not the dog.'

They smiled dutifully. 'Do you know where he lives? Or where he works?'

'No idea. I've just seen him around a few times. It's the dog I've noticed. Not an animal I'd like to get close to.'

They thanked him and walked on. 'If he's been seen in Hatfield several times, he might well live here,' Daniel said. It was encouraging.

Another hour circling the town led them to two more people who thought they'd seen Mick and Samson out and about, but neither knew where Mick might be found.

'We should eat something,' Alice suggested, wanting Daniel to be well fed during his leave.

They found a tea shop offering potatoes baked with cheese but didn't linger long over their meal.

They made another circuit of the town, this time further out, but still made no progress – until one man told them, 'Sounds like Mick Briggs. Lives out on the Hertford road. Somewhere around there, anyway.'

It was a lead!

They headed for the Hertford road but it was dauntingly long. A woman was out walking her dog so they stopped her to ask for help. 'Why do you want to know about this man?' Her tone was suspicious.

Might she be a friend of Mick's? 'He left some tools at the house of a friend by mistake. She needs to return them to him,' Alice said, hoping her mission sounded harmless.

It was the wrong thing to have said, though. 'If the man you want is who I think it is, I don't see why I should help him to get his tools back,' the woman told her. 'His dog bit my poor Eleanor.' She picked up her little dog and cradled her as though the attack still caused her pain.

'We're sorry to hear that, but our friend will worry if she can't return the tools.'

'She's old and frail,' Daniel added for good measure.

The woman relented. 'Oh, very well. He lives on the corner of Becket Street. Ramshackle old place.'

'Becket Street is . . .?'

'Straight ahead then turn left at the Golden Fleece pub. The house is a bit further along, on the right.'

'Thank you,' Alice told her warmly. 'We hope Eleanor won't encounter Samson again.'

Energized now, they made their way to Becket Street. 'Not the most salubrious part of town,' Daniel observed.

The Golden Fleece failed to live up to its name, since it was rough and seedy-looking. The properties around it were mostly poorly maintained terraced houses, but at the end there was an even more dilapidated house that stood on its own behind a high brick wall. 'Looks promising,' Alice said.

'Mmm.' Daniel took a few steps back then ran at the wall, grasping the top and pulling himself up so he could see into the yard on the other side.

Immediately, there came a snarl and the sound of claws scratching on the ground as a dog raced towards him.

Daniel dropped down again. 'I suggest we make a run for it before the savage's owner comes out to investigate.'

Hand in hand, they ran back the way they'd come and ducked into an alley to get their breath back. 'There was a cream-coloured van in there. Ladders, too. It looks as though we've found Mick,' Daniel said. 'But with that dog on the loose we need reinforcements before we confront him.'

'Bert?' Alice asked.

'Bert,' Daniel agreed.

CHAPTER TWENTY-FIVE

Naomi

Alexander had long considered buses and trains to be beneath his dignity, and today was no exception. He appeared in an unfamiliar car which he'd probably borrowed from someone with a mysterious supply of petrol, rules about rationing applying only to lesser mortals than him and his cronies.

'Not precisely a picture of happiness,' Bert observed, as Alexander got out of the car and scowled up at the house.

Standing beside him at the sitting-room window, Naomi had to agree. Alexander might look immaculate in his crisply cut suit, pristine white shirt and tasteful tie, but he gave off as much warmth as a glacier.

To spare Suki from the discomfort of opening the door to such a thundercloud of ill will, Naomi went to the door herself. 'Good day,' she said, determined to be the politer, better person.

Alexander grunted and barged into the house. 'Where is he?'

'Do you mean your son?'

'Who else would I mean? Don't try to be clever, Naomi. It doesn't suit you.'

She led the way into the sitting room where Alexander came to a hostile halt, seeing Bert instead of William. 'What's he doing here?' Alexander demanded. 'The boy has nothing to do with him.'

Bert answered for himself. 'I'm going to sit here quietly and be nice,' he said, lowering himself into an armchair and folding his arms over his substantial middle. 'Just as long as you sit quietly over there and behave nicely, too.'

He gestured towards another armchair, leaving the sofa free for Naomi.

Alexander merely sneered. 'Where is the boy? I haven't got all day to waste playing childish games.'

Naomi forbore to mention that it was already afternoon. She didn't wish to antagonize Alexander more than necessary because it was William who'd suffer the consequences. 'I'll call him,' she said instead.

She'd suggested earlier that William should take Basil into the garden, her hope being that the little dog would distract the boy from his nervousness. She found him throwing a stick for Basil, who was looking weary, as though he was too old for such capers but trying his best to cooperate.

Seeing Naomi, William's face paled. 'He's here?'

'He is, but remember, William: try not to get upset or angry but explain yourself calmly.'

'I'll try,' he said, but he looked as though he were going to his execution.

Basil had already come to Naomi's side in what she guessed was relief, so she led the way into the house. 'Stand tall,' she whispered to William outside the sitting-room door. Then she walked in.

Alexander had sat down but now he rose up again, tall and chilling, the gaze from his cold eyes piercing William like rapiers. 'Well?' he demanded.

William opened his mouth only to flounder, his shoulders drooping like the stalks of flowers deprived of water. He was no match for his icy brute of a father.

'You've caused no end of trouble with your selfish,

foolish behaviour,' Alexander spat at him. 'You've caused uproar at your school – an expensive school, I might add – upset your mother, and here you are inconveniencing me when I should be at the office.'

'Oh dear, oh dear,' Bert said, heaving himself back to his feet.

Alexander rounded on him. 'You said you'd be quiet!'

'I said I'd sit quietly and be nice as long as you did the same,' Bert corrected him. 'You've broken the deal.'

'Deal? There is no deal!'

'Then it's fine for me to be up on my feet, isn't it? What I want to say – and I'm going to say it whether you like it or not – is that you shouldn't condemn the boy for what he's done without at least hearing his reasons for it.'

'It's obvious why he came here. To spite me!'

Bert laughed. 'You're deluded, man.'

'What other reason could he have had?'

Naomi judged it wise to intervene. 'Shouting triggered William's flight from school and we'll get nowhere if we shout now. No one say a word until we're all sitting down.'

'This is ridiculous,' Alexander snarled, but Naomi simply sat and raised an eyebrow to signal that she was waiting.

Bert sat down, too, and so did William, though the boy's drooping head suggested his father's verbal attacks had already punched all the fight out of him. Naomi would have to fight on his behalf.

'William didn't come here to annoy you but to confront me,' she explained, when Alexander had thrown himself back into his chair, looking disgusted. 'He was in some distress because things he overheard at Christmas led him to believe that I was making demands that were impoverishing you. He wanted me to stop. He was also upset because he'd learned that he was . . . well, born outside a true marriage. The thought of the other boys at school taunting him if they found out about it dismayed him. Understandably. The bad temper you exhibited all over the Christmas holiday didn't help.'

'Nonsense,' Alexander declared, but a slight flush in his cheeks betrayed the fact that he was embarrassed at having his poor behaviour so exposed. Being a snake, however, he was quick to try to pass on his humiliation to someone else. 'Did you confront her?' he asked his son, only to sneer and answer his own question. 'Obviously not, because here you are, all pals together.'

'William and I *did* talk,' Naomi said. 'I put him right on a few things.'

Another slight flush of humiliation rose to Alexander's bony cheeks but he wasn't the man to accept blame. 'You poisoned him against me,' he accused Naomi.

'Seems to me the poison is all on your side of the room,' Bert said.

'No one asked for your opinion,' Alexander snapped.

'You're getting it anyway. You treat that boy badly and we'll all know you're hurting him on purpose, and what sort of father will that make you?'

Alexander glowered but a clever answer appeared to elude him. He turned back to William. 'Get your things. We're leaving.'

'Not yet,' Naomi said calmly. 'If you don't wish to be the sort of father Bert just described, you should *talk* to William. That doesn't mean shouting at him, but listening to what he has to say about what's happening in the family and what he wants out of his life. Listening with an open mind, too. You've made choices for your life, Alexander. William should be free to make choices for his.'

'Have you finished? Because I'm not wasting any more time on the sort of rubbish you're talking. Don't just sit there, William. Get your things.'

Alexander got up again and, after giving Naomi an agonized look, so did a defeated William. Naomi could do no more.

William's things were already packed and waiting in the hall. He picked up the bag and swung it over his shoulder. Alexander opened the front door and marched at speed towards the car. No goodbye. No thank you for looking after his son. Nothing.

Naomi gave William a hug and so did Bert. 'Write to let us know how you are,' Naomi urged. She'd put note-paper, envelopes and stamps in his bag.

'Hopefully, your father will think twice about being nasty again,' Bert said, though it was more of a hope than an expectation.

'Thanks for letting me stay,' William said. 'I wish . . .' He let the words trail off, shaking his head.

He wished he could stay longer, Naomi guessed, but William was a minor and the law was on Alexander's side. She gave him another quick hug and watched him slope out to join his father in the car. With a scrunch of gravel, the car moved off.

'It's a pity we can't do more to help that boy,' Naomi said.

'We did what we could. The icicle knows William has people like us on his side now, so with luck he'll think twice about shouting, knowing it makes him look like a bully.'

It was the best outcome they could hope for, but Naomi still suspected William was on his way to more unhappiness.

Bert put his arm around her and squeezed comfort-ingly. 'I liked having young William around,' he said.

'So did I.'

'You'll have more young 'uns tomorrow with Victoria's two arriving.'

'I will.' If only she could look forward to their arrival with enthusiasm instead of dread.

'Victoria must be looking forward to seeing them again. Why don't I go home and fetch more veggies for you? You'll need them with two extra mouths to feed.'

'Three extra mouths for lunch, since Victoria's friend is bringing the children and I can't send her on her way back to London unfed.'

'Course not.'

Bert left and Naomi helped Victoria to prepare a room for the children. Mrs Kitts had slept in an attic room but Victoria had slept in a guest room since her arrival and Naomi proposed that she should continue to do so, with the children having the room next door. That way they wouldn't be far from Victoria in the night.

'You're very thoughtful,' Victoria said.

Naomi could only smile tightly.

Bert returned with a basket of vegetables and Naomi opened the door to him just as Alice and Daniel appeared between the Foxfield gateposts.

'You two have springs in your steps,' Bert observed. 'Have you had a fruitful day?'

'We believe so,' Daniel said, and told the story of their visit to Hatfield.

'We need reinforcements and thought of you, Bert,' Alice said. She explained the plan they had in mind for the following evening. 'What do you say, Bert?'

'I say count me in.'

Something else for Naomi to worry about!

CHAPTER TWENTY-SIX

Naomi

'May I have permission to go into the village to meet my friend and the children off the bus?' Victoria asked. 'I was up early to get ahead of my work.'

'Of course,' Naomi told her. 'I'm heading into the village as well but I'll keep a distance so you have some time with the children on your own.'

'It was a lucky day for me when I met you,' Victoria said, smiling.

'Even if it did involve falling into a ditch?'

'A price worth paying.'

Naomi was emerging from the post office when she heard the bus approaching. Victoria stood waiting, visibly excited.

The bus pulled up and passengers began to alight. A little girl with brown hair came first. Running straight to Victoria, she wrapped her arms around her guardian's waist. 'I missed you too,' Naomi heard Victoria say.

A boy came next, looking unsure of himself until Victoria gave his shoulder a playful punch and drew him close for a hug. 'Soppy!' he protested, but he was grinning when Victoria released him.

How Naomi wished she'd had children to hug.

Victoria welcomed a woman off the bus next. 'Thanks for bringing them, Mags.'

'My pleasure.' Mags was a tall, solid woman with an

abundance of auburn hair. She looked to be older than Victoria, well into her thirties.

Two more children jumped off the bus and Victoria looked disconcerted to see them. 'Lewis and Orla,' she said faintly, folding the red-haired children in her arms but clearly worried.

She must have assumed Mags would leave her own children back in London. Now there'd be another two mouths to feed at lunch. The meal would have to be spread thinly.

But that wasn't the end of it. Victoria's mouth dropped open as more women and more children got off the bus, sweeping Victoria into their midst for hugs and kisses.

Were they all expecting to be given lunch? How on earth would Naomi and Foxfield cope with this lot? Oh, heavens! Not that Victoria was to blame. Naomi could see in her bewildered expression that she hadn't antici-pated this.

Naomi's alarm mounted as she realized Mags was unloading bags, cases and gas masks from the bus, and handing them round. It looked as though the group had brought all their worldly goods with them. Surely, they didn't think . . . No, it wasn't possible. They must have plans to go on somewhere else.

But then Naomi heard the eldest woman speak: Ivy, judging from the sadly bowed legs. 'It was such a relief to receive your letter and hear there was room for all of us at this Foxfield place.'

Victoria's bewilderment turned to horror. 'I didn't mean . . .' Her words were snatched away as a young girl tugged on her arm and announced that she needed the toilet. Urgently.

Naomi was reeling in shock, too, but she pulled herself together and hastened to Victoria's side. 'I know I said I'd give you time alone with your friends, Victoria, but I just thought I'd come over and say hello.'

She forced a smile at the women and children. 'I'm Naomi Harrington, Victoria's employer.'

'Our heroine,' the woman called Mags said.

Victoria almost exploded in anxiety. 'Actually, I didn't—'

'I suggest we don't stand around in this cold wind,' Naomi said, 'especially not with rain threatening.' And not with one little girl jigging up and down and saying again that she needed the toilet. 'Let's all head for Foxfield for a proper chat.'

'That sounds like music to my ears,' Ivy said. 'I won't pretend I find travelling easy any more. Even sitting on trains and buses takes it out of old bones like mine.'

'Straight down there.' Naomi pointed along Churchwood Way.

The group began to shuffle onwards but Victoria held back, clearly mortified. 'I'm so sorry,' she began, but Naomi cut her off.

'Clearly, there's been a misunderstanding, but we can't resolve it here in the street. The children must be cold and hungry, not to mention the adults.'

'But we haven't anything to feed to them.'

'You go on with your friends and I'll see what I can buy now. Hopefully, some bread at least.'

Victoria looked reluctant but obviously saw the sense in Naomi's proposal. She turned to catch up with the group but Mags was walking back, looking concerned. 'Something's wrong, isn't it?' she asked Victoria, turning pale as she realized what had happened. 'When you said *we* were all welcome, you meant *we* as in you, Arthur and Jenny. Not the rest of us.'

'I'm sorry, Mags, I should have been clearer.'

'We shouldn't have jumped to the wrong conclusion.

153

It's just that we were desperate and it seemed too good to be true when we heard from you. It *was* too good to be true.'

'We'll talk about this soon enough,' Naomi said, shooing Mags and Victoria forward.

She was relieved when she saw Alice in the street, watching in surprise as the troop of women and children walked through the village. Alice made eye contact with Naomi and crossed the road to join her. 'Do I detect a problem?'

'It seems that Victoria's friends thought they were all moving to Churchwood.'

'To stay with you? Good grief!'

'Quite.'

'Tell me how I can help.'

Trust Alice to get straight to the practicalities. 'I need food for them all. Milk, too.'

'Leave it to me. You get off home with your visitors.'

Thank heavens for Alice.

CHAPTER TWENTY-SEVEN

Naomi

Naomi hastened after the arrivals, trying to work out the various family groups. Arthur and Jenny had been first off the bus so Naomi could identify them. She could also identify Mags and her two children. The older woman was clearly Ivy, and her little granddaughter was easy to spot since she was a tiny thing and even now she was coughing. Arthur walked at her side, holding her hand and encouraging her forward. 'It can't be far, Flower. You'll soon be in the warm . . .'

It was hard to split the others up, though, as the women chatted and the children skipped and danced about in wonder at finding themselves in a place that was so unlike London.

Victoria was lingering by the gateposts when Naomi arrived. 'This is all my fault, Mrs Harrington. But please don't worry. Mags and I will explain that there's been a misunderstanding and they'll catch the next bus home.'

'Are you sure they still have a home?' Naomi asked. 'They might have given the keys back and, anyway, isn't the house due to be demolished any day now?'

'Yes, but . . .' Victoria couldn't find the words but looked despairing.

'First things first,' Naomi said. 'Let's get everyone inside.' She moved towards the house.

The families had come to a halt by the front door and were looking up at the house in awe.

'Cor!' one boy said.

'Blimey!' said another. 'Are we really going to live here?'

'It's like a palace,' said a girl.

'Would you prefer us to use the kitchen door?' Victoria asked miserably.

'Don't be silly.' Naomi turned to the families. 'Someone needs to knock.'

There was a scrabble of 'Me! Me! Me!' from the children. The door knocker was made of brass and shaped like a lion's head, and they were all keen to use it. Naomi didn't see who got to it first but a loud knock finally sounded.

Suki took a startled step backwards when she opened the door to a crowd of strangers.

'It's all right, Suki,' Naomi called. 'The sitting room isn't large enough, so perhaps you could show everyone into the drawing room?'

'But the carpet, madam!' Suki took pride in the sumptuous carpet.

'I'm sure it'll survive if the children remove their shoes.'

Suki opened the door wider and the children surged inside, voicing more 'cors' and 'coos' and 'blimeys' at the sight of the spacious hall with the wide staircase rising to the upper floors. 'This hall is ten times bigger than the one at Straker Street,' a boy said, Straker Street presumably being his previous home.

'Shoes off, everyone,' Suki instructed, and Naomi was moved to see that a couple of children had holes in what were clearly very old socks.

The maid led them into the drawing room – more 'oohs' and 'ahs' – and then worked her way to Naomi's side, lowering her voice. 'There isn't enough lunch for everyone.'

'Hopefully, Mrs Irvine will be along with some supplies soon,' Naomi told her. 'It may have to be a picnic sort of lunch, but as long as everyone gets fed . . . The priority now is to get the kettle on for hot drinks.'

'Right you are, madam.'

The maid hastened into the kitchen while Victoria shepherded those children who needed the toilet up to the bathroom.

Naomi headed into the drawing room. 'Oi, Davie!' one of the women yelled as a boy ran to the French windows. 'Don't you dare touch that glass with sticky fingers.'

'And no bouncing on the furniture,' Mags boomed.

'If you'll excuse me . . .' Naomi went to help in the kitchen. Suki had the kettle on the stove and Naomi joined her in setting out extra cups and saucers. 'Have we much milk?'

'Not enough for that lot.'

'Let's hope Mrs Irvine can help.'

A knock on the door soon signalled Alice's arrival. She burst in with a shopping basket and a bag. 'I managed to get bread and a tin of custard powder from the shops, and I've brought some eggs laid by my chickens. Also, apples to stew for dessert, though I imagine Bert can keep you supplied on that front. Luckily, I made a batch of soup myself this morning, so Daniel will bring that over. There should be enough for everyone and we can make sandwiches, though they'll need to be an assortment of whatever we can cobble together.'

'We've got meat paste in the cupboard,' Suki said. 'And a bit of cheese.'

'I saw Adam and he's going to bring whatever he can lay his hands on, too,' Alice added. 'I've brought a pint of milk for the children since we can get along with the dried stuff at home. Not that a pint will go far among so many.'

Daniel arrived with the pan of soup, bringing Alice's father, who said he'd pop his head around the drawing-room door just to be sure that everyone was all right. He was always ready to help with medical advice should anyone need it.

Adam came next, bearing two pints of milk, more bread, some margarine and a fruit pie. 'I hope this will help,' he said.

A meal was put together and carried into the dining room. Naomi winced at the thought of the damage the children might cause to the polished mahogany furniture but the adults gave them strict instructions to be careful. Everyone sat, although some children had to perch on laps as there weren't enough chairs.

The children's eyes had widened at the sight of the food but no one snatched and eventually it was distributed fairly.

Had Mags told the other adults of the awful misunderstanding that had occurred? Naomi guessed not, as the women would surely have been more anxious.

Dr Lovell slipped away after saying into Naomi's ear, 'Keep an eye on that little girl, Flower. She has a weak chest.'

Naomi nodded. The child looked as delicate as a fairy.

She waited until the meal was over and then introduced Alice, Daniel and Adam to the Londoners. 'Perhaps you could introduce your friends, Victoria,' she said afterwards and made a big effort to remember the names and ages.

Mags was Margaret Brennan and her children were Lewis, just turned eight, and Orla, six. Flower Percival was four and Ivy's only grandchild. A woman called Jessie Smith had a son, Mattie, of seven, and a daughter, Ruth, of six. Another woman called Pat Nicholls had Davie, seven, and Sue, six, while Sheila Blair had one child, a daughter called Mary who was also six.

'Perhaps the children would like to play in the garden for a few minutes,' Naomi suggested, wanting to speak to the adults. 'They'll need to wrap up warmly.'

The children put their outer clothes back on – clean but terribly shabby and ill-fitting – and Suki, Daniel and Adam were deputized to keep an eye on them.

'Don't worry about the washing-up,' Naomi told Victoria. 'We can see to it later.'

With the children out of earshot, Mags spoke up and explained the misunderstanding to the other women. Their aghast expressions tore at Naomi's heart but Mags was amazingly brave. 'We're all grateful to you for feeding us just now, Mrs Harrington, but please don't worry. We'll leave on the next bus.'

Naomi let that pass and said, 'Why don't you tell me something of yourselves. I know Victoria's story, of course.'

Mags went first. She was a widow, having been married to Liam, who'd worked on the docks before his death from lung disease. Jessie's husband had walked out on her and the children. 'He left one night and never came back. I've no idea where he went.'

Pat Nicholls's husband had been killed in the Blitz. 'My Andy was a good man but not so good with money. He left us with nothing.'

Ivy had long been a widow. She had a daughter, but Flora was a flighty thing who had had Flower at seventeen and, being uninterested in babies, had left the child with her grandmother. 'I haven't heard from her since,' Ivy said.

Some of the children had been evacuated at the start of the war but hadn't been happy. 'I brought mine home

159

after Liam died,' Mags said. 'They were grieving and needed me.'

Pat had retrieved her children for the same reason. 'They lost their father. They couldn't have their mother a hundred miles away. They weren't coping,' she explained.

Sheila Blair was mother to Mary, six. Her husband had died of tuberculosis when Mary was small.

'How did you all get together?' Naomi asked next.

'I rented a room in a different house but moved in with Joan, Arthur and Jenny when Joan became ill and needed help,' Victoria said.

'I worked at the wireless factory with Victoria and Joan,' Mags said next. 'My landlord was a nasty man who wanted more than just money for his rent, if you take my meaning. When I slapped him around the face for putting his filthy hands on me, he said we had to leave. Joan and Victoria let us move in with them.'

'I lived in a house down the road from Mags,' Jessie said. 'After it was bombed I moved in, too.'

'My landlord evicted me when I couldn't pay the rent,' Pat said. 'Jessie was a friend so she got me into the house with the others.'

'I met Victoria when she helped after Flower had a bad coughing fit in the street,' Ivy said. 'She took us into a cafe to warm up and when she heard that we lived in a damp basement, she invited us to move to the house. It was very crowded but it worked well for all of us. I'm no longer fit to work but I looked after the children while their mothers went out to their jobs. None of us had other family. Not family that was willing or able to help out, anyway.'

'And now you want to live in the countryside.'

'If we have a choice,' Mags said. 'Cleaner air, fewer bombs . . . But we don't want to turn the children back into the sort of evacuees who are sent off to live away from us.'

No wonder Victoria's letter had felt like a gift from heaven.

'I imagine you all gave up your jobs before coming here?' Naomi said.

'There'll be other jobs,' Mags said, her chin jutting with determination.

'What about your house? Is it still available to you?'

Mags's lips tightened. 'You've no need to be worrying about that, Mrs Harrington. You've no need to be worrying about anything. We're grateful for your kindness in feeding us but we'll be on our way in minutes.'

Which meant that, no, their old house wasn't available but Mags and her friends had their pride. It was fighting talk and Naomi admired the courage and dignity behind it. But how would a troop of women and children manage with nowhere to go and probably little money?

Sudden rattling on the window had Naomi's head turning. The rain had begun in earnest. It was followed by another sound, this time from inside the house as, squealing, the children rushed back in from the garden.

'Mind your feet!' Suki called. 'You're treading mud in!'

'I think Suki and Daniel might welcome some help,' Alice said, getting up and gliding from the room.

'Who likes stories?' Naomi heard her ask, and there was a babble of 'Me!'

'Then come this way.' A moment later the drawing-room door closed and quietness descended.

The rain rattled against the window even harder. It was coming down like silver darts, caught by the wind and launched at the glass.

Mags glanced at it, frowning. She chewed on her lip for a moment before asking Naomi, 'Do you know of any cheap lodgings near by? Just for tonight?'

'No one in Churchwood offers lodgings, as far as I know,' Naomi told her.

'Then we'll have to go further afield.'

'No, you won't.' Naomi saw no alternative to what she was about to propose. 'You can't drag the children all over Hertfordshire in this weather with no certainty of finding beds. You can stay here tonight. In fact, you'd better stay tomorrow night, too, since it'll be hard to find anywhere else to stay on a Sunday.'

'All of us?' Mags exchanged glances with the other women, who all looked desperately hopeful.

'All of you,' Naomi confirmed. 'It's a large house, though it still might be a squeeze. I suggest Victoria and I make plans while the rest of you return to the children.'

'You're a kind woman, Mrs Harrington,' Mags said, and the others murmured agreement.

As the adults rejoined the children, Alice, Daniel and Adam came to Naomi's side. 'Everyone will be staying here until Monday,' Naomi told them.

Alice nodded as though she'd guessed as much. 'We have a spare bed at The Linnets.'

'And someone can have my bedroom at the vicarage,' Adam said. 'I can make do with the sofa.' The vicarage hadn't yet been fully repaired after being damaged in the plane crash so not all rooms were usable yet.

'Thank you both, but it's been an unsettling day for the families so I think they should all be together, at least for tonight,' Naomi answered.

She fetched a pen and paper and with the help of Victoria – still appalled by the misunderstanding – worked out who would sleep where. Foxfield had six bedrooms. Naomi occupied one and Victoria another. 'I know we said Arthur and Jenny would have their own room, but perhaps they could bunk in with you for one night, Victoria?' Naomi suggested.

'Of course,' she agreed.

It was settled that Ivy and Flower should share the third bedroom, Mags and her children the fourth, Jessie and her children the fifth, and Pat and her children the sixth. 'I suggest Sheila and her daughter take Mrs Kitts's old room in the attic next to Suki's,' Naomi said. 'There are two more attic rooms, but one is used for storage and the other isn't furnished. Not that I've enough beds for everyone, anyway, but hopefully the children won't object to sleeping top to toe or camping on the floor.'

'You'll need a lot of blankets and pillows,' Alice said.

'And I haven't enough.'

'Daniel and I will bring some from home,' Alice offered.

'I'll do the same,' Adam said.

They left to fetch the bedding.

'We need to think about food for this evening and for breakfast, too,' Naomi told Victoria. 'Would you mind making up the beds while I telephone Bert? He'll probably have some vegetables going spare.'

'Of course.'

Naomi was relieved to find Bert at home.

'I've got myself in a bit of a pickle,' she began.

'What is it this time, woman?'

She explained about the unexpected visitors.

'That *is* a pickle, but you wouldn't be the woman I love if you hadn't offered shelter. What you need from me is food.'

How lovely it was to be speaking to someone who understood.

'Leave it with me and I'll see what I can pull together,' he said.

'You're wonderful, Bert.'

'Course I am. That's why you love me.'

Naomi went next to the kitchen. 'I'm sorry about all the extra work, Suki, but there's more to come,' she said.

'They're all staying the night?'

'Tomorrow, too. They've nowhere else to go, and those poor children . . .'

'We'll manage, madam.'

Pausing in the hall to get her breath back – Naomi's head was reeling – she opened the door to Alice and Daniel, who had their arms full of bedding they were keeping dry under large umbrellas.

'I brought towels, too,' Alice said.

'Goodness, yes. I didn't think of towels,' Naomi told her.

The next step was to show everyone where they'd be sleeping. The relief on the adults' faces was Naomi's reward and the children appeared to regard sleeping somewhere new as an adventure.

Bert arrived with a basket of vegetables, which he carried into the kitchen. 'Potatoes, onions, carrots and parsnips,' he reported. 'Also, some of the apples and pears I've laid out in my loft. I called in at the shops and managed to get a bag of porridge oats for breakfast, along with tins of dried milk and custard powder. I also picked up some liver and kidneys from the butcher. All in all, you should have enough here to cobble together some sort of meal.'

'I shall. Thank you.'

'You know, it's days like this that remind us how much we need our bookshop back,' Bert said. 'When the bookshop was running, everyone heard what was going on and pitched in to help.'

'Talking of the bookshop, are you still planning to go to Hatfield with Alice and Daniel tonight?'

'Certainly, I am. I want that rogue builder brought to justice. Luckily, the rain has eased off.'

'Take care,' Naomi urged him. 'I want the con man brought to justice, too, but not if it means you, Alice or Daniel getting hurt.'

'We'll be fine,' he told her.

Would they? Naomi would worry about them until they were home safe and sound. She seemed to be collecting more and more worries these days: her divorce, her settlement, the bookshop, Ellen, William and, of course, all these London women and their children. Hopefully, they'd find a way to move on soon so Foxfield could regain some of its customary peace. Not that they'd all be leaving, since Arthur and Jenny would stay.

They seemed to be nice enough children, but already Naomi had felt a pang when she'd seen Jenny wrap her arms around Victoria's neck and kiss her. Perhaps Naomi should have been over her childlessness now, but she wasn't, and knowing she'd never have a little Jenny in her life . . . Well, it hurt.

CHAPTER TWENTY-EIGHT

Alice

'I think I've got everything we're likely to need,' Bert said when he collected Alice and Daniel in his truck. 'Climb aboard and let's get going.'

They said little on the journey to Hatfield. Alice was outwardly calm – at least, she hoped she was – but inside, her nerves were twisting like writhing snakes. Was it the same for Daniel and Bert?

Parking near to Mick Briggs's house, they unloaded the truck and headed for the rogue's back wall.

'Let me take a look,' Daniel said.

Moving quietly so he wouldn't alarm the dog, he set up the stepladder they'd brought a couple of feet from the wall and climbed just high enough to peep over the top. Climbing down again, he whispered, 'The van is there and so is the dog. I expect Mick is at home, too, because there's a light showing where he hasn't closed his curtains properly. Maybe he leaves a gap deliberately so he can keep an eye on the yard and the dog.'

'I imagine he's upset a lot of people in his time and some may want to fight back,' Alice said.

'As we're doing,' Bert said.

He moved towards the big double gates that led into the yard and directed a torch at them to see how they were fastened. 'Chain and padlock,' he reported. 'You'll need to go to the front door, but wait while I do my bit.'

The dog growled: he must have seen the torchlight or heard the whispers. They all fell silent, allowing time for the dog to relax again.

Then, creeping stealthily despite his considerable size, Bert moved the stepladder closer to the wall and armed himself with what he needed – a rope lasso and a long-handled hook speared with liver. 'Everyone ready?' he murmured.

Everyone was, Alice and Daniel being poised to run around to the front of the house the moment Bert told them to go.

Bert climbed the stepladder and dangled the liver down the other side. 'Come and get it, Samson,' he crooned.

The dog's sharp claws gouged the paving slabs as he raced to grab the meat. Bert must have lassoed him at the first attempt because his call came softly but urgently: 'Now!'

Alice and Daniel raced around to the front door and Daniel banged on it hard before Mick had a chance to register that his dog was whining and fighting for freedom. They heard movement inside, a door being opened – presumably the back door – and a voice calling, 'Here, Samson! Now!'

Would he see that the dog had been captured? All was lost if so. But it appeared that he'd merely thrown the door open, expecting the dog to come bounding in to act as his protector or even his weapon.

Mick looked taken aback to find two nicely dressed, pleasant-looking people on his doorstep, though it didn't inspire him to courtesy. 'What?' he demanded.

Daniel smiled. 'Sorry to disturb you, but I wonder if we might come in for a chat?'

'A chat?' Mick probably hadn't had a cosy chat in his entire life.

'It's hard to explain in just a few words,' Daniel continued.

'Try.' Mick glanced back over his shoulder and Alice guessed he was wondering why Samson hadn't appeared.

'We don't need more than five minutes of your time,' she said.

'If you're selling something, I'm not buying. If you're wanting something, I'm not giving. Samson!' He barked the name over his shoulder.

'Samson is rather – er – tied up at the moment,' Daniel told him.

'Eh?' Puzzlement gave way to alarm as Mick realized something was afoot.

He turned to investigate Samson's predicament, slamming the front door behind him, but Daniel had placed his foot in the way and the door simply bounced off it to open again. 'Shall we?' Daniel invited Alice, and they walked into the house, stepping past dirty plates and empty beer bottles on their way to the back yard.

They arrived in time to see Bert brandishing the hook, now minus the liver, in one hand and keeping a tight grasp on the lasso in the other. 'This could do a lot of damage,' Bert warned, giving the hook an experimental stab in Mick's direction.

'Release my dog!' Mick demanded.

'The quickest way to have your dog freed is to cooperate with us,' Alice said.

Mick whirled around and saw her and Daniel. 'How did you . . .?' Anger took over. 'Get out of my house!'

'We wiped our feet before we stepped in,' Daniel said. 'Though, arguably, there's more dirt inside the house than outside it.'

'Get out!'

'It will be our pleasure to get out,' Alice said. 'Just as soon as we've concluded our business.'

'We don't have any business.'

'That's where you're wrong. Remember Ellen Bates? You tricked her out of money and we want it back.'

'I don't know who or what you're talking about,' Mick lied.

'You're not a very good liar, Mr Briggs,' Alice told him. 'Do you really want to waste time pretending you don't know why we're here? Or would you rather conclude matters swiftly so you and your dog can be more comfortable?'

'I didn't trick anyone,' he insisted, but his fight was in its death throes.

'Hand the money over or I fetch the police,' Alice threatened. 'I'll leave my two friends here to keep guard over you while I'm gone.'

Daniel was young and fit. Bert was neither but, just in case Mick was nurturing ideas, he said, 'I may be a few years older than you, Briggs, but I was a champion boxer in my youth and I haven't lost my touch.'

Seconds ticked by as Mick glanced from Bert to Daniel to Alice and back again, looking fit to burst as he tried to decide what to do. Alice began to worry about Bert's arms. Holding a dog as big as Samson while brandishing the hook and balancing on a stepladder would be taking a toll on his muscles.

'As you're not ready to give us what we want, Mick, I'll invite the police to come along,' Alice said, turning.

'All right!' Mick howled.

'You'll repay the money?' Alice asked.

'I've just said so, haven't I?'

Not quite. 'We'll take it now, please.'

'I don't have that sort of money lying around the house.'

'Scared there might be someone like you on the prowl?' Alice asked. 'Another common thief?'

'I'll have it in a few days.'

'We'll take it now,' Alice said.

'I just told you, I don't—'

'I don't believe you.'

'Neither do I,' Daniel said.

'Nor me,' added Bert.

Mick muttered a curse. 'Wait there. I'll fetch it.'

'Oh, no,' Daniel said, and Alice guessed he wasn't going to give Mick the chance to arm himself with some sort of weapon. 'I'll come with you. You're worried I'll see where you hide your money – other people's money, I should say – but I'm only interested in what's due to Ellen.'

He stood aside and made a mock bow to signal to Mick to walk past him into the house. Mick stalked by and Daniel gestured to Alice to accompany him.

'Be quick!' Bert called, and it was clear that he couldn't keep up his position for much longer.

Inside the house, Mick had got down on his knees. He sent a glower over his shoulder but appeared to accept that he couldn't keep his hiding place from them. Pulling back some stained linoleum, he prised up a floorboard. They couldn't see how much money he had because he huddled over it then slung an arm backwards with some pound notes in his fist. 'There.'

Daniel took it and counted it. 'You're ten pounds short.'

'No, I'm—'

'Beginning to get on my nerves,' Alice told him. 'Hand over the missing ten pounds and a further five to compensate for our inconvenience.'

'Are you—'

'Serious? Mad? I'm both,' Alice said.

He handed over the extra money, covered his hiding place and heaved himself to his feet. 'Now get out of my house.'

'It'll be a pleasure,' Alice told him. 'This house is a hazard to health.'

They left by the front door again and ran around to the back. 'We've got the money,' Alice told Bert. 'All of it.'

'Thank goodness for that. My arms are killing me.'

Bert threw the end of the lasso into the yard and they packed up the rest of the equipment, hastening back to the truck before Mick could set the furious Samson on them.

'Well, that was a decent evening's work,' Daniel said as they drove away.

'Justice was done,' Bert agreed.

Alice smiled, guessing the release of tension was making them all feel light-headed. 'Were you really a champion boxer in your youth, Bert?' she asked.

'Perhaps I wasn't a champion, exactly. I went along to a boxing club as a boy and had a couple of matches, which I won. The trainer told me I had talent but I couldn't take pleasure in bashing other lads and making their noses bleed, so I packed it in.'

They went first to Ellen's house. Invited inside, Alice handed over the money. 'Every last penny and a little extra, too.'

Ellen was overcome. '"Thank you" doesn't feel nearly enough. But I can't take this extra five pounds. You three went to the trouble of recovering my money. Share the extra between you. Call it repayment of your bus fares and petrol costs.'

'I've got a better idea,' Alice said. 'Why don't we put it towards the costs of setting up the bookshop again?'

'I'd like that,' Ellen agreed. 'It could buy a few books.' But then her face sagged. 'I'll have to find someone else to do the plastering now.'

'I'll be glad to look around for someone,' Bert offered.

'Would you? I don't trust myself to choose the right person after the last fiasco.'

'Leave it with me,' Bert said.

Back in Churchwood, he pulled up outside The Linnets. 'Make sure you have some rest, young man,' he told Daniel. 'You and Alice have done a fine job in getting Ellen's money back, but it's time to step back and relax while you can.'

'I will,' Daniel said at the same time as Alice said, 'He will.'

They all smiled. 'You won't mind if I tell Naomi about our night's adventure?' Bert said.

'Of course not,' Alice answered. 'She's probably feeling overwhelmed by all her visitors, so the news might cheer her up.'

'My thoughts exactly.'

Bert drove off and Alice let Daniel and herself into the cottage. 'Well?' her father asked, emerging from his study with his dandelion-clock hair floating around his cherubic face in disarray.

'We got the money,' Alice told him.

'Splendid! This calls for sherry.'

They followed him into his study to toast their success. Surely, all would go well with the bookshop now?

CHAPTER TWENTY-NINE

Naomi

'I hope we didn't wake you?' Mags asked as Naomi came downstairs in her dressing gown on Monday morning.

'Not at all,' Naomi told her, though the truth was that she'd been roused by a child shouting that his socks had another hole in them.

She didn't normally sleep in late, but worry about the London families – about William, too – had made sleeping difficult. Besides, the past two days had been filled with bustle and Naomi was exhausted from it. Yesterday, the families had been out and about in the village and had come to church, too, but even that had been awkward since Arthur had led the children in a light-hearted run around the churchyard, not realizing that some residents considered such behaviour to be disrespectful.

Afterwards, Marjorie had hastened up, agog at the sight of so many visitors and desperate for information about them. Somehow, she'd heard about William's visit, too, though she didn't know his identity. 'I'm surprised you didn't tell me about him,' she'd complained. 'Not that I'm the sort of person who sticks her nose into other people's business, but we're such good friends.'

Marjorie was exactly the sort of person who stuck her nose into other people's business.

The boy was a relative of Alexander's, Naomi had told her, keeping to the agreed story.

'How nice that you're keeping in touch,' Marjorie had said, burning with the desire to know more but not having quite enough nerve to ask.

Now Naomi felt flustered at being still in her dressing gown.

Mags's boy, Lewis, came up and Mags told him, 'Have a good look around so you don't leave anything behind, then stack your bag by the front door.'

Naomi saw that two bags had already been placed there.

'You were an angel for putting us up, but we don't want to outstay our welcome by taking up more of your time,' Mags explained. 'Besides, we've a busy day ahead of us. We've decided to go to a town called Hatfield, since we might stand a good chance of getting work there. We want to make an early start so we can look for a place to stay as well.'

Her attention was caught by her son. 'Lewis, you've one sock on inside out, so you have.'

Naomi moved into the kitchen where Victoria, Suki and Alice were busy making porridge and slicing bread. 'I'm sorry I'm down so late,' Naomi said, though a glance at the kitchen clock told her that she wasn't particularly late. Everyone else was early.

'I hope you don't think we're taking liberties with your kitchen,' Victoria said.

'Of course not. You're helping and I'm grateful.'

'Bert managed to buy some bread and he's donated a pint of fresh milk,' Alice said.

'How kind. Well done for recovering Ellen's money on Saturday.'

Alice smiled. 'It was a good result for Ellen and the bookshop, too. They're both due some good luck now.'

'They certainly are.' Feeling at a disadvantage in her

dressing gown, Naomi added, 'I'll get dressed then come and help.'

She hastened back upstairs. It was her routine to take a bath in the mornings but today she opted for a quick wash and dressed in her usual winter garb of warm lisle stockings, cream blouse, tweed skirt and matching jacket.

Breakfast was already under way when she returned downstairs and she could see that everyone was on their best behaviour. 'Don't wave your bread around like that, Davie,' Mags urged. 'We don't want to have to clear up a mess.'

All the adults appeared to be anxious to be gone, since none of them knew what the day would hold or where they'd rest their heads that night.

Naomi answered a knock on the door to find Evelyn Gregson and her boys in the porch. 'Forgive me for intruding when I know you must have your hands full,' Evelyn said. 'Adam told me about your visitors and I've brought a few of my boys' old books in case they're of interest to the children.'

'How thoughtful,' Naomi told her. 'Step inside for a moment. It's horrid out there.' Rain was falling again. No, not just rain. Icy sleet.

'We'll only stay a minute or two. I need to get the boys to school.'

Naomi led them into the dining room where breakfast was winding down. 'This is Mrs Gregson, a neighbour. These are her sons, Alan and Roger.'

'I'm pleased to meet you all,' Evelyn told them. She took the cover off her shopping basket and brought out five or six books. 'I thought these might help to keep the children entertained.'

'You're a kind woman, so you are,' Mags said. 'It seems to me that there are a lot of kind people in Churchwood. We'll take the books gladly.'

'You're leaving today?' Evelyn asked. 'If so, I'll wish you all good luck.'

'Heading for Hatfield, we are,' Mags confirmed.

Wind blew the sleet against the window. Knowing there was a better course of action than for all the visitors to go to Hatfield when the outcome was so uncertain, Naomi shrugged her tiredness aside to do what she knew to be the right thing. 'Why don't the children stay here today? It'll be easier for you to look for work without them trailing along.'

'Wasn't I just saying there are kind people in Churchwood?' Mags exclaimed. 'We appreciate the offer, but we'd have to come back to fetch them later and we need all our time for finding somewhere to stay.'

'I meant that you can all spend another night here.'

The relief in the room was like a living creature that slumped in its chair, sighing and murmuring, 'Thank God!'

'We're already in your debt, Mrs Harrington, but if you're sure about letting us stay, we'll make that debt even bigger by accepting your kind offer,' Mags said. 'Did you hear that, children? We're staying here tonight. What have you to say to that?'

There was a chorus of 'Thank you!'

'Ivy will look after you while your mammies and I search out jobs and a place to live,' Mags continued. 'I don't want us coming back to the news that you've behaved badly, though.'

'I can help with the children,' Evelyn offered. 'I can come back after I've taken my boys to school. I was a teacher once and I'll be teaching again after Easter, so I'm used to entertaining young people.'

'That would be wonderful, wouldn't it, Naomi?' Alice said. 'I was going to offer Daniel and myself but that would have meant letting the patients at the hospital down.' She explained to the visitors about Stratton House and her volunteering. 'I don't like to disappoint the patients if I can help it.'

'To be sure, you don't,' Mags agreed. 'And thanks to another of Churchwood's kind women – Mrs Gregson here – there's no need for it.' She smiled at Evelyn.

It was a weight off Naomi's mind to know she'd have help about the place.

'We must leave money for the children's food,' Mags said.

Naomi wouldn't hear of it. 'You'll need all your money for getting settled somewhere.'

The women went off shortly afterwards, heading for the bus stop: Mags, Jessie, Sheila and Pat. Alice left too, but promised to look in later.

It was a busy morning. Evelyn and Ivy took care of the children while Victoria, Suki and Naomi saw to the house, Victoria clearly feeling guilty still and trying to make up for her blunder by working incredibly hard.

Bert arrived, took stock of the situation and went home for more vegetables before driving Naomi into the village to see what the shops might have in the way of food supplies.

Adam approached from across the village green. 'Nasty weather,' he remarked, grimacing at the sleet that was plastering his unruly brown curls to his head. 'Have your unexpected guests moved on?'

'Come into the grocer's with us and we'll tell you all about it,' Bert said. He was used to being outside in all weathers but Naomi guessed he was thinking of her comfort.

They moved into the shop and Naomi filled Adam in on the latest situation with the visitors. 'I'll ask around the village for food donations,' he proposed.

It would be a miserable job knocking on doors in this weather but the young vicar would do it uncomplainingly. To buoy his spirits, Naomi also told him about the recovery of Ellen's money. Adam had rushed off after the Sunday morning church service yesterday to spend time with another clergyman who was sick, so she hadn't had a chance to tell him then.

One of Adam's sweet smiles lit up his face and he went off with a bounce in his step.

Naomi moved with Bert towards the counter. Using their own ration allowances, they managed to buy a packet of tea, a bottle of Camp coffee, another tin of custard powder, some dried egg and a small quantity of cheese. 'We've no chance of getting butter or margarine, but I've a pot of honey in the truck and more vegetables,' Bert said. 'You could make one of those Lord Woolton pies with mashed potatoes on top.'

They were all tired of the Minister of Food's recipe but it was a good suggestion since the pies were nutritious and filling.

'What's this I'm hearing about a bunch of evacuees?' the grocer's wife asked.

'Several mothers with their children and one grandmother with her grandchild,' Naomi explained.

'They're not staying permanently?'

'Just for a couple of nights.'

'Must be hard to feed them all.'

'It's requiring some sacrifice but we're muddling through.'

Mrs Miles put a bag of biscuits on the counter. 'Take that from me. I've no sweets or chocolates, but a biscuit apiece will be a little treat.'

'That's very kind of you, Mrs Miles,' Naomi told her.

They moved on to the baker's and bought two loaves of bread. 'At least bread isn't rationed yet,' Bert said.

The baker asked about the visitors, too, and donated apple cake.

They'd been home for about an hour when Adam arrived with a basket, which he unloaded in the kitchen. 'People have been as generous as they could,' he reported. There were two tins of rice pudding, gravy browning, a small bag of flour, a jar of home-made jam, apples, pears, onions and parsnips.

Lunch was soup again followed by a small portion of rice pudding for each child.

The sleet eased off during the afternoon. The air was still damp and the clouds looked ready to drop more rain at any moment, but the children were becoming restless.

'They need to work off some energy,' Evelyn said.

'Might they play in the garden?' Victoria asked Naomi, obviously concerned that something might be damaged if the boisterousness increased.

'Of course.' Victoria's guilt touched Naomi's heart. At twenty-two, the girl should have been travelling lightly through life, enjoying romances, adventures and fun before she settled down with a husband and children of her own. Instead, she had years of supporting her parents behind her, and a future of caring for two young orphans ahead of her. Just now, she was also feeling responsible for her friends and their children. 'I wish you'd stop blaming yourself for the misunderstanding,' Naomi told her yet again.

'If I'd been more careful with my words, my friends wouldn't have given up their jobs or their home.'

'The house might have been snatched from under them at any moment,' Naomi reminded her.

'They might have had a little more time in which to organize themselves.'

'Sometimes unplanned events can turn out for the best.'

Victoria looked as though she wanted to point out that at other times they could turn out for the worst, but a screech from one of the children distracted her. 'Arthur, stop that now, please,' she called.

Naomi hadn't seen what he'd been doing but it had involved Lewis. Now Arthur sank down, looking vexed, but little Flower patted his hand, and the boy let go of his resentment to smile back at her.

'You can play in the garden, but keep to the paths and the grass,' Victoria announced. 'Don't go near the soil or plants, and make sure you wipe your feet thoroughly when you come back in.' She turned back to Naomi, still anxious. 'Do you mind if I go out and supervise them? I'll make the time up, I promise.'

'Victoria, you're already working very hard. Just go out with them and try to relax.'

'I'll come too,' Evelyn offered. 'Naomi, I hope you don't mind, but I asked my boys to come along after school.'

'Of course I don't mind.'

The children dressed in their outdoor clothes. From the outset, Naomi had formed an impression of old and ill-fitting clothes that had probably been passed down from child to child. Now she was noticing details. Like a hole in little Flower's shoe that her grandmother had tried to fill with newspaper. Like the way one of Arthur's boots was separating from the sole and Lewis's jacket was too small for him. Then there were patches on Davie's short pants that left his knobby knees exposed to the elements, and mismatched buttons on Mary's coat. Yet there was dignity in the adults who cared for them. They were doing their best in difficult circumstances.

Naomi saw them outside then tottered to her sitting room and sat down, feeling shattered already. 'Tea, madam?' Suki asked, following her in with her usual gentleness.

'I'd love some, but the mothers will be home soon and I expect their need for tea will be greater than mine after being out all day in this weather.'

'I'll make you a weak cup,' Suki suggested.

'You're a treasure.'

Naomi drank her tea gratefully but didn't linger over it, feeling she should be doing more to help.

Alice returned at the same time as Evelyn's boys, bringing Daniel with her. After greeting everyone, she and Naomi went to the kitchen to make a start on the dinner preparations. Alice's injured hand made her slow at peeling vegetables but there was something capable about her that made all things seem possible. Naomi wasn't much faster, as she'd never needed to learn to cook, but she was eager to be useful and it wouldn't hurt to gain experience for when she married Bert. He'd said he'd have no objection to some paid help, but Naomi guessed he'd be more comfortable with self-sufficiency.

Suki got to the door first when the mothers returned, so Naomi had no chance to ask privately if their mission had been successful before they joined their children in the drawing room, more sleet and approaching darkness having driven them back inside. 'It's good to see the house still standing,' Mags joked, but she was obviously tired and Naomi saw a worried look pass between her and Ivy.

No one wanted to upset the children, though, and a few minutes were spent giving hugs and kisses, and hearing about the children's day.

'You ladies must be in need of tea,' Naomi said then.

Leaving Evelyn and Alice with the children, Naomi and Victoria led the women to the sitting room to hear about their trip to Hatfield.

Mags was a plain-speaking woman. 'You want to know how we got on, and the answer is mixed. There's work to be had in aircraft construction but our references need to be checked before we can start. It's understandable, since we could be German saboteurs, but it's likely to take a week or two at least.'

Victoria's pretty face pinched up with dismay at the thought of the women having no work – and no incomes – for so long.

'As you say, Mags, it's understandable,' Naomi said, trying to keep her own dismay hidden.

'We looked at places to live as well. There was a house up for rent but it was too near the factory for our liking. One reason for bringing the children out of London is to get them away from any bombing, and an aircraft factory might be just the sort of place the enemy could have in its sights as a target.'

'It might,' Naomi agreed.

'Somewhere just outside Hatfield would suit us best. Safe for the children and easy for us to get to work. We made a few enquiries, but to be honest . . .' Mags looked embarrassed. 'We couldn't manage it with no money coming in. We'll have to get by with a bed-and-breakfast sort of lodging for a while.'

'For all of you?' Naomi asked, suspecting their finances couldn't stretch to lodgings, either.

'Don't you be worrying your head about that,' Mags said staunchly. 'We're strong women and we'll cope. Won't we, girls?'

The others nodded but Naomi read the truth of the situation in Victoria's face. The women would pay for Ivy and the children to stay somewhere but sleep rough themselves. In the dead of winter.

'You're staying here until you can find somewhere suitable to settle.' Naomi's tone was firm, though heaven knew how she was going to cope.

Victoria's hands went to her mouth in a show of distress at having brought so much trouble to Naomi's door. Mags sent her friend an apologetic look and said, 'If it was just us women, we wouldn't dream of trespassing on your hospitality longer, Mrs Harrington. But there are children to consider and we've no right to let our pride get in the way of their welfare. Thank you from the bottom of our hearts.'

Naomi mustered a show of cheer, hoping that Churchwood could come to her rescue with more offers of help.

As if the village had been listening, she answered a knock on the door to find Edna Hall with an offering. 'I've brought you all a pie,' Edna said. 'Apple and blackberries preserved from last summer. Milk, too. Only half a pint, but I hope it'll be welcome.'

'It will indeed, Edna, if you're sure you can spare it.'

'I can spare it. Children need milk for strong bones.'

'They certainly do,' Naomi agreed, thinking of poor Ivy's bowed legs.

'I also came to repeat my offer of my spare room for one of your families. My house is small but my second bedroom is standing empty.'

'Edna, you're an angel. I think everyone will manage here for tonight, but perhaps tomorrow . . .?' Boarding out one of the families might relieve some of the pressure on Foxfield.

'Just say the word.'

CHAPTER THIRTY

Kate

Kate's journey started well. She was at the bus stop in good time to reach St Albans for the train into London. She also crossed London in good time to catch the train to Cheltenham. After that, things went downhill rapidly.

The train she wanted was packed with troops, who had priority, so Kate had to take a later one. She didn't panic at first, since she'd allowed for delays, but, after giving up her seat to a wounded soldier, she had to stand and found herself being jostled this way and that, while her feet were trodden on several times. Then the train broke down and was stuck out in the countryside for two hours while the problem was fixed.

She was flustered and dishevelled when she finally reached Cheltenham. What a terrible impression she was going to make on the Kinsellas. She'd been expected for tea but it was long past teatime now. Had they gone ahead without her or were they waiting still and drumming impatient fingers on the tabletop?

She thought of telephoning to explain that she'd be along in a taxi just as soon as possible, but the queue for the telephones was long and she feared the queue for taxis would be even longer. She was right. She joined the back of the queue, annoyed at herself for forgetting an umbrella because heavy sleet was falling and making her even more bedraggled.

184

'Kate!'

She turned – and there was Leo, waving through the open window of a car. She hastened towards him and he leaped out to open the passenger door for her, lifting a hand in apology to a taxi driver who wished to pass.

'I'm sorry I'm so late!' Kate cried, but Leo only lobbed her case into the back, got in the car and drove off as the taxi driver tooted his horn.

Was Leo angry with her? Alarm flared inside her as he turned into a side road and brought the car to a halt. Was he about to tell her that she'd blotted her copybook with his family and was no longer welcome?

He turned to her and Kate felt a flood of relief because he was grinning. 'Now I can drink my fill of you without that impatient driver behind us,' he said.

'I couldn't get on the train I wanted,' Kate explained, gabbling. 'Then the train I caught got stuck and—'

'I know,' he soothed. 'I telephoned the station and heard all about it.'

'Your parents—'

'Perfectly understand that delays happen, especially in wartime.'

'They're not annoyed with me?'

'It isn't your fault you're later than planned.'

'No, but—'

'Shh, my darling. You're making it hard for me to kiss you and I've been looking forward to this moment for weeks.'

'Oh,' Kate said.

He held out his arms and she moved into them, delighting in the velvet nuzzle of his lips on hers. Then the kiss grew serious and for a moment Kate forgot that she was sitting in a car in full view of anyone who happened to be passing, and dreadfully late for a visit, too. She existed only in the moment.

'Goodness,' she said when they finally separated. A blush warmed her cheeks despite the dampness of her clothes.

'Goodness, indeed,' Leo said. 'I've missed you.'

'And I you,' Kate admitted, suddenly shy.

They stared at each other for a moment then Leo roused himself. 'We'd better be on our way.'

He drove off again and Kate chewed her lip in anxiety over the forthcoming meeting with his parents. Leo must have sensed her tension because he glanced over and smiled again. 'Stop worrying! I'm in the lucky situation of having parents who love me and want nothing more than for me to be happy. You're the girl who makes me happy so they'll welcome you with open arms. They'll love you for yourself, anyway. You're a great girl, my darling.'

She was also a stranger to the sort of gracious living the Kinsellas probably took for granted. She hated the thought of being considered uncouth, not just for her own sake but for Leo's, too.

'Is this your father's car?' she asked, to stop her nervousness from rendering her mute.

'It is. A sedate old thing. The car, not my father, though he's growing old and sedate, too.'

He smiled and Kate forced a smile in return, though nerves were cramping her stomach.

'He isn't using it much due to the petrol rationing but we agreed that collecting you should be treated as a special circumstance.'

'How kind. It isn't hurting you to drive?'

One of Leo's hands had been burned when his plane crashed. 'The back of my hand was hurt worse than my palm,' he explained. 'Besides, I'm wearing dressings and soft cotton gloves beneath these leather gloves.'

She was glad he was coping, though the faster he

recovered, the sooner he might be sent on active duty again. Kate felt he'd done his bit for the war effort already, having flown from its earliest days and all through the Blitz, but Leo's sense of duty was strong.

It wasn't long before he steered the car between tall white gateposts which bore the name Claremont. The house appeared to be on the outskirts of town. Even so, it had a long drive that opened into a circular sweep in front of an achingly beautiful house. Elegant was the word that sprang to Kate's mind. It was painted white with a central porch and three long windows to each side, with more windows above them. Even in the darkness, it looked immaculately cared for, and so did the garden of trees and bushes that grew around a lawn.

'I suggest you make a dash for the porch,' Leo said, as the sleet was still heavy. 'I'll bring your things in.'

She followed his suggestion and ran for the porch, but she left it to Leo to knock on the door, not wanting to meet his family until he was beside her.

A maid in a traditional black dress, white apron and cap appeared. 'Here we are at last, Dora,' Leo said.

'Come away in, sir. It's a vile night out there.'

They stepped into a large square hall which contained a graceful staircase rising to the upper floor. There was a table to each side of the door, and some sort of cabinet beside the staircase. All were highly polished and topped with lamps and photographs framed in sparkling silver. How different from Brimbles Farm!

A man and a woman emerged from a room to Kate's left. Leo's parents, she assumed. They were a little past middle age but well preserved, and, even to Kate's in-expert eye, their appearances whispered care and expense. There was nothing flamboyant about them, but it was there in the quality of Mr Kinsella's suit and the cut of

Mrs Kinsella's neat navy dress trimmed in velvet. It was there, too, in her pearl necklace, matching earrings and dazzling rings.

'Mother, Father, this is Kate,' Leo announced, and Kate thought there was pride in his voice.

But what did his parents think of her sodden coat and hair? 'Poor thing, you must be frozen in those wet clothes,' Mrs Kinsella said.

Her words couldn't be faulted, but were they spoken out of convention or with real warmth? It was too soon for Kate to judge but she suspected that the senior Kinsellas cared more for social class than Leo realized.

Mrs Kinsella offered a hand, which Kate took briefly but firmly, wishing she wasn't so tall that she loomed over the smaller woman. Mr Kinsella stepped forward and offered his hand in turn. 'Delighted to meet you, my dear,' he said.

Was that true? Again, it was hard to gauge. But at least Kate didn't feel too tall beside him. Clearly, Leo got his height from his father.

'Dora.' Mrs Kinsella gestured for the maid to take the visitor's coat and then coaxed Kate into the drawing room where a fire was burning. It was a large room with sumptuous velvet drapes at the windows, a lush carpet atop a parquet floor and more gracious furnishings.

'I hope I'm not dripping everywhere,' Kate said.

'It can't be helped,' Mrs Kinsella assured her.

'It's so kind of you to invite me to stay.' More than ever Kate suspected that her presence had been imposed upon them by their son.

'I'm sorry you had such a difficult journey,' Mrs Kinsella said, which neither confirmed nor denied that Kate was an imposition.

She was relieved when Leo entered with his father. She

only caught the end of their conversation, though it seemed to be about the car rather than Kate. Did that mean his father was at least neutral about her, or was he only saving his criticism for later, when he had Leo to himself?

'Do sit.' Mrs Kinsella gestured to the chairs near the fire.

Kate sat, hoping she wasn't taking one of their favourite chairs. 'I'm sorry I didn't arrive in time for tea,' she said, only to fear it might be taken as a hint that she wanted some refreshment.

'I can ask Dora to bring you a cup of tea now,' Mrs Kinsella offered.

'Or would you prefer a pre-prandial glass of sherry?' her husband asked.

Pre-prandial? What did that mean? Before dinner?

Leo raised an eyebrow to prompt an answer. She felt like saying she'd have whatever was easiest for them to provide, but would that sound gauche and awkward?

Seeing Mr Kinsella heading for a silver tray on which stood crystal decanters and glasses, Kate said, 'A sherry would be lovely, thank you.'

'Do you have a preference?'

For what? Different types? Kate didn't even know that there were different types.

At that moment there was a knock on the outer door and the Kinsellas exchanged the sort of looks that suggested they were wondering who could be calling halfway through an evening. Two minutes later, Dora showed a young woman into the room. She was wet too, but, far from looking drowned by it, the raindrops merely glistened like diamonds on the sort of hat and coat May Janicki would have been proud to design. Beneath the hat the young woman's hair looked beautifully coiffed and she too was wearing pearls in her ears.

'Oh, I'm sorry!' she declared, her voice sounding as crisply clear as the crystal glasses with which Mr Kinsella was busying himself. 'I didn't realize you were entertaining.'

'Julia, dear, there's no need to apologize.' Mrs Kinsella moved towards the arrival, who bent to kiss the older woman's cheek. There was no doubting Mrs Kinsella's warmth for *this* young woman.

'I only called to say I'm newly returned from Scotland,' Julia said. 'I was hoping to cheer Leo up, but if he already has company . . .'

Her eyes – blue and chilly – turned to Kate, but there was no friendliness in their gaze. Instead, there was . . . challenge?

Leo, too, kissed Julia's cheek. 'It's good to see you, Ju Ju,' he said, though the shortened name didn't suit her. He drew her forward. 'I'd like you to meet Kate Fletcher. Kate, this is Julia Kingsley, a neighbour and old family friend.'

'A pleasure,' Julia said, her glittering gaze turning the words into a lie. 'I'm sorry to turn up unannounced but I've run tame in this house for years.'

Kate took the offered hand and saw Julia's lip curl at the work-worn roughness she encountered. 'Well, I won't intrude,' Julia said, but she was like a prompt delivering a cue to an actor in a scene – in this case Mrs Kinsella, who duly said, 'You're not intruding.'

Julia smiled in satisfaction.

'Sherry?' Mr Kinsella offered.

'Amontillado, please. I recall I had a lovely amontillado the last time I was here.'

'From Webster's,' Mr Kinsella confirmed.

'Mummy and Daddy's favourite vintners,' Julia said.

Mummy and Daddy? Julia looked to be in her early

twenties. Surely that was too old for such terms? Perhaps not in her circle.

Julia cast her coat into Dora's waiting hands and glanced at herself in the mirror. 'I must look a fright after all that travelling.'

'Nonsense,' Mrs Kinsella assured her.

Indeed, Julia looked lovely in a midnight-blue dress that must have cost more than Kate earned in several months. 'I only hope you had a better journey than poor Kate.'

'Oh?' Julia looked at Kate enquiringly.

Kate explained about the trains.

'Unlucky. And then you got caught in the rain.' Julia's gaze moved pointedly down to the hem of Kate's trousers. May's trousers, rather. They'd looked stylish when Kate had first put them on but now there was a ring of water at the bottom and the weight of it had pulled the trousers out of shape.

'Heavens, what am I thinking?' Mrs Kinsella said, as though chiding herself. 'You must want to get out of those wet clothes before dinner, Kate. Not that we're wearing formal clothes tonight, but you'll feel more comfortable in something dry.'

'Let the girl drink her sherry first,' Mr Kinsella said, handing both young women glasses of sherry the colour of amber. 'It'll warm her from the inside out.'

Amontillado? Both drinks looked the same. Kate tasted hers and found it soft and warming but then realized that perhaps she should have waited until everyone had been served.

Certain that Julia had noticed but hoping that no one else had, Kate drank no more until Mrs Kinsella took a sip.

'Have you come far?' Julia asked then.

'From Hertfordshire. My family has a farm near a village called Churchwood.'

'Your family manages the estate?'

Estate? It was just a smallish farm with a tumbledown farmhouse. 'My father farms himself. So do my brothers, and so do I, actually. We have two land girls helping, too.' Much as Kate felt out of her depth, she wasn't going to put on airs and pretend to be something she wasn't.

'How . . . splendid.'

'Julia helps with the war effort, too,' Mrs Kinsella said.

'I'm with the War Office,' Julia explained, though she didn't mention what she was doing there. One thing was certain: it wouldn't involve turning compost, removing slugs from crops or using a plough to try to break into iron-hard winter fields while her fingers felt lacerated by the cold.

'How is old Chumleigh getting along?' Mr Kinsella asked Julia and the conversation turned to some high-ranking personage in the War Office whom Kate didn't know.

She glanced at the ornate clock that stood on the mantelpiece, wondering if she should get ready for dinner but not knowing if it was polite to ask to be shown to her room. She was relieved when Leo came to her rescue. 'I think Kate needs to change into dry clothes now,' he said.

'Of course.' Mrs Kinsella stood and put her glass on a table. 'Let me show you to your room, Kate.'

They walked up the wide staircase, the carpeted runner in the middle as soft underfoot as the carpet in the drawing room, and the brass stair rods that held it in place gleaming with care. Kate's room was four times the size of her little bedroom at home. There were more sumptuous drapes at the window, massive walnut wardrobes and dressing table, a double bed with a satin eiderdown the colour of old gold and a fire burning brightly in the hearth. There was also a sink in a corner with a washstand beside it on which fluffy towels were piled. What luxury!

'I hope you'll be comfortable,' Mrs Kinsella said.

'I'm sure I shall.'

'The bathroom is to your right as you enter the landing.'

'Thank you. You're very kind.'

Mrs Kinsella looked as though she wanted to know more about her visitor but time was marching on and dinner would surely be served soon. 'Ring the bell for Dora if you need anything and come down when you're ready,' she said.

Mrs Kinsella left and Kate resisted the temptation to throw herself on the bed, not wishing to risk staining the beautiful eiderdown. She'd hoped the sherry might relax her but, while it had given her much-needed warmth, Kate felt as wound up as an actress forced onstage when she didn't know the words of the play.

But no one had forced her to come to Cheltenham. Kate had chosen to come, to see Leo and to try to build a relationship with his family. It was just a pity that her arrival – late and bedraggled – had battered her already fragile confidence.

Julia's appearance hadn't helped, but had Kate only imagined that smart young woman's hostility? After all, insecurity could make the most innocent of circumstances feel threatening. Not in this case, Kate decided, certain that Julia hadn't warmed to her. The question was: why? Because she was disappointed at being unable to spend time with an old friend since he already had company? Or because she had hopes of making Leo more than an old friend? Was she, in fact, setting her cap at him? Not that Julia would use such a vulgar expression as that.

With a jolt, Kate realized her mind was drifting when she needed to prepare for dinner. She kicked off her shoes and opened the case Dora had brought up, taking out the forest-green dress she'd worn to Alice's wedding. It was a little creased but Kate shook it vigorously and hung it on the wardrobe door while she stripped off, washed and stepped into a borrowed petticoat and stockings.

May was right about the dress suiting Kate's brown eyes and chestnut hair, but what a mess that hair was. Kate brushed it out in front of the fire, hoping the heat would help to dry it. Usually, she kept it off her face in a braid down her back, but a childish hairstyle was the last thing she needed in front of the glamorous Julia. Kate pinned the front parts back in wings, trying to emulate the way May had dressed it in the past. May had nimble fingers, though. Kate's felt like thumbs.

She tossed the rest of her hair over her shoulders. It was much longer than was fashionable but, back in the old days when she'd been isolated on Brimbles Farm with only her brothers' cast-off clothes to wear, she'd kept her hair long as a defiant symbol of her femininity. She was through that stage of her life now, but had still never brought herself to chop her hair off. Maybe she should ask May to trim it once she was at home again. In the meantime, there was nothing Kate could do to look more sophisticated.

She fixed some amber-coloured beads around her neck and went downstairs to find that Julia had left. That was one weight off Kate's mind, but the evening with Mr and Mrs Kinsella still stretched before her like an ordeal to be endured.

At least she had Leo by her side. 'You look beautiful, darling,' he whispered as they walked through to the dining room.

This was another splendid room, furnished in highly polished mahogany, and although Mrs Kinsella described the dinner as an informal family meal, it bore no resemblance to any dinner Kate had experienced before, not even at Foxfield. Here everything sparkled – the silver cutlery, the crystal glasses, the china edged with gold . . . The tablecloth was pristine white. So were the napkins. And Dora was far more formal than Foxfield's Suki, a girl of whom Naomi was clearly fond.

'Unfortunately, our dinners aren't what they were before the war,' Mrs Kinsella said. 'But we do our best.'

Their best was magnificent. They began with soup, accompanied by a delicious wine. Not that Kate drank much of it, being unused to alcohol and not wanting to let her guard down.

'I believe this is your first visit to Cheltenham,' Leo's father said.

'It is,' Kate confirmed. 'It looks a pretty place, though I couldn't see much of it in the dark and the rain.'

'Leo will give you a tour tomorrow, I expect.'

'Just as long as he doesn't tire himself out,' Leo's mother said.

'I wouldn't want that!' Kate hastened to assure her.

'Kate will look after me as well as any nurse,' Leo told his mother, wryly.

'I'm pleased to hear it,' Mrs Kinsella said, but did she believe it?

Leo sent Kate a wink, which was lovely but also made her worry that Mrs Kinsella might take it as a sign that he considered his mother to be an old fusspot and out of sight would be out of mind.

'You'll make me wish I hadn't come if you overtire yourself,' Kate told Leo, and that at least won a nod of approval from his mother.

The soup was followed by fish, and Leo's parents led the conversation on to Kate and her life. They were delicate about it, and Kate couldn't blame them for wanting to know the sort of person their son had entangled himself with, but she still felt she was taking part in an interview she was destined to fail.

She had no wish to lie or pretend to be grand. On the other hand, she didn't want the Kinsellas to take fright at the sort of life she led, since that would be awkward for Leo. She decided on a middle course, telling the truth but not the whole truth. She talked about the farm but described the farmhouse as old and picturesque rather than ramshackle, making no mention of the fact that the only lavatory was out in the yard and the only bath was the tin sort that had to be dragged before the kitchen hearth and filled with water boiled in the kettle. She explained that she'd gone to the village school but omitted to mention that she'd rarely turned up after the age of about nine and her only education since then had comprised whatever she'd managed to pick up from newspapers and books.

She focused on the positive things in her life instead – the beauty of the Hertfordshire countryside and the helpfulness of the land girls. Mrs Kinsella looked dismayed at the thought of young ladies plunging daintily manicured hands into soil but had no fault to find with their willingness to support King and country.

They looked approving when Kate spoke of having two brothers serving in the war, too, and made suitably sympathetic murmurs when they heard about Fred being injured. They also listened with apparent interest when Kate described the bookshop and the village.

But had Kate passed muster with them? She hoped she hadn't disgraced herself – a glance at Leo had another wink coming her way, which was a comfort – but she couldn't help thinking that his parents would have been far more at ease if he'd brought home a girl like Julia.

After a casserole and fruit pudding, they returned to the drawing room for coffee and Mrs Kinsella apologized for the fact that the war had made it impossible for her to offer anything better than 'that awful syrup that comes in bottles'.

It tasted fine to Kate but she was no connoisseur.

'I'm afraid we don't keep late hours at the moment,' Mrs Kinsella finally said, a discreet glance at Leo suggesting that they wanted him to rest.

'We don't keep late hours on the farm,' Kate replied, trying to make things feel comfortable.

'I expect you're tired after your journey, anyway,' Mr Kinsella said.

Kate and Leo headed upstairs, and Kate was glad to have a few minutes alone with him. 'I hope that wasn't too much of an ordeal,' he said, smiling ruefully.

'Of course not.'

'A first meeting with parents is bound to be awkward. Best behaviour and all that.'

Kate wanted to ask about the sort of impression he thought she'd made. But she feared it would not only sound craven but also place him in a difficult position if he had to lie.

'I hope you like your room?' he asked as they paused outside her door.

'It's lovely.'

'I wish I could say the same of my room, but it hasn't changed since I was a boy. It's still full of model aircraft, school sports trophies and the books I had as a five-year-old. Hardly manly stuff befitting a flight lieutenant in the Royal Air Force.'

'I suspect you love all that old stuff.'

'My secret is out!' he declared. Then he drew her into his arms. 'We'll have more time alone tomorrow,' he promised, and kissed her. Not for long, but deeply and hungrily, lighting a fire inside her.

He was the first to draw away, rolling his eyes and saying, 'We mustn't shock Mother!'

With a final stroke of her cheek, he moved along the landing, just as his parents' footsteps sounded on the staircase. Kate dived into her room, closed the door and leaned against it. Leo had been as affectionate as ever, but he was a kind man who wouldn't want her to know if his parents had taken against her, especially since staying in their house would make her feel awkward and vulnerable.

Keep faith, she told herself. *See what tomorrow brings.*

CHAPTER THIRTY-ONE

Kate

'I'm sorry there isn't more choice,' Mrs Kinsella said as they sat at the breakfast table. 'At least kidneys aren't rationed. Both Leo and my husband are fond of those.'

Kate was happy to settle for porridge sweetened with stewed apples, declining to partake of the Fortnum & Mason preserved cherries that Alice had given her to present to the Kinsellas as a hospitality gift, since she wanted Leo's parents to enjoy them.

She answered questions about how well she'd slept as though she'd never slept better, though the truth was that she'd slept badly.

'What are your plans for the morning?' Mr Kinsella asked.

'I'm taking Kate for a tour of Cheltenham,' Leo said.

'A short tour,' his mother insisted. 'You mustn't overdo it.'

'You'll take the car?' his father said. 'I can spare the petrol on this occasion.'

Kate was glad for Leo's sake. He was recovering well, but it was still early days. Upstairs again, she got ready for the outing. She was wearing May's smart skirt, blouse and cardigan today. Over them she put on a coat, gloves and scarf that also belonged to May.

Mrs Kinsella was fussing over Leo when Kate returned downstairs. 'Not too much parking up and walking around.'

Leo gave Kate a pained look but Kate said, 'I don't want Leo to exhaust himself either.'

They set off in the car and Kate waited, wondering if Leo would mention anything about how she was fitting in. Instead, he began acting as her tour guide. 'Do you know much about Cheltenham?' he asked.

'It's an old spa town, isn't it?' Kate had asked Alice about it. While Alice had never visited in person, she knew a little of its history.

'That's right. It was an ordinary market town for centuries until so-called medicinal waters were discovered.'

'As happened in Bath, Harrogate and Tunbridge Wells,' Kate was pleased to be able to say.

'People flocked to those places and this one to drink the waters. It meant new buildings sprang up and many of them are beautiful.'

'Like your parents' house.'

'Indeed.' They were driving past more gracious, white-painted houses from the Regency period.

'I've read some of Jane Austen's books.' Kate had borrowed them from Alice. 'It isn't hard to imagine her heroines and heroes staying in these houses.'

'And going out to the Theatre Royal and dancing at the Assembly Rooms,' Leo said. 'It was an elegant age, but I'll hazard it was a cold one for the females in their flimsy muslin dresses. We're more practical these days. Talking of which, are you warm enough?'

'I'm fine. Don't forget I'm used to working in the fields in all weathers at home.'

The fields of Brimbles Farm felt a world away, but Kate's relationship with Leo would never thrive unless his image of her was grounded in reality.

'That's one of the things I admire about you.' Leo

glanced over, his eyes warm and glowing. 'You shoulder your workload without complaint.'

'I do complain sometimes. Things like bad weather, insect infestations and birds eating our seeds can even make me curse.'

'We all complain at times, but you have a lot to bear and you put up with it remarkably well.'

'At least I'm not fighting in the war,' she said, only to regret her words as it occurred to her that the war was probably the last thing he wanted in his thoughts.

'That's a pretty crescent.' Keen to change the subject, Kate pointed towards a terrace of smart houses that overlooked a swathe of green.

'Cheltenham is a pretty town in a pretty part of the country,' Leo agreed. 'Some of the nearby Cotswold towns and villages are lovely, too. We've neither time nor petrol to go sightseeing now, but one day . . .'

'I'd like that.'

They returned to his parents' house, parking the car in an old coach house. Standing in its shadows, Leo took her in his arms and kissed her. 'I wish I could have you to myself for a while longer,' he said.

But good manners dictated that they rejoin his parents. Even so, the kiss and Leo's hand holding hers as they walked into the house boosted Kate's confidence – until they reached the drawing room and Mrs Kinsella said, 'You've just missed Julia. She called in to say her parents have invited us all for cocktails and dinner tonight. Isn't that lovely?'

Dread settled in Kate's stomach. She managed a smile but it was stiff enough to make her muscles hurt. It didn't help when Mrs Kinsella added, 'It'll be nice for you to meet some of our friends and neighbours, Kate. You'll see how we live.'

Which would be different to the way Kate lived.

Later, Leo managed to whisper, 'I hate having to share you this evening but we mustn't disappoint my parents.'

'Of course not,' Kate said. She didn't wish him to feel guilty.

The forthcoming dinner preyed on Kate's mind all afternoon, despite her attempts to convince herself that she was being ridiculous on several counts.

1. She might be making more of Julia's hostility than it warranted. After all, Julia could be over her disappointment now.

2. Julia's parents and friends might be friendlier.

3. The conversation was bound to flow between old friends even without Kate contributing, so she needn't fear excruciating silences.

4. She had Leo on her side.

And finally:

5. Wealth and important connections were nothing when set against integrity, kindness and concern for others.

Frustratingly, Kate's insecurities clung on and her stomach churned to the point of nausea.

Over tea, Mrs Kinsella drew Kate aside. 'Julia mentioned that you may not have brought suitable clothes for a dinner. She said you're welcome to borrow something of hers. Dress, shoes, jewellery . . .'

'How considerate,' Kate said, suspecting that Julia simply wanted a chance to dig into Kate's background and make her feel small, perhaps even sending her away with an outfit which would make her look like an imposter instead of someone who was at home in this sort of world.

'Julia is a lovely girl,' Mrs Kinsella answered, and the

wistfulness in her expression left no doubt that she'd hoped to be her neighbour's mother-in-law one day.

'I don't need to accept her kind offer on this occasion,' Kate was glad to say. 'I brought a dress with me. Just in case it was needed.'

'How sensible, my dear.' Mrs Kinsella patted Kate's hand but the gesture left her feeling second best.

Leo came over when his mother walked off. He touched Kate's cheek as though he sensed she was ill at ease. 'Meeting new people can be difficult. I'm sorry you've been thrust into this dinner party.'

'I can handle a bunch of strangers,' Kate assured him, her hatred of appearing weak making her more forceful than necessary.

'You can handle anyone. Lions and tigers, too,' he joked, and Kate managed a smile, though it faded when she entered her room and prepared for the evening.

Thank heavens for May, she thought, laying a copper-coloured dress on the bed together with clean underwear, forest-green shoes and a matching wrap.

She washed, dressed and studied herself in the mirror, deciding against cosmetics for fear that her lack of skill with them would only make her look like the pantomime dame she'd once seen in a magazine. Opting for a natural look instead, she simply brushed out her hair and held it back from her face with a comb on each side. May's amber beads were her only jewellery.

She paused for a final look in the mirror. The dress was sleeveless and utterly plain but the shape suited Kate's tall, slender frame, while the colour did wonders for her chestnut hair. She'd be admired in Churchwood. But in Cheltenham . . .

The Kinsellas had suggested sherry in the drawing room before they set out. Kate tried hard to steady her nerves as she descended the graceful staircase and joined them. Warmth glowed in Leo's eyes when he came to kiss her cheek. 'Simple but spectacular,' he said, admiring her dress.

'Dashed pretty, my dear,' his father agreed.

'Indeed,' his wife said, though Mrs Kinsella's appearance had Kate's confidence wilting even more.

It wasn't because Mrs Kinsella had what May would call style. In fact, her dress did little to flatter her rounded body. But it was made from black velvet and edged with beaded braid and black lace that looked as though it had cost a lot of money. So did her triple row of pearls, diamond and pearl brooch and matching earrings, especially since her easy manner suggested she was as accustomed to wearing jewels as she was to washing her face. The dinner jackets and silk scarves of Leo and his father also spoke of quiet wealth going back generations.

Mr Kinsella passed around glasses then asked his wife, 'Who's going to be there tonight?'

'Ferdy and Celia from the golf club. And the Wards with their daughter, Anne.'

'Charming girl.'

'She and Julia are as close as ever.'

A good friend of Julia's felt unlikely to become a good friend of Kate's, though perhaps that was an unfair judgement.

It wasn't long before Mr Kinsella looked at his watch. 'Time we were leaving.'

The Kingsleys lived only a few houses away and the intention was to walk, but Mrs Kinsella still rang for the maid to bring long dark coats for the men and two of Mrs Kinsella's evening cloaks for Kate and herself. Probably, it was obvious that Kate was wearing a borrowed cloak since it wasn't long enough, but it was more appropriate than an ordinary winter coat so Kate accepted it gratefully.

The Kingsleys' house was as lovely as expected, glowing with care and luxury.

Kate felt like a specimen under a microscope as she was introduced as Leo's young friend. She didn't miss the way Anne gave her a long assessing look and then whispered something to Julia which made the predatory girl smile.

Leo squeezed Kate's hand reassuringly but, oh! She wished they were a hundred miles away. The guests asked about Leo's recovery and he was generous with the praise he directed her way. 'I'm recovering well, thank you, and it's all thanks to this incredible young woman. And the staff at the hospital, too, of course.'

But inevitably the conversation moved on to Kate's circumstances, with Ferdy Fisher taking the lead.

Had she come far?

'From Hertfordshire. A village called Churchwood.'

Were her family in business there?

'They run a farm.'

One old gentleman went off into an anecdote about his uncle's terrible land agent. He hoped Kate's father had a better one.

'Actually, my father works the land himself.'

She didn't mean . . .?

'He does everything. Ploughing, planting, harvesting . . . He has help, of course. Two of my brothers work on the farm and we have land girls as well.'

'How very commendable.'

It was a natural leap from farming to rationing. 'We can't promise you splendour tonight,' their hostess announced. 'Not with rationing . . .'

One of the guests knew the Minister of Food personally. Did Kate's father know him, too?

'I doubt it,' Kate said.

'I hope you're not boring the poor girl with war talk,'

Julia's mother called. 'Come along with me, my dear, and enjoy more congenial company.'

Kate was drawn away from Leo and towards Julia and Anne.

'You've met my daughter, I believe. This is her friend Anne.'

'Delighted.' Anne's smile was insincere.

'I'll leave you three girls together,' Mrs Kingsley said. 'I'm sure you must have plenty to talk about.'

Anne's and Julia's expressions put Kate in mind of spiders relishing prey. Julia was in blue satin, set off to perfection by sapphire and diamond jewellery. Anne was in what May would describe as eau de Nil, also satin and also set off by sparkling jewels.

'You live on a farm, I understand?' Anne said.

Kate confirmed it. Beginning to feel a return of her old rebelliousness at the way these superior girls were treating her, she added tauntingly, 'I work on it, too. Manual labour.'

'Good grief. Still, you must have horses to enjoy.'

'Only an old pony.'

'You don't ride?' Anne looked even more shocked.

'I don't.' Kate had never had a chance to try it.

'Anne is horse mad,' Julia said. 'She's a great rider to hounds and she's taken dozens of prizes at gymkhanas.'

'Fancy,' Kate murmured.

'How do you know Leo?' Anne demanded, suddenly changing the subject.

'We met when he asked for directions to the military hospital near my home,' Kate explained. 'His cousin was a patient there and Leo wished to visit him.'

'He took you dancing at the air base, I believe.'

'At Hollerton, yes.'

'I expect lots of young women hang around air bases.'

Anne made it sound as though Kate was just a girl Leo had picked up for a good time so he could forget the war temporarily.

'Do you know the Morleys?' Anne asked then. 'They have a house in Hertfordshire. Sivyer Park.'

'I've never heard of them,' Kate said. 'Hertfordshire is a large county.'

'Even so, one tends to get to know—'

Leo swept in to take Kate's arm. 'Anne, Julia – how are you?'

'We're well,' Anne answered. 'But how are you? I'm glad to see you back in Cheltenham. We must meet for—'

'It's good to be back in the old place,' Leo said, cutting off whatever suggestion Anne had planned to make. 'I gave Kate a whistle-stop tour this morning.'

'Kate tells us she works on a farm. Actually works on it.'

'Admirable, isn't it? They say an army marches on its stomach and it's equally true of the air force and navy. Without the food our farmworkers produce to keep us strong, we'd be no match for the enemy. Everyone at home needs feeding, too. I wonder where the food we'll eat tonight came from? It makes you think about all the people whose hard work keeps our lives going, doesn't it?'

'Well, I . . .' Clearly, it wasn't something Anne had considered before or wanted to consider now. 'We need to make the most of having you in our midst again, Leo, so perhaps—'

'Excuse us, Anne, but there's someone I'd like Kate to meet.'

He drew Kate away and bent towards her to whisper, 'Have I done the right thing? You looked to be in need of rescue.'

Rescue? Kate hated the fact that she must have looked feeble to him, though she couldn't deny that she'd been uncomfortable. 'I don't think Julia and Anne have particularly warmed to me,' she admitted.

'The loss is theirs if they've let their privileged, protected upbringings make them narrow-minded. Now, I said I wanted to introduce you to someone, so I'd better do it. Here comes Iolanthe Frobisher.' An elderly woman and her husband had arrived late. 'She's a nice old girl but deaf, so conversation can be somewhat interesting. Mrs Frobisher!' he called. 'There's someone I'd like you to meet.'

'We're going to eat, did you say?' Mrs Frobisher asked. 'Is this young woman going to escort me into the dining room?'

'Later, perhaps. This is Kate.'

'We're late? It takes a long time to get ready at my age. Now, don't just stand there, Leo. Introduce me to this young woman. What's her name?'

'It's—'

At that moment dinner was announced. 'Allow me to take you in,' Leo said, offering his free arm to the elderly lady.

He kept hold of Kate's arm, too, but she drew back when they reached the door, judging that it would be difficult for the three of them to pass through together. She walked into the dining room just behind them and was promptly invited – or was that directed? – to sit by Ferdy instead of Leo. Realizing what had happened, Leo sent her an apologetic look, but Kate only smiled, not wishing to appear feeble again.

'I'm afraid we're more women than men, thanks to the war taking so many of our young men away,' Julia's mother said, from which Kate gathered that it was conventional for men to sit in alternate seats to women.

The numbers meant that, while Kate had Ferdy on her

right-hand side, she had Anne on her left, and it was ever more obvious that Anne was to be Julia's ally in making Kate feel small.

'Play golf, do you?' Ferdy asked Kate.

'I'm afraid not.'

'You should take it up. It's good to get out of the shops and beauty parlours and into the fresh air.'

'Kate doesn't frequent beauty parlours,' Anne told him spitefully. 'She labours on the land.'

Ferdy looked momentarily startled and then lost interest, shouting to someone across the table about getting his golf ball stuck in a bunker.

'We've missed Leo badly,' Anne told Kate. 'He's always been such fun. Terribly good at tennis. A genius at charades, too. Do you enjoy charades, Kate?'

'I can't say I've ever played them.'

'It's a must at Christmas in our circle. Then there's fancy dress. Julia's parents always hold a New Year's Eve party and everyone dresses up. Leo was Antony to Julia's Cleopatra once.'

'Is that so?'

'I say, Mother,' Julia said loudly. 'Did you hear that the Robinsons' marriage has failed? Such a pity.'

'Especially for their children,' Mrs Kingsley agreed.

Ferdy's wife took up the subject. 'I can't say I'm surprised. Bette Robinson was never . . . I hate to seem unkind, but she was never quite the thing. It's always a mistake to marry outside one's class. Does no good to anyone, I say.'

Kate was sure Julia had manipulated the conversation to make her feel awkward, even before she saw Julia's gloating little smile. Willing her cheeks not to fire up, Kate speared a carrot and ate it, relieved that, thanks to tutoring from Alice and Naomi, there was nothing to condemn in her table manners.

And so it went on. For hours.

'I hope that wasn't too much of a trial,' Leo murmured as coats were brought and they finally left to go home.

'It was fine,' Kate lied, hating to be pitied. 'Cheltenham seems to be a lively sort of place. Tennis, golf, parties . . .'

'It has its moments, I suppose.'

It wasn't possible to be alone that evening, but in the morning Leo offered to drive her to the railway station. 'I'm happy to walk,' Kate insisted, determined to be true to herself instead of pretending to be a spoilt young woman like Julia. 'Let your father save his petrol.'

'I'll walk with you.'

'There's no need. You shouldn't overtire yourself.'

'I *want* to walk with you. It's been lovely having you to stay but we haven't had nearly enough time to ourselves.'

They set out after breakfast, Kate thanking his parents for their hospitality but unsure what they were thinking as she left.

She imagined Leo's father saying, 'A nice enough girl who doesn't put on airs.'

'But . . .' Leo's mother might reply.

'Precisely, my dear. *But.*'

Unsuitable for their son and the circle in which he moved.

'I hope you won't let whatever Anne and Julia said get you down,' Leo said as they walked.

'I wouldn't give them the satisfaction,' Kate retorted, and Leo laughed.

'I see you got the measure of them. Not that they're all bad. Julia and I have been friends since our childhood. We had a lot of fun together then and Anne soon became part of our circle.'

'But you're not children now and Julia resents me

because she wants you for herself. Anne is trying to help make that possible.'

'I didn't like to mention it in case it made me sound conceited, but yes, that's exactly what they want. It's a pity because they're dooming themselves to disappointment, since I don't feel the same.'

'Julia is very attractive.'

'Many young women are attractive. But the only one I want is you. Think about it, Kate. I've known Julia for years and she's made her interest in me obvious for years. If I felt anything of a romantic nature for her, I could have done something about it. I didn't, because she doesn't interest me that way.' He squeezed her hand. 'Understood?'

'Understood,' Kate confirmed, but her doubts about the future remained.

They reached the station and Leo bought a platform ticket so he could see her on to the train. Before she boarded he put her case down and drew her close. 'I love you, Kate Fletcher. You and only you. Tell me you believe it.'

'I do believe it, and I love you in return.'

She saw the tension leave his body like air escaping a puncture. It wasn't as simple as that for Kate, though. She needed to do some hard thinking.

The sound of doors being slammed reached them. The train was about to depart. Leo kissed her.

'No time for that,' a passing guard told them and, parting, they laughed.

But there was agony in Leo's face at the thought of her leaving and Kate felt equally distraught.

He held the carriage door open as she mounted the steps and then passed her case over. As he closed the door behind her, she raced into the nearest compartment – thankfully empty – and opened the window to wave and blow him a kiss.

Steam from the engine made a mist around him, but fleetingly so. As the train chugged out of the station, she saw him touch his heart and blow a kiss back to her. Then he was gone from sight and she sat down heavily, her head hanging forward as she felt the needle sharpness of tears.

The door to the corridor opened suddenly and a man called back over his shoulder, 'There's more room in here!'

He entered the compartment and sent Kate a smile. 'You've no objection if we join you?'

'Of course not,' Kate said, though she wished him and his two companions a million miles away.

Swallowing her tears, she stared sightlessly out of the window. She loved Leo as deeply as ever and believed that he loved her in return. For the moment, that was – while the war was raging and life was turning somersaults, bringing strangers from different walks of life together.

But what would happen when peace came? Doubtless, the world wouldn't simply fall back into old patterns. There were bound to be *some* changes. But it was hard to imagine that they'd be far-reaching enough to make Kate feel both welcomed and at ease in the company of the Kinsellas and their kind. Last night she'd seen that, deep down, even Leo knew she didn't fit. Hence his urge to rescue her.

It wasn't only Cheltenham society that mattered, either. Leo had a promising career ahead of him. She'd heard of regimental dinners for army officers and presumably there were similar formal occasions in the RAF. Rubbing shoulders with his superiors – the people who could influence his future – would Leo feel on edge if he had to take Kate with him, knowing she wasn't from that world? Would he be embarrassed, especially if she let her temper get the better of her and retaliated with anger to curious looks or pity? It had already taken an effort to keep her temper in check with Julia and Anne.

Yes, Kate and Leo were in love. But would she be making a huge mistake if she encouraged him further when it might hinder his career as well as expose him to sympathy at best, and at worst maybe even ridicule? In short, would it be kinder – less selfish and more loving – if Kate let him go?

CHAPTER THIRTY-TWO

Alice

Daniel wiped a tear from Alice's cheek. 'You don't need to come to the bus stop,' he said.

'I want to come.'

'But if it upsets you . . .'

'I want to be with you until the last possible moment,' Alice insisted.

Daniel smiled. 'And I want to be with you. At least let's be glad we've had longer together than expected.' His orders had come through later than anticipated and every extra day had been precious.

He said goodbye to her father and they walked to the bus stop arm in arm. 'It was Shakespeare who said, "Parting is such sweet sorrow", wasn't it?' Alice asked.

'Mmm. When I was at school I was told it meant that while there was sorrow over the current parting, there would be sweetness in the next meeting.'

'All I can feel is the sorrow just now, because the sweetness might be a long time away.'

'I'll do my best to see you again before I return to Africa,' Daniel said.

'I know.' But he might not have the chance. If the war continued, they might not see each other for a year or more.

A pang of loss swept through her but she swallowed hard. This was difficult for Daniel, too, and she didn't want to make it worse for him.

They neared the bus stop but stayed on the other side of the road beside the village green so they could be private as they waited – arms wrapped around each other – for the bus to appear. All too soon it rumbled towards them.

'Stay safe,' Alice urged.

'You too, my love. And write as often as you can. Your letters mean so much.'

They crossed the road and kissed for one last time before Daniel got on the bus and leaned towards a window so he could wave.

Alice waved back, barely seeing him through a shimmer of tears. The moment the bus was out of sight she hastened home to cry for a while. But then she wiped her eyes and blew her nose. Enough moping. Alice was tired of feeling mired in helplessness. The time had come to fight back until it was vanquished once and for all.

She went downstairs to make lunch and then headed up Brimbles Lane towards the hospital, intending to call on Kate on the way to hear about the visit to Cheltenham. The Fletcher men had improved since Alice had first met them, but Ernie was the exception and she was glad to be spared the possibility of encountering him when she saw Kate up by the farmhouse and called out to her.

Kate half galloped over on her long, graceful legs. 'Has Daniel gone?' she asked.

'This morning.'

'I'm sorry.'

'I won't tell you how I'm feeling because I'm sure you can guess. The war will end one day and I can only hope that it'll be sooner rather than later. But how was your visit to Cheltenham?'

Misery passed over Kate's face like a shadow. Oh dear.

'It was lovely to see Leo, and his parents were perfectly polite,' she said.

'*Polite?* Was that all the warmth they could muster?'

'I'm being unfair,' Kate corrected. 'They were considerate and friendly.'

'And yet . . .?'

'Oh, Alice, they're much higher up the social scale than me. I didn't fit in, especially not when . . .'

'When what?'

Kate grimaced. 'There was another girl there. The daughter of a family friend, and she slotted right into the Kinsellas' world. Leo's parents like her and she's just the sort of girl they hope he'll marry one day.'

'Would *she* like to marry Leo?'

'Without a doubt.'

Alice gave it some thought. 'An old family friend, you say?'

'Something like that.'

'Then Leo must have known her for years. If he was half as interested in her as she is in him, wouldn't he have done something about it long ago?'

'That's what Leo said.'

'Then you've nothing to fear.'

'I don't think it's as simple as that. Being in the RAF has taken Leo away from that style of living. But in time he'll return to it and then . . . Well, I'll hardly be an asset to him.'

'Leo isn't a fool. He knows what he does and doesn't want. He wants you and, unless I'm much mistaken, he'll never choose a stuffy sort of life ever again. He wasn't propelled out of his social circle by the war. He left it long before then and joined the RAF because he wanted to live differently. Doesn't that tell you something about him?'

Kate shrugged.

'You need to have more faith in Leo,' Alice urged.

'Maybe.'

'*Certainly*. I'm sure you'll receive a letter from him soon, singing your praises and declaring undying love for you regardless of this other girl setting her sights on him. What's her name, by the way?'

'Julia Kingsley.'

'She may or may not be a nice girl, but—'

'She isn't a nice girl.'

'All the more reason for Leo to have no interest in her.'

Kate still looked unconvinced. 'Julia isn't the only issue. There's Leo's career as well. I may hold him back.'

'Leo's been in the RAF for years. He's the best judge of what may hold him back and he obviously doesn't think you'll do anything of the sort. You'll see I'm right when that letter comes.'

Alice parted from her friend with a hug.

Poor Kate. Alice understood what a strain it must have been for her to stay with a family that was rich in social graces and expectations as well as money. Leo had appeared to be a lovely man on the few occasions when Alice had met him. Hopefully, he was lovely through and through, because it would devastate Kate if he turned out to be shallow. The sooner he got in touch with words of reassurance, the better.

Alice reached the hospital where Tom the porter, her nursing friend Babs Carter and Matron all sympathized with her over Daniel's departure, though Matron took her usual bracing approach. 'You're doing the right thing in keeping busy and helping others,' she said. 'The patients are waiting for you, Alice, and Doctor Marwood is waiting for you, Nurse Carter.'

Babs rolled her eyes behind Matron's back but went about her business. Alice headed for Ward One to collect and distribute the diminished supply of books. 'Have you got *Murder on the Orient Express*?' Private Andy Hughes asked.

'That book went up in flames when the plane crashed, I'm afraid. I've got *Flying Colours* by C. S. Forester, if that's of interest?'

'I've read that one.'

'I'm afraid I've nothing else today.'

'This hospital needs more books.'

So did the village.

'How's the new bookshop coming along?' his neighbour asked.

'It's hit a hiccup but we're hoping it'll move forward soon.'

'Will that mean more books?'

'If we can raise the funds. Now, who'd like to hear a story?'

There was a chorus of 'Me!' and Alice settled down to read 'Darkness over the Arctic', a story about racing across the frozen wastes on sledges pulled by huskies.

Afterwards, she walked home, letting ideas for a story of her own play through her mind, and this time she managed to force down the doubts about her ability. She settled on a story she was going to call—

Her thoughts broke off at the sound of shouting up ahead. What was happening? She quickened her pace to find out.

CHAPTER THIRTY-THREE

Naomi

'I'm sorry,' Naomi told her farming neighbour, Alec Mead. 'No harm was intended and I hope no harm was done.'

'No harm?' he bellowed. 'I don't call running over my crops no harm. A man has a living to earn.'

'The children didn't know the field had crops in it. They're not used to country ways.'

'They shouldn't have been on my land anyway! That boy shouldn't have led them there.' He pointed to Arthur.

Naomi had begun the conversation apologetically but Alec Mead was trying her patience. 'The children ran on to your land after a dog. They were trying to catch it in case it was lost. It was *your* dog, the very one that got loose once before and caused an accident to my housekeeper. You're lucky she didn't sue you.'

'All right, all right,' the farmer grumbled, reining his temper in a little. 'Just keep these children off my land in future.'

Irritated, he called his dog to heel and the pair walked away.

Naomi turned to the children. 'That was unfortunate. Please let it be a lesson to you to respect other people's property. Now, in you go.' She gestured towards Foxfield and the chastened children passed through the gateposts to troop along the drive.

Naomi saw that Alice had approached. 'Trouble?' she asked.

'High spirits more than mischief.'

'The children are finding their feet.'

'Unfortunately, that involved treading on Alec Mead's crops.'

'They'll learn.'

'I hope so. They're not bad kids but lively, Victoria's Arthur especially. He's always the first with the suggestions and ideas because he feels responsible for making the others happy. I can't fault his good intentions, but his judgement doesn't always measure up to them.'

'Look at him now,' Alice said, and Naomi turned, her feelings softening as she saw that he'd crouched down to fasten little Flower's shoe. Flower wrapped her arms around him and Arthur picked her up gently to carry her the rest of the way into the house.

'Flower dotes on him,' Naomi said, 'and he's amazingly gentle with her. I think it's her delicate health that brings out his protective instincts.'

'That cough,' Alice said.

'Indeed.'

'Is he close to his sister, too?'

'He's wonderful with her.'

'And how are *you* coping with such a busy house, Naomi?'

'The women are doing their utmost to be as light a burden as possible, so they're pitching in with cleaning, washing, cooking . . . Food is still a struggle but they're using their ration books now, and people are still being generous with gifts. People like you, Alice.'

'I'll do everything I can to help.'

'I'm grateful. The house isn't quite as crowded now since Ivy and Flower have moved into Edna Hall's spare room. It's a small room with a single bed, so unsuitable for the larger families or those with older children, but it gives Ivy and Flower a bit more peace and quiet. They're still coming to Foxfield for meals, and Evelyn Gregson is including Flower in the lessons she gives the children.'

'What about school?'

'Arthur and Jenny will start in the village soon, but the others will go to school wherever the families make their new homes.'

'You're not exhausted by it all?'

'I won't pretend I'm not tired, but it's a temporary situation. I'll manage.' What other choice had she?

'Have you heard from William?' Alice asked then.

'Not yet. I'd like to think it's because he's settled down after his wobble.'

'But you don't believe it?'

'It would be nice to be sure. What about you, Alice? Would it be foolish to ask how you are, since you've just had to say goodbye to Daniel?'

'It's never easy when he leaves, but there's a chance I might see him again before he leaves the country. It depends if he can get away from his training. Meanwhile, I'm keeping busy.'

'If Bert manages to find another builder, you'll have the bookshop to help keep you busy soon.'

'Fingers crossed.'

Parting from Alice, Naomi headed indoors, where Victoria was hovering in the hall, looking anxious. 'Arthur told me what happened with the dog,' she said. 'I'm terribly sorry he got you into trouble with your neighbour.'

'Alec Mead never gets involved in village life so you needn't fear that Arthur has put a friendship under strain.'

'Even so, it was wrong of him to trespass.'

'He'll learn.'

221

Arthur himself appeared a moment later. 'Sorry for treading on that man's crops.'

'Don't let it worry you unduly,' Naomi told him. 'But do make an effort to respect other people's property. It's important.'

'I will.'

'Off you go, then.'

Obviously relieved, he ran to join his friends.

Bert arrived, looking cock-a-hoop. 'I've got some men to work on the bookshop,' he reported. 'A plasterer, an electrician and a plumber who've worked together before. I've been to their houses to check that they're genuine and I've taken references from several happy customers. The electrician is at Joe's house now. The plasterer and plumber will start tomorrow. And, before you ask, I'm keeping a tight rein on the purse strings.'

'That's so good to hear. I hope your market garden isn't suffering with you being away so much?'

'I'll catch up. On that note, I'll leave you to let the other bookshop organizers know, if that's all right?'

'Of course. Thank you, Bert. I don't know what we'd do without you.'

'Careful, woman. You'll give me a swollen head.'

She laughed and kissed him, and from behind her she heard a childish giggle and smoochy kissing sounds.

'Children, eh?' Bert said, shaking his head.

He turned to go, but then paused and looked back. 'Have you heard from young William?'

'Alice just asked me that question. The answer is no. I hope it means he's feeling a little easier about things.'

'Just as long as his icicle of a father isn't stopping him from writing.'

That possibility had occurred to Naomi, too. It really would relieve her mind to know William wasn't desperately unhappy. She wished she could also be sure that Alexander's resentment of her interference in his son's life wouldn't fuel some sort of spiteful skulduggery over her settlement. It was hard to imagine what he could do, given her evidence of his bigamy, but Alexander was a wily man.

CHAPTER THIRTY-FOUR

Kate

'What are you *doing*?' Timmy screeched and all heads turned to see what disaster had befallen Brimbles Farm.

Fred was throwing his wooden animals into the fire.

'Fred, stop!' Kate cried, because he'd spent hours making them and Timmy loved them. 'I'm sorry if you're feeling low, but destroying your crafts isn't the answer.'

'Don't go all Florence Nightingale on me with your *feeling low*,' Fred told her. 'I've decided these are just practice animals. I'm going to make better ones.' He turned to Timmy. 'You want better ones, don't you?'

'Well, yes. If you think you can make them.'

'I'm learning as I go along, but I think I can.' He turned to Kate. 'What's your problem? Do you think I'm too stupid to make better ones?'

'No.'

'What she thinks,' Pearl said, 'is that you're stupid because you didn't explain what you were doing.'

'I've just explained what I was doing.'

'I mean before you threw the animals in the fire and panicked Timmy, you dolt.'

'You're just being horrible,' Fred told her.

'I'm telling the truth. If you don't want to be *thought* stupid, don't *act* stupid.' Pearl paused then said, 'I don't suppose this idea of making better animals has anything

224

to do with the fact that Frank wrote and said he wanted to try whittling too?'

'Why should that bother me?'

Because Fred wanted to do something better than his still able-bodied twin, of course.

'Anyway, I'd rather make animals than put papers into piles,' Fred said, but Kate knew he was simply fishing for a compliment about how good a job he'd made of organizing the farm's paperwork. 'That was boring.'

'But useful,' Kate told him.

'What's boring is listening to you moaning,' Pearl said. 'We all have to work round here, and that includes you.'

'Meaning what?' Fred demanded.

'Meaning the shears need mending and so do the scissors I use for cutting twine.'

'That's because you're rough with them.'

'It's because I work hard with them. I'll fetch them from the barn along with the jar of screws so you can find ones that fit.'

'But—'

'Just shut up and get on with it,' Ernie snapped.

'Yes, do,' Kenny agreed, wrapping an arm around Ruby and squeezing her briefly.

Ruby leaned into the hug with apparent willingness. It had been a relief to Kate to return from Cheltenham and find that there'd been no arguments or parting of ways in her absence. But while Kenny appeared to think that Ruby was back to normal, Kate still wasn't convinced. The sparkle had gone from the way she looked at him and something else had taken its place. Disappointment, though she appeared reconciled to it since it meant she and Timmy could remain on the farm, perhaps reminded of the value of security by the new arrivals at Foxfield who had no permanent homes and depended on Naomi's kindness for food and shelter at the moment.

'I hope you don't mind, but I took a pie down to them,' Ruby had whispered on Kate's return from Cheltenham. 'I didn't tell Ernie – obviously – but I don't want you thinking I'm making free with our food supplies behind your back.'

'It was kind of you,' Kate assured her. 'It must have been nice for you to chat to some fellow Londoners.'

'It was. Timmy came and made friends with the children. I was tempted to invite them for a look around the farm but I didn't want to give Ernie apoplexy.'

'Wise decision,' Kate said, 'though a sad one. Those kids need to be made welcome.'

'It's hard for them,' Ruby agreed. 'Seeing those families made me count *my* blessings.'

Settling for Kenny as a convenience still seemed unfair to Kate, though he was looking as happy as a morose man could ever look. But she couldn't judge Ruby harshly for making the most of a difficult situation and putting Timmy's interests first. She'd have to wait and see what happened between the land girl and her brother. In the meantime, Kate had her own dilemma to face.

She slipped out of the house to be alone and think about the letter she'd received.

Darling Kate,

It was sweet of you to write to my parents so quickly to thank them for their hospitality. It was sweet of you to write to me quickly, too, since I was relieved to hear you got home safely.

It was wonderful to see you, my darling. I hope you enjoyed your visit? Forgive me for saying so, but you seemed a little quiet at times. I've been telling myself that it was only because

226

you were tired and a little overwhelmed by all the company we
had to endure. I can't bear to think that you were bored with
my company.

Write back soon and let me know all is well with you. I love
you, Kate. I need to know that you're happy . . .

All my love,
Leo x

Unable to bear the thought that she might have made
him *un*happy, she decided to write back to assure him that
she loved him as much as ever. It was true and it would
give her more time to decide on her answer to the awful
question: would it be the loving thing to let him go?

CHAPTER THIRTY-FIVE

Naomi

'You're making excellent progress,' Naomi told the new builder, Eddie Waite.

The electrician and plumber had needed only a couple of days for their work on the bookshop. Now Mr Waite was busy replastering.

'It's coming along,' he agreed. 'This weather won't help to dry the plaster, though.'

It was raining outside, a cold winter rain that kept many people indoors.

'I brought you a flask of hot tea,' Naomi said, placing it on the window ledge. 'I can collect the flask again later. Good day to you, Mr Waite.'

'Good day to you, Mrs Harrington. And thanks.'

Naomi stood at the door to consult the list she'd drawn up of people who might benefit from a visit. Until the bookshop was up and running again, she and her fellow organizers were visiting as many Churchwood residents as possible, prioritizing the old and infirm who were more likely to need help. Deciding to call on Florrie Philips, Naomi grimaced at the rain, put up her umbrella and walked on as quickly as her short legs would carry her.

'It's good of you to come,' Florrie said, inviting Naomi inside. 'Especially in this awful weather.'

'I just wanted to say hello and ask if there's anything I can do for you, Florrie?'

'That's kind, but I don't wish to be any trouble.'

'It's no trouble, Florrie. We help each other in this village.'

'We're lucky in that way. As you can see, I've lots of coal for my fire – thanks to Bert, who filled up my scuttle from the coal hole. I'm a little low on bread, though. I've been hoping the rain would ease off so I could go out but it looks like being one of those all-day soakers. I hope that doesn't sound feeble, but I've been warned to stay warm and dry to keep my bronchitis away.'

'It isn't feeble to follow a doctor's advice. It's sensible. I'll pop to the baker's for you. Is there anything else you need?'

'Custard powder, if you can get it. Oh, and some sort of fruit.'

'I shan't be long, Florrie.'

The rain actually eased as Naomi scuttled along to the baker's, where she bought bread. The greengrocer had apples so Naomi bought four. She'd joined the queue in the grocer's when the door was flung open behind her and several of the London children burst in, Arthur leading them with Flower on his back. 'You've won the race, Flower!' he cried jubilantly, only for Lewis to speed past him, shouting, 'It's the first to touch the counter that matters!'

'No, it isn't—' Arthur argued, but broke off as Lewis almost collided with Molly Lloyd.

'What on earth . . .?' Mr Miles, the grocer, spluttered. 'Take care, you fools! And look at my floor!' The children had trodden in mud and the pulp of last autumn's fallen leaves.

Now they stood wide-eyed and frozen in surprise at the wave of anger. 'Sorry,' Arthur said.

'Racing, were you? Your idea, I suppose?' Mr Miles barked.

229

'Yes,' Arthur admitted, 'but—'

'Out!' Mr Miles pointed towards the door. 'Go on! The lot of you. And don't come back until you've learned some manners.'

'We didn't mean—' Arthur tried, but Mr Miles wasn't in the mood to listen.

'Out!' he roared again.

Chastened, Arthur beckoned for the other children to follow him outside.

'I'm sorry about that,' Naomi said.

'Those children are a menace.'

'Hardly that, Mr Miles. Lively, I'll accept.'

'They need discipline.'

'They're getting it. We all want the children to settle down, but they're going through a difficult time and the bad weather isn't helping by keeping them cooped up indoors so much.'

'I've no fight with you, Naomi. You're a force for good in this village. But those children, especially that lad . . .'

'Lewis? The one who almost collided with Molly?'

'The other one.'

'Arthur.'

'He's the ringleader.'

'Hardly that, Mr Miles. He's simply trying to cheer the others up with a bit of fun. He doesn't mean to cause trouble.'

'Maybe not. But he *does* cause it. If there's running, shouting and rampaging in this village, that boy is at the front of it. And now this. People could be hurt if they slipped on the mud he's brought in.'

Naomi sighed. 'Can I mop your floor for you, Mr Miles?'

'I wouldn't dream of letting you. I'll do it myself.'

He stepped through the door behind the counter and

returned with a mop and bucket. 'There,' he finally said, when he'd finished mopping. 'The floor is still wet, so watch your step, ladies.'

He paused, leaning on his mop, and said, 'I meant what I said, Naomi. Those children aren't welcome in this shop until they've learned some manners, that Arthur especially.'

Oh dear.

There was tension in the air when Naomi reached home and, once again, Victoria was desperate to apologize for what had happened. 'They'd been well behaved for hours while Mrs Gregson taught them their lessons. They went out to run off some energy and took it too far. I'd given them money for biscuits to share as a reward for being good and they were overexcited.'

'No real harm was done, but I suggest they don't go to the grocer's for a while. Mr Miles's temper needs to cool.'

'I can't apologize enough.'

'Did Arthur tell you what happened?'

'Yes, he's mortified with himself.'

'He's a good boy at heart.'

'He is, he is!'

'I'm impressed by the way he admits when he's at fault.'

'That's because he's genuinely sorry.'

'That said, it was actually Lewis who nearly bumped into an elderly lady.'

'Really? Arthur didn't mention that. He's only a few months older than Lewis but sees himself as responsible for all the children, Lewis included. We're all trying to protect them from worry, but they've had a lot of heartache in their young lives and they don't know what their future holds. Arthur just wants to take their minds off it by encouraging them to have fun.'

'It's to his credit,' Naomi assured her.

'His intentions are excellent. It's his judgement that lets him down sometimes, but he's only eight. Churchwood is a different sort of place from London, too. Quieter. Less anonymous. The children haven't quite adapted to it yet.'

'They'll adjust.'

'I hope they do it soon enough to preserve your reputation, Mrs Harrington.'

Naomi looked in on the children later and saw Arthur sitting on the floor between Jenny and little Flower. He was helping them to complete a jigsaw puzzle. 'Look for the corner pieces first,' he advised. 'And then the pieces with flat sides so we can make the outside of the puzzle before we fill it in. That's right, Jen. Well done. You next, Flower. That's it.'

How patient he was. How kind to two small girls.

She was roused by a visit from Alice.

'I came to see how you all are,' Alice said, following Naomi into the sitting room. 'I heard about Mr Miles and did my best to calm him down, but he was still cross when I left him. It was wrong of Arthur to have the children racing into a shop, but Churchwood needs to be kinder, Mr Miles especially.'

Alice could be fierce in her defence of underdogs.

'What this village needs is a pick-me-up,' she continued. 'The new builder seems to be making excellent progress, so perhaps we should start thinking about a bookshop opening event. A party to bring the village together again.'

'It's a terrific idea,' Naomi said. 'If we can let people see the good side of the children, Arthur especially . . .'

'Exactly. We need to start fundraising for books and equipment, too. I wouldn't want anyone to miss the party because they can't afford to pay towards it, but we could have a donations box in a discreet position, and a raffle.'

'I like both of those ideas.' Naomi only wished her financial settlement would come through soon so she could make a generous donation instead of living frugally, but she'd heard nothing from Alexander or William.

'I'll sound out the other bookshop organizers and we'll get started,' Alice said.

CHAPTER THIRTY-SIX

Kate

'A party sounds wonderful,' Kate told Alice, having met her in Brimbles Lane while Alice was heading for the hospital and Kate was heading for the village on her bicycle.

'I'm hoping it'll bring the village together again, especially as we have newcomers in our midst who are struggling to be accepted.'

'Oh?'

'Arthur has caused some bother and word is starting to go around that he's a troublemaker.'

'Is he?'

'Accidentally, perhaps.'

Kate had heard about the incident in the grocery shop. 'Sounds like he has a good heart but poor judgement and rotten luck,' she said.

'That summarizes the situation perfectly,' Alice agreed. 'I'd like the party to be a fundraiser as well. We desperately need more books, not to mention chairs, cups, saucers and so on.'

'I could ask Fred to donate a wooden animal as a raffle prize,' Kate suggested. 'He's getting better and better at making them, and it might give his confidence a boost if people like his creations.'

'A wooden animal will make a lovely prize,' Alice said, then she put her head on one side and studied Kate. 'Is everything all right with you?'

'I'm fine,' Kate insisted. 'Overworked, but that's nothing new.'

'Leo hasn't written?'

'Not for a few days.' Kate smiled because she didn't wish to appear anxious. A wait of a few days for a letter was hardly a crisis, though Leo was writing through the regular post these days so his letters had neither to work their way through the RAF postal system nor to travel from overseas.

'I hope you're not imagining some terrible significance in that?' Alice said, for she knew how Kate's insecurities could rise like tentacles to squeeze all peace of mind from her. 'Trust me – better still, trust Leo – you'll hear from him soon.' With that prediction, Alice went on her way.

Kate hoped she was right. Leo's silence was torturing her. Did it mean that his parents – perhaps the awful Julia, too – were succeeding in persuading him that he needed a different sort of girl? One who'd fit in with his life and make him happier in the long term than an outsider like Kate ever could?

She knew her feelings were inconsistent, given that she herself thought that Leo might be better off without her. But she loved him desperately and the reality of him drawing away from her made her distraught.

She cycled on and had nearly reached the end of Brimbles Lane when she saw Arthur kicking up twigs on the verge.

He stiffened when she approached and looked positively scared when she got off her bike.

'I haven't done nothing wrong,' he said.

'I'm not suggesting you have.'

His expression relaxed a little but remained wary.

'I hear you've been in trouble, though.'

He shrugged, his urchin mouth turned down in misery.

'There was a time when I was always in trouble in this village and people said mean things about me,' Kate told him.

Arthur blinked in surprise.

'It's true. They didn't like my family, and because I was a Fletcher they didn't like me, either.'

'That wasn't fair.'

'No, it wasn't. But I didn't help myself. I was hurt and that made me angry. One of my biggest flaws is my temper.'

'You have a bad temper?' Arthur looked even more surprised.

'Shocking. Ask Naomi. Ask anyone around here. Anyway, I brought more harshness on myself by picking arguments and taunting people. It didn't help, though. It only made things worse. What I'm trying to say is that, if I were in your shoes now, I wouldn't feel resentful or angry. Instead, I'd try to prove people wrong by being nice. It's satisfying, proving people wrong, you know, and it works out best for everyone.'

Arthur nodded thoughtfully.

'Don't despair,' Kate said, getting back on the bicycle. 'Churchwood people are mostly friendly. They just need a bit of help before they can show it sometimes.'

She waved and cycled on. Poor boy. Had she done him any good? She could only hope so.

Kate continued into the village and completed her errands. Arthur was nowhere to be seen as she cycled homewards, but when she reached Brimbles Farm she saw the postman was on his way there and sped up to intercept him.

'A few letters today,' he said, handing them over.

'Thanks.' Kate looked at the envelopes. Another bill from Pearson's. A letter from Pearl's family. A letter from Frank. But nothing from Leo.

Fred was due at the hospital soon. Keeping her inner turmoil to herself, Kate locked up the bicycle, carried the post into the house and helped him to get ready. He was stronger now and able to manoeuvre himself into the ancient truck's cab instead of needing to ride on the back in his wheelchair.

Tom the porter came to their aid in getting Fred out of the truck when they arrived at the hospital.

'Rum business, this fighting in the East,' Tom commented once Fred had gone off. 'There seems to be no stopping those Japanese. They've taken Malaya and it looks like it'll be Singapore next.'

The end of the war seemed as remote as ever. Kate could only hope Leo wouldn't be posted out to the Far East if he were found medically fit for active service.

Leo. Just the thought of him twisted her insides with worry and the desolation of possible loss.

She was glad to see Ruby emerge from the house when they returned to Brimbles Farm. It was hard for Kate to get Fred out of the truck by herself, despite his increasing strength. 'Thanks for coming to help,' Kate told her.

But then it occurred to her that Ruby looked agitated. 'What's wrong?'

'Nothing. I hope. But you have a visitor.'

'Oh?'

'Go and see. Here's Pearl.' The big land girl was approaching, her steps long and bouncing. 'She'll help with Fred.'

Puzzled and more than a little wary, Kate headed for the kitchen door. She walked through to find Leo sitting at the table in his RAF uniform. 'Surprise!' he said.

It was a surprise, all right. Kate's heart leaped in shock and joy combined and then hammered against her ribs. She shook her head in wonder. 'I wasn't expecting . . .'

'It wouldn't be a surprise if you were expecting me, would it?' Leo got up, walked around the table and drew her to him. 'I've been worried about you,' he said.

Thoughts and emotions crashed wildly through Kate's head. Surely, Leo wasn't well enough to be travelling to Churchwood. And why was he here? Without giving her notice, too?

The door opened and Leo released her as Pearl, Ruby and Fred trooped in. Then Ernie entered and pulled up short at the sight of Leo. 'Who are you?'

'I'm the man who's in love with your daughter,' Leo answered.

He loved her still? Relief and euphoria made Kate's limbs feel as though they were floating. Only for a moment, though. The doubt that was torturing her – that love might not be enough to bridge the gap between their different worlds – could have begun to torture Leo, too. He might even be here to break off with her, since he wasn't the sort of man who'd consider it honourable to do so in a letter.

Kate tried to tell herself that if Leo broke things off, she'd be spared the anguish of having to do it herself, since even now her conscience was telling her that what she wanted – needed – for herself wasn't necessarily best for Leo. But the truth was that it wouldn't spare her even an iota of pain because, whoever called time on their relationship, it would leave her distraught.

'If you're here to ask my permission to marry her, you can go whistle,' Ernie said. 'She's to do her duty on the farm.'

Belatedly, another emotion barged into Kate's head. Shame. Leo was here on the farm. The squalid farm with its mean and truculent master. Her embarrassment was acute.

But Ernie's rudeness and aggression left Leo uncowed. 'I've several answers to that,' he said calmly. 'Firstly, we don't need your permission since Kate is no longer a child. Secondly, she isn't a chattel to be passed from pillar to post. She's a person in her own right with a good head on her shoulders and a warm heart in her chest. She can make her own decisions. And thirdly, she's spent years doing her duty on the farm, so she's earned the right to break free and pursue a different sort of life if she chooses.'

Ernie looked taken aback by the visitor's untroubled authority. But he rallied with a crafty look. 'There's a war on, as I suppose you know, judging from that uniform you're in. You need to help the war effort in your way. She needs to help the war effort in her way. That's here on the farm. You lot would soon starve without farmers growing the food you need in your bellies.'

'Kate's work here is valuable,' Leo admitted. 'You're lucky she puts such long hours into both the farm and the house, and I imagine you'd find it almost impossible to replace her with someone half as willing or half as efficient. But there are many other ways she could contribute to the war effort. Easier ways, probably. Staying here – or not – is her choice. I hope we don't need to fall out about it, though.'

Ernie turned scornful. 'You want me to be your friend?'

'By no means. Neither do I aspire to be *your* friend. I'm talking about tolerating each other, Mr Fletcher. And about you showing your daughter some respect because, without it, I suspect you and your farm are going to be the losers.'

Ernie's hands bunched into fists but he was no match for cool and collected Leo, who turned to Ruby and said, 'You offered tea. I'll accept it gladly.'

Ruby brought the pot to the table and poured tea for everyone. Pearl brought over the plate of bread that Ruby had sliced, managing not to drop it.

As for Kate, she felt struck dumb, though her thoughts were racing. Leo had met her awful father and squared up to him . . .

'I've met Kenny and Vinnie, so you must be Fred,' Leo said.

Fred was looking awed by this confident visitor who'd taken Ernie in his stride, but he managed an inarticulate grunt that conveyed agreement that yes, he was indeed Fred.

'This war has battered us both about a bit,' Leo said, gesturing to his burns, which were red and angry still. 'I've been treated very well by the medics I've seen. Have you been treated well by yours?'

'I suppose.'

'My cousin was a patient at Stratton House for a while. He spoke highly of it. He lost half a hand, which was particularly unlucky considering he earned his living in civilian life by playing and teaching the piano. But he survived, and he's glad of it. He's looking into other ways of earning a living now. I'm hoping to fly again, though whether that will involve missions remains to be seen. At the very least, I should be able to help with training other pilots. That's what I've been talking about today at my air base.'

So he'd been to Hollerton earlier. It explained his uniform, and it wasn't a great distance from Hollerton to Churchwood.

Kate's thoughts continued to race. He'd spoken of her in glowing terms to her father but it didn't follow that he wanted their relationship to continue. Leo was a decent man and might simply be laying the ground for her to save face with her family by pretending that she had broken off with him. Again, he might be doing his best to increase her father's respect for her and buck up Fred's ideas as parting gifts to make her life easier. Then again, Kate's doubts might not have infected Leo yet, and he might be here because he suspected she was troubled and wanted to talk about it face to face. If that proved to be the case, could she find the strength to do the right thing by setting Leo free?

A pang of desolation cut through her. She couldn't decide what she was going to do, given a choice. The selfish thing? Or the best thing for the man she loved?

Leo was still talking to Fred. 'It doesn't do to sit idly on the sidelines while life goes on around you, does it?' he said. 'I hear you've done some wood carving.'

'It's not worth looking at,' Fred said hastily, but Pearl got up to fetch the little horse he'd been working on.

'This is good,' Leo said, studying it.

Fred's eyes narrowed as though he suspected Leo of patronizing him, but there was nothing condescending in Leo's manner.

'Good enough to sell,' he said. 'You could try making chess pieces, too. Castles, queens, knights, pawns . . . If you're interested, I could send you a chess set of mine so you can see what I mean. My father, for one, collects chess sets, but he hasn't got a wooden one.'

'I dunno,' Fred muttered, but Pearl said firmly, 'That would be smashing, Leo. Thanks.'

'Would you show me a little more of the farm?' Leo asked Kate when the last slice of bread had been eaten and the last drops of tea consumed.

'There's work needs doing,' Ernie grumbled, but Leo simply stared at him until Ernie blushed. Ernie blushing! Whatever next?

Leo thanked Ruby for the tea and shrugged into his coat, cap and scarf. Kate wrapped up in her old work jacket. Leo was already seeing her at her worst.

'Is there somewhere we can talk undisturbed?' he asked outside, and nerves squeezed Kate's stomach.

'The orchard is the best place. But—'

'Let's talk when we get there.'

CHAPTER THIRTY-SEVEN

Kate

Leo took her arm for the short walk to the orchard. Once there, he rested an arm on a branch of an apple tree and looked down at her. 'I've missed you,' he said.

'It's been mutual.' Kate had missed him dreadfully.

'Something happened in Cheltenham, though. Something that changed things between us. Your letters have been as loving as ever but also tinged with . . . I'm not sure how to describe it, but it's made me feel as though you're pulling away.'

Kate couldn't deny it.

'Was it because of something Julia or Anne said? Something mean that upset you?'

'I don't care about Julia and Anne,' Kate told him. 'I don't respect them enough to care about their opinions. But they were right about one thing.'

'Which was . . .?'

Kate took a deep breath and forced the words out. 'I'm not a part of your world, Leo. I don't fit into Cheltenham society.'

'Darling Kate, I wish you could see yourself through my eyes. I see someone who's bold, beautiful and brave. Kind and loving, too. They're the qualities I want in my world, darling. I don't give a fig for what school anyone went to, who their parents are and whether they're more used to dancing a jig around a maypole than performing a waltz at the Lord Lieutenant's ball. You're overlooking something crucial.'

Which was . . .?

'I don't fit into my parents' idea of good society either,' Leo said. 'Oh, I can dress up and make polite conversation well enough. But I hate that narrow, blinkered world. If I'd wanted my parents' sort of life, I could have become a banker or a solicitor or an accountant. But I joined the RAF precisely because I wanted a different future. Don't get me wrong. My parents are good people. I love the old dears and I'm even fond of some of their friends. But I'm only a visitor to their life these days. I've chosen my own path and I want to tread it arm in arm with you.'

'But after the war . . . When things return to normal . . .'

'Our normal won't be the same as theirs.'

Kate didn't doubt his sincerity. But would the day come when adventure palled and he wanted to settle into a steady life like his parents, after all? Would Kate become a hindrance then? A millstone around his neck? Would it be selfish to take the risk?

'I'm older than you, darling,' he pointed out. 'I'm not going to claim it makes me wiser, but it does mean I've more experience of the world. I've met all sorts of girls from all sorts of backgrounds but I've never come close to experiencing what I feel for you. I love you, Kate. More than that, I want to spend the rest of my life with you. Which is why I'm here to beg you to do me the honour of marrying me.'

Kate gasped.

'Will you, Kate?' he asked. 'Will you marry me?'

She felt winded. As though all the breath had been knocked out of her body. 'I . . . don't know what to say!'

'"Yes" would be nice.'

'I do love you, Leo. With all of my heart.'

'But?'

'I'm . . . scared, I suppose.'

'Scared that your feelings for me won't last?'

'I can't imagine ever not loving you, Leo.'

'Then you're scared that my feelings for you won't last?'

'Not exactly. I'm worried that I won't be the sort of wife who'll make you happy. I don't mean just now, but in the future.'

'We're back to Julia, Anne and Cheltenham society. Please don't play into their hands.'

Kate wasn't playing into their hands. The fact was that they had a point. A valid point. And Kate needed to look beyond what *she* wanted to what was best for Leo. Self-sacrifice – wasn't that real love?

'No one can know what the future holds,' Leo argued. '*I* may turn into Ferdy and think of nothing but golf and what I'm going to be given for dinner. *You* might turn into Julia's mother and become a crashing snob.'

The idea of Kate turning into Julia's mother was so absurd that Kate let out a bark of laughter.

'You see,' Leo said. 'You think it's impossible that *you'll* ever change that much. Well, I think it's impossible that *I'll* ever stop loving you and feeling proud of you. I could shout about my pride in you from the rooftops, and the more your father is a surly boor, the more remarkable that makes you.'

Was that true?

'Life's full of risks but I can assure you of one thing. If, by some jinx of nature, I do turn out to be like Ferdy, I won't fight you if you decide to divorce me.'

Leo was joking but then he turned serious again. 'What's the alternative? We go our separate ways because we're too afraid to take a chance?'

'The last thing I want is for us to part!' It was a cry from the heart because it was indeed the last thing she wanted. For her. Even the thought of it had anguish tearing claws into her soul.

'But you don't want to marry me?'

She could see the emotion in his face – crushing disappointment mixed with dignity in defeat.

When she didn't answer he nodded slowly, as though silence equalled rejection. 'Fair enough,' he said, attempting a crooked smile.

Seeing him hurting – aware of her own suffering, too – Kate couldn't bear it. The future suddenly felt remote and unreal. With the war raging, they couldn't even be confident of a future. It was the here and now that mattered. This moment.

'I'll marry you, Leo,' she said, clinging to him.

'But you just said—'

'I'm scared,' she repeated. 'Scared I'll let you down.'

He smiled, wrapped his arms around her and breathed in deeply, this time in obvious relief. 'You've nothing to worry about. I know myself and I know that you're the woman for me.'

He kissed her forehead tenderly and then he lowered his head to nuzzle her mouth. It was delicious. Groaning, Leo deepened the kiss and she swayed towards him, savouring the delight.

'We're made for each other,' he said, smiling again when the kiss came to a slow and lingering finish.

'I can't argue with that.' The kiss had left Kate feeling light-headed.

'An engagement requires a ring,' he said then.

Releasing her, he dug in his pocket and brought out a small box. 'I have my grandmother's ring at home, but something from the past doesn't feel quite right for two people who are fashioning a whole new style of future.

I chose an emerald because the green reminds me of nature and nature reminds me of you. Fresh and full of promise. But if you don't like it . . .'

He held out a ring – an oval-shaped emerald surrounded by diamonds – and Kate's breath caught in her throat.. 'It's beautiful,' she told him.

'It may not fit but it can be altered,' he said, sliding it on to her finger.

It fitted perfectly.

'It occurred to me that engagement rings and farming aren't the best of companions,' Leo continued. 'It would be a shame to spoil the shine with mud, and horribly unlucky if you lost the ring in a field or – worse – a compost heap, so I suggest you wear it on this chain when you're working.' He pulled another box from his pocket. Inside was a gold chain. 'Keep the ring on your finger just now, though,' he urged. 'I want to see it sparkling.'

Kate's fingers were long and straight but, being workworn, she felt they didn't do the ring justice. Leo didn't complain. He raised her hand to his mouth and kissed it. 'The sooner we marry, the happier I'll be,' he said.

'You're not returning to active service already?' Kate said, horrified.

'Not quite yet. I went to Hollerton to offer myself for duty but the doc I saw there says I need to wait for another month or so. Don't look so forlorn, my darling.'

'I can't help it. I want you safe.'

'You know I can't stand by and let others fight when I'm able to help them.'

Kate did know. But she didn't have to like it.

'What sort of wedding do you want?' he asked. 'A big event with a white dress and bridesmaids, or something smaller? More intimate?'

Whoa! Leo's words brought the future back into focus.

They'd only just got engaged and Kate had envisaged that many months would pass before she had to make plans for a wedding, months in which they could both think about whether they were truly right for each other in the longer term.

'I haven't thought about it.' Though, now he'd raised the subject, she realized there was no way Ernie could put on the sort of lavish occasion Leo's family might expect. It was hard to see him laying out a single penny of the costs, and while her friends would do their best to help out, the wedding would need to be modest in the extreme. 'A small wedding, probably. Here, in Churchwood.' A smart venue in London or even St Albans would be out of the question.

Not that Kate imagined it happening for a long time yet. She was about to tell him that there was no need to rush when he said, 'Suits me. I don't really care about the sort of wedding we have. I just want it to be soon. As soon as possible, in fact.'

As soon as possible? Kate's head whirled. She hadn't anticipated this.

'Can I leave it to you to think about wedding plans and let me know what you decide? We should tell your family about the engagement now, though.'

He took her arm and led her back towards the farm-house, and he was so obviously happy that she hadn't the heart to urge him to take things more slowly to avoid rushing into a terrible mistake.

Ruby was in the yard and, seeing them, raised an enquiring eyebrow.

'Kate?' Leo prompted, and she pushed through her panic to hold up her left hand to show the ring.

'Wonderful news!' Ruby declared, hastening forward to hug them. 'This girl deserves some happiness,' she told

Leo. 'You'd better look after her well, or you'll have me to answer to. And I'm from the East End of London where we don't take any nonsense.'

'No one appreciates Kate more than I,' Leo assured her.

Ruby turned and yelled in the direction of the barn, 'Get out here now, Kenny!'

Kenny emerged looking puzzled. 'What?'

'You need to congratulate Kate and Leo,' she told him.

'On what?'

Ruby rolled her eyes and the penny dropped inside Kenny's brain. 'Oh, I see.' He loped forward and came to a halt in front of his sister, looking as though he didn't know what to do next.

'Hug her, you idiot,' Ruby instructed.

He gave her an awkward squeeze. 'Congratulations.'

Standing back again, he offered a hand to Leo only to realize that it was filthy. He dug in his pocket for a handkerchief, spat on it and redistributed some of the dirt. 'He doesn't want to touch your spit!' Ruby told him and he shrugged ruefully.

'Settle for saying "Congratulations",' Ruby advised, and Kenny did so, adding in a rare moment of affection, 'Make sure you look after my sister well.'

'What's this?' Ernie demanded, also emerging from the barn, doubtless to investigate the interruption to work.

'I'm engaged to your daughter,' Leo told him, a light of challenge in his eyes.

'Humph.' Ernie looked at Kate. 'If you're expecting money for a fancy wedding, you're going to be disappointed. There isn't any.'

'I'm not expecting anything,' Kate told him, though she was mortified by such boorish behaviour in front of Leo. Ruby looked embarrassed, too, and even Kenny cringed.

'We may be able to manage something,' Kenny muttered, but Leo took the situation in his stride.

'We don't care about fanciness,' he said. 'A simple wedding will suit us fine, and I can pay the expenses of that.'

Vinnie and Pearl came up. Vinnie looked mystified that anyone should want to get married, but Pearl grinned and folded Kate into an embrace. 'What super news!' She punched Leo on the shoulder. Quite hard, because Pearl was strong, but he took it manfully. 'Let's have a look at the ring,' she demanded.

Kate held out her hand again.

'Smashing!' Pearl declared.

'Beautiful,' Ruby said, and the wistfulness in her voice and face gave Kate sudden insight into the land girl's dissatisfaction with Kenny. Maybe Ruby liked him still – loved him, even – but was disappointed that he hadn't proposed. Maybe she felt his declarations of love had no real substance to them without marriage.

How upside down the world could be. Here was Ruby appearing to want nothing more than to get married, and here was newly engaged Kate feeling terrified at the thought of it.

'A ring like that must have cost a fortune,' Vinnie said, only to look surprised when everyone winced. 'What?' he said.

'It's bad manners to mention the cost,' Pearl explained.

'I don't see why.'

Fred yelled from the kitchen door, 'Is anyone going to tell me what's going on?'

'Kate is engaged,' Pearl announced.

'Blimey.'

'I don't think "blimey" is what Kate and Leo need to hear.'

'Eh?'

'The traditional thing is to wish them every happiness.'

'Right. Well, yeah. *That.*'

Pearl sighed at him and then turned back to Kate, saying, 'You'll need to take care you don't lose that ring in the fields.'

'Leo's already thought of that. I'm going to wear it on a chain around my neck when I'm working.'

'Talking of work, is anyone round here going to bother doing any, or are you planning to waste the day gossiping?' Ernie said, acidly.

'Kate deserves a break to celebrate,' Ruby told him.

'She's already had a break.'

'A proper break.'

Muttering curses, Ernie stomped off. The others melted away, too.

Leo put his arm around Kate's shoulders and squeezed her. 'Don't worry. I couldn't care less about your father's attitude. I'm not marrying him. I'm marrying you.'

'Even so,' Kate said.

'Even so, nothing. My parents have their flaws, too.'

'At least they're polite.'

'They're also snobs, bless 'em. When it comes to embarrassing parents, we're equal.'

He was being kind, but he was also being sincere about loving her. It showed in the soft yet determined look in his blue eyes. She was beyond lucky to be his fiancée, but still the voice whispered frantically in her ear that she'd been selfish to accept his proposal when she wasn't sure she should go through with the wedding.

'Unfortunately, I have to leave,' he said. 'I need to return the motorbike to Hollerton. I'm spending the night there and returning to Cheltenham in the morning. I wish I could stay longer, even if it meant camping in one of your fields, but duty calls.'

He eased a stray hair from her face and left his hand on her cheek as though cherishing it. 'I'll miss you, my darling. Write and reassure me that you won't change your mind about marrying me. I know I sprang my proposal on you. And let me know when you'd like to marry, too. As I said before, the sooner the better for me, and I meant what I said about meeting the expenses. It may not be traditional for the groom to pay but, as I've already said, we're forging our own path.'

He led her towards the motorbike, which he'd left around the side of the farmhouse, but turned her to face him again, rubbing his hands up and down her arms as though hating to let her go. 'Don't let your father or anyone else get you down or give you doubts,' he urged. 'I love you, Kate Fletcher. That's all that matters. The rest . . . We'll navigate a way through any problems.'

He paused to let his words sink in and then said, 'Of course, your father may be worried that he'll lose your labour on the farm once you're married. If you want me to set you up in a home of our own from the beginning, then that's what I'll do. But if you prefer to stay here for the time being, that's fine too.'

'I couldn't leave the farm,' she said. 'It would be hard on everyone else.'

'That's what I thought you'd say, though if living here becomes too much, just tell me. But right now, my darling, I need you to kiss me goodbye.'

Kate never needed persuading to kiss him. She loved kissing him. But in time they had to ease apart. Leo pulled on his helmet and gauntlet gloves. 'I'm going to love thinking of you wearing my ring,' he said. 'Whether you wear it on your finger or close to your heart on the chain, it'll bring me joy.'

He rode off into the distance and Kate wanted to cry.

She thought of walking down the aisle to meet him, his eyes aglow with love for her and her eyes aglow with love for him. She thought of waking up beside him, too. Sharing breakfast while chatting about the news on the radio or in a newspaper. And then going their separate ways for the day but thinking of each other often and feeling excitement at the thought of going home . . .

It could be perfect. If only she could rid herself of that insistent voice of doubt.

CHAPTER THIRTY-EIGHT

Alice

Alice heard Kate's news when she paused at Brimbles Farm on her way to the hospital. 'I'm so happy for you! Leo is a lucky man!'

'I'm the lucky one,' Kate said.

'You're both lucky and that's how it should be. I know you've only been engaged for a day and need to catch your breath before you make any plans. And I don't want to interfere. But I'll gladly help with the wedding arrangements if you'd like that . . .'

'I don't know where to begin,' Kate admitted.

'I don't suppose Ernie will help towards the expenses.'

Kate laughed. 'Not a chance. Leo has offered to pay but I'd rather keep things simple and inexpensive, though the thought of his parents turning their noses up at that type of wedding terrifies me.'

'It's *your* wedding, and Leo's too. If you're both happy with a small event, his parents will just have to lump it. Have you thought about a possible date?'

'Leo wants to marry soon.'

'That rules out an outdoor reception in Naomi's garden. It's too cold at this time of year.'

'I wouldn't impose on Naomi anyway, now she has her hands full with the evacuees. But there's nowhere on the farm that's suitable. Certainly not the house. It's far too ramshackle, with just one toilet in a tumbledown shed. Besides, I couldn't trust Ernie to behave himself.'

'He's taken the engagement badly?'

'You know Ernie.'

'That man should be ashamed,' Alice said. 'Adam would love to marry you at St Luke's and you're more than welcome to have your reception at The Linnets, though the cottage won't fit many people inside. But I'm thinking too far ahead. You need time simply to bask in the joy of being engaged.'

Alice paused and then said, 'Kate, you are happy about this engagement?'

'I love Leo as much as ever. More, if that's possible.'

'But?' Alice asked.

'I suppose I'm still in shock. I feel as though I'm on a runaway train with everything happening so quickly.'

'Just as long as you've got rid of that ridiculous notion that you're not right for him.'

Kate smiled, but a second too late to hide her vulnerability. She was indeed still thinking that she wasn't right for him.

'Leo is intelligent and thoughtful,' Alice insisted. 'He knows you'll make him happy. If his family can't see that you're an amazing person, they'll be the losers, not you.'

Kate only shrugged. Her confidence had come a long way since Alice had first met her, but there were times when it still hadn't come far enough.

'Love is an amazing thing, Kate. I believe in grabbing it with both hands.' Alice let that sink in, then said, 'Now then, do you have a ring?' She couldn't see one.

Kate brought the chain out from under her shirt and showed Alice the ring Leo had given her.

'It's stunning,' Alice said, 'and an emerald is perfect for you.'

'I'm keeping it on a chain so I don't lose it in a field.'

'That really would be unlucky,' Alice said, only to wish she hadn't spoken because a look of dismay passed over Kate's face. Vulnerability must be making her suspicious of bad omens.

Alice changed the subject. 'Did you manage to ask Fred about donating a wooden animal to the bookshop raffle?'

'I did, and he said his work isn't good enough. I assured him it is, but we'll see. If I don't persuade him to give something, Pearl will snatch something from him anyway.'

'How are they getting along?'

'With non-stop bickering, but she's doing Fred the world of good and she knows it. Which is lovely, since it's boosting her confidence.'

If only Alice could boost Kate's confidence. 'Do you still think they might become a courting couple?'

'Perhaps, though I doubt they'll ever be the sort of couple who whisper sweet nothings to each other.'

'Insults and clips around the ear are probably Pearl's style,' Alice agreed.

'Definitely. Have you been given any other donations for the raffle?'

'Home-made wine from Bert, sherry from Naomi, lavender bags from Janet and Betty, a small hamper of unrationed food from Churchwood's shopkeepers, a potted aspidistra from Edna Hall, a baby's matinee coat and matching hat knitted by Molly Lloyd . . . Oh, and May has offered an hour of her time to help someone make a child's dress. Hopefully, we'll raise enough to buy several books and perhaps make a start on the equipment we need as well, though we've already had offers of a few things.'

Edna Hall had given a set of six matching cups and saucers and other people had given random pieces of crockery, glasses and teaspoons. 'As long as they hold liquids safely, it doesn't matter if they're of different designs,' Adam had said.

Ellen had donated the table and four chairs that Joe had left behind and Jonah Kerrigan had offered another four. 'They've been in my shed for years so I can't promise they're still fit for use,' he'd cautioned.

'I can take a look at them and make any necessary repairs,' Bert had promised.

Walking on, Alice thought about her own wedding. Having taken place in August, the reception had been held in Naomi's garden. It hadn't been grand but it had been perfect. Wanting Kate to have a perfect wedding too, Alice wondered if the new bookshop might be ready in time to host the reception. It wouldn't be well kitted out but it could accommodate quite a few people indoors and be convenient for the church as well. She decided to ask if the rest of the bookshop team agreed.

At the hospital, Matron offered a lady's scarf for the raffle. 'It was given to me as a gift a couple of years ago and I forgot all about it,' she said. 'Bilious green isn't my colour, you see.'

'I'm sure it'll be someone else's colour,' Alice assured her.

She went about her usual job of collecting and distributing books, glad to be able to tell disappointed patients that, with the fundraiser planned, there might soon be more books for them. Then she took a deep breath and held up the magazine she often took to the hospital: *Tales of Adventure*. 'Would anyone like to hear a story?'

There was a clamour of 'Me!' and 'Yes, please' and Alice pulled up a chair, trying to still her fast-beating heart because she was only going to pretend to read from the magazine. Inside, she'd slipped pages torn out from her notebook, pages on which she'd finally written a story of her own: 'The House on Blackwell Point'.

It was an adventure story of the sort she often read to the patients, featuring Abel, a lonely old man, and an equally lonely evacuee boy called Jonny. They were strangers, though both lived by the sea and took separate walks along the beach when no one else was around. Their walks took them in sight of a long-abandoned clifftop house and one night they each noticed lights shining from the windows. Intrigued, they ventured out for a closer look and were scared half to death when they bumped into each other. But, working together, they uncovered the fact that German spies were using the house. Thanks to them, the spies were caught, and man and boy became firm friends.

She reached the end and took a deep breath. 'What did you think of that?' she asked.

It was a question she regularly asked, as it helped to get the men talking and often laughing. But this time she awaited the verdict with a dry mouth and fluttering nerves.

'It was a corker, miss,' Private Andy Hughes said.

'A belter,' Corporal Eddie Mayes agreed.

'I loved the old man,' Private Lawrence Higgs said. 'Reminded me of my granddad. Crusty on the outside. Melting with kindness in the middle.'

'I liked the boy. It's sad the way so many kids have been separated from their families by this war.' That was Sergeant John Miller.

There were murmurs of sympathy.

'Thank you for listening,' Alice said.

Well, she decided, the story might not be the best one ever written, but she felt proud of having worked through her self-doubt in order to write it. Whether she could make Daniel proud by selling it to a magazine remained to be seen, but at home that night she read through the story again, made a few alterations here and there and decided to send it to the editor of *Tales of Adventure*.

Needing to type it out if it was to look professional, she asked her father to carry the typewriter into the kitchen for her. 'Bookshop business?' he asked.

Alice simply smiled as though to confirm it, not wanting her father – or anyone else – to know what she was doing yet so they wouldn't worry about her feelings if the editor rejected the story. Of course, if the editor accepted it . . . No, she'd try not to think of that, because anticipating happiness and building up hope might only make rejection feel all the worse.

She'd typed only the first page before her hand cramped. She'd expected it, though, so wasn't downhearted. Even if it took several days to type the story, the important thing was that she'd finish the job in the end.

She typed another page the following morning and then went out on a mission to speak to the bookshop team. Afterwards, Alice walked up to Brimbles Farm to tell Kate the news. 'We're all agreed that you should have the bookshop for your wedding reception – if you want it . . .'

'Goodness, how kind! It sounds ideal.'

'It'll be spartan,' Alice cautioned, 'but it'll be a bigger space than any other in the village.'

'It's a weight off my mind, anyway.'

Alice was glad. 'Do you know how many people you're likely to invite?'

'I haven't thought that far ahead. I'm still reeling from the engagement, to be honest.'

And she was still suffering doubts about whether she was the right girl for Leo, Alice guessed.

'It'll be a small occasion,' Kate said. 'Leo's friends are

all away at the war and he hasn't a large family. I'll have to invite everyone at the farm, of course. You and the rest of the bookshop team, too. Oh, and your father. It'll be tricky enough having all those eyes on me. I couldn't face a crowd.'

'Have you spoken to Adam about the service?'

'Not yet.'

'The entire village is delighted for you,' Alice said. 'You deserve some happiness, Kate.'

'You're all so kind.'

'Not kind. Honest.' Kate had simply to trust it.

Just as Alice needed to trust in herself. She hastened home to type another page of her story.

CHAPTER THIRTY-NINE

Naomi

'They're here!' Mags said, entering the drawing room with a handful of envelopes.

There was one for each of the London women except Ivy. They tore them open, slumping in relief as they read the letters.

'All confirmed in post?' Mags asked. 'All to start next Monday?'

They nodded.

'We'll be out of your hair just as soon as we can, Naomi,' Mags told her, on first name terms now at Naomi's insistence.

'You'll need at least a week or two's wages before you can take on a house,' Naomi pointed out. 'It needs to be the right house, too. Or the right couple of houses, if you can't find one to fit all of you. You're welcome to stay here in the meantime instead of wasting your money on temporary lodgings.'

'Saint Naomi of Churchwood, that's you,' Mags said, and the others agreed.

It was tiring having so many people in the house, especially when they included lively children, but Naomi couldn't have lived with herself if she hadn't offered more help to these admirable people. She liked all of them and was getting to know their individual personalities.

There was something of the warrior in Mags. She

stood for no nonsense from anyone. Ivy was a kind woman whom life hadn't always treated well. She grieved for the daughter who'd left without as much as a glance over her shoulder, but doted on little Flower. Pat Nicholls was a great homemaker, always tidying and making things comfortable. Jessie Smith liked to laugh and tell jokes, while Sheila Blair loved reading. Her eyes had lit up at the sight of Naomi's book collection. 'Borrow anything you wish,' Naomi had told her and she'd been revelling in the luxury of reading ever since.

None of the children had a bad bone in their bodies, either. Arthur was especially considerate, despite the reputation he'd acquired in the village. Naomi understood Victoria's concern about him taking too much responsibility to heart, though. He was on the watch continuously in case any of the other children needed help and he always put them before himself.

'You can play first, if you like, Lewis,' he said, when he organized a ball game in the garden and Lewis was desperate to get started.

'Let's swap biscuits, Jenny,' he said another time. 'My biscuit is bigger than yours and I know they're your favourites.'

'Shall I read you a story?' he said, when Mary was growing bored.

And so it went on.

He was particularly careful with Flower, mindful of her weak chest. 'Let's wrap this scarf around you, Flower . . . I've saved you this chair near the fire . . . Eat up so you grow strong . . .'

'It's such a shame that bad luck seems to follow him around,' Victoria remarked, when he incurred the wrath of Miss Gibb for failing to hold the post office door open for her. 'He didn't let it close in her face deliberately. He was holding it open when Jenny tripped on the pavement and he forgot the door when he ran to help her.'

In the shops, in the street and in church, Naomi had noticed smiles turning to suspicion when Arthur was near by. Poor Arthur – Naomi could see that his bad reputation upset him. Poor Victoria, too. It was unfair for life to have burdened her with such weighty problems at her age.

'Time will settle everyone down,' Naomi said, but it was beginning to feel a hollow assurance.

As for Naomi herself, she was struggling too, as whichever way she turned there was a reminder of her childlessness. The bleakness of it crept around her when she heard Victoria reading Jenny a bedtime story and saw them snuggled together against Jenny's pillows.

It crept up again after Flower banged her knee on a chair when Naomi was the only other person in the room. 'There, there, it'll stop hurting soon,' Naomi said, patting Flower's head.

'Please will you kiss it better?' Flower asked. 'Grandma always kisses my hurts better.'

Naomi hesitated. She'd never kissed a child's hurt better before. Swallowing, she sat on a sofa and bent forward to kiss the tiny knee. 'Is that right?'

Flower nodded and then took Naomi by surprise by reaching her arms around her neck, climbing on to her lap and making herself comfortable.

How warm the little body was! How soft!

'Are you crying?' Flower asked suddenly, reaching a small hand to Naomi's cheek. 'Have you got a hurt, too? I'll kiss it better if you like.'

'A speck of dust came into my eye, that's all,' Naomi said.

Flower couldn't help with this hurt. No one could. Blast Alexander Harrington.

*

On the day Mr Waite finished work on the new bookshop, Alice, Bert and Naomi gathered there to thank him and have a look around. 'Let's leave the door open so the air can circulate while it's dry outside,' Bert suggested. 'It'll be a while before this plaster dries out fully but, as you can see, I've started putting on a thin mist of paint so it doesn't look quite so bare.'

'We should fix a date for the opening party,' Alice suggested.

'It'll give people something cheerful to look forward to,' Naomi agreed. 'Hopefully, it'll take their minds off Arthur, too. Trouble seems to follow that boy around.'

'Humphrey Guscott?' Alice asked.

'Mmm.'

After Naomi had discovered an old cricket bat of Alexander's in the attic, Arthur had taken the others on to the village green to play, thinking they'd be out of anyone's way there. Unfortunately, old Humphrey Guscott had walked by with his stick and the ball had struck his shoulder. Davie had hit the ball but old Humphrey hadn't been aware of that. 'I suppose you're responsible for this game?' he'd snapped at Arthur.

'Well, yes, but—'

'It's true what everyone says. You're a menace, boy, and you're leading these others astray.'

'Did you see what happened in church, too?' Naomi asked.

'I did.'

'Arthur collected in all the children's marbles so they wouldn't drop them on the floor, only one of them fell out of his pocket during the sermon.'

'Unlucky,' Alice said. 'Particularly unlucky that it rolled to a stop at Mr Miles's feet, just as Arthur was crawling on the floor trying to retrieve it.'

'A party should put everyone in a better mood,' Naomi said.

They turned in surprise as a woman and a much younger man walked into the house and stared around it. Naomi didn't recognize them and, judging from their expressions, neither did Alice nor Bert.

The woman was middle-aged and . . . The word that came into Naomi's mind was 'buxom', for there was substance to this woman and much of it was packed on to her chest. She had dyed blonde hair that had been styled to provide volume, and a face that looked hard and knowing. As for her clothes, the tight skirt and low-cut blouse she wore beneath her open coat would have Churchwood's eyes out on stalks.

The man was cut from a different sort of cloth. Far from being hard and knowing, his grin was loose and floppy, while his pale eyes were vacant in a way that suggested there was nothing much stirring behind them. His hair was brown and cut short, drawing attention to his ears, which stuck out from the sides of his head like the handles on a child's beaker. Jug ears. He was around thirty but a limp provided a possible explanation for why he wasn't away in the forces.

'I think this will suit us nicely, Maurice,' the woman said.

Naomi exchanged another baffled look with Alice and Bert before taking the initiative, walking over and saying, 'Good morning. I don't think we've met.'

'I'm sure we haven't,' the woman said, 'but we can put that right, seeing as we're about to be neighbours, assuming you live near by. I'm Gloria Gumble. This is my son, Maurice.'

'I'm Naomi Harrington. My friends are Alice Irvine and Bert Makepiece.'

'Delighted, I'm sure. Well, it's good to see the place

being given a lick of paint. But we're here now so we can finish it off.'

'I think there may have been a misunderstanding,' Alice pointed out. 'This house isn't available to rent. Mrs Harrington has already agreed to rent it and then buy it.'

'That's what she thinks,' Gloria Gumble said. 'If there's been a misunderstanding, it's on your side. This is Joe Simpson's house?'

'Yes, but—'

'Then we've inherited it. Or rather, Maurice has. We're going to be living here.'

CHAPTER FORTY

Naomi

A moment of silence followed Gloria's bombshell. Then Naomi roused herself. 'Actually, Joe's sister, Ellen, inherited this house.'

'Got Joe's last will and testament, has she?'

'I didn't think there *was* a will, but—'

'That's because *I've* got it. Joe left everything to Maurice, fair and square. And so he should have done. Can't you see the likeness? Maurice is Joe's son.'

Naomi stared at him then looked over at Alice and Bert, who were staring at Maurice too.

There was definitely something familiar in those pale eyes, while the sticky-out ears were exactly like Joe's.

'I didn't know Joe ever married,' Naomi said.

'Well, I'm not saying he did the right thing by me when I fell with his kid. Not that I minded, because we wouldn't have suited as man and wife. But he's done the right thing by Maurice and that's what matters now. It would have been harsh if Joe had cut his own flesh and blood off without a penny, marriage certificate or no marriage certificate. But Joe wasn't a bad man and he did what was decent in the end.'

Naomi looked at Maurice, who simply grinned.

'We'll need furniture, of course,' Gloria said. 'That's why we're here to reconnoitre. Are there beds?'

'Not any more.'

'No matter. We'll have to hire a man and his van to bring our other things from Hove, so adding a couple of beds to the load shouldn't make much difference to the cost. Joe must have left some money behind as well as this house, so that should cover it. A careful man with money was Joe. Not that I'm calling him mean, because he wasn't. But . . . cautious. Holding on to a little nest egg.'

'Does Ellen know about all this?' Naomi asked.

'About me and Maurice?' Gloria shrugged. 'Search me. I never met the woman and I don't know what Joe told her about us *or* the will. But it's all done proper. The will, I mean. It's . . . Oh, what's the word that means it'll be held up in a court of law? Legal, that's it. Not that it's going to see the inside of a court, because why would anyone question what a man did with his possessions when he used them to benefit his own son?'

'Would it be possible for me to see this will?' Naomi asked.

Gloria frowned. 'I don't like to be rude, but I can't see that it's any of your business, you not being family.'

It was a fair response but it still made Naomi blush and feel like a nosy neighbour. 'I think it would be advisable to speak to Ellen as soon as possible,' she said.

'Lives in a place called Barton, doesn't she?'

'That's right.'

'Is there a bus that runs there?'

'No need for a bus.' Bert stepped forward. 'I can take you there in my truck. I'll take you too, Naomi, since you must want a word with Ellen on your own account. Your lad won't mind travelling in the back?' he asked Gloria.

'Maurice won't mind at all and a lift will save my feet. Thank you.'

Maurice said nothing. It seemed likely that he rarely spoke.

Bert turned to Alice. 'Would you—'

'I'll stay here. We shouldn't overwhelm Ellen.'

Bert nodded. 'Let's talk later.'

Gloria sat in the middle of the truck's bench seat on the drive to Barton. Far from trying to keep a discreet distance from Bert, she was happy to rub shoulders with him. Was it unkind of Naomi to suspect that Gloria had rubbed shoulders with a lot of men in her time?

'So kind of you to give us a lift,' Gloria told him. 'You and me are going to be friends.'

Hmm.

'It'll be nice to settle in a village,' Gloria continued. 'Not that I dislike Hove, where we've been living. But it doesn't hurt to have an adventure somewhere new, does it?' She gave Bert a suggestive dig in the ribs with her elbow.

Heavens. If Gloria settled in Churchwood, she would set the village alight with scandal. That was the least of their problems, though. If Gloria was right about the will, Ellen would lose out on her inheritance and the bookshop would be homeless again.

'Looks like Ellen's at home,' Bert said as they reached Barton. Smoke was emerging from her chimney.

She was wiping her hands on a tea towel when she came to the door. 'Naomi. Bert,' she said, but then she noticed Gloria and Maurice and did a double-take. 'My goodness,' she said. 'I don't know who you are, young man, but you remind me of my brother.'

'That's because he's your brother's son,' Gloria said, smirking.

The announcement struck Ellen dumb.

'Can we come in?' Gloria asked. 'It's freezing out here.'

'What? Oh, of course.' Ellen led them into her sitting room. 'I don't understand,' she said then.

'It's simple, really.' Gloria told her story and Ellen sank into a chair, looking pale and overcome.

'But why wouldn't Joe have told me if he had a son?' she wailed. 'We were so close!'

Gloria's shrug suggested Ellen had been fooling herself on that point. 'What Joe did or didn't tell you is beside the point. We're here now to claim Maurice's inheritance.' She turned to Bert and Naomi. 'Thanks for the lift, but we're discussing family business now.'

In other words, it was time they left. Naomi looked to Ellen, but Joe's sister appeared to be unaware that she was being invited to voice an opinion. 'Would you like us to leave, Ellen?' Naomi asked gently.

'What?' Ellen glanced up, though her eyes looked unfocused. She made a visible effort to concentrate. 'I'm sorry, did you say you needed to leave? Of course. I know you're busy and I don't want—'

'We can stay if you wish,' Naomi said.

Gloria narrowed her eyes and straightened her shoulders as though squaring them for a fight. 'That won't be necessary. Ellen and me just need to get acquainted.'

Ellen was no match for Gloria. 'Perhaps it would be best if you left,' she said.

'Of course.' Naomi patted Ellen's arm. 'We'll see ourselves out.'

She headed into the hall, Bert following. They were closing the door behind them when they heard Gloria say, 'Joe must have left money as well as the house . . .'

Back in the truck, they sat in shocked silence for a moment before Naomi said, 'We should report to Alice. She'll be waiting for news.'

Alice opened the cottage door with an alacrity that suggested she had indeed been waiting. They settled in the dining room and Naomi brought Alice up to date with developments.

'Do you think she's genuine?' Alice asked.

'The delightful Gloria?' Bert shrugged. 'Hard to say, though Ellen was certainly struck by Maurice's resemblance to Joe.'

'Did you see the will?'

'It was made clear that we should remove our noses from family business,' Naomi said.

Alice was quiet for a moment. Then she shook her head. 'I didn't know Joe for as long as you two, but he never struck me as the sort of person who'd leave a mess like this behind him.'

'Perhaps he was ashamed of having fathered a child out of wedlock and couldn't find the courage to admit it to a beloved sister for fear of disgusting her,' Naomi suggested.

'But to let Ellen think she was going to inherit . . . To let her think she was going to be financially comfortable after a lifetime of scrimping and saving . . . Able to help her children, too . . .'

'It doesn't sound like Joe,' Bert agreed. 'Maybe he tried to tell her but the words just wouldn't come.'

'It's possible, I suppose,' Alice admitted. 'It's a pity we haven't seen the will. It might be worth warning Ellen to check its authenticity before handing over the keys to Joe's house.'

'That's a job for another time,' Bert said. 'I don't think we'll be allowed near Ellen today.'

'Let's talk again tomorrow,' Naomi suggested.

Alice nodded and showed them to the door, looking thoughtful.

'Any news from William?' Bert asked as he and Naomi walked back to the truck.

'No news from William. No news from Alexander, either.'

CHAPTER FORTY-ONE

Alice

Please give Kate my very best wishes on her engagement, Daniel had written. *I couldn't be happier for her. I'm doing some useful work here but my time is fully occupied and it may not be possible for me to visit you again before I return overseas . . .*

Alice's disappointment was intense. She wanted desperately to see Daniel. To touch him and kiss him, too. But the war was ever cruel and, like couples all over, they'd have to make the most of letters instead.

She blinked back tears, determined that she wasn't going to let herself slip back into dark times. Feeling the bookshop situation was more urgent than typing her story, she called on Naomi at Foxfield and then caught the bus to Barton.

'Is this a bad time?' she asked, when Ellen opened the door. It was the day after Gloria's arrival and poor Ellen looked as though she'd barely slept. 'You don't already have company?'

'Gloria and her son? No. They wanted to spend the night here but I wasn't up to it. Not after the shock I'd received. Perhaps it was unkind of me, but I suggested they try Mrs Hamilton's guest house on Spencer Street.'

'Tell me if I'm being intrusive, but I wonder if I could talk to you about Gloria's claim?'

'I owe you and your Daniel for recovering the money

I paid out to that awful Mick Briggs. Of course I'll talk to you.'

'I'll try to be brief.'

Ellen made tea and they sat at her kitchen table.

'The way I see it, there are two things to consider,' Alice began. 'The first is whether or not Maurice is Joe's son.'

Ellen got up and fetched some photographs from a drawer. They showed Joe as a boy and then as a young man. 'I'd say the evidence speaks for itself.'

Alice looked at each photograph in turn. Joe was pictured as a cheeky urchin of about six, in a line-up of fellow pupils at school, on his first day as a newspaper delivery boy, at a wedding, in army uniform following his call-up to the 1914 war . . .

'That must have been our cousin Mabel's wedding,' Ellen said. 'We were a large family back then, with four aunts and three uncles. The older generation have all gone now, and the rest of us haven't kept in touch much, though Joe and I remained close.' Ellen smiled sadly. 'I miss him badly.'

Alice squeezed her hand and Ellen passed over another photograph. 'Gloria gave me this yesterday. It's Maurice as a boy, and as you can see . . .'

The resemblance to Joe was marked.

'Forgive me if I'm straying on to painful ground,' Alice said, 'but weren't you surprised to hear that Joe had a son?'

'I was. I still am. I can only think that Joe must have been ashamed. Not only of fathering a son out of wedlock but also of entangling himself with a woman like Gloria. He'd have known I wouldn't warm to her.'

'Was Joe a secretive sort of man?'

'I never thought so. But perhaps some things are too hard to share.'

273

It certainly looked that way. 'Did Gloria mention how she met Joe?'

'It was in London, apparently. Joe did work there for a while, but he didn't like it so he soon came home. I can't remember exactly when it was, but it could well have been around the time Maurice came into being. Gloria knew things about Joe, too. That he loved boiled eggs but hated kidneys. That he had a way of saying "champion" when something was good, though I believe that's a Yorkshire expression and he'd never been to Yorkshire in his life. Little things like that make me think she must be genuine.'

Alice could think of no grounds for disagreeing. But the will was a separate issue. 'Did Joe never even hint that he'd be leaving everything to Maurice?'

'Not that I remember. To be fair, I don't recall him ever saying that *I'd* be comfortably off after he'd passed. Not in so many words. It just seemed to be an understanding between us.'

'Did you see the will?'

Ellen nodded. 'It was one of those home-made wills but typed on a typewriter. Joe had terrible handwriting, you see.'

'What did it say?'

'Just that, being of sound mind, he was leaving everything to his son, Maurice Gumble.'

'Did it include an address for Maurice?'

'It did, and I wrote it down, more to give myself time to digest the shock than for any other reason.'

'May I see it? Copy it down?'

Ellen fetched a piece of paper from the drawer. 'Be my guest.'

The address was in Hove on the south coast. Alice wrote it in her notebook, together with the date Joe had signed the will and the names and addresses of the two witnesses.

'I appreciate that you're trying to help,' Ellen said. 'But if Maurice really is Joe's son – and I think he must be – it seems only right that he should inherit the house and the money Joe left behind.'

Ellen was a good woman.

'Not that there's any money left, because I used it to pay for the work on Joe's house.'

'Is Gloria aware of that?'

'Not yet. I couldn't face telling her. I'd had enough upsets for one day, but I expect she'll be coming back today so I'll tell her then.' Clearly, Ellen was dreading it.

'I don't wish to cause trouble between you,' Alice told her. 'I just want to be sure everything is as it should be.'

'You'll be discreet if you're going to question anyone else? I wouldn't feel I was a good sister to Joe if I caused unpleasantness for his boy and his boy's mother. I can't warm to Gloria, but I'd like to get to know Maurice better and that won't happen if Gloria thinks I'm challenging her son's inheritance.'

'I'll be discreet,' Alice promised. 'Just one more question, though. How did Gloria hear that Joe had passed away?'

Ellen looked blank. 'I've no idea. Maybe Joe had arranged for someone in the family to tell her. I wrote to a few family members to let them know about Joe. Not that any of them came to the funeral.'

It was time to leave Ellen in peace.

Alice walked back to the bus stop, deep in thought. Instinct was telling her that Gloria was conning Ellen, but was it really instinct or just wishful thinking because she wanted Joe's house to benefit Ellen and become the bookshop's new home?

At home again, she wrote to let Daniel know what had happened. *I want to do something about it, though I haven't yet worked out a course of action*, she told him.

Given the eagerness with which he'd pursued the awful Mick Briggs, she was sure Daniel would approve and wish her luck.

CHAPTER FORTY-TWO

Kate

'I suppose you can have this for your raffle, but don't blame me if no one wants it.' Fred pushed one of his carvings across the table.

Kate picked it up and held it to the light. 'It's beautiful.' Fred's talent was going from strength to strength. This carving of a sparrowhawk was extraordinarily lifelike, the feathers realistic and the bird's facial expression proud. It was a pity she had to let Fred down. 'Unfortunately, the raffle has been cancelled.'

'*What?*' Fred's question was a wail of dismay. Clearly, he'd been secretly hoping this carving would be admired. It would have made him feel that he still counted for something.

'Isn't the bookshop opening any more?' Ruby, too, sounded dismayed.

Kate explained what Alice had reported after walking up to the farm early that morning to let her know about Gloria and Maurice. 'I didn't want you to hear about it from anyone else,' she'd said, and Kate had guessed that her wedding reception was one of Alice's concerns.

'My wedding is a minor issue compared to Ellen losing her inheritance and the bookshop having no home. Again,' Kate had insisted, but she couldn't help feeling that fate had judged her marriage ill-starred.

Superstitious nonsense? Alice would certainly think so.

'You'll have a lovely reception somewhere else,' she'd insisted. 'The Linnets will be a squeeze but you're still welcome to it.'

'It's a kind offer,' Kate had told her. 'Can I let you know?'

'Of course.'

'I was so looking forward to the bookshop party,' Ruby said now.

'Me too,' Pearl agreed. 'I wanted to spin Fred's wheelchair around so fast that he'd be sick and I'd get to eat his share of the food.'

'Charming,' Fred said, rolling his eyes.

Despite the teasing, Kate saw genuine disappointment in their faces. The new bookshop had been a bright spot on all their horizons. Clutching her ring on its chain around her neck, Kate tried to tell herself that there were no such things as bad omens.

She'd watched Ruby closely since the moment it had dawned on her that the land girl's unhappiness might arise from Kenny's failure to propose. The more Kate had thought about it, the more sense it made.

She left the house thinking that even if she could do nothing about her own worries, she could at least try to help Ruby. She found Kenny tossing a bale of hay down from the loft and told him about Gloria and Maurice. Kenny only grunted.

'I know Pearl was looking forward to dancing at the bookshop party,' she said. 'Were you looking forward to dancing with Ruby?'

'I never dance.'

'No matter. I'm sure Ruby would have found people to dance with. Other men, I mean.'

'Eh?'

'That's what happens when you neglect a woman,

Kenny. She thinks you're not serious, so why shouldn't she look around for someone else?'

'Ruby wouldn't do that.'

'Wouldn't she? Of course, there aren't many young men around at the moment, but there are a few farmers and Leo knows a lot of men at Hollerton. Not just pilots but all the ground crews as well. It isn't as though you've asked Ruby to marry you, is it?'

She left him staring after her, his mouth wide open.

Having already stuffed two carrots into her pocket, she walked over to the field where Pete the ageing pony lived. Since Ernie had consented to buying a rusting truck, Pete was less in demand for pulling the cart, but he'd worked hard over the years and deserved to ease up. She was almost there when she realized Pete already had a visitor. Arthur.

The boy whirled around when he heard a twig snap under Kate's boot. 'I wasn't—' He broke off, looking relieved that it was Kate rather than one of the Fletcher men who'd caught him.

'I know you weren't doing any harm,' Kate told him, for she'd heard him crooning how the pony was a beautiful boy. 'Would you like to feed him a carrot?'

'Yes, please!'

Kate told him how to avoid getting bitten and let him feed both carrots to Pete.

'Feeling a bit out of sorts?' Kate asked then.

'I've been in trouble again. I don't mean it to happen but it does.'

'You're having a run of bad luck. It won't last.'

'Won't it?'

'Bad luck tends to be followed by good luck.' Kate wasn't entirely sure she believed it but Arthur needed to cling to the hope that his fortunes would change.

'I should go,' he said. 'I don't want to get into trouble yet again.'

'That's the right attitude,' Kate approved. 'Help that good luck along.'

He hesitated as though unsure if he should thank her. He settled for a nod. 'Bye, Kate. Bye, Pete.'

He patted the pony's neck and ran off, and Kate watched him go, wishing his luck really would change.

Fred was still looking glum when she returned to the house. She gestured to the chess set Leo had kindly sent. 'Are you going to try making one of these?'

'Dunno.'

That wasn't good enough for Pearl. 'Yes, you are going to try making one,' she told Fred. 'Leo went to trouble and expense to send that to you. The least you can do is show gratitude by doing as he suggested.'

'All right, all right! Can a man get no peace around here?'

'Not when he behaves like an idiot.'

Leaving Pearl to bully Fred out of his despondency, Kate went upstairs for a rare few minutes alone in her room. She'd done her best to help others: Ruby, Kenny, Fred and Arthur. Could she bring some sort of resolution to her own troubles?

She took out the letter that had been included with the chess set.

Darling Kate,

I hope you weren't cross with me for arriving at the farm unexpectedly. I was desperate to see you and ask you to be my wife. It brings me such joy to think of you wearing my ring.

The last thing I want is to put you under pressure, especially since I know you're always busy, but I really would like to marry soon, if you're agreeable. As I said before, I don't care

about a grand wedding. All I care about is becoming your hus-
band and whisking you off on a honeymoon before I take up my
duties again and a honeymoon becomes problematic. Having
said that, my parents would be hurt if our wedding involved
just the two of us and a couple of witnesses dragged off the
street, but I'll happily limit my side of the guest list to them.

I've investigated getting a special licence so we don't have
to wait for the banns to be read. It's expensive but worth every
penny. Tell me what you think, my darling. I'm sorry if I'm
going faster than you'd like. If you'd rather take things more
slowly, then that's what we'll do. Your happiness matters above
everything else . . .

But what about *his* happiness? Not just now but in the
future when, despite his current expectations, he might
want a different sort of life and need a different sort of
woman to fit into it. Leo was too good a man ever to blame
her if she let him down, but Kate would blame herself.

On the other hand, if she broke things off now, he'd
be unhappy for quite some time. He'd win through to
happiness again eventually, but what if he returned
to active service and was killed before that could happen?
Kate would never forgive herself if he died feeling full
of sorrow.

Might talking things through with someone else clarify
her thoughts? She already knew Alice's opinion and suspected both Ruby and Pearl would share that view. Kate
didn't wish to disturb Naomi when she had her hands
full. Maybe Adam would have some advice to offer. As
a vicar, he must have married numerous couples and
have thought deeply about the ingredients of a successful marriage.

She cycled down to the vicarage and was greeted with
one of his sweet smiles.

He led her into the sitting room, where an ancient bicycle occupied space on newspapers spread in front of the hearth. 'I decided a bike would help me to get around my parishioners and up to the hospital to visit patients. Petrol rationing means more people want bikes, though, so they're hard to come by. This old thing belonged to the grocer in Barton and he let me have it for a song. It was used by his delivery boy years ago, hence the basket on the front, but that'll come in handy. I'm just rubbing some of the rust off and oiling the bits that need oiling. Don't tell Mrs Harris I brought it in here, though. She thinks her job as my housekeeper includes trying to make a civilized young man out of me, but she's not having much luck, I'm afraid.'

Adam's clothes were as well worn as the bicycle and the room was positively spartan, but he had neither money nor inclination for luxury. Whenever he had a spare penny or two, Kate suspected he donated it to the poor and needy.

'But enough of me,' he said. 'How are you, Kate?'

'Leo has been asking about wedding plans.'

'Let me guess. He wants to marry you soon?'

'By special licence.'

'That's excellent news! Shall we fix a date? Assuming you want me to conduct the service? If you'd rather have someone else, it can—'

'I don't want anyone else.'

Adam smiled again. 'I'm glad, because there's nothing I like more than marrying people who are in love.'

'But is being in love enough for a successful marriage?' Kate asked, feeling her emotions overflowing.

'I can't think of a stronger foundation for it.' Adam frowned at her obvious distress.

'That's what Alice says, more or less.'

'Alice is wise.'

'None wiser. But she and Daniel come from similar worlds. Leo and I . . . don't.'

Understanding cleared Adam's brow. 'You're not defined by Brimbles Farm any more than Leo is defined by his birth and family. You've forged your own paths as individuals and you'll forge your own path as a couple. Of course, if you feel Leo isn't actually the right man for you . . .'

'He *is* the right man for me! It's whether I'm the right woman for him that's the issue.'

'Have faith, Kate. Faith in Leo and faith in yourself. Shall we fix that date?'

'Now?' She'd come only to talk. Not to make actual plans.

'You love him, don't you?' Adam asked. 'You want to marry him?'

'Yes, but . . .'

'Faith, Kate. Besides, fixing a date will concentrate your mind. Help you to realize what it is you really want.'

Adam made it sound as though a revelation would strike her, signalling the best way forward clearly and free from lingering doubt. Kate wasn't entirely convinced but she was desperate. 'If you're sure . . .'

He asked various questions about full names, ages and so on, and wrote the answers down. And the date was duly fixed. Saturday 28 February, provided it suited Leo and his parents. Less than two weeks away.

'Congratulations,' Adam said.

Kate was too stunned to answer. No revelation had struck her yet, but perhaps she needed to calm her muddled mind to make space for it.

Leaving the vicarage, she saw Naomi over by the shops

talking to Marjorie. Unable to face Marjorie's beady eyes and questions, Kate turned away, but no sooner had she got on her bike than Naomi came across.

'Don't worry. Marjorie didn't see you,' Naomi said, when Kate glanced around warily. 'You needn't fear your private business will be all over Churchwood by morning. Since you're not a regular churchgoer, do I take it you've been calling on Adam to arrange your wedding?'

'We . . . er . . . talked about it,' Kate admitted.

'Did you fix a date?'

Oh, heck. Kate hadn't planned to mention the date to anyone yet since there was every chance the wedding wouldn't actually take place. She'd wanted time for the revelation to strike first. But Naomi deserved better than a lie. 'Adam suggested 28 February but it's only provisional. It might not—'

'That's wonderful! You and Leo are perfect for each other and I wish you every happiness. If it helps, Leo and his parents can stay with me. I can host the reception at Foxfield, too.'

'You have a houseful of people already!'

'It'll take some working out, but I'm sure we can come up with something. I imagine Alice has offered The Linnets but Foxfield is larger. No pressure to decide now, though. Just let me know what you'd like me to do. I may have misjudged you when you were growing up, Kate, but I couldn't be fonder of you now. I'm delighted that you've so much happiness ahead of you.'

Ah, but had she? Had Leo?

'What are you going to wear?'

'I don't know. I thought I'd speak with May and see if she has any ideas.' Not yet, though. Only if she decided the wedding should go ahead.

'There's May over there.' Naomi waved and May came

to join them. 'Kate needs help with a wedding dress,' Naomi said.

'Not now,' Kate said hastily, feeling ambushed and more panicked than ever. 'Another time. Perhaps.'

'Nonsense,' Naomi told her. 'You need to act fast if you're getting married on the twenty-eighth of February.'

'Goodness, yes,' May agreed. 'A wedding dress is a challenge in wartime – obviously – but leave it with me, Kate. I won't let you down.'

'It's only a provisional date. It might not be convenient for Leo,' Kate argued.

'It's still best to get started even if the wedding gets delayed for a week or two,' May insisted.

Oh, heavens. Kate really did need to make a decision soon. The thought of becoming Leo's wife in less than two weeks was exciting. But it was also frightening when the voice of her conscience kept hissing, *Selfish, selfish, selfish* . . .

CHAPTER FORTY-THREE

Alice

'I'm going away for a day or two,' Alice told her father.

'Oh?'

'To Hove.'

'Feeling a need for sea air? In February?'

'I'm sure the breeze coming off the Channel will be perishing, so I'll wrap up warmly. I just want to see what I can learn about Gloria Gumble and her son.'

'My darling girl, I wish you wouldn't,' he told her, frowning. 'If this woman isn't who she says she is, your questions might get you into trouble with a nasty set of people.'

'I won't take any chances.'

'Perhaps I should come with you.'

Alice kissed his cheek. 'There's no need for that, but thank you.'

'Take care,' he warned.

She had another task to complete before she travelled. Returning to the kitchen, she read through the story that had now been typed out in full. Was it any good? Finding it impossible to judge her own writing, Alice could only hope so.

She slotted a sheet of paper into the typewriter and addressed a letter to the editor of *Tales of Adventure* magazine. But then she paused. Was there a form of wording that authors used when addressing editors? Not liking to come across as an amateur but seeing no help for it, she wrote simply.

Dear Sir,
I am an admirer of *Tales of Adventure* and often read the stories out loud to the patients at the military hospital where I volunteer. Based on my understanding of the sort of story the patients enjoy, I have written a story of my own and enclose it in the hope that you will think well enough of it to publish it.

Unable to think of anything else to say, she finished the letter with standard words about looking forward to a reply and signed her name.

She addressed an envelope, too, and added a stamp. Then she sealed the story and letter inside and headed for the pillar box in the village to post it.

Alice travelled to Hove by bus and train the following morning, after checking that Gloria was still busying herself painting Joe's house. The sea air was more than bracing. It was bitter. But she sank her neck into her scarf and went in search of somewhere to stay, settling on a tall, narrow house that offered bed and breakfast at modest rates. 'We don't have much call for rooms at this time of year,' the landlady told her, and Alice guessed that the few shillings she was paying were welcome.

'I'm afraid I can't stretch to a fire in your room,' Mrs Roberts continued, 'but I can provide a hot-water bottle for your bed and there's a fire in the parlour downstairs.'

'I don't have a fire in my room at home,' Alice reassured her, though this house was much bigger than the cottage, where heat from the fire took the chill off all the rooms. Alice could tough it out for a night or two.

The important thing was to save money, since she still had no income apart from her share of Daniel's service pay. She'd brought a notebook and pen with her in the hope of beginning another story later, though whether it would be good enough for publication remained to be seen.

She went first to what was Maurice's address, according to the will. Probably, it was Gloria's address too. Much of Hove was beautiful but the terraces of Fuller Street were shabby. Aiming to be discreet, she glanced at number fifteen but continued walking. It looked to be the sort of house that was divided into rooms or small apartments let out at budget prices. The paintwork on the door and window frames was a dull, flaking brown.

Reaching the end of the street, Alice was turning to walk back when a woman emerged from the nearest house. 'Excuse me,' Alice said. 'I'm sorry to trouble you, but I was hoping to look up a friend, only I've forgotten her house number. Her name is Gloria Gumble.'

'Oh?'

'I used to work with her,' Alice said.

'At the cafe?'

'That's right.'

'She lives in the house with the broken step just along there. I don't know the number.'

'Thank you.'

Alice set off towards it, slowing her steps when the woman began walking in the same direction. 'Are you a friend of Gloria's too?' Alice asked.

'We're not friends. I just know of her.' The woman spoke as though many people probably knew of Gloria and not because she was popular.

There wasn't time to ask more because they'd almost reached number fifteen. The woman would surely think it odd if Alice didn't knock on the door, but Alice wasn't ready to do that. Faking a sneeze, she came to a halt and fished in her bag for a handkerchief. By the time she'd found one, the woman had rounded the corner and moved out of sight.

Alice blew her nose to give herself thinking time. With Gloria and Maurice in Churchwood, it was probably safe enough to knock on their door and speak to a neighbour. If nothing else, Alice might learn more about the cafe where Gloria worked. There had to be numerous cafes in a seaside town like Hove and it could take hours to find the right one.

She realized someone was watching her through the window. Perhaps this grey-haired woman was Hove's equivalent of Marjorie Plym. A gossip. Waving, Alice walked up to the door and knocked. Moments later the woman opened it.

'I'm hoping to see Gloria,' Alice said.

'I'm afraid you're wasting your time. She isn't here.'

Alice feigned disappointment. 'Will she be back later, do you know?'

'All I know is that I saw her and that son of hers go off a few days ago and they haven't come back yet.'

Clearly, it would suit this woman if they never returned. 'You're not friends?' Alice asked.

The woman hesitated and Alice guessed she was afraid of word getting back to Gloria that bad things had been said about her. Gloria wouldn't respond to criticism by turning the other cheek. She'd wade into a row like a galleon in full sail. 'I'm not Gloria's friend either,' Alice said. 'I'm only here to pass on a message from a mutual acquaintance.'

'I thought you looked too wholesome to be in Gloria's circle. I can't say as I've warmed to Gloria. She's loud. Aggressive, you might say.'

'Her son isn't like that, though. Or so I've heard. I believe he's the harmless type.'

'He's certainly the brainless type. He must be close to thirty but seems happy to live in his mother's shadow.'

'Does he hold down a job?'

'Hardly! I think his mother bullies people into giving him jobs like sweeping up or washing pots, but he never lasts long, as far as I can tell. He's too . . .'

'Brainless?'

'No gumption, that boy.'

'Thanks for the chat,' Alice said. 'I might call in at Gloria's workplace to ask when she's expected back there. I know she works in a cafe but the name has slipped my mind.'

'It's the Bridge Tea Rooms on Bridge Street.'

Alice suspected this woman made sure to take her tea elsewhere.

'Thank you.' Alice went on her way, thinking about what she'd learned. Clearly, Gloria and her son weren't much liked, but it was a big jump from being disliked to forging a will.

Locating the tea rooms, Alice went inside and ordered tea and a bun. 'Gloria isn't working today?' she asked her smiling waitress.

The smile lost some of its sparkle. 'Not today.'

'Might she be working tomorrow?'

The waitress shrugged. 'Maybe.'

Alice decided on the same approach she'd tried on the neighbour. 'I'm not Gloria's friend. I just have a message for her from a mutual acquaintance.'

Some of the wariness left the waitress's face. 'I heard her telling the boss she had bigger fish to fry than him and he'd be hearing more about it soon. I haven't seen her since.'

'She gets along with the boss?'

'Hardly.'

'He's afraid of her?'

'Yes, but he wouldn't like anyone saying so.'

'Has Maurice ever worked here?'

'Him! The boss gave him a job in the kitchen but he was useless. That's when I heard Gloria telling the boss she had bigger fish to fry. She said something about it not mattering if Maurice broke plates because he was a goose that was going to lay golden eggs. I've no idea what that meant.'

Alice suspected that the golden eggs were Joe Simpson's house and money. 'Did Gloria have any friends here?'

'I can't imagine Gloria having friends anywhere.'

The door opened and more customers entered. With a parting smile at Alice, the waitress went to attend to them.

Alice paid her bill, slid a sixpence under the saucer for the waitress and went on her way. She'd still learned nothing that pointed to actual dishonesty on Gloria's part, but Alice hoped for better luck in the morning when she investigated the men who'd signed their names as witnesses to Joe's will.

The wind suddenly whipped her scarf into her face. A storm was forecast for the evening and it seemed to be getting under way already. As the rain started, Alice ran back to Mrs Roberts's guest house, reaching it just as the rain gathered strength and began to pummel the pavements.

CHAPTER FORTY-FOUR

Naomi

Grey clouds were darkening the afternoon as Naomi hastened home from the shops. She let herself into the house and heard Victoria's voice in the drawing room. 'Not again, Arthur!'

What had happened this time?

Naomi went to find out. 'I'm afraid there's been more trouble,' Victoria told her, looking vexed and embarrassed.

'I didn't mean to cause trouble,' Arthur said, but he never did.

'Just tell us what happened,' Naomi encouraged.

'We were out in the street and Flower saw a bird's nest in a tree. It was an empty bird's nest from last spring, so I didn't think it would do any harm to let her have it.'

'But you had to climb the tree to reach it?' Naomi guessed.

'I climbed up on a wall so I could reach the branches and pulled myself up from there. I got the nest and dropped it down to Flower but then I slipped and . . . Well, I landed on the wall but then fell off the other side.'

'Into someone's garden?'

'It belonged to an old man. Mr Atkinson. He rushed out of his house, shouting because I'd broken one of his flowerpots and squashed the plant that lived in it. I told him I was sorry. I *am* sorry. But he said I was a bad 'un who was nothing but trouble. Mr Miles from the grocer's walked past – he was delivering shopping – and he shook his head at me too. I really am sorry.'

'All right, Arthur. Off you go,' Naomi told him. 'I'll speak to Mr Atkinson in the morning and try to calm him down.'

'Will you have to pay for the broken pot? The squashed plant, too?'

'I'll certainly offer.'

Arthur nodded regretfully. 'I wish I could pay for them.'

'Just stay out of trouble,' Naomi advised him. Not that he went looking for it.

Victoria waited for him to walk away before saying, 'I'll pay for the damage. I know I keep repeating it, and circumstances keep trying to prove me wrong, but Arthur really is a nice boy. I sincerely regret that we're making things awkward with your neighbours, Mrs Harrington. It must be difficult for you to know people are talking about the children – Arthur especially – and not in pleasant terms.'

Naomi had indeed heard the children called rough and ill-mannered, with Arthur even being called a bad lot. Naomi had waded into the conversation on his behalf but doubted she'd convinced anyone that a series of unfortunate incidents didn't make a child a bad lot.

'Things will settle down,' Naomi said, but the words were beginning to sound hollow.

She changed the subject. 'The storm is blowing up from the south. I suggest Ivy and Flower leave for Edna's sooner rather than later so they don't get caught up in it.'

'I'll tell them.'

Naomi went into her sitting room but heard Ivy and Flower getting ready in the hall. Arthur must have come to bid his little friend goodbye because his voice joined theirs. 'Wrap up warmly, Flower. It's windy out there,' he said.

'I'm sorry you got into trouble over my bird's nest, Arthur.'

'I should have been more careful.'

'I love you, Arthur.'

There came the sound of movement. Probably a hug. She went out to the hall so she too could say goodbye. Ivy and Flower duly left and Arthur slunk away with dejection like a weight on his shoulders.

Within minutes the rain began lashing down. It kept up for a full hour. Two hours. 'Awful night,' Naomi commented as she drew up a shopping list with Victoria. Feeding so many mouths took careful planning.

A knock sounded on the front door. 'Who's out in this weather?' Naomi wondered.

'I'll find out.' Victoria got up and went into the hall. Moments later, she reappeared, looking puzzled. 'There's a half-drowned boy at the door,' she reported.

'A half-drowned . . .?'

'He says his name is—'

'William,' Naomi guessed, heaving herself to her feet and rushing into the hall. What had brought him here this time?

He was drenched and his teeth were chattering with cold. 'Come in,' Naomi urged.

He stepped into the hall and stood dripping. 'Off with that coat,' Naomi said, but his fingers were purple from the cold and he couldn't unfasten the buttons.

Naomi unfastened them for him, relieved when Victoria reappeared with towels for William and a mop for drying the floor.

'I'm sorry to be a nuisance, but I couldn't bear it,' William said.

What couldn't he bear? The time for talking was later, though. Right now, William needed warmth. She helped him out of his shoes and socks then led him upstairs and ran him a bath. 'There are clothes—' He broke off, shivering so violently that he could barely speak. 'In – in my bag.'

Naomi investigated while he bathed. There were indeed clothes, though they were damp and badly creased. She pulled some out and aired them, then called to William that they were outside the bathroom door and she'd see him downstairs.

It was just like the first time he'd come to Foxfield, but what had happened in the interim?

She waited in the sitting room to find out.

William looked awkward when he shuffled in to join her. 'I didn't realize there would be people here,' he said, doubtless having heard the children chattering. 'I'm in the way. Sorry.'

'Never mind that. Tell me what's been going on in your life. If you're able?'

He nodded, but just then Victoria arrived with tea and soup for him. Naomi made the introductions. 'This is William, a young friend of mine. William, this is Victoria, my new cook-housekeeper.'

Both said, 'Pleased to meet you.' Then, being kind and tactful, Victoria left them to talk.

Naomi gestured towards the tea and soup. 'Tuck in.'

William ate and drank like a starving man but looked better for having something warm inside him. Not that his eyes lost any of their misery.

'I tried to follow your advice,' he finally said. 'I tried to talk to my father calmly about how I felt and how I didn't want a high-flying career. He didn't shout at first. He just simmered as though he might explode at any moment. Then he heard me telling Mother how much I'd enjoyed working in Bert's market garden and how I'd like to do it as a job.'

'That's when your father exploded?'

'He shouted louder than ever. He told me I shouldn't dare to mention Bert's name or your name ever again and that I should forget the idea of being some sort of poverty-stricken farmer because it was no job for a gentleman. He said I was a spineless, snivelling embarrassment for even thinking of it. Ungrateful, too, considering the education I was being given at vast expense.'

Clearly, the words had hurt.

'My mother tried to say I was young and I'd grow out of it, but my father snapped at her and made her cry. She can never stand up to him. My sister hid in her room but afterwards she was angry with me for causing another row. The next morning my father put me on the train for school, telling me I should knuckle down like a man and that there'd be serious trouble if I dared to run away again. As soon as I got there, the headmaster called me to his study to say my father had telephoned to insist I should be kept on a tight leash.'

'The headmaster wasn't sympathetic?'

'He said that not only had I let my family down, but the school too, because Carstairs boys had backbones and went on to fulfil important positions in the world. He warned me he was going to make sure I grew a backbone and didn't disgrace the school.'

Oh dear.

'I tried to work hard. Really, I did. But the headmaster must have spoken to the other masters because almost all of them insisted I should sit at the front of their classes so they could keep an eye on me. They picked on me to answer questions, too. Constantly picked on me, I mean. The music teacher was nicer but had to watch his step since he was new, so he was only kind when no one else was looking.'

'Did anything in particular happen to make you run away again?'

'I suppose it was the headmaster telling me he was writing a report to my father every week. It made me feel like a prisoner and something inside me just snapped.'

They sat in thoughtful silence for a moment then William said, 'I shouldn't have come here but I didn't have anywhere else to go. Besides, you and Bert are the only people I've ever seen stand up to my father. You made me realize it could be done.'

Oh, good grief. She hadn't meant to turn him into a rebel, exactly.

'I don't want to be a burden to you, though,' William continued. 'I want to find a job and earn my own living. Do you know of a farmer who might take me on and let me sleep in his barn? I don't mind what I do. I just want to make a start on being independent.'

'William, I hate to pour scorn on your wishes, but you're still a minor and your father has rights over you.'

'He can keep dragging me back to school but I can keep running away. He won't like that and neither will the school. They'll wash their hands of me.'

'If you abandon your education now, you might never have a chance to resume it,' Naomi pointed out. 'Isn't it worth sticking with it for just a little while longer to give yourself more choice over your future? It would be terrible if you let a hasty decision now cause long-term regret.'

'I wouldn't mind a different school. A day school, perhaps. But if that isn't possible, I'd rather work. My father called me spineless but that isn't actually true. I do have a backbone and I'm willing to work hard to make my way in the world. I'll even study at a night school or teach myself from books if that's what it takes to get on in the way I want.'

He looked as thin and awkward as ever – not quite in control of his lanky limbs – but a glow in his eyes revealed that he'd grown up since his last visit and had indeed found his courage.

'Have you talked to him about another school?'

'I tried. I even wrote a letter explaining how I felt. It was easier to put my reasons into a letter.'

Because William could express himself in writing without being reduced to a shaking wreck by his father's shouts.

'He wouldn't even think about a different school?'

'Of course not.'

Naomi tried a different approach. 'What about your mother and sister? Won't you miss them if you leave home?'

'I don't see much of them anyway when I'm at boarding school. I'll miss not being around them in the holidays, but I'll still meet them as much as I can.'

'What if your father forbids it?'

Clearly, the possibility had already crossed his mind, because a ripple of distress worked over his face. But he took a deep breath and straightened the backbone his father doubted existed. 'If he does . . . Well, I hope my mother and sister will see me anyway, even if it needs to be in secret.'

'Your father might never forgive you,' Naomi pointed out.

'That will mean he doesn't love me, so it won't be much of a loss.'

It appeared that he'd thought through everything – apart from the possibility of her already having visitors. 'I don't wish to be an inconvenience, but would it be all right if I stayed here tonight?' he asked. 'I can curl up in a corner so I don't get in the way.'

'Of course you can stay. We'll manage somehow.' Naomi was doing a lot of managing somehow these days.

She told him about Victoria and the London families. 'Gosh,' he said. 'The way you've taken all those people in . . . You couldn't be further from my father's description of you than . . . well, the Angel Gabriel from Jack the Ripper.'

Naomi smiled at that. 'If you're game for it, why don't I take you through and introduce you to your fellow visitors?'

'They won't think I'm intruding?'

'On the contrary, I suspect they're going to enjoy meeting a new face. Be warned, though. They're not from the best part of London. They're a little rough in their speech and in their ways. But they have hearts of gold.'

'I'm not like my father,' William said. 'He wouldn't know a heart of gold if he fell over it.'

All eyes turned towards William as they entered the drawing room. 'Who's that boy, Ma?' Davie asked loudly.

'We're going to find out, aren't we?'

Naomi introduced William as a friend who might be staying for a while. Thinking it would do him good to get to know the Londoners by himself, she returned to the sitting room where she telephoned Bert. 'You'll never guess what just happened.'

'Does it involve more waifs and strays?'

'It does.'

'William?' he hazarded.

She filled him in on the latest developments. 'He seems determined to break off with his school this time. With his father, too.'

'You must be getting crowded over there,' Bert said.

'Would it help if William stayed here? I haven't had anyone stay the night in years, so I'm out of practice as a host and this place is hardly a smart hotel, but he's welcome. I shan't be offended if he'd prefer to stay at Foxfield, though.'

'I'll keep him here tonight, but thank you,' she told him. 'He's meeting the others at the moment.'

'Just give me a ring if you need anything. Good luck!'

'You're a wonderful man, Bert Makepiece.'

'You're a wonderful woman.'

She wondered if Alexander would ring that evening. When the phone stayed silent, she suspected he'd heard from the school that William had bolted again but was hoping the boy would be making his way home. It would humiliate him to have William run to Naomi again and he'd spare himself the mortification of having to call her for as long as possible.

Should she call him? Probably. But she decided to give them one night of peace first.

CHAPTER FORTY-FIVE

Naomi

Naomi never got the chance to ring Alexander because he telephoned her early in the morning. 'Is he there?' he snarled.

'I'm glad you've called, Alexander. You've saved me from having to get in touch.'

'He *is* there! How dare you entice my son away? You're interfering with my parental rights, and all because you're a bitter, petty woman.'

'William is well, if you're interested?'

'I don't need your advice about my son.'

'No? If you're such a good father, isn't it odd that William should have run away from school and come here? Twice?'

'He's being weak. And you're encouraging him.'

'Nonsense. Do you want to come and talk to him or are you washing your hands of him?'

'He's my son, not yours!'

'Indeed. That doesn't answer my question. I have an idea for a compromise, if you're willing to hear it.'

'Keep out of my private business, Naomi.'

'I didn't choose to be *in* it. But your son has turned up on my doorstep and asked for my help.'

Naomi caught the sound of distant sobbing. William's mother? The suspicion was confirmed when she heard Alexander snap, 'Oh, do be quiet, Amelia. You know I can't abide tears. You too, Emily. William is perfectly all right. He's just making a nuisance of himself.'

'Do you want to hear about the compromise or not?' Naomi asked. 'You'll need to come here if you do. There's a perfectly efficient train and bus service if you haven't the use of a car.'

'Expect me soon, but be warned. That boy is trying my patience to its limits.'

'Goodbye, Alexander.'

'If you're wondering why I'm here, it's because Naomi is more than just my friend,' Bert told William. 'I'm going to marry her and I won't have the icicle bullying her.'

'The icicle is my father?'

'Sorry. Is that—'

'No, it's fine. It suits him.' William grinned as though trying the name on for size. 'Actually, I guessed that you were more than friends, but I won't tell the *icicle*. He'll be spiteful about it.'

Wise boy.

Alexander arrived in a different car from last time but brought the same sort of scowl.

'You're a disgrace!' he snapped when he entered the sitting room and saw William.

'Shall we all sit down?' Naomi suggested.

Alexander sent her a scathing look but sat on an armchair while Naomi settled beside William on a sofa and Bert took another chair. 'Much more civilized,' Bert declared.

Alexander sent him a scathing look, too, and then pointed a finger at his son. 'You should be heartily ashamed of the trouble you're causing.'

Would William crumple again in the face of his father's anger? Not this time. He raised his chin and said, 'I told you I was unhappy, but you wouldn't listen.'

'What has happiness to do with anything? You're at school to gain an education that will hold you in good stead for the rest of your life.'

'It's the wrong sort of education for me,' William said.

Alexander sneered. 'You want a better one, do you? Eton College? Harrow? I'm already paying a fortune in fees.'

'I don't want a more expensive education. I want a different one. I want to learn about working on the land.'

'No son of mine is becoming a *labourer*!' Alexander was apoplectic.

'I want to earn an honest living doing something I enjoy. I'm seventeen. Lots of people leave school and start working at fourteen.'

'Failures do that, you fool. Not people like us.'

'But I'm not like you,' William pointed out. 'I've spent my life trying to please you but I can't keep pretending to be someone I'm not.'

'You may think you're grown up but you're just a boy. And I'm not going to let you throw your future away.'

'It's *my* future!' William said, voice rising.

Naomi judged it time to try to pour calming oil on troubled waters. 'Why don't you both consider a compromise?' She turned to William. 'Your father thinks you should continue your education until you're eighteen, and I agree.'

William looked betrayed.

'But it's obvious that your current school is unsuitable,' Naomi continued, and William unbent a little. 'What I suggest is not only a different school but a different arrangement, so that you board during the week but are allowed to leave school at weekends.'

'To go home? Is that what you mean? But I can't learn horticulture at home. I want to stay here in Churchwood. I'll work to pay my way.'

'You could spend some weekends here. Part of your holidays too, perhaps. This way you could discover if working on the land is really what you want, but finish your education too.'

Resistance played across William's face but was followed by acceptance of an arrangement that was sensible even if it wasn't perfect. His gaze slid towards Alexander.

'This is ludicrous,' Alexander said. 'Can't you see what she's doing?' He flapped a contemptuous hand in Naomi's direction. 'She's trying to take you over to spite me.'

'Naomi isn't like that,' William argued. 'She's a good person. So is Bert. They want to help me, not control me.'

Alexander made a scoffing sound.

'What's the alternative?' Naomi asked.

'I'm not going back to that school.' William was forceful now. 'If you drag me back, I'll run away again. They can't keep me locked up for ever. They might not even want me back. A boy running away can't reflect well on them.'

'How dare you threaten me?' Alexander roared.

William winced but kept his chin raised. 'I don't mean to threaten. I just want you to listen. To understand.'

Alexander's lip curled. 'This is all the stuff of fantasies, anyway. You don't really think a good school will take you on a part-time basis?'

William's face fell and for a moment Alexander gloated with triumph.

'Actually, there is such a school,' Naomi said. 'It's called Hammondswick and it isn't far from St Albans. William could catch the train from there for his weekends at home and he could catch the bus for his weekends here.'

Alexander fought back. 'It can't be a good school.'

It was satisfying to have the power to knock some of the smug arrogance from his face. 'Its reputation is excellent,' Naomi told him. 'The boys do well in life. Most boys board full-time, but William wouldn't be the only one who left at weekends. Not that he'd be obliged to leave. On the contrary, the school would be happy for him to board any weekend he chose if he wished to take part in a particular activity or simply preferred to stay.'

William brightened, but Alexander got up, clearly angry that Naomi had proved him to be in the wrong. 'Do as you like, William. You've turned out to be tiresome and ungrateful. I've no more time to waste talking nonsense with you.'

Rapid strides took him into the hall, Naomi following at a calmer pace. 'I'll ask the school to get in touch with you,' she said.

He pointed a finger in her face. 'I blame you for all of this.'

'Of course you do. It's because you never bothered to get to know me, and you're blind to your own faults.'

'Spiteful and vindictive, that's you.'

'So you've said before. You're being tedious, repeating it.'

Cursing again, he opened the front door, went out and slammed it hard behind him. Gravel flew into the air as he drove away.

Naomi returned to the sitting room where William was on his feet and waiting. 'Thank you!' he said, wrapping his spider-like arms around her in an awkward hug.

Naomi hugged him in return, delighting in his affection. But then she drew back and said, 'Sit down, William.'

The boy obeyed her.

'I don't want you to think that you needn't put effort into your schoolwork from now on. A good education is a privilege and Hammondswick will cost your father a considerable amount of money. Many children aren't nearly so lucky. Just look at the children here. Arthur,

Jenny, Lewis . . . They'll receive whatever education the local school can offer. I'm not saying it'll be bad, but it won't offer the advantages you'll enjoy with a private education.'

'I'll do my best,' William promised.

'I don't mean this as an insult, but you're still very young with little experience of either the world of work or of being financially independent and making your own way through life. You may find that you always want to work on the land. But you may change your mind. Even people as old as me can change their mind about a lot of things.'

'I understand.'

'Good. I suggest you telephone your mother to inform her of developments and write to your sister, too. I hope you'll stay in touch with them and also try to repair your relationship with your father.'

'It takes two to repair a relationship,' William said.

'But not necessarily the same amount of effort on both sides. Sometimes we need to do more than our fair share of repairing. If not for your own sake, think how uncomfortable it's going to be for your mother and sister if you and your father are at daggers drawn every time you go home.'

William grinned. 'Point taken. I'll try to be a better person than him. More generous. More forgiving.'

'That sort of attitude can take you far,' Naomi approved. 'Now, you've thrown your lot in with us at Foxfield and that means there's little time for idleness. I suggest you go and make yourself useful, either here or at Bert's.'

'I'll be glad to,' he said, getting up again with hopefulness and happiness energizing his lanky frame.

Naomi wasn't naive enough to think that the fighting with Alexander was at an end. He'd called her spiteful and vindictive because those flaws were close to the surface in his own personality. If he could hit back at her in the divorce or over William, he'd do so and gain malicious satisfaction from it. Naomi would have to hope she was ready for him.

In the meantime, she had domestic headaches to resolve. The first involved finding a bed for William. He'd fallen asleep curled up on a sofa last night and, not liking to disturb him, she'd simply covered him with an eiderdown. But he needed a proper bed tonight. The second headache involved feeding him, since who knew when his ration book might turn up?

CHAPTER FORTY-SIX

Alice

Alice had taken the train from Hove to Brighton after spending a chilly night in the unfamiliar bed of Mrs Roberts's guest house. At least the storm had blown itself out, leaving the day cold but fresh.

Only a few months earlier, Alice had spent her honeymoon here. It was tempting to revisit the scenes of that happy time – the hotels where she and Daniel had taken tea, the pavilion, the seafront . . . But she was here on business and treading in those happy footprints would have to wait.

Charles Pitney, the first witness to Joe's will, lived in another dilapidated terrace in another run-down street not far from the station. It was two doors down from the Sailor's Rigging pub. Noah Hurst, the second witness, lived in similar accommodation just around the corner. Studying her street map, Alice wondered if the Sailor's Rigging might be the common denominator between the two men and perhaps also the connection to Gloria.

Alice had never visited a pub on her own before. She'd rarely visited pubs, even in company. It was a particularly daunting prospect now because the Sailor's Rigging looked rough from the outside.

And so it proved to be on the inside. Alice stepped into a dark space that smelled of stale beer and was fuggy with cigarette smoke. Conversations suddenly stopped and Alice felt that every gaze in the bar turned to her with a curiosity that bordered on rudeness. Women weren't welcome here, she guessed.

She walked up to the bar, where a man was wiping a glass with a limp and none-too-clean tea towel. 'You'll be better off in the saloon, miss,' he said.

Alice didn't understand.

'This is the public bar. The saloon bar is on that side.' He nodded towards a door.

Alice didn't know the difference but assumed that the saloon bar must be more respectable. 'I'm looking for Gloria,' she said. 'Gloria Gumble?'

'Gloria hasn't worked here for months.'

So Gloria was indeed connected to the pub. Alice felt a burst of triumph but hid it behind a slump of fake disappointment. 'You don't know where she's working now?'

'No idea. Moves on a lot, does Gloria.'

Upsetting people along the way, Alice guessed. 'What about Maurice?' she asked. 'Gloria's son.'

The barman's expression said, *That idiot!* but he simply shook his head. 'Haven't heard from either of them in a while.'

Alice took a chance and said, 'What about Charles Pitney?'

'He moved on, too. Did a flit in the night, I heard. Owed money.'

'Noah Hurst?'

'Died a week or two back. Got into a fight after cheating at cards and collapsed in the middle of it. A stroke, I heard. Not having much luck, are you, miss?'

'I don't suppose you know of a Joe Simpson?'

'There's a Joe Henderson who comes in here sometimes, when his wife lets him out of the house. But Joe Simpson? I can't say he's *never* been a customer, but he isn't one of our regulars and hasn't been for the ten years I've worked here.'

'I see. Thank you.'

Alice left the pub and walked down to the seafront to think, looking out across the English Channel towards France, only a few miles away but under German occupation. Sometimes it was hard to suppress panic at the thought of an invasion and the terrible way of life it would bring. Even young children like May's Rosa, Samuel and Zofia might be snatched away and sent who knew where, with who knew what consequences, merely because they were Jewish.

But Alice could do nothing about the war. She could only focus her energy on the problems that were closer to home: Gloria and Maurice Gumble. She'd learned some useful information on this visit – that Gloria could well be the sort of woman who'd forge a will and that she shared common ground with the witnesses in the form of the Sailor's Rigging. But where was the proof of a conspiracy? Of a forgery? There was none. Not yet.

Frustratingly, a niggle had begun nudging the back of her mind. It was suggesting she might be missing something important but she couldn't work out what it might be. With luck, it would come to her. Meanwhile, Alice could see no benefit to remaining in Brighton. Turning, she set off for the train station, pausing to buy a picture postcard of the pier to send to Daniel as a reminder of the happy times they'd spent here.

'Any luck?' her father asked when Alice reached home.

She told him what she'd learned.

'It certainly sounds suspicious, but do keep an open mind, my dear,' he urged. 'Suspicions can be unfounded.'

Wise words, and Alice was keen to heed them. For all she knew, there might be a decent person beneath Gloria's brash exterior, a woman who deserved a chance to settle into village life. But Alice's instincts were telling her otherwise and she wanted to leave no stone unturned before she abandoned the idea that the woman was a fraud. It was the thorny issue of proving it that taxed Alice's mind.

CHAPTER FORTY-SEVEN

Kate

With both Naomi and May aware of the date fixed for the wedding, any chance of keeping it quiet until Kate decided the best way forward had shrivelled to nothing. She'd felt obliged to tell others, too, not least Leo. She'd hoped the date would be inconvenient for him so she could gain more thinking time, but it wasn't to be.

> *My parents will be delighted to stay with Naomi for the wedding,* Leo had written, *just as I'll be delighted to accept Alice's offer of a bed at The Linnets, though I only need it for the night before the wedding. Afterwards, I'll be whisking you off on honeymoon. It's only going to be a few nights on the south coast but it'll be perfect because we'll be together. I can take you to Paris or somewhere similarly glamorous when peace comes, as surely it must eventually.*
>
> *If you're even half as excited about the wedding as I am, that's very excited indeed. I'm counting the days . . .*

Kate doubted that Leo's parents were delighted about any aspect of the wedding. Probably, they were simply bowing to the inevitable.

> *Everyone in Churchwood is being kind, it seems, with so many people contributing ingredients to the cake Janet is making and May helping you with your dress.*

Churchwood was being generous because Churchwood wished her well, but, oh dear, how Kate's nerves were slipping and sliding inside her!

Far from clarifying matters, fixing the date had only stirred up her panic and Kate was as confused as ever. Worse, in fact, as each passing day increased the awkwardness of any break-up and added to Leo's likely pain.

She'd received the letter that morning and thought of little else ever since. She'd even come out to work specifically to be alone with her thoughts, first in Five Acre Field and now in the kitchen garden. Not that it was helping. Nothing was helping. Why, oh why, couldn't she reach a decision?

Knowing Ruby would be making tea, Kate heaved her spade from the earth and headed indoors. She was the first to arrive and, after washing her hands, she helped Ruby to put teacups on the table. The situation between Ruby and Kenny was unchanged as far as Kate could see. But at least Kate had tried to—

She became aware that Ruby was staring at her. 'What is it?'

'Probably nothing, but is your necklace tucked under your shirt?'

'Yes, it's . . .' A cold chill swept over Kate as the hand she'd raised to her throat found no chain there – and therefore no ring, either.

Panicking, she looked inside her shirt and patted her waist in case they'd slipped down, but once again . . . nothing.

'Maybe you forgot to put the necklace on this morning,' Ruby suggested.

'I'm sure I didn't forget.' Kate kissed the ring every morning. But might she have forgotten just this once? It wasn't as though she was thinking clearly just now.

She raced upstairs, hoping to see the precious jewellery

on the cupboard by her bed. It wasn't there. But perhaps it was elsewhere in her room, having fallen off because she hadn't fully secured the clasp. She looked on top of her bed, under the covers and pillows, and then got down on the shabby linoleum to search under the bed. She even tugged the cupboard away from the wall to look behind it. Nothing.

Kate's heart beat faster and her mouth dried.

'Any luck?' Ruby asked from the open door.

'Not yet.'

They looked along the landing, down the stairs and in the small hall at the bottom of them. Still nothing. The kitchen was next. They searched the floor, chairs, table, dresser, cupboards, sink, stove and even the baskets holding potatoes and other vegetables . . . All in vain.

'Fred's room?' Ruby said.

Kate gave his door a curt knock and then stepped inside. 'Oi!' he protested, but Kate was in no mood for sensitivities.

'Have you seen my ring?'

'What ring?' Understanding dawned quickly. 'Not *that* ring?'

'Yes, *that* ring.'

'Oh, heck.' They looked around his room, drawing a blank yet again.

'Let's retrace your steps,' Ruby suggested. 'Obviously, you've been out in the farmyard, so let's start there.'

They peered into every nook and cranny without success. Kate began to feel sick. 'Did you go to the chickens?' Ruby asked.

'Timmy saw to the chickens this morning.'

'But you helped me with the laundry.'

They headed for the outhouse where the mangle was kept, but once again the search proved fruitless.

'Barn?' Ruby said then.

Between Kate, Ruby and Fred, they looked behind tools, under hay bales, on the cart . . . Nothing.

'Where else have you been?' Fred asked.

'The kitchen garden.'

They made a painstaking effort to search under each plant, but in vain. Of course, it was possible that the jewellery had been trodden into the mud or slipped down between leaves, but no one voiced the possibility out loud, probably because it would overwhelm them with hopelessness.

'Anywhere else?' Ruby asked.

'Five Acre Field.'

Kate saw the dread on the faces of both Ruby and Fred. The prospect of finding something small in such a vast space filled with soil, crops, grasses and bushes was daunting, but they tried it anyway.

Only Ernie – bad-tempered as ever – did farm work that afternoon. Everyone else walked up and down Five Acre Field with their gazes cast down at the earth and swinging from side to side as they searched.

'Mind those crops!' Ernie yelled as Vinnie tripped into some cabbages.

There was a moment of excitement – of hope – when Ruby caught sight of a metallic glint, but it was just a bolt from a broken tool. Kate herself discovered an old penny with Queen Victoria's head stamped on the back but otherwise they only found stones. Before long, it began to rain, making Kate despairingly aware that every step might drive the missing objects deeper into the soupy earth.

'You should go inside,' she finally told the others.

No one was prepared to abandon the search quite yet, but gradually, with the light fading from the grey, rainy day, even Kate had to admit defeat and give up until the morning.

'The ring may still turn up in the house,' Ruby suggested comfortingly.

'Or you might come out tomorrow and find the chain dangling from a tree branch you passed earlier, and the ring hanging with it,' Pearl said.

Kate struggled to believe in anything so convenient. More likely the beautiful ring was sinking into the earth of Five Acre Field. Perhaps the tractor might unearth it one day, or maybe it would lie undisturbed for centuries before being discovered as seemingly buried treasure. Either way, it would be too late for Kate.

As ever when she was feeling out of sorts, there was one person in particular whose company she craved. Alice.

CHAPTER FORTY-EIGHT

Alice

Even in the darkness Alice realized that Kate's face was a picture of misery and angst. 'Come in out of the cold, Kate,' she urged. 'Tell me what's wrong.'

'Are you sure it's convenient?'

'Of course it is.'

Kate stepped inside the cottage and Alice closed the door behind them. 'Kate's here!' she called to her father in his study, and then led Kate into the kitchen.

'You're soaked,' Alice said. 'Give me your jacket and I'll hang it near the fire.'

Kate shrugged it off and passed it over. Alice hung it up, gestured Kate to sit at the small table and sat down opposite her. 'Well?'

Alice already knew Kate was conflicted about her forthcoming marriage but there was more to her friend's distress than that. Something new.

'It's my ring.'

'Your wedding ring? Has Leo ordered the wrong size?'

'My engagement ring.'

'It hasn't—'

One look at Kate's face confirmed that the ring had indeed been lost. Goodness. Her unhappiness tugged at Alice's heart, but what she needed now was bracing talk. 'It's a blow,' Alice admitted. 'I'd be upset if I lost Daniel's ring. But don't start thinking it's put a jinx on your marriage. Losing it was an accident, not an omen.'

Yet, coming on top of the doubts she already held, there was no doubt that it felt like an omen to Kate.

'Here's what we're going to do,' Alice said. 'Tomorrow I'm going to recruit some helpers to come and search the farm. I'm sure your father won't like it, but that's tough. If we find the ring, it'll be wonderful. But if we don't, you'll simply have to tell Leo what happened and he'll relieve your mind by assuring you it makes no difference at all to how he feels about you. Knowing Leo, he'll be all kind sympathy.'

'He will,' Kate agreed.

'But what? The Fates plan to tear you apart anyway? That's nonsense, Kate. The ring may be lovely, but when all's said and done, it's just a circle of metal and sparkling stones. And even though it was given as a symbol of love, it's the love itself that matters more than the token. That love will survive an accidental loss and more besides.'

Kate attempted a smile but it was weak.

'I'm going to make you some tea,' Alice said. 'And you're going to sit there and rid your mind of superstitious nonsense.'

Alice busied herself with the kettle. She'd intended to spend tomorrow on the quest to expose Gloria Gumble as a fraud. That would have to wait, though. Looking at Kate's woebegone face, Alice knew that friendship came first.

CHAPTER FORTY-NINE

Kate

'What on earth . . .?' Ernie sounded outraged.

'Here comes the cavalry,' Pearl joked.

Kate looked through the kitchen window to see a troop of people walking into the farmyard. Alice was at the front, a slight figure but a force of nature. Beside her came Adam Potts. Next came Bert and Naomi with a tall, spider-limbed youth Kate took to be William Harrington. May Janicki and Janet Collins were behind them and others followed: Alice's father, Victoria and the London women, apart from Ivy, whose rickety legs made walking a trial.

Ernie raced to the door and raised a fist. 'Get off my land! You're trespassing!' he yelled.

'Do shut up, Ernie,' Alice told him. 'You can be tedious at times.' She walked up to Kate who, along with every-one else, had spilled out of the house. 'Several pairs of fresh eyes reporting for duty. Just tell us where you'd like us to search.'

'If you damage my crops, I'll sue!' Ernie threatened.

'Why don't you go about your business and we'll go about ours?' Alice said.

Ernie fumed but he was no match for her. He stalked away, muttering curses.

'This is incredibly kind of you all,' Kate said. 'I'm afraid you're all going to get extremely muddy.'

'That doesn't matter,' Alice told her.

Kate was introduced to William, who looked more than a little like his father but whose grin made him infinitely more likeable. She waved to everyone else, including the London women, touched that they'd turned out to help a virtual stranger on a chilly winter morning. Rain wasn't falling now but everywhere was sodden. Unpleasant.

They split into groups to search the farmyard, the kitchen garden, the paths that led around the farm, and Five Acre Field. An hour passed. Two. 'At least the rain is holding off,' Naomi said.

Bert looked skywards. 'Not for much longer,' he predicted.

He was right. The rain began again in earnest.

'Enough is enough,' Kate finally said. 'I'm grateful for all your help but I don't want anyone catching a chill on my behalf. I need to accept that the ring is lost. For the time being, anyway. Please go home now. All of you.'

'Very well,' Alice said. 'But remember what I said yesterday. Losing the ring is an unfortunate accident. Nothing more.'

Kate hugged her before Alice could see the doubt in her face.

Victoria came up next. 'I'm sorry we didn't find your ring,' she said. 'Arthur was desperate to join the search but we thought the children should stay at home.'

'That was sweet of him, so please tell him thanks. I don't think he could have made a difference, though.'

'Probably not, but he may still be keen to search himself. I expect you've heard how he's been labelled as a troublemaker in the village. He's keen to do something to prove that he isn't all bad.'

'He doesn't need to prove anything to me,' Kate said. 'I know he's a nice boy.'

'He likes you too. But the village . . .'

320

'Can be too quick to judge sometimes.'

'People have been swift to jump on his mistakes without seeing his better side,' Victoria agreed, 'though, to be fair, Arthur hasn't helped himself. Anyway, I hope you won't run him off the land if he turns up.'

'I can't answer for my father, but I'll tell everyone else to leave him alone. I really don't want Arthur or anyone else catching a chill, though.'

Victoria joined the other helpers and they all trudged homewards. 'About time, too!' Ernie yelled. Before barking at Kate, 'Time to get to work.'

Kate walked away, her thoughts back in Cheltenham and replaying all the comments that had pointed out the difference between her world and Leo's, not least: 'It's always a mistake to marry outside one's class. Does no good to anyone.'

The missing ring really did feel like a portent of doom.

CHAPTER FIFTY

Alice

'Don't go out in wet clothes,' Alice's father cautioned as she prepared to leave the house shortly after returning from the search of Brimbles Farm. As both a loving father and a retired doctor, he was always concerned for her health.

'Don't worry, I've changed my stockings.'

'But your coat must be wet from tramping across that field for hours,' he pointed out.

'Can't be helped. I need to go out and right wrongs, if I can find a way to do it.'

She kissed his cheek and hastened into the village to catch the bus to Barton.

She was relieved to find Ellen at home. 'I'm so sorry to trouble you again, but would you mind if I took another look through those photographs of Joe?' Alice asked.

'I don't see what good it can do, but by all means come in.'

'I shan't keep you long.'

'Keep me as long as you like.' Poor Ellen looked exhausted.

Alice sat at the kitchen table. 'How are you coping?' she asked. 'Have you seen much of Gloria?'

'Not much, though that's a good thing. She complained about the way I spent Joe's money. I explained that it was spent on repairing his house but she pointed out that it only needed spending because I hadn't bothered to get the chimney swept or taken out insurance. Negligent, she called me.' Ellen blinked back tears.

'I'm sorry,' Alice said. 'I don't suppose she offered to repay the money you contributed from your own savings?'

'Hardly. She called it compensation for my negligence.' Ellen's smile was a fragile, trembling thing that deepened Alice's wish to expose Gloria as a fraud.

Not that she had any idea how to go about it, but coming here in the hope of identifying the niggle at the back of her mind felt like a good beginning.

Ellen produced the photographs and Alice looked through them slowly: Joe as a cheeky urchin of about six, Joe in a line-up of fellow pupils at school, Joe in a playground, Joe on his first day as a newspaper delivery boy, Joe at his cousin Mabel's wedding . . .

She reached the final photo, still feeling that something vital might be eluding her. She looked through the photos again. And again.

But this time the instinct that had been nudging at the back of her mind stepped forward into the daylight. 'Who's this?' she asked, pointing to someone in the background of the wedding picture.

Ellen squinted, for the background was indistinct. Even so, the outline of a head was clear enough. 'I reckon that must be our cousin Jack.'

'A cousin with sticky-out ears,' Alice pointed out.

'Yes.' Ellen smiled at times past, but then Alice's meaning caught up with her and her eyes widened. 'Good grief, you can't think . . .'

'I don't know what to think yet. But tell me about Jack.'

Ellen pleated her apron between agitated fingers. 'He's a year or two older than Joe. As boys they could pass as brothers instead of cousins.'

'He's still alive?'

'He is. Not that I'm in touch with him. I haven't seen or heard from him in . . . ooh, it must be thirty years – but I exchange Christmas cards with his sister and she'd have mentioned if anything had happened to him.'

'What sort of man is he?'

'He wasn't what you'd call an easy boy, to be honest. If there was trouble, he was usually in the middle of it. Pranks, fights . . .'

'Stealing?' Alice asked, and Ellen winced.

'We made allowances because his father was a drinker who beat the lad. But Jack didn't mend his ways even when he grew up. His poor mother and sister have had a lot to put up with over the years, since he's often been in trouble. He even spent time in prison.'

'Do you think he might know Gloria?'

'I've no idea.'

'So you wouldn't know if Jack was Maurice's father?'

'I wouldn't.'

'Did Joe keep in touch with him?'

'I don't think so. Not often, anyway. Joe didn't approve of Jack. Then again, Joe was a kind man. He might have written occasionally.'

'If he did, Jack would have seen Joe's signature.'

'And forged it on the will? Oh, my goodness!'

'I might be doing a grave disservice to Jack by suspecting him,' Alice said. 'But it sounds more likely that he would have fathered a child outside of marriage than Joe. And not beyond the realms of possibility that he would have conspired with that child's mother to get their hands on Joe's property. It's worth considering, anyway. I assume you told Jack's sister about Joe's passing? Perhaps you also mentioned that you expected Joe's house to go to you?'

'I did.'

324

'She could have passed that information on to Jack.'

'True, but wouldn't it be obvious what he'd done if he came to live in Joe's house?'

'He might have no intention of living in Joe's house or even of letting it be known that he's connected to Gloria. He might simply want to give his son a home. Or maybe Gloria intends to sell the house eventually and give Jack a share of the sale proceeds. Gloria doesn't strike me as the sort of woman who'd be happy living in Churchwood for long.'

'Me neither.'

'Ellen, I'm only guessing. Please don't mention my suspicions to anyone else. If I'm wrong and they come to Gloria's ears, there could be unpleasantness.'

'I won't breathe a word, but what should I do?'

'Do you have Jack's address?'

'Only his sister's.'

'Might you get his address from her? You could write to tell her you've found some photos of Joe and Jack together and would like to send one to Jack as a keepsake. Unless you've a better idea?'

'Hardly. I'm all at sea, Alice. But if Jack, Gloria or anyone else is trying to take Joe's house by fraud, then I want them stopped. Leave it with me, Alice. I'll write today.'

Alice headed for the bus stop. She had a ten-minute wait, but no sooner had the bus arrived than she heard her name being called. Turning, she saw Ellen hastening towards her, waving a piece of paper.

'Do you want this bus or not?' the conductor asked when Alice hesitated to get on.

'I do, but could you wait just a moment?'

'I need to keep to a timetable. People will complain if we're late.'

'Please,' Alice begged, and his eyes softened.

'You can have a moment. That's all.'

'You're a treasure,' Alice told him, and he blushed.

Ellen was out of breath when she caught Alice up. 'I thought of a quicker way of finding Jack's address. I looked through Joe's old papers and there it was. I've written it down for you.'

Alice took the paper and jumped on to the bus. 'Thanks, Ellen,' she called. 'But remember: not a word to anyone!'

The bus rumbled away from the kerb. 'Take care,' Ellen called back.

'You need to sit down, miss,' the conductor told her. 'And I need to sell you a ticket.'

Alice found a seat, paid her fare and studied the paper Ellen had given her. Jack lived in Brighton. Surely, it couldn't be coincidence that Gloria and the two dubious witnesses to Joe's will lived in Hove, just a short distance along the coast from Brighton?

Reaching home, she looked up Jack's address on her map of Brighton and wasn't surprised to discover that it was close to the Sailor's Rigging. 'I'm returning to Brighton tomorrow,' she told her father. 'I hope to be home again the same day, but I'll take overnight things just in case I need them.'

Her father looked troubled. 'Why are you going?'

Not wanting to lie, she told him about Jack but made no mention of his prison sentence. Even so, her father's frown deepened.

'My dear, I hate to act the strict father, and I know you're a grown woman, but I'm not comfortable with you confronting this man. If he's guilty of fraud, who knows what he'll do to protect himself if he thinks you're about to expose him?'

'I won't take any risks.'

'You'll be taking a risk in simply confronting him.'

'I shan't confront him. He'll send me packing if I do that. I'm hoping to draw him into a confession.'

'By tricking him? That could make him even angrier. He might lash out at you.'

Alice couldn't deny it was a possibility. 'I can't just stand by and let Ellen be cheated out of her inheritance, especially not when it leaves the bookshop homeless. You know how much the bookshop benefits the village.'

'Perhaps if I come with you . . .'

But Alice's father radiated integrity – which wouldn't suit Alice's slowly forming plan at all.

'It's lovely of you to offer, but I've already decided to ask Bert,' she said. 'You won't object if Bert comes with me?'

Some of her father's worry lifted. 'Bert will be a good man to have on your side. But you won't go to Brighton without him?'

Alice kissed his cherubic cheek. 'I won't.'

With no time to waste, she hastened to Bert's market garden.

'It certainly sounds as though you're on to something,' he said, when she'd told him about Joe's cousin, 'though how you'll get a confession . . .'

Alice explained what she had in mind.

Bert's eyebrows lifted in astonishment but then he shrugged. 'All right. It's got to be worth trying. Count me in.'

There was one more person Alice needed to see, so she went straight to May Janicki's house and told the story of Joe's cousin all over again. 'You want me to *what*?' May said.

CHAPTER FIFTY-ONE

Alice

Bert chuckled when Alice emerged from the ladies' cloak-room at Brighton station. 'And to think you normally look so wholesome!'

'Wholesome won't get the job done,' Alice reminded him. 'I don't feel much like myself, but that's the point of the exercise, isn't it?'

May had taken in one of Alice's flannel skirts to hug her slender curves and loaned her a blouse which, on Alice's shorter body, opened low on her chest. 'Stuff some stockings into your bra,' May had recommended. 'They'll help to give just the sort of impression you're aiming for.' Tucked into the skirt, the fact that the blouse was too long was hidden. There wasn't much May could do about Alice's shoes, since the girls took different sizes, but Alice had changed into her best court shoes, which gave her a little more height, and she planned on swinging her hips from side to side.

To help the brazen look along, May had shown Alice how to brush her hair back from her face and give it volume. Then she'd demonstrated how cosmetics could give her a bold, brash appearance with bright-red lips, rouged cheeks and thick, dark eyebrows.

'Your father would have a fit if he saw you,' Bert said.

'So would Daniel, but I need to look like the sort of woman Gloria might befriend. Come on. The sooner I can revert to my normal self, the better.'

They headed straight for Edsell Street and knocked on Jack's door, keeping their fingers crossed that he'd be at home.

He was, though he looked none too pleased to see them. 'What?' he demanded, a half-smoked cigarette dangling from his lips.

The similarities to Joe were striking – similar height and build, same sticking-out ears and same squashy nose – but so too were the differences. Joe had been neat and clean. This man looked as though he'd lived a life of dissipation. His sparse hair was greasy, his teeth brown and small veins made patterns across his cheeks. As well, his shirt looked grimy and there were food stains down the front of his ancient sweater. He also smelled bad, though Alice did her best not to recoil.

'Gloria asked us to look you up and let you know how she's getting on in Churchwood,' she said.

He relaxed at the mention of Gloria and his debauched eyes almost twinkled. But then they narrowed suspiciously. 'How do you know Gloria? She wouldn't have sent you all this way just to look me up.'

'She didn't,' Alice answered coolly. 'We're only looking you up because we happen to be in the area to collect a debt from someone who thought he could cheat my father and run away.' Her aim was to give the impression of being part of a family that operated on the wrong side of the law, with Bert as her henchman and protector. After all, Bert was a large man who'd done hard physical work all his life. 'We're parched, though. We need hot tea – or something stronger.'

Alice stepped forward into the hall, practically barging Jack out of the way. 'Which room?' she demanded.

He waved towards the first room on the left. Alice walked in and wrinkled her nose at the squalor of it. There was an unmade bed with filthy sheets in one corner, an armchair in another, a small table with two mismatched wooden chairs by the grimy window and a low-built cupboard beside it on which stood bread, butter, food-encrusted plates and a disgustingly dirty tea towel. Here and there were bags, one spilling clothes across the shabby linoleum floor. An ashtray filled with old cigarette butts sat on the arm of the armchair.

Alice regretted asking for tea, fearing she wouldn't be able to stomach anything from these surroundings.

'Whiskey for me,' Bert said. 'Or brandy?'

She guessed his stomach was rebelling too, and that he judged alcohol to be safer, given its antiseptic properties. 'Brandy sounds good,' Alice said.

Jack took a bottle from the cupboard along with two glasses into which he poured small measures of brandy. They appeared to be the only two glasses he possessed, because for himself he emptied a cup by throwing the contents into the grate before pouring a larger amount of brandy into it. He passed the glasses to Alice and Bert and raised the cup in a toast. 'Cheers!'

'Cheers,' Bert echoed, and Alice forced a smile, surreptitiously wiping the outside of the glass on her skirt before taking a sip. Unused to spirits, her eyes watered and fire burned down her throat. 'We'll sit here, shall we?' she asked, gesturing towards the wooden chairs. She certainly didn't want to sit in the armchair, which was stained with who knew what.

'How do you know Gloria?' Jack asked, taking the armchair for himself.

'My father knows her,' Alice said. 'She worked in one of his pubs back in . . . I don't know when, actually. A long time ago. One of the pubs is the Feathers in Luton. She came to say hello and I suppose you could say the friendship was renewed.'

'Luton, eh? That's not far from Churchwood.'

'It's a few miles away but a bus runs between them.'

'So what's the news of Gloria?'

'She's doing well. She introduced Maurice as Joe's son and produced the will.'

'No one challenged her?'

'Apparently, not everyone was pleased by them, but what could they say? Maurice looks like your dead cousin and Gloria has a will that your cousin appears to have signed.'

Jack chuckled. 'I might have known Gloria would pull it off. Good for her.'

'It'll probably mean prison if she's found out.'

'Who'll find her out? It was a good plan. Has she given you any money for me?'

'No.'

He looked disappointed but then shrugged philosophically. 'I suppose it might take a while for her to get her hands on the cash, especially if Joe's sister is kicking up a stink.'

'You don't like Joe's sister?'

'She's all right, I suppose. But she doesn't need what Joe left behind.'

'Why's that?'

'She's already got a house.'

'Your son hasn't?'

'Exactly. Not the brightest of lads, my Maurice, but his mother has brains.'

'You didn't think enough of her to marry her,' Alice pointed out.

'Marry Gloria? I'd have been sticking myself in a spider's web. She'd have killed me sooner or later. If I hadn't killed her first. No, Gloria and me had fun, but we weren't the marrying kind.'

'I believe Churchwood is a quiet place,' Alice said next. 'Gloria doesn't strike me as the sort of woman who'd like a quiet sort of place.'

Jack laughed, showing more of the hideous teeth. 'She ain't. But she'll live there for a while and then sell up. It depends how much money Joe left and how long it lasts.'

'Especially after you've had your share of it,' Alice said.

'Fair's fair. Gloria wouldn't have got her hands on a penny without me.'

'Whose idea was it? The forged will?'

'Hard to say. Gloria was here when a letter came from my sister telling me Joe had passed on. I said it was a pity I wouldn't benefit from anything he left behind and . . . Well, we got talking about how we might make it happen. Gloria looked into how to make a will and I practised signing Joe's name. I had it on an old card he'd sent years ago.'

'Clever,' Alice said.

Jack grinned, rubbing his hands together in a way that suggested he couldn't wait to get them on some money.

Alice stood, trying to hide her disgust. 'We came to attend to other business, so we'd better attend to it, Bert.'

'Right you are.' Bert got up too. 'Thanks for the brandy, Jack.'

'Tell Gloria I'm expecting some money soon.'

'We'll be talking to her shortly,' Alice promised. It just wouldn't be the sort of chat Jack had in mind.

They left the grubby house and moved out of earshot. 'Mission accomplished?' Bert asked.

'For the moment,' Alice confirmed.

The next task was to talk to Gloria. What an interesting conversation that promised to be.

CHAPTER FIFTY-TWO

Kate

He was back, his small figure walking slowly up and down Five Acre Field, his face angled downwards as he searched for Kate's ring. As Victoria had predicted, Arthur had turned up yesterday long after everyone else had left.

Kate had walked down to see him. 'Does Victoria know you're here?' she'd asked. The poor boy had looked chilled to the bone.

'She said I could search for a little while.'

'You don't have to search at all. It's a terrible day and the ring doesn't seem to want to be found.'

'I want to search,' he'd said, and Kate had guessed that he meant he *needed* to search because doing something helpful might restore his reputation in the village.

'You mustn't let a few unkind comments get you down,' she'd advised, but Arthur had only shrugged.

'Easy for me to say, I know,' Kate had conceded. She too had burned at life's injustices over the years, but Arthur had also to contend with guilt at believing himself to have let down the people who were closest to him – his sister, his friends, Victoria, Naomi . . .

'I want to find the ring for you, too,' he'd said, and she'd smiled, appreciating the spirit of friendship.

She'd helped him search for fifteen minutes then sent him home to get dry and warm.

Now Kate took a slice of apple pie from the larder and went along to see him again. 'No luck?' she guessed.

He shook his head. 'Sorry.'

'It's good of you to bother searching, but you must be cold. Hungry, too. Perhaps this will help?' She held out the pie and his eyes widened.

He raised it to his mouth only to hesitate, as though he'd changed his mind about eating it now. 'You won't mind if I take it home and share it?' he asked.

'Share it with whom?'

'My sister. And my friend.'

'Flower?'

'She isn't strong. Some pie might build her up.'

'Sharing would be kind,' Kate confirmed. He really was a nice boy.

'Don't stay for more than a few minutes,' she told him. 'It'll be dark soon and Victoria will worry if you're not home.'

She walked back to the house thinking that both she and Arthur were misfits. The difference was that Arthur hadn't chosen to be snatched from his old life and dropped into a country village which appeared not to want him. If Kate left Churchwood for Leo's world, she'd be doing so of her own free will, with her eyes wide open to the hazards. And if it went wrong, the fault – the responsibility – would be hers.

CHAPTER FIFTY-THREE

Alice

Gloria was giving instructions to Maurice when Alice and Bert approached Joe's cottage. 'Not there, Maurice. Put it over there.'

'Knock, knock,' Bert said, walking inside.

Maurice put down the chair he was holding and gaped at the unexpected visitors. Gloria looked around, too, her expression souring when she saw who was calling. 'Yes?' she demanded.

'We're wondering what you'd prefer?' Alice asked. 'To hand the keys to this house to us now and go on your way, or to hand them to the police?'

Wariness narrowed Gloria's eyes but she fell back on bluster. 'What are you talking about? This is Maurice's house fair and square.'

'Looks like we're going to have to fetch the police,' Bert said to Alice.

'It does,' she agreed.

'The police can't do anything about a perfectly legal will just because you're sulking about losing your precious bookshop,' Gloria mocked.

'They can do something about a perfectly *il*legal will,' Alice countered. 'By that I mean a fraudulent will. One bearing a forged signature.'

'Forged? What nonsense!' Gloria said, laughing, but her darting eyes signalled that she was searching her mind for a way out of trouble.

'You should know that we went to Brighton,' Alice said.

'And had a little chat with Jack,' Bert added.

'As if Jack would have told you anything!'

'He told us *everything*,' Alice said.

'I don't believe you.'

'He admitted that he's Maurice's father. And he admitted that you conspired together to produce a fraudulent will.'

'Jack wouldn't have admitted anything,' Gloria insisted, but her face was registering growing desperation. 'As if he'd even let you holier-than-thou people past his door!'

'He thought we were very different people from a doctor's daughter and a market gardener,' Bert explained.

'What do you mean?'

Bert told her about the visit to Jack's.

'If he did confess, and I'm not saying he did,' Gloria argued, 'the confession was worthless. There weren't any witnesses.'

'Do you really think Jack will hold up against police questioning?' Alice asked. 'He hasn't the brains for it – or the steadiness of mind. He'll flounder. And if he can get a lighter sentence for his part in the fraud by implicating you, then he'll do it.'

'No, he won't.'

'There's more,' Alice continued. 'A barman at the Sailor's Rigging told me that you used to work there and knew the two men who pretended to witness Joe's will. With Jack's confession as well, I don't think there's any doubt that you'll be found guilty of fraud and sent to prison. Maurice, too.'

'Rubbish!' Gloria spat, but she was fighting a losing battle and, from the vexed look on her face, she knew it.

'I'll repeat the question,' Alice said. 'Do you want to hand the keys to us or the police?'

Gloria almost exploded in frustration.

'Where are we supposed to go? You can't throw us out on the street!'

'You have a home in Fuller Street in Hove. I went there too,' Alice said. 'Pack up now and you can be home before teatime.'

'Need a hand with the packing?' Bert asked calmly. 'We're busy people so don't want to be waiting here for long.'

Gloria's anger boiled over into a scream. She grabbed the keys from the window ledge and threw them at Bert, who caught them easily.

'We'll just wait to see you off the premises,' he said.

'Pack your stuff!' Gloria barked at Maurice.

'Eh?'

'We're leaving.'

Ten minutes later the Gumbles left and Bert locked the cottage door. 'Good riddance,' he said, watching Gloria march furiously to the bus stop with a bewildered Maurice half running behind her.

'And here comes Marjorie, so it'll soon be all over the village that the Gumbles have left,' Alice said as the tall, lanky figure of Marjorie Plym trotted across the road to intercept Gloria.

A moment later Marjorie backed away in fright. Gloria must have snarled at her. Alice felt a burst of sympathy for Marjorie, though doubtless the snub would spice up the gossip she'd spread.

'To Ellen's?' Bert asked Alice.

And to Ellen's they went, Bert driving them in the truck.

Ellen clutched her throat and sat down hard when she heard the news. Then her tears began. 'To think that the house and money my poor brother worked so hard for were almost snatched away by that scheming woman!' she said, groping in her apron for a handkerchief and blowing her nose. 'It's such a relief to know the house is mine so I'll be able to help my children and the bookshop, after all.'

She stuffed her handkerchief back into her pocket and reached out to clasp a hand of each of them. 'Thank you! From the bottom of my heart.'

'It's young Alice who did the thinking and planning,' Bert said. 'I just went along as her protector.'

'And did a first-rate job,' Alice said.

Bert placed the keys on the table but Ellen pushed them back towards him. 'Give them to Naomi and tell her to open the bookshop just as soon as possible. And tell Kate she's welcome to hold her wedding reception there, if it suits.'

'I'll tell her,' Alice confirmed.

Surely now Kate could be persuaded that omens could be favourable and good times lay ahead?

CHAPTER FIFTY-FOUR

Kate

Kate heard the news of the Gumbles' departure from Alice, who walked up to Brimbles Farm especially to tell her. 'Isn't it wonderful?' Alice asked.

'It certainly is,' Kate agreed. 'This village needs the bookshop badly.'

'It's excellent news for your wedding, too.'

'Oh, of course.' Kate smiled, but it couldn't have looked convincing because Alice sighed.

'Kate, I don't believe in omens but, if you believe in them, can't you see that this is a good one? Your luck has changed!'

Kate nodded, but again Alice sighed.

'You're still upset about the ring. I don't mean ordinarily upset – who wouldn't be? – but you're not seeing it for what it is: an accident, not a portent. Leo hasn't been unkind about it?'

'He's been sympathetic.'

Please don't feel bad, my darling, he'd written. *You may have lost the ring, but I bought a chain with a clasp that wasn't strong enough. If you wish to apportion blame, that makes us equal, but I don't feel either of us is to blame. Accidents happen . . .*

'Leo loves you, Kate. Please don't do anything drastic, like call the wedding off. You'd break both of your hearts.'

But Leo's heart would heal and he'd be free to pursue happiness with someone better suited to deliver it into the future. Kate couldn't imagine her own heart healing, but wasn't selflessness an integral part of love?

'Just promise you won't make any decisions that may cost you your happiness,' Alice urged, but Kate wouldn't make a promise she knew she might break. Not to as cherished a friend as Alice.

'I have to get back to work,' Kate said.

Turning, she walked away, hearing Alice call out behind her, 'Don't do it, Kate!'

Omens, symbols, portents . . . Kate decided that superstition wasn't the cause of her doubts. It merely confirmed the doubts she already held – doubts that were rooted in the inescapable fact that she and Leo were from different worlds. Incompatible worlds, perhaps.

With the wedding only three days away now, she needed to reach a decision about the future urgently, but opposing wishes still held her fast between them. Kate couldn't bear the thought of trapping Leo into a marriage that might ultimately make him unhappy, yet she was also unable to bear the thought of breaking off with him. In fact, the very idea of it tore the air from her lungs and stabbed her heart.

She returned to work and later went indoors for tea. Sharing the news of the bookshop, she was met with universal delight – except from Ernie, of course, but his power to dominate and depress the family was weakening day by day now that not only the land girls but also his own sons stood up to him.

Afterwards, Kate stole a precious few minutes of solitude in her room. It was raining again, water wriggling down the window like a game of snakes and ladders in which the ladders had disappeared and the snakes were racing each other to the bottom. Kate felt like one of them.

Sighing, she leaned her forehead against the glass,

feeling the coldness of it on her skin. She breathed out slowly then breathed in again, letting images and conversations flash through her head in rapid succession. Leo's smile. The feel of his lips on hers. The relief in his eyes when he realized she loved him despite his burns. Julia and Anne. The Cheltenham dinner party . . .

She frowned at the sight of the familiar small figure trudging up and down Five Acre Field. 'Just popping out,' she called to Ruby as she ran downstairs and unhooked her jacket from the pegs near the kitchen door.

Shrugging it on, she shoved her feet into her boots and stepped outside, wincing as wind drove icy rain into her face.

Seeing her approaching, Arthur paused his search and waited for her to reach him.

'You really shouldn't be out in all this rain,' Kate said. 'Look at you. You're drenched and you're shivering.'

'I want to find the ring.'

'I know, but your health comes first.'

His small face was blue with cold, but there was fervour in his eyes. 'Finding the ring . . . it's important,' he insisted.

'I understand that. Really, I do. But the chances of finding it are tiny, while the chances of you catching a chill are high.'

'Please,' he insisted. 'Just a few more minutes. It's hardly raining any more so I'll soon dry off.'

Kate glanced up and saw that the rain was indeed easing off, though the air was so damp and wintry that she doubted his sodden clothes would dry off for hours. 'You've already proved that you're my friend, Arthur, and I'll be sure to tell everyone in Churchwood that I think so.'

It wasn't enough. The mention of the village had brought hurt into Arthur's eyes.

'Please,' he said again, and she saw that he was desperate to redeem himself in the village's eyes. To prove that, far from being a mindless troublemaker, he cared about others and was useful. Honest.

Kate was cold too, but she felt the heat of anger flood her veins. How dare the people of Churchwood judge this vulnerable boy so harshly, after all he'd been through and when he was trying so hard to find a niche for himself and his little friends? 'You know, Arthur,' she said, 'you're worth ten of those nasty people down in the village. You're a good person, which is more than can be said for some of them. You deserve to hold your head high.'

Arthur blinked at her sudden passion. Kate found herself blinking in surprise, too, for the things she'd said to Arthur applied equally to herself. She too was a good person, or at least trying to be, and she'd be a fool if she let petty snobbery and doubts about her own worthiness drag her down. Adam's revelation had struck her at last.

Leaning forward, she kissed Arthur's frozen forehead.

'What was that for?' he asked, looking astonished.

'For being a friend and helping me more than you'll ever know. Ten minutes of searching and then you go home,' she instructed. 'And make sure you stand up tall next time you venture into the village. Be proud of who you are, because you're fabulous.'

Arthur's grin was just lovely.

She walked back to the house, deep in thought. She arrived to find Pearl in the kitchen.

'Was it a wedding present?' Pearl asked. She must have seen that Kate didn't understand because she added, 'The parcel that came for you?'

Ruby walked to the dresser and picked up a package wrapped in brown paper and tied with string. 'I did tell you it had arrived,' she said.

'I'm sure you did,' Kate conceded. With her thoughts caught up in her dilemma, she probably hadn't heard.

'Well?' Pearl asked, as eager as a child awaiting the unwrapping of a Christmas gift.

Kate unfastened the string and opened the parcel. There was a box inside that bore the name *Turlington's Fine Shirtmakers of Savile Row, London*. Had it been sent to Kate to pass on to Leo? An envelope on top bore her name.

She read it quickly then eased the top off the box and stared down at the contents.

Well, well, well.

A shout from outside caught her attention. Kate looked out of the window to see Arthur racing across the farmyard. He burst into the kitchen, spraying mud in all directions. 'I've found it!'

Breathlessly, he held up the chain with one hand and opened the palm of the other hand to show the ring. Both were filthy but they were the most precious treasure Kate could imagine.

'Arthur, you're a wonder!' she declared.

'I found the chain first,' Arthur explained. 'There was just a little bit of it sticking out of the dirt. I dug it out with my fingers but the ring wasn't with it, so I dug around some more and found it squashed deeper into the mud. I think it's all right, though.'

Kate took them from him and rinsed them under the kitchen tap. 'They look perfect,' she said. 'Thank you so much!'

'I knew I'd find them if I kept looking long enough.' He'd known nothing of the kind, but desperation had given him purpose.

Ruby and Pearl made a fuss of him too, Ruby insisting he should change into some of Timmy's dry clothes and Pearl cutting him a large slice of apple pie.

'What's this?' Ernie came in from the barn. 'Am I expected to feed every waif and stray in Churchwood now?'

'Arthur found Kate's ring,' Pearl said. 'Her chain, too. He deserves a slice of pie.'

'Not at my expense,' Ernie grumbled, but no one bothered to respond with more than eye-rolling.

'Take no notice of him,' Kate advised Arthur. 'You're the hero of the moment.'

When he was warm again, Kate insisted on driving him home in the truck, turning a deaf ear to Ernie's objections about wasting precious petrol. She shovelled Arthur's wet clothes into one bag, then placed the parcel and the note that had accompanied it into another. 'Don't wait tea for me,' she advised Ruby.

She turned on to the Foxfield drive and brought the truck to a halt. 'I want you to have this as a reward,' Kate said, handing over a ten-shilling note from her savings.

Arthur's eyes widened. 'It's all for me?'

'You deserve every penny and more besides. The ring and chain you found are worth a lot of money and they're even more precious because of the person who gave them to me.'

'But ten shillings! I've never had more than sixpence before.'

'You've earned it.'

He gazed at the note in wonder but then shook his head and offered it back. 'Thanks, but I didn't find the ring to get money.'

'I know. I want you to have this money anyway. In fact, I'm going to insist on it.'

She closed his hand around it and said, 'Come on. Let's get you inside.'

The door was opened by Victoria, who took in the

fact that he was wearing someone else's clothes and said despairingly, 'What's happened now?'

'Arthur is a hero, that's what's happened,' Kate explained. She handed over one of the bags. 'Arthur's clothes are in here. They're wet so he's wearing some of Timmy's things. I'll let Arthur tell you the story.' She ruffled his hair. 'Thanks again, Arthur. You're an amazing boy.'

She nodded goodbye to Victoria and was walking back to the truck when she heard Victoria say, 'Well, I can't wait to hear about your heroics . . .'

Kate drove only as far as The Linnets and was glad when Alice opened the door. 'Have you got time for a chat?' Kate asked.

'I'll always make time for you, Kate. You look . . . calmer. You've reached a decision, I suppose. I only hope it's the right one.'

They settled in the kitchen.

'Look,' Kate said, holding out her hand on which Leo's ring sparkled brightly again.

'You found it!'

'Arthur found it, bless him.'

'He's a determined boy.'

'Luckily for me.'

Alice made tea and brought it to the table. 'You thought losing the ring was a bad omen. I hope you think that finding it is a good omen.'

'There's more,' Kate said.

She showed Alice the note that had come with the parcel. Sitting side by side, they read it together.

Dear Kate,
    My husband and I have been talking and we both feel that our welcome when you came to Cheltenham may not have been as warm as it should have been.

I hope you'll allow me to explain. As you know, Leo is our only child and we love him dearly. For years we've been nursing the hope that, once this war is over, he'll decide to return to Cheltenham and take up the reins of the sort of life that we enjoy. I don't mean to cause you pain when I say this, but I suppose we envisaged him settling down with a girl who would enjoy being the sort of wife I am. By this, I mean that she would enjoy shopping, organizing lunches, dinners and cocktail parties, sitting on charity committees and supporting her husband at dances, balls and the like. We've long known that Julia has had hopes of being the girl Leo would choose, and it pleased us to think of them marrying, too.

When we met you, we admired your spirit and weren't blind to your beauty, but we feared you wouldn't enjoy our sort of life at all. In fact, after years of wanting Leo to return home, we feared you'd take him further away than ever. It meant we lost sight of the most important considerations for parents – our son's nature and happiness.

The truth is that it's unlikely that Leo will ever wish to settle for our tame style of living. As a boy, he loved to explore and have adventures. He swam, climbed trees and rode a bicycle long before anyone expected it of him, and his schoolmasters reported that he was always the first to step forward to try anything new or daring. As you know, he rejected the idea of office life to join the RAF years before the outbreak of war.

In our imaginings about the future we tried to mould our son to suit our own convenience, but what Leo really needs is a wife with a spirit to match his own. That isn't a Cheltenham miss whose idea of an adventure is trying a new cocktail. It's someone like you, my dear. Someone to challenge him and keep him on his toes. Someone to share his spirit of adventure.

I hope we haven't damaged ourselves for ever in your eyes, Kate. Leo tells us you're kind and generous, so we're asking – humbly – for you to give us a second chance. I can assure you that our eyes are open to your excellent qualities now, and our arms are open in welcome. We hope that the wedding will provide us with a chance to prove it to you, though we don't wish our troubles to distract you from your enjoyment of what should be the happiest day of your life.

On the subject of weddings, Leo has no taste for grandness and we're anticipating a simple but heartfelt occasion. You may have no patience with the tradition of wearing something old, something new, something borrowed and something blue, or you may already have everything in hand to go along with it. But just in case you haven't, I'm enclosing my own bridal veil, which was also worn by my mother and her mother before her. Perhaps it could be your something borrowed or something old? Please don't feel obliged to wear it if it doesn't feel right to you, though.

With fondest regards, Cecilia Kinsella x

'Is that the veil?' Alice nodded towards the shirt box.

Kate took the lid off and parted layers of tissue paper to reveal a froth of beautiful lace.

'You're going to wear it?' Alice asked.

'I think I might. I know you offered to lend me the veil that you and your mother wore—'

'But this one has more meaning for you, and for Leo, too. Of course, you must wear it.'

It was typical of Alice to be understanding.

'I take it that finding your ring and receiving this veil have convinced you that you're right to marry Leo, after all?'

'Actually, they've made no difference,' Kate said. When Alice looked baffled, she added, 'It was Arthur who helped to send the doubts packing.'

She explained about the conversation in the field. 'You always said I was good enough for Leo – for anyone –

but I let my old insecurities persuade me otherwise for a while.'

'But now you're fighting back with your head held high. You've always been a fighter, Kate. Every day of your life you've had to fight against being soured by Ernie and your brothers. I've no doubt that you'll vanquish all doubts and be blissfully happy with your flight lieutenant. I'm so glad you've come to your senses at last. Nothing will go wrong now!'

Kate remembered those words later. When time proved Alice wrong.

CHAPTER FIFTY-FIVE

Kate

Kate was deeply touched to see friends rallying round to make her wedding as lovely as possible. May was busy with the dress and Janet had baked a cake using ingredients contributed by well-wishers. Bert had promised his home-made wine and beer as a wedding gift and Naomi had promised sherry. The food was to be simple, but even simple food was tricky in wartime. 'The chickens don't seem to be laying well,' Pearl had announced at Brimbles Farm one morning. 'Perhaps a fox is spooking them.'

Ernie had fired up at that suggestion. 'The day I see a fox near my chickens will be the day it feels the blast of my shotgun.'

'Maybe they'll lay better tomorrow,' Pearl had said blithely. Then she'd winked at Kate and hidden six eggs at the back of the dresser.

Bert and Alice had been saving eggs, too. They'd go into sandwiches, as would any other foods that could be spared – cheese, fish paste, potted meat . . . Ruby had raided the store of apples and pears to make fruit pies as well, and more pies were being contributed by Alice and Victoria using bottled fruits from Bert's market garden. None of the guests should go hungry.

Alice and May were full of enthusiasm over how they'd decorate the bookshop with greenery to hide its starkness, and Bert was planning to use his truck to collect tables and chairs on loan from various village residents. Crockery, cutlery and glasses were being loaned for the occasion, too.

'It's because we all love you dearly,' Alice had explained, reducing Kate almost to tears of gratitude.

And then there was Leo, writing every day to tell her he couldn't wait to make her his bride.

Only a couple of years ago, Kate had been lonely and more than a little bitter at being an outcast in Churchwood. Now, bliss awaited her. Or so she hoped.

The first hiccup came from Alice, calling at the farm on the way to the hospital. Seeing her worried expression, Kate felt her heart slide downwards. 'What is it?'

'I may have done you a disservice, suggesting you hold your reception in the bookshop.'

'Not more problems with the bookshop!'

'The building is fine,' Alice assured her quickly. 'But people seem to be assuming that your wedding is a bookshop event so they're all welcome.'

'The whole village?' Kate was aghast.

'Pretty well. People from the hospital, too.'

Kate's head reeled. 'There won't be room for everyone. And I can't possibly feed them.'

'Food and drink isn't the problem. People are talking as though it's one of our bring-and-share events. Space is more of an issue, since it'll be a crush even if we spread into the bedrooms. But the most important consideration is how you feel about it. And how you think Leo will feel. If you don't like the idea, I can make sure people realize there's been a misunderstanding. I'll tell them that they're welcome at the church – I imagine you won't object to them watching the ceremony – but that the reception afterwards will be a small, private affair.'

'I can't make you disappoint so many people!'

'I should have made things clearer from the outset.'

How Alice-like to take the blame and want to put it right.

'Let me think for a moment.' Kate shuffled her feet a few times then took a deep breath and said, 'Let's leave things as they are. Leo won't mind and his parents will be outnumbered by the guests on my side, anyway. As long as everyone knows it'll be a crush . . .'

'I'll make sure they do,' Alice promised, giving a relieved but wry smile. 'You really don't mind too much?'

'I suppose it wouldn't be Churchwood without a little chaos in the community. And I suppose most weddings have a hiccup. Just as long as it's the only hiccup . . .'

She called in at the post office later to send a package to Frank, who'd miss the wedding since he was still serving in North Africa. Finding herself greeted by so many beaming faces, Kate was glad she hadn't let the village down. 'We hear you found your ring,' Janet said. 'It's wonderful news.'

'Arthur found it in one of our fields.'

'We heard that, too,' Janet said. 'He's incredibly proud of the reward you gave him.'

'Ten shillings doesn't seem much considering the value of the ring,' Kate reasoned.

'It's a huge amount to a boy like Arthur,' Janet said. It was a large amount to Kate, too.

Other people came forward to say how pleased they were. Kate thanked them all and, after dropping off her parcel, moved on to the grocer's where she was greeted by more happy faces.

'Arthur was such a hero,' Kate told them, but Mr Miles dismissed the praise with a humph.

'That boy is nothing but trouble,' he said. 'It wouldn't surprise me if he stole the ring then pretended to find it so you'd give him some money.'

'Erm . . .' Molly Lloyd dipped her head towards the door.

Glancing around, Kate saw that Arthur had come in and, judging from his woebegone expression, he'd heard Mr Miles's every word.

He turned suddenly and left the shop. 'Blast!' Kate said, following.

'Arthur, stop!' she called, seeing him running down the street.

He didn't stop so she chased after him, finally catching hold of his shoulder. 'Arthur, stop.'

Tears of hurt and anger were spilling from his eyes. 'I didn't steal your ring, Kate. I didn't!'

'I know that, Arthur. I saw how hard you had to work to find it. Don't feel bad about what Mr Miles said. It was wrong of him to jump to a false conclusion like that. I'll explain the full story to him. Put it right.'

'Won't do any good.' Arthur sniffed and wiped his nose on his sleeve. 'People here have decided I'm a bad 'un and they're not going to change their minds.'

'They will once they understand. Now go home and put Mr Miles from your mind. It's my wedding tomorrow. You're my guest and you're going to have a good time.'

He nodded, but only as though he saw little point in arguing.

'I mean it, Arthur. Churchwood people can be . . . unpleasant when they don't know someone very well. But once they do, they're the best people in the world. You just have to give them time to see the person you really are. Now, did you go into the grocer's for anything in particular?'

'I just went for a look so I can decide how to spend my reward, but I won't be spending it there now I know that man still thinks badly of me.'

'Mr Miles might be regretting what he said already.'

'He might not.'

'He'll come round in time. Off you go now, and I'll see you tomorrow.'

He trudged off, his slight shoulders drooping under the weight of injustice.

Deciding to speak to Mr Miles, Kate returned to the grocer's. 'You upset Arthur with what you said,' she told him.

'I speak as I find.'

'Arthur spent hours out in the field in terrible weather searching for my ring.'

'Maybe he did. But he's been a terror since he came to Churchwood, so you can't blame people for thinking the worst of him.'

'He may have made mistakes,' Kate admitted. 'But what you said about the ring wasn't true.'

'Neither you nor I know what really happened. He could have been pretending to search when the ring was in his pocket all the time. I don't want to fall out with you, Kate, especially since it's your wedding day tomorrow. If the boy wants people to look kindly on him, he needs to behave better. Once he does that, I'll be the first to speak well of him.'

'Searching for my ring in the cold and rain *was* behaving better,' Kate pointed out.

'Then all he needs to do is to keep behaving better.' Mr Miles looked over her shoulder to Mrs Hutchings. 'Good morning,' he said to her. 'How can I help you today?'

Sighing, Kate left the shop but called at Foxfield to tell Victoria what Mr Miles had said.

'I guessed something bad had happened, but Arthur wouldn't talk about it,' Victoria said. 'Obviously, it's going to take more than finding your ring to improve his reputation in the village. It's such a pity.'

Kate headed home, regretting that Arthur was going to be a dejected little soul at her wedding.

'Feeling excited?' Ruby asked on her return.

Kate tried to shrug off the disappointment. 'Indeed I am. Leo and his parents are arriving today, though I won't see them until the wedding.'

'Naomi and Alice will make them welcome.' Ruby was all confidence and goodwill, though underneath there was still a wistfulness about her. It appeared that Kenny had still made no move to make things official between them.

There were no undercurrents to Timmy's excitement. He had a role to play in the wedding and went around telling everyone that he couldn't wait to play it. Seeing his happiness turned Kate's thoughts back to Arthur. She wished there was something she could do to make him happy, too. What, though?

CHAPTER FIFTY-SIX

Naomi

Leo brought his parents to Foxfield late in the afternoon. Keen to make a good impression on them for Kate's sake, Naomi had briefed everyone in the house on the importance of being warm and welcoming. 'Does that mean we should all say hello?' Lewis had asked.

'It does. But not too boisterously, hmm? Mr and Mrs Kinsella may be tired after their journey and we don't want to overwhelm them.'

Arthur had hung his head miserably. Was he thinking that Naomi had him in mind as someone likely to be too boisterous? Since overhearing Mr Miles's unfortunate comment, he'd been the opposite. Subdued, in fact. He was going to need time and love to get back to his usual self.

It was arranged that Suki should open the door to the visitors, and Naomi was touched to see how the little maid made sure her white apron and cap were clean and straight. It was also arranged that she'd hand them over to Naomi and Victoria and then return to the kitchen to make tea. Charming and well spoken, Victoria would make a good impression on all but the most ungracious of people.

'It's most kind of you to put us up,' Mr Kinsella said when Naomi led them into the sitting room.

'In such a beautiful house, too,' his wife added.

'It's my pleasure,' Naomi told them. 'Kate is a dear girl and a dear friend. She hasn't been brought up with the advantages given to some young women, but that makes her all the more admirable, in my opinion. She's clever, kind, hard-working and passionate about justice. But I imagine Leo has already sung her praises, so you don't need to hear them from me.'

Leo grinned. 'I certainly have.'

Naomi had simply been making sure his parents knew how special Kate was. Realizing it, Victoria sent her a wink.

'It's especially kind of you to accommodate us when I believe you have several guests already,' Mrs Kinsella said.

'Our evacuees from London? You'll meet them soon, but I thought you might be glad of a quiet few minutes first. The children are full of energy, but they're also packed with courage and goodwill. They've had a difficult few years, since most of them have lost at least one parent. They came here to escape a condemned building and find safety. Their mothers are admirable, too. They've taken jobs in aircraft construction while a grandmother looks after the children.'

'How marvellous.'

'I also have a young man staying. William Harrington. He's a relative by marriage. Life is busy here, but I like it that way.'

Suki brought in tea and Victoria handed it round, joining Naomi in chatting to the Kinsellas with easy grace. Afterwards, she offered to show them to their room. The bedrooms had already been reorganized to accommodate William, and now Naomi was giving up her room to the Kinsellas since it was the best in the house. She was to manage in a single bed in a much smaller room, but she was happy to make the sacrifice.

'Thank you,' Leo told her as his parents were led away. 'You're a good friend to my beloved.'

'No more than she deserves,' Naomi told him.

'She deserves the moon, the stars and the entire world,' he agreed. 'I can't wait to marry her.'

He folded Naomi into a hug and left for The Linnets, where he was to spend the night with Alice and her father.

Dinner that night was a lively affair. The Kinsellas looked a little bemused but also rather taken with the warmth of the merry gathering. 'You're a remarkably hospitable woman, Mrs Harrington,' Mr Kinsella said, in a quiet aside to Naomi.

'Remarkable,' his wife agreed.

'I'm just doing my bit for the war effort and for anyone who needs help,' Naomi insisted.

But the conversation brought to a head something she'd been mulling over in her mind. A short time later, she approached Victoria and Mags. 'I know you've been looking for accommodation near Hatfield.'

'We'll find something, don't you worry,' Mags assured her.

'I've been thinking that it would be a shame to uproot the children again,' she said. 'They have everything you wanted for them here – safety, fresh air, space to play . . . They're thriving – even little Flower, who isn't coughing half as much these days. The village school is excellent, too.'

'All true, and it's a wonder to behold, especially Flower looking so well,' Mags said. 'But there are no houses for rent in Churchwood. Even if there were, we probably couldn't afford them. It's a lovely place but I imagine rents are high.'

'What I mean is, you can stay here. Not for ever, perhaps, but for the foreseeable future while the war is on.'

Mags gaped at her. Victoria looked thunderstruck, too. 'Are you sure?' Victoria finally got out.

'It seems the best solution,' Naomi confirmed. 'We've grown used to each other and settled into a routine. And feeding you all should get easier now you've registered your ration books in the village.'

'You're a saint,' Mags declared. 'A blessed saint. Hear that, everyone?' She looked around the drawing room. 'We've no need to move to a damp, smelly place, after all. We're staying here!'

There were cries of wonder and gratitude from adults and children alike. Except for one child, who looked as though conflicting emotions were passing over his face. Arthur.

Naomi went to him. 'You don't feel that staying here is the best thing for your friends?'

'No, I do!' he said.

'But?' she prompted.

He shrugged.

'You think you've got a bad reputation and you're worried it'll rub off on them?' she asked.

'It's already going that way,' Arthur said.

'Things will change,' she told him, but he'd heard it numerous times and things hadn't changed.

'You need to be patient,' Naomi said, patting his arm with what she hoped was reassurance.

In bed that night, Naomi lay back against the pillows, thinking over what she'd done. She'd committed herself to organized chaos for the foreseeable future. That much was clear. But had she also committed herself to more heartache, since the little ones would continue to remind her of her own childlessness? Naomi didn't think so.

Something had happened to her over the past few weeks. Certainly, there'd been times when her soul had been crushed by the familiar bleak sense of loss, but, gradually, those times had been driven out by a growing sense of joy in the children's presence. It warmed her heart when Jenny or Flower put up their arms to be lifted on to her lap for a story. She laughed with them when she attempted to braid their hair and it turned out badly. She took pleasure in praising Arthur, Davie and the others for doing their best in their lessons. And then there was William.

How he was thriving in the life she was offering him! And how wonderful it felt when he turned glowing smiles to her and gave her spider-like hugs before he went to bed each evening.

In loving other people's children and being loved by them in her turn, she'd finally come to terms with her loss. She might not have given birth to children, but she could rejoice in being surrounded by them and giving them a home.

Naomi smiled, anticipating what Bert was bound to say when he heard. 'Proud of you, woman!'

CHAPTER FIFTY-SEVEN

Naomi

'It isn't fairy-tale weather,' Naomi said when the morning dawned wet and cold, with the forecasters warning of another storm. 'But it'll be a fairy-tale wedding even so.'

'With Kate looking radiantly beautiful,' Victoria agreed. 'Have you seen Arthur this morning, by the way?'

'Perhaps he's in the garden,' Naomi suggested.

'You're probably right. The rain won't have stopped *him* from going out and he may be trying to hide from the Kinsellas for fear of doing something wrong.'

'He certainly kept himself in the background yesterday,' Naomi said. 'It was as though he thought breathing might get him into trouble. Poor boy.'

'I'll have another chat with him once the wedding is over,' Victoria said. 'Ah, good morning, Mrs Kinsella . . .'

They went about the business of breakfast, but afterwards Victoria came to Naomi again. This time she was frowning. 'Arthur missed breakfast. He isn't in the garden and no one seems to have seen him.'

'Might he have gone to see Flower at Edna's so he could keep out of the way?'

'Flower and Ivy have just arrived. Arthur didn't go there.'

'Maybe he went to Bert's.' Naomi rang Bert from her sitting room, but he'd seen neither hide nor hair of Arthur that morning.

'Let me know when he's been found,' Bert said, and Naomi felt worry settle in her stomach.

She returned to Victoria and shook her head. 'He could be playing in the woods, I suppose.' But it seemed unlikely.

Victoria crouched down in front of Jenny. 'Did Arthur tell you he was going out this morning?'

'No.' The little girl had begun to look troubled, doubtless sensing Victoria's growing concern.

'I expect I've just missed him,' Victoria said, giving the child a quick squeeze of assurance.

But afterwards she ran upstairs. Following, Naomi saw her pretty face whiten when she looked up from the drawer in which Arthur's few things had been kept.

'Gone?' Naomi guessed.

'This is my fault,' Victoria said. 'I should have talked to him more. Helped him.'

'You did talk to him, and you did your best to help him. But this isn't the time for debate. We need to find Arthur and bring him home. So, let's take a moment to think about it. I can't believe he'd have run off without leaving a note. He wouldn't want Jenny to worry about him. Or you.'

'A note. Of course.'

Victoria looked on the cupboard next to Jenny's bed and there it was, tucked under the lamp. It was addressed to Jenny but she mustn't have noticed it.

Dear Jen, I'm going away so I don't keep spoiling everythink for you and the others. It's for the best becos I want you all to be happy. Remember I love you. Tell Viktoria, Mrs Harringtown, Mags, Flower and everyone else that I love them too. Arthur x

'Where might he have gone?' Naomi asked.
Bewildered, Victoria only shook her head.

361

'Someone else might know,' Naomi said.

Downstairs again, she gathered the London families together. 'As you can all see, Arthur isn't with us this morning. Does anyone know where he's gone?'

Blank looks were exchanged, and if anyone had something to hide because they'd been sworn to secrecy, they hid it well.

Mags stood up and addressed the children, too. 'It won't help Arthur if you don't tell us where he's heading. He may run into trouble. They're forecasting a storm, for one thing. Arthur may catch flu. He may injure himself and be unable to get help. He might . . . Oh, there are all sorts of hazards out there.'

Including bad people, though obviously Mags hadn't wished to mention them specifically.

'Please think hard,' Victoria urged. 'Even if Arthur didn't share his plans, has he ever mentioned a favourite place? Somewhere he'd like to go or people he'd like to see?'

'He just said he wished we were still in London,' Jenny said. 'He hadn't been in trouble so much there.' The little girl began to cry. Mags drew her on to her lap and rocked her.

Rain rattled against the window. The sky was a cauldron of roiling dark clouds and the strengthening wind was causing trees to sway and creak. 'We need to organize a search party,' Naomi said.

She telephoned Bert and he agreed to come over immediately. She also dashed out to The Linnets to explain the situation to Alice.

'You go home and start making plans while I try to recruit some others,' Alice said.

'What's this?' Dr Lovell appeared at his study door, Leo just behind him. The anxious murmur of voices must have reached them.

'I'll be glad to help, too,' Dr Lovell said, when he understood the circumstances.

'And me,' said Leo.

'Not you, Leo. Not on your wedding day,' Naomi argued.

'I insist. A little boy is missing in atrocious weather. He needs to be found.'

'Very well. Hopefully, we'll find him soon. Come over to Foxfield when you're ready.'

Naomi ran back across the road just as Bert arrived from one side and Pearl came up on Kate's bicycle from the other. 'I've got a note for Arthur,' she said. 'It's from Kate.'

The weather didn't appear to be bothering Pearl in the least but her cheerful expression dropped when she heard that Arthur was missing. 'Oh, heck.'

'Would you mind searching the outbuildings and woods around Brimbles Farm?' Bert asked her.

'Be glad to.'

'But tell Kate not to worry,' Naomi said. 'We don't want her upset on her wedding day.'

'Right you are.' Pearl set off and Bert entered the house with Naomi.

Mr and Mrs Kinsella emerged from the sitting room where Naomi had left them reading the newspaper. They were looking concerned. 'Forgive us if we're being intrusive, but we couldn't help overhearing people talking,' Mr Kinsella said. 'Are we to understand that a little boy has gone missing?'

'I'm afraid so,' Naomi confirmed. 'We're organizing a search party.'

'Then I must be part of it.' He turned to his wife. 'Not you, my dear. You should stay and help with the other children.'

In the drawing room, Naomi grabbed a pencil and paper and drew a rough sketch of the village and the surrounding area. 'Some of us need to search the woods, some the roads and some the fields,' she said.

It was a daunting prospect. No one knew what sort of head start Arthur had. No one knew whether he really would head to London. And no one knew whether the storm would persuade him to stay local, at least for a while.

A thought occurred to her. She was only assuming he'd be on foot. 'Does Arthur have any money?' she asked.

'He has the ten shillings Kate gave him as a reward for finding her ring,' Victoria said.

'Yes, of course.'

With ten shillings Arthur could have caught a bus. A train, too. How on earth were they going to find him when he might be miles away? It felt hopeless but they had to try.

Leo and Dr Lovell arrived, wrapped up in coats and holding umbrellas. 'Alice will be along in a moment,' Leo said. 'She's rounding up more helpers.'

They divided the map into sections and worked out who would search each one. Ivy would stay at home with Mrs Kinsella and the children. William, Victoria and the other London women would join in the search.

More helpers arrived: Alice, Adam, May – who'd left her children with Janet – and several others. 'I didn't ask any of our older or frailer residents,' Alice reported. 'I didn't think it wise for them to turn out in this weather.'

Naomi and Bert filled everyone in on their search areas. The sound of gravel crunching had them all looking out of the sitting-room window. 'It's Kate in the Brimbles Farm truck,' Bert observed.

'She can't see Leo on her wedding day! It's unlucky!'

Naomi declared, but Leo simply glided past her, saying, 'My wife and I will make our own luck.'

He opened the door as Kate got out of the truck and she ran into his arms. Holding her close, Leo said, 'Happy wedding day, darling.' And then he kissed her.

Pearl got out of the truck, too, along with Kenny, Ruby and Vinnie. 'What are our orders?' Pearl asked, after grabbing Kate's bicycle from the truck bed.

Orders were duly given out. 'We can cover more roads if we have two vehicles,' Bert said. 'I suggest we have a driver and a lookout in each. Naomi and I can cover the roads south and east of here. Perhaps Kate and Leo could cover the roads to the north and west.'

He lowered his voice to whisper to the Kinsellas, 'The truck will keep Leo dry. He needs to have a care for his health, having only recently left hospital.'

'That he does,' Mr Kinsella agreed.

'But Kate needs to get ready for her wedding!' Naomi protested.

'I want to give an hour or two to the search first,' Kate insisted.

What a dreadful let-down the wedding was going to be. Not only was a storm brewing, but many of the guests might miss the ceremony if they were still searching for Arthur. 'I suggest anyone who finds Arthur or learns anything about him telephones Foxfield as soon as possible,' Naomi said. 'In fact, I suggest we all telephone Foxfield when we have the chance. We don't want to continue searching if Arthur has already been found.'

'Come on, woman,' Bert told her then. 'The sooner we set out, the better our chances of finding the lad.'

They all departed. Bert kept his eyes mostly on the road while Naomi looked from side to side. Seeing a bus up ahead, she urged Bert to catch it up and then got out to speak to the driver. 'I'm not a passenger,' she explained. 'It's just that a boy from this village has gone missing. Would you mind keeping an eye out for him and asking any other drivers you see to do the same?'

'I'll be glad to,' he said.

Naomi produced several of her old visiting cards that were printed with her name, address and telephone number. 'Please take one for yourself and pass any others on. The boy is eight years old with brown hair and blue eyes. He's unlikely to be smartly dressed and he speaks with a London accent. But he's clever, too. He may try to change both his appearance and the way he speaks if he thinks it'll help him to avoid detection.'

'I know the sort,' the driver said.

Thanking him, Naomi returned to Bert, glancing up at the clouds in dismay. The worst of the storm was approaching.

'I know we want to find Arthur quickly, but it won't help if we miss him because I'm driving too fast in poor visibility,' Bert said. 'I'll go slowly and carefully instead, even if it frustrates us both.'

He took the Barton road. 'The more people we have searching, the better,' he said, bringing the truck to a halt outside Ellen's house.

He told her the story quickly.

'Leave it with me,' she said. 'I'll get as many people as possible to keep an eye out for any wandering urchins. I'll also ask them to look in their sheds and even their coal bunkers. Arthur might be sheltering inside one of them on a day like this.'

Thanking her, Bert and Naomi continued on their way. Once, Naomi spotted movement across a field, but it turned out to be a fox. Another time, Bert spotted a distant figure that turned out to be a scarecrow.

They paused so Naomi could ring Foxfield, but no one had reported finding Arthur yet so they pressed onwards. 'It's difficult to see anything at all!' Naomi wailed as rain lashed down on them.

Squinting through the windscreen, she spotted another bus coming towards them. Jumping out of the truck, she ran into the middle of the road and waved her arms to force it to stop. The driver hadn't seen Arthur but he too promised to keep an eye open for him and took some old calling cards.

Wet and unpleasantly cold, they drove on, looking this way and that but seeing nothing except a scrap of cloth caught on some barbed wire and a hardy farmer braving the weather to check on his livestock.

'This dratted storm is keeping most folk indoors,' Bert complained, because few people on the streets meant few people to ask about Arthur. 'But let's not forget that Arthur is no fool. He might have got on a bus hours ago and be miles away, but it's equally possible that he's holed up in some sort of local shelter waiting for the storm to pass.'

The first growls of thunder shuddered in the air.

They came to another village with a public telephone and Naomi rang Foxfield again. Suki answered. 'Still no news,' she said.

'If you wouldn't mind, Suki, would you walk into the village and ask everyone you see to look in their garden sheds and other outbuildings? I know Alice asked a few people, but she couldn't have asked everyone. Marjorie is often looking out of her window so you might call to ask if she saw the boy.' Marjorie's nose for gossip might actually prove useful for once. 'I'm sorry you'll get drenched, Suki, but—' Naomi broke off, hearing panicked voices in the background.

'What is it, Suki?' she asked. 'What's going on?'

Suki came back on the line. 'It's Flower, madam. She was crying earlier so Ivy put her to bed but now it seems that she's gone missing, too.'

Oh no. It was bad enough having Arthur out in the storm, but for delicate little Flower a soaking could be even more serious. Her health might have improved in leafy Churchwood, but Dr Lovell had warned that her chest was still weak so she needed to be kept warm and dry.

'Ivy thinks Flower must have gone looking for Arthur,' Suki said.

'I'm sure she's right. If anyone else telephones, ask them to change tactic and search nearer to the house. Flower can't have gone far. I'll come back too.'

'That dainty baby won't last long in this weather,' Bert said, when Naomi told him what she'd heard.

They headed back to Churchwood, finding that, despite thunder and lightning raging overhead, the village was astir. Mr Miles from the grocery waved them to a halt. 'Suki says that two children are missing,' he said.

'That's right. We don't know how long Arthur has been gone, but Flower can't have left much more than an hour ago. We need to find them urgently.'

'I regret being so harsh on the boy now,' Mr Miles said, 'but this isn't the time for voicing regrets. This is the time for action.'

He stepped back into his shop and Naomi heard him bellowing at his customers, 'Sorry, but you're going to have to come back later. This shop is closing. We all need to be out looking for these missing little ones.' He turned the sign on his door from *Open* to *Closed*.

The same thing was happening in the other shops along the row. People were emerging from houses, too, dressed to keep out the weather in hats and boots and carrying umbrellas. Marjorie was among them. 'I didn't see the little boy or girl but I wish I had,' she said.

'Just do your best looking for them now,' Naomi told her.

Some of the original searchers returned. Pearl, half drowned on the bicycle but clearly game for more. Alice and her father, too. William and the London women.

'Churchwood at its best,' Naomi murmured.

'There's no better place in the whole of England when there's a crisis,' Alice answered.

Hollering for attention, Bert strove to raise his voice above the thunder and driving rain. 'Thank you for turning out to help. I know you all understand the urgency. The missing little 'uns may not be Churchwood born and bred, and they've had their ups and downs while they've been with us. But they're Churchwood folk now and we need to bring them home where they belong. I suggest we all spread out and report back to Foxfield as often as we can.'

They began to disperse. 'Suki, could you go back to Foxfield and put the kettle on?' Naomi said. 'I suspect a lot of people are going to need hot drinks as the search goes on.'

'What about Miss Kate's wedding, madam?'

'Good question. Kate deserves the most beautiful wedding possible, but—'

'Look!' someone shouted. It was Pearl. Having just set off on her bicycle, she'd skidded to a halt. Now she was pointing down the street to where two small figures – one carrying the other – were trudging towards them.

'Arthur and Flower,' Naomi said, exhaling in relief. She hastened towards them but Alice got there first.

'Thank goodness you're all right!' she said, taking

Flower from Arthur's arms and opening her own coat to wrap it around the little girl.

Flower clung to her.

'You look freezing too, Arthur,' she said.

'He does,' Bert agreed, whipping off his jacket to drape it around the shivering boy. 'Welcome back, lad. You've had us all worried sick.'

'I didn't ask Flower to come with me,' Arthur said. 'I wouldn't have gone if I'd known she'd follow.'

'Follow where?' Naomi asked.

'I was going to London but the weather was horrid so I decided to wait in Farmer Mead's barn.'

'Did no one look for you there?'

'Mags came but I hid under the straw. But then Flower came. She remembered I like Farmer Mead's dog so guessed I might have gone there. But Flower was so wet and cold! I couldn't let her stay, so here we are . . . Have all these people been looking for her?' He stared round at the crowd with wide, worried eyes.

'They've been looking for both of you,' Naomi told him.

'For *me*?' Arthur looked stricken. 'I didn't think anyone would come looking for *me*. Not after I'd let everyone down by causing trouble. And not with the wedding and all. I just thought people would like Jenny, Flower and the others better without me spoiling things for them.' The stricken look gave way to one of horror. 'I haven't made everyone late for the wedding, have I? I didn't mean to, but—'

'But nothing,' Bert said. 'You've made a few mistakes, lad, but you belong to Churchwood now, and Churchwood looks after its own.'

'We do.' That was Mr Miles the grocer. 'I'm sorry for what I said about the ring, Arthur. It was unfair of me.'

370

Arthur gaped at him.

Mr Miles ruffled the boy's wet hair. 'You'd best be going home to dry off and warm up. As had we all.'

Bert jogged back to where he'd left the truck and drove it up to them. 'Kids in the front with Naomi. Everyone else in the back.'

Naomi opened the truck door but then paused. 'It looks like we need to add another person to the guest list,' she said, smiling at Alice.

Puzzled, Alice turned. Then she let out a shriek as Daniel walked up. 'Am I too late for the wedding?' he asked.

Alice launched herself into his arms, leaving Naomi to answer his question. 'We're *all* late for the wedding. But actually . . .' She paused, struck by a rather horrifying realization. 'We've a bigger problem than that. We've no bride and no groom, either.'

Kate and Leo were still out looking for Arthur and Flower.

CHAPTER FIFTY-EIGHT

Kate

Leo glanced at his watch. They'd telephoned Foxfield to be told Flower was missing too, but that had been a while ago. 'Should we look for a telephone so we can call again?' he asked Kate. 'Or will that only waste precious minutes that would be better spent looking for the missing children?'

'Let's try along here first.' Kate turned the truck down a narrow lane.

Of course, if the children didn't want to be found, they could duck behind trees or bushes at the truck's approach. Not that they'd be together. Arthur might risk his own health in this terrible weather but he wouldn't risk Flower's. If Flower had found him, he'd have taken her home. Probably, they were both alone. Cold, wet, afraid . . .

'Stop!' Leo said suddenly and Kate brought the truck to an abrupt halt.

'What is it?' she asked, looking around eagerly.

'I heard something.' Leo wound down his window.

And there it came again: the tooting of a vehicle horn.

'There!' he said, pointing.

Kate's gaze followed the direction of his arm. In another lane on the far side of a field, she saw someone waving frantically above the hedgerow. But how was that possible? The hedgerow was high and a person would need to be twelve feet tall to . . .

'It's Pearl,' Kate said. 'She must be standing on the roof of Bert's truck! She'll break her neck if she isn't careful.'

Setting off in her own truck to investigate, Kate found Pearl back on the ground but jigging about impatiently. 'Arthur and Flower are found!' she yelled as Kate's truck drew near. 'You need to get ready for the wedding. Shift over and I'll drive.'

Kate scooted into the middle of the bench seat while Pearl climbed up beside her. Bert tooted his horn again and saluted them through his window as they drove off with Pearl's large boot stamping down on the accelerator.

'Out!' she barked at Leo when they arrived at The Linnets.

'Wait!' Kate cried, and she smiled up at Leo as he took her in his arms and kissed her.

'For heaven's sake!' Pearl protested. 'There'll be time for all that smoochy nonsense later.'

Neither Kate nor Leo took any notice. When the kiss finally ended and Kate opened her eyes, she blinked at sudden brightness, for the clouds had parted to let the sun blaze through and were scudding away at speed. 'It's clearing up!' she declared. 'And look! A rainbow! How lucky!'

'I don't need to search for a pot of gold at the end of it,' Leo told her. 'I have all the treasure I need right here.'

Beside them, Pearl rolled her eyes.

Grinning, Leo got out of the truck. 'Thanks, Pearl. You're an angel.'

'At six feet tall with hands and feet like shovels? Not likely!' Her voice rose as Kate leaped out too. 'Where are *you* going?'

'Did you deliver my note to Arthur?'

Pearl's face told her no.

'Thought not. Back in a moment.' Kate raced through

the Foxfield gateposts and up to the house. Not bothering to knock, she opened the door, stepped inside and kicked off her boots. 'Only me!' she called.

Victoria emerged from the drawing room.

'I'm looking for Arthur,' Kate explained.

'He's in here. But—'

Kate hastened into the drawing room where Arthur and Flower were swathed in towels and blankets as everyone else fussed around them. Sketching a general wave of greeting, Kate crouched down beside the boy to whisper the suggestion she'd made in the note.

His eyes widened. 'Really?' he asked.

'Really.'

'I won't let you down, Kate.'

'Of course you won't. You're my hero.'

Waving again, she rushed from the house to see that Pearl had moved the truck on to the drive.

'Hurry up!' she bellowed.

Kate climbed back inside and Pearl drove away even before the door was shut. Minutes later, she pulled up outside May's house, where Kate was to get ready. 'Go on. Shoo! I'll see you later.'

Alice had come to get ready, too, and must have heard the truck's engine because she flung open the door. 'At last!' she said, dragging Kate into her arms.

Pearl tooted the horn by way of farewell and drove off.

An hour passed in the whirl of a hot, scented bath and hair wash followed by May wielding a hairdryer and brush, Alice helping Kate into her dress and then May sitting her down again to secure the veil and apply just a little rouge, mascara and lipstick.

Finally, May announced, 'There! You're ready.'

'You look absolutely beautiful,' Alice said, laughing as her eyes teared up in the emotion of the moment.

Led to the full-length mirror to see for herself, Kate gasped. May had rung around her old contacts in London and begged a length of ivory satin which had been just large enough for her to make a slender sheath of a dress for Kate. Then Alice's father had come up trumps by donating his clothing coupons for a remnant of ivory lace that May had fashioned into an over-bodice with long sleeves. 'Consider it a wedding gift,' he'd said. 'I've enough clothes to keep me going for a decade, so coupons are wasted on me, my dear.'

Edna Hall had donated tiny pearl-like buttons from her own wedding dress, which had succumbed to mildew years previously, and May had used them to decorate the front of the bodice.

Kate's hair had been swept off her face but May had created artful wings on each side and coaxed the remainder into a tumble of chestnut waves down her back. The veil sat on top, secured by a headdress that Alice had made from greenery and sprigs of winter jasmine, the small yellow flowers flattering Kate's healthy colouring perfectly. Sweeping down over her shoulders, the veil reached the floor to spread out behind her.

On her feet Kate wore the ivory satin shoes May had worn to her own wedding. And in her hands she carried the bouquet Alice had made to match the headdress, adding in delicate primroses and violets.

'You're marvels,' Kate declared. 'Both of you. Utter marvels.'

'It isn't exactly difficult to make *you* look good,' May said. 'Now don't move a muscle while Alice and I get ready.'

Alice was to be matron of honour in a pale-blue dress she'd had for some years but which always looked pretty. May changed into a superbly cut copper-coloured dress from her London days.

Downstairs, the door opened and Pearl shouted up, 'Your carriage awaits you, Kate.'

They headed down and May opened the door. Outside, all was sunshine and freshness, the leftover raindrops sparkling like diamonds.

They all laughed when they saw that, instead of the truck, Pearl had brought the cart, decorated with swags of foliage along the sides and with more sprigs of greenery in Pete's browband. Pearl herself wore a top hat and gentleman's morning suit. 'Ruby did the flowers and stuff,' she reported. 'Naomi loaned the hat and suit. Apparently, they used to belong to Awful Alexander. Well, Kate, I wouldn't know fashion if I fell over it, but you look spectacular. That doesn't mean you should stand there gawping, though. Get in the cart! You've a wedding to attend!'

Kenny was with her, looking uncomfortable in a new white shirt and a suit borrowed from May's husband. It was Kenny who was to accompany her to church and walk her down the aisle. It should have been Ernie's role, but he'd looked horrified at the prospect of being on show, though he'd tried to hide his fear behind grumpiness. 'It's all nonsense, this wedding stuff,' he'd complained. 'If a man and a woman want to get wed, they can do it by themselves without dragging everyone else into a fuss.'

But he'd put up no serious resistance to attending the wedding, even if he preferred to stay in the shadows.

The drive to the church took only moments.

They all climbed out of the cart and May blew Kate a kiss before slipping inside. Pearl tied Pete to a railing and followed rather less elegantly. Lingering, Alice tidied Kate's veil at the church door and Arthur and Timmy came out to fulfil the roles Kate had given them. 'You know what to do?' she asked them, and they nodded, puffed out with importance.

Kate linked arms with Kenny. 'Blimey,' he said, looking flustered, because he wasn't relishing the thought of walking down the aisle with so many gazes turned on him. 'Who'd have thought a day like this would ever come? My little sister getting wed!'

'We've seen a lot of changes over the last couple of years,' Kate told him.

'We certainly have.'

'Time to go,' Alice said. 'Leo must be waiting.'

Leo. Kate's stomach flipped in joy.

She took a deep breath and stepped through the open door. Immediately, the organist began playing the wedding march and everyone stood. Arthur and Timmy led the procession down the aisle, holding a satin cushion from Naomi's bedroom on which the wedding ring sat. They couldn't have been more careful if they'd been guarding the Crown jewels. Kate and Kenny went next, with Alice following.

Kate was aware of smiling faces – Victoria, Mags and the others from Foxfield, including little Flower, looking none the worse for her adventure . . . Older friends such as Janet, May, Daniel, Alice's father and dearest Naomi . . . The Brimbles Farm party: Ruby beaming, Vinnie and Ernie looking awkward and Fred arguing with Pearl over the flowers she'd used to decorate his wheelchair. 'So soppy!' he grumbled as Kate moved past.

Leo's parents were there, too, and Kate was glad to catch smiles from both of them. At the end of the aisle, Adam stood waiting in his crisp white robes. And just in front of him stood best man Bert and Leo himself in his RAF uniform – tall, trim and everything she could desire. He turned to greet her and Kate's breath caught in her throat at the soft glow in his eyes. Such love!

Alice took Kate's bouquet and sat down. And Adam

raised his hands to signal that the ceremony was about to begin.

Kate hadn't relished being the centre of attention, but everyone except Leo faded into the background as they made their vows and the gold wedding band was slid on to her finger. Then Leo kissed her, the register was signed and the guests came back into focus as they clapped and someone said, 'Aw, how lovely!' before a child made everyone laugh by calling out, 'Kissing is horrid!'

It was time to process back up the aisle, this time on the arm of Leo, her husband.

Her husband! How wonderful that felt.

They reached the steps and Leo turned to kiss her again in the brief moment before everyone else spilled out of the church. 'You're a beautiful bride, Mrs Kinsella.'

'You're not looking badly yourself, Flight Officer.'

There was no time to say more as people began to emerge and congratulate them, shaking Leo's hand and kissing Kate's cheek. 'You're lovely, Kate,' Leo's mother said, and there were tears in her eyes. Happy tears, which she dashed away, laughing.

'Lovely indeed,' Leo's father agreed, kissing her too. 'Welcome to the family.'

Photographs were taken, then Pearl drew up in the cart. 'Oi!' she called. 'It's time for a glass of Bert's beer.'

Leo helped Kate up and got in beside her for the short journey to the new bookshop. 'Oh, how pretty!' Kate cried, because there were pots of flowers around the door and on the windowsills.

Still more flowers were inside on the borrowed tables that had been laid out. 'I've no idea where everyone will fit,' Kate said, because the downstairs room was hardly a ballroom.

'They'll manage,' Leo replied confidently.

They *did* manage, with goodwill all round. The elderly and infirm were shown to seats before anyone else, and others sat on laps, on the stairs or on window ledges. The afternoon had turned glorious so the garden was thrown open to revellers, too, as were the bedrooms upstairs. One became a quiet room for chatting, another became a children's playroom and the third became a games room with Pearl showing off Fred's hand-carved chess set, which aroused considerable interest. So too did the wooden animals which she'd displayed on the fireplace downstairs. 'What have you done that for?' Fred protested. 'You're an embarrassment.'

'Don't care,' Pearl told him blithely, and was rewarded by the comments that were made.

'That's beautiful,' Leo's father declared on seeing the chess set.

'Cor, look at that 'orse!' Mags's son, Lewis, cried. 'Looks real!'

'Is that kingfisher for sale?' Jonah Kerrigan asked Fred.

'How much would you charge for a special commission?' Matron enquired. 'My nephew is due to be christened soon and a Noah's Ark would make a lovely gift.'

'It's about time you earned your keep,' Pearl told Fred.

Food was the usual village bring and share, so Fortnum & Mason delicacies from Leo's parents sat side by side with fish paste sandwiches from Marjorie and Edna Hall's apple tart.

Janet's wedding cake was a triumph and Bert's beer and wine went down a treat.

Ernie would rather have died than make a speech and Kenny had been pale with dread the day he'd asked Kate, 'I don't have to make a speech, do I?'

Seeing that he was genuinely terrified, Kate had let him

off, and the speeches were given by Leo, who made her blush with his compliments, and by Bert, who was just as vocal about her best qualities – courage and kindness being two of them. He welcomed Leo as the rare sort of man who actually deserved her.

'Now I have a presentation to make,' Bert said. 'We haven't bought presents since you're not setting up home just yet, but we've collected a little money instead.' He handed a small box to Leo. It had probably once held seeds but now it had been painted white, presumably in honour of the occasion.

'Goodness, it's heavy!' Leo said. 'Thank you all for your kindness.' He hesitated, looking at Kate questioningly. In answer, she smiled and whispered in his ear.

Leo nodded and then addressed the guests again. 'My wife and I – how wonderful that sounds! – would like to do something special with this money. The Churchwood bookshop means a great deal to my darling Kate, and to many of you in the village and at the hospital, too. To help the bookshop get off the ground again, we'd like to donate this money towards replacing some of the books and equipment that were destroyed in the plane crash. How does that sound?'

There were cheers of approval, with whistling from the hospital contingent. 'I'm beginning to feel part of Churchwood myself,' Leo said, grinning.

Dancing followed, space being made in the large down-stairs room and spilling out into the garden.

'It's my privilege to have the first dance with the bride,' Leo said, drawing Kate into his arms and smiling down at her with a warm regard that lit an answering warmth in her.

They danced to 'Moonlight Serenade', then others joined in and the pace picked up. Arthur danced with

Jenny and Flower in one corner, while a spider-legged William and shy Suki danced in another.

'Will you do me the honour?' Adam asked, drawing Leo's mother on to the floor, while May walked up to his father and said, 'If you're not a dancing man already, you soon will be.' With that, she pulled him forward as Glenn Miller's 'In the Mood' came on the gramophone.

'Such fun, Leo!' his mother cried in passing.

'Look, Son,' his father called, twirling May in a circle. 'There's life in this old chap still.'

Leo bent to speak into Kate's ear. 'You're good for me and you're good for them. They're broadening their horizons and enjoying it, too.'

'I'm glad,' Kate said, 'because my family is certainly a challenge!'

Ernie was sitting in a corner drinking beer. His face was as sour as ever but she could see his foot tapping in time to the music. He'd looked awkward when Leo had introduced his parents to him, and they'd looked bemused. But afterwards Kate and Leo had heard his father say to his wife, 'You know, it shows what a remarkable girl Kate is, coming from such difficult people.'

'It does,' Leo's mother had agreed. 'I realize now that she's perfect for Leo. A Cheltenham miss like Julia would never have made him happy.'

Leo smiled down at Kate again. 'Life is going to be one long adventure with you, my darling.'

'Likewise,' she told him, grinning, but then she pushed him away. 'Go on. Shoo! Do your duty by dancing with Churchwood's womenfolk, starting with Marjorie. You'll make her day.'

Kate danced with old Jonah Kerrigan and Leo's father. With Daniel, too, while Leo danced with Alice. Kate had been thrilled by how enthusiastically Daniel and Leo had taken to each other. After all, Alice was Kate's best friend and it would be terrific if their husbands became good friends too.

Eventually, Kate stood at the side of the room for a breather, smiling as Adam tried to fend off the village children who were clamouring around him. 'All right, all right!' he said. 'We'll start the children's club next week. Yes, we can play football in the garden, Roger. And yes, we can sing songs, Davie. You like making things, Mary? I'm sure we can manage that . . . And games, Timmy? Yes, we can play games . . .'

Alice and Naomi glided across to join her. 'Adam's going to have his hands full with the children's club,' Kate predicted.

'We'll all help out when we can,' Alice said. She looked up at Kate. 'Have you enjoyed your wedding?'

'It's been the best day of my life,' Kate said. She savoured her contentment for a moment before saying, 'It'll be your turn next, Naomi. The moment you're rid of Awful Alexander, Bert will be sweeping you into marriage.'

Naomi looked pleased. But then a cry from near by caught their attention.

'Yes!' Ruby was saying. 'A thousand times yes!' She threw her arms around Kenny and kissed him.

'It looks as though yours won't be the only wedding we have to look forward to,' Kate said, and glancing at Pearl spinning Fred in his wheelchair, she wondered if they too might make it down the aisle one day. Even Vinnie had managed to ask a girl to dance with him.

'What a lovely day we're having,' Alice said, and something secret in her smile had Kate's instincts prickling.

'Alice, has something happened?'

'I've sold a story to *Tales of Adventure* magazine.'

'A story you wrote?'

'Mmm.'

'That's wonderful news!' Kate cried.

'Wonderful news indeed,' Naomi agreed. 'Congratulations.'

'It'll be the first of many, I hope,' Alice said.

'I'm sure it will.' It was lovely to see her friend looking happy and fulfilled again. But then it occurred to her that there was more to Alice's happiness than a story, amazing though that was. She looked . . . radiant. 'Forgive me if I'm prying, but are you . . .?'

'Expecting again? I think so. We're keeping quiet about it, but we're hopeful that this time the outcome will be happier.'

Kate glanced towards Daniel, who was watching Alice with love in his eyes. 'This is even better news,' Kate said.

'It certainly is,' Naomi agreed, and they both folded Alice into their arms.

'Wedding bells, babies and a new bookshop,' Kate said, feeling satisfaction deep inside her. 'Hasn't Churchwood got a lot to look forward to?'

Acknowledgements

Evacuees is the fourth book in the 'Wartime Bookshop' series and I've been thrilled and humbled by the generous response the series has received from readers, reviewers and bloggers. Writing can be a lonely and uncertain business, but the kind reviews and messages I receive never fail to lift my spirits. Thank you so much, lovely readers!

Of course, my books aren't written in complete isolation and I'm grateful for the wonderful editorial input I've received from Alice Rodgers and Francesca Best at Transworld who sprinkled fairy dust on the manuscript to make it so much better than it was. Further thanks are due to eagled-eyed copy editor, Eleanor Updegraff, and to Vivien Thompson for readying the book for publication. A big hello and thank you is also due to the rest of the Transworld team, not least proofreaders, cover designers, marketeers . . .

As well, I'm hugely grateful to my superagent Kate Nash and all at the Kate Nash Literary Agency for their tremendous support. I'm so lucky to have you in my corner.

Finally, I'd like to thank another team for their support – my family and friends, without whose cries of, 'You can do it!' this book may never have been written.

About the author

Lesley Eames is an author of historical sagas, her preferred writing place being the kitchen due to its proximity to the kettle. Lesley loves tea, as do many of her characters. Having previously written sagas set around the time of the First World War and into the Roaring Twenties, she has ventured into the Second World War period with *The Wartime Bookshop* series.

Originally from the northwest of England (Manchester), Lesley's home is now Hertfordshire where *The Wartime Bookshop*'s fictional village of Churchwood is set. Along her journey as a writer, Lesley has been thrilled to have had ninety short stories published and to have enjoyed success in competitions in genres as varied as crime writing and writing for children. She is particularly honoured to have won the Festival of Romance New Talent Award, the Romantic Novelists' Association's Elizabeth Goudge Cup and to have been twice shortlisted in the UK Romantic Novel Awards (RONAs).

Learn more by visiting her website:
www.lesleyeames.com

Or follow her on Facebook:
www.facebook.com/LesleyEamesWriter

Don't miss the start of *The Wartime Bookshop* series . . .

The Wartime Bookshop
Book 1 in *The Wartime Bookshop* series

Alice is nursing an injured hand and a broken heart when she moves to the village of Churchwood at the start of WWII. She is desperate to be independent but worries that her injuries will make that impossible.

Kate lives with her family on Brimbles Farm, where her father and brothers treat her no better than a servant. With no mother or sisters, and shunned by the locals, Kate longs for a friend of her own.

Naomi is looked up to for owning the best house in the village. But privately, she carries the hurts of childlessness, a husband who has little time for her and some deep-rooted insecurities.

With war raging overseas, and difficulties to overcome at home, friendship is needed now more than ever. Can the war effort and a shared love of books bring these women – and the community of Churchwood – together?

AVAILABLE NOW

Land Girls at the Wartime Bookshop
Book 2 in *The Wartime Bookshop* series

The residents of Churchwood have never needed their bookshop, or its community, more. But when the bookshop comes under threat at the worst possible time, can Alice, Kate and Naomi pull together to keep spirits high?

Kate has always found life on Brimbles Farm difficult, but now she is struggling more than ever to find time for the things that matter to her – particularly helping to save the village bookshop and seeing handsome pilot Leo Kinsella. Can two Land Girls help? Or will they be more trouble than they're worth?

Naomi has found new friends and purpose through the bookshop and is devastated when its future is threatened. But when she begins to suspect her husband of being unfaithful, she finds her attention divided. With old insecurities rearing up, she needs to uncover the truth.

Alice has a lot on her plate. Can she fight to save the bookshop while also looking for a job and worrying about her fiancé Daniel away fighting in the war?

AVAILABLE NOW

Christmas at the Wartime Bookshop
Book 3 in *The Wartime Bookshop* series

Alice, Kate and Naomi want to keep the magic of Christmas alive in their village of Churchwood, but a thief in the area and a new family that shuns the local community are only the first of the problems they face . . .

Naomi is fighting to free herself from Alexander Harrington – the man who married her for her money then kept a secret family behind her back. But will she be able to achieve the independence she craves?

Alice's dreams came true when she married sweetheart Daniel. Now he has returned to the fighting, but Alice is delighted to discover that she's carrying his child. Will the family make it through the war unscathed?

While **Kate**'s life on Brimbles Farm has never been easy, she now has help from land girls Pearl and Ruby. But what will it mean for them all when Kate's brother returns from the war with terrible injuries? And why has pilot Leo, the man she loves, stopped writing?

As ever, the Wartime Bookshop is a source of community and comfort. But disaster is about to strike . . .

AVAILABLE NOW

And pre-order the next book in the series:

A Foundling at the Wartime Bookshop
Book 5 in *The Wartime Bookshop* series

Victoria is astonished when she discovers an abandoned
newborn baby on her doorstep, along with a note begging
her to 'take care of little Rose'. Who is the mother? Victoria,
Naomi and the Churchwood bookshop organising team set
about trying to identify her, concerned for her welfare and
hoping to give her a chance to reclaim her baby.

As they piece together the heartbreaking story, all sorts of
surprises emerge. But they can't keep the baby a secret for
long: can they reunite the little family before the authorities
take Rose away?

AVAILABLE TO ORDER NOW